# The Houses of Elliot

by

Robert McNamara

*The Houses of Elliot*
by Robert McNamara

Printed in the United States of America

ISBN 978-1-60791-728-1



Reg. #Txu1-326-457
3/22/08

www.xulonpress.com

It was such an ordinary, little accident. If Susan Reed hadn't been pregnant, she would most probably have laughed about it and certainly would not have thought about mentioning it to anyone. It was just one of those silly little things, a slight jarring slip, grabbing out for support, and catching herself, at the most a half-fall. Nothing more! But she felt a pull inside and had a momentary fear, just enough to cause her to call her doctor.

The doctor suggested that they meet at the hospital. He advised her to take a cab rather than driving her own car, just in case, since her husband was away on business. She agreed, and they met in the lobby. She smiled at him, shrugging at her own foolish, uneasiness, as he put his arm around her, and they moved to the elevator. He led her upstairs to Ultra Sound, where tests discovered internal bleeding. Immediately, he decided on surgery.

Her husband, Bertrand Reed, was traveling in a nearby city. Upon being contacted, he returned, arriving at the hospital within two hours. When he entered the lobby, Susan's doctor was waiting for him. Bertrand had met him once and knew that Susan had high regard for him.

"What is it?" Bertrand asked.

"She slipped at home. We found internal bleeding and had to take the baby." The doctor paused, knowing there was no exact explanation for what happened next.

"After it was over, when she was in the recovery room, Susan went into shock, and we couldn't bring her back."

Bertrand's eyes searched the doctor's face. He wanted him to repeat the message, hoping he'd heard incorrectly. Then Bertrand felt things shutting down inside of him, as if open doorways were being closed, lights turning off, and a hollowness coming up through a sudden closed-in darkness.

Bertrand knew that he really didn't want to hear the message again. Once was enough. He had lost Susan.

The doctor was unsure of what to do. Mr. Reed was standing before him with his mouth open. Then, it closed without saying a word. There was little doubt that the man was in shock. Should he tell him now about the condition of the baby? The doctor had a feeling that the man, at this moment, really didn't care about anything more than Susan. Yet, the doctor certainly knew his obligations, and a full report needed to be made.

"The baby is doing fine." The doctor waited. He had been right in his assessment of Mr. Reed's state. If the man had taken in the information just given him, the doctor certainly couldn't tell it.

"Why don't we sit?" the doctor said, as he led the way to a small waiting room. The place was empty, and the doctor motioned to a seat near the window. He waited for Mr. Reed to sit first.

"Four years was not enough," Bertrand said abruptly. "She wanted the baby. I didn't. <u>She</u> was all I wanted." Bertrand continued looking at the doctor for another moment, then turned and looked out the window.

"You don't have to stay," Bertrand said. There was little doubt that the doctor was being dismissed. As the doctor stood, he wanted to say something, but what, then, thought better of it. Mr. Reed had already shown, he was not interested in hearing anything the doctor had to say about the child, so he walked from the room, wondering if he would later face this man in the courts.

Bertrand's mind seemed almost a blank in this new darkness. He could hear the receding footsteps of the doctor as he walked away and could partially concentrate on a colorful tree across the parking lot, but what about his feelings? He felt nothing...no anger, no sorrow, and no concern. Nothing! He looked at his watch.

He was supposed to be at a board meeting. He thought about the meeting then told himself, "No, I don't give a damn about that right now. What do I care about?" He searched his darkened mind. Nothing! He cared about nothing. So this is what shock is like, he thought. How does the mind do it? How does it just shut down on its own? Does everybody react like this? That's a foolish question, he thought. No, he was well aware that some people would go berserk by now, and others would be deep in tears, but not him. He felt nothing.

A man with two small kids came into the waiting room. Bertrand stood, adjusted his suit coat, as was his habit, and walked steadily from the room. He went to the information counter.

"Yes, sir?" the smiling volunteer asked.

"Maternity?" he asked.

"Fourth floor, east wing," she answered, pointing to the closest elevator.

Bertrand felt calm as he got off on the fourth floor and looked both ways. He saw two men standing in front of some windows at the far end of the hall. He could tell, by the way they were looking through those windows and smiling at each other, what was behind the glass. He walked slowly toward them. As he reached the large windows of the nursery, the two men walked away, laughing between themselves. Bertrand looked inside. All the cribs were lined up in rows.

One of these is my baby, he thought. He realized he didn't care. He shifted his attention to the nurses. There were four of them, all seemingly there to take care of the newborns. Two young ones, probably in their twenties, were talking to each other in the back of the room. By their relaxed attitudes, Bertrand could see that their conversation had little to do with the business at hand. Another of the nurses, somewhat older and rather heavy set, was in a small side room having a cup of coffee and reading a magazine.

The last nurse, most probably in her early fifties, seemed to be both proficient and dedicated to her job. She was moving from crib to crib looking, touching, and talking to each baby no matter if the infant was crying, peaceful, or asleep. Bertrand watched her movements and wondered how she could stay so calm in what he imagined was an entirely stress-laden job. He had always found tiny babies irksome to be around. In the past, by making up some timely excuses, he had gotten away from the demanding little creatures as quickly as possible.

He stopped short. He paused and then stopped short again. He had always prided himself on his capacity for unique ideas. In the business world it had made him a fortune, far surpassing even what his family had handed down to him. He closed his eyes for a moment, concentrating. "Yes", he said to himself.

Though he was never sure where these ideas came from, he was always quick to take hold of them, believing that they were his alone. So it was with this one. It had struck quickly, and he was surprised at the ease and clarity with which it had come. He was aware he should be in mourning and in some way feeling his loss. Instead, he was clear-minded and easily able to organize the steps to this extraordinary idea. He wasn't sure how long he had stood by the window, but when he was ready, he tapped on the glass, getting the last nurse's attention.

She turned, looked at him and smiled. He knew that she expected him to point to one of the babies, but instead, he motioned toward the side door, gesturing for her to meet him there. He moved toward the door, and with only a brief hesitation, she did the same. She opened it.

"Yes?"

"My name is Bertrand Reed." He waited to see if his name had any effect on her, but it didn't. "My wife's name was Susan Reed."

"Oh, I'm sorry, Mister Reed. I'm terribly sorry. What may I do for you?"

"I wondered if you could spend a few minutes with me?"

The woman didn't know exactly what to say. She certainly couldn't refuse, and yet she had her obligations. "Why, I guess so." She turned back to the nursery. "Girls, I'll be gone for a few minutes."

Bertrand saw the two young nurses break from their long conversation and separate. The nurse then came into the hall with Bertrand.

"Yes?"

"Is there a place we might talk?"

"There's a room down the hall for the nurses. It might be empty." She led him to it and, seeing that it was empty, motioned him to a chair. They sat down.

"Would it be too much to ask if you answered some personal questions for me?" Bertrand asked.

"I don't understand," she said, searching his face.

"I know that this is very irregular, but if you could bear with me. The questions won't be that difficult or embarrassing."

"I wasn't in the delivery room or the recovery room."

"What?" he responded, momentarily not understanding her intent. "Oh, it's nothing like that. It has nothing to do with this hospital or the doctor."

The nurse paused for a moment then said, "All right. If it will help, I'll answer whatever I can."

"Thank you." He hesitated and then asked, "Are you married?"

"I was for twenty-three years. I lost my husband two years ago from lung cancer. He was a heavy smoker."

"What about children?"

"Two, but they're grown and married...a boy and a girl."

"Do you still have contact with them?"

"My daughter moved down South with her husband. His work transferred him there. But my son lives in the city and takes care of anything that goes wrong with the house."

"Did you go back to work after your husband died or have you always worked?"

"I stopped for seven years when my kids were little, but then I went back."

"Why?"

"My husband worked hard all of his life but never made that much money. It took both of us."

"You said you have your own home?

"Yes."

"Is it paid for?"

"No. I had to take out a second mortgage after my husband's death."

"How much is the balance?"

"Mr. Reed," she said quietly, "I really don't understand the reasons for such questions."

"There's a good reason for them, Mrs....? Oh, I'm sorry; I haven't asked your name."

"Ida Wilcock," Ida sighed. As she thought about it, she really didn't care if he knew these things anyway. "I owe a little over sixteen thousand I think. I'm still not too good about finances, but I'm learning."

"I noticed that you really like babies."

"Yes. I'm doing the work that I like best."

Ida was struck with the directness of his gaze and decided he certainly must have a point to all these questions. So, why doesn't he tell me what this is all about? As she watched him, he momentarily looked down at his hands, then back up at her. He smiled for the fist time.

"Mrs. Wilcock, would you be willing to quit for five years?"

"Working?"

"At this hospital,..yes."

"Why would I do that?"

"To take care of one baby. Mine."

"You mean you want me to go to work for you?"

He paused at this question, then said, "In a sense, yes, but not in the usual way. I want you to raise the child. To take the child into your own home, as though..." He stopped abruptly, his face showing concern, almost fear.

Well, she thought, there's finally a little emotion from the man. And she could see that his next question was not coming easily, almost as if he were afraid to ask it.

"Is it a boy or a girl?"

Amazed that he didn't already know, she answered, "It's a boy." She could see that he was relieved.

"Good," he said. "We thought it would be." Then he seemed to collect himself before he went on with what he wanted.

"I want you to have full control of the child. For five years, I want you to raise him."

"And you said in my own home?"

"That's right, just as if he were your own."

"And you'd visit him there?"

There was no hesitation with his answer. "No. You will have a phone number where I can be reached, but for the next few years, I won't be available."

"You won't be seeing him at all?"

"No."

This stopped her completely. I really don't know what to think at this moment, she thought. How can a man say such a thing? Should I be angry with a man who's willing to give up his child? And yet, what business is that of mine? I know nothing about this Mr. Reed except that he's just lost his wife. But then again, why would he ask such a thing from a complete stranger?

"Mr. Reed, you don't even know me."

"That's true," he said as he looked at her questioningly. "Is there something I should know that might stop you from taking the job?"

"Stop me?"

"Yes. Are you an alcoholic?

"No. I don't drink at all."

"Narcotics?"

"No. Nothing like that either."

An almost imperceptible smile passed across his face. "It seems to me you're exactly the kind of person I want. But before you say anything else, let me tell you what I'll do for you. If you agree, I'll pay off your mortgage immediately. And for the five years I'll pay you three thousand dollars a month. And at the end of the fifth year, you'll receive a bonus of stock options and T-bills that should be well over one hundred thousand dollars."

He smiled and paused. Then, he continued. "Everything I'm promising will be drawn up by my lawyers in a binding contract. You can take the contract to any lawyer you want for verification. Naturally, I'll pay for that too."

Once again, the man's words brought her mind to a dead stop. She didn't know how to talk to this man. Even though he had told her exactly what he planned to do, it seemed to her that he sounded as if he were discussing some business plan instead of the life of a child!

"What if I say no?"

"Then, I'll find someone else.

Just like that, she thought. How can he say such an important thing so quickly? If I don't do it, he'll find someone else! Where ...out in the street?

"Do you want to say no?"

Ida really hadn't thought what it would be like to raise a child once again, to have only one baby to hold, to change and to care for?

"I feel...almost numb. You're asking me to change my whole life."

"That's true. And I'm also saying that after five years, the baby will no longer be yours. The contract will be airtight in all aspects. Do you understand what that would mean?"

He's done it again, she thought. This man wants everything handled just like a business agreement! But then again, how should he handle it, when he doesn't even know the person he's talking to?

"If I become too attached, it wouldn't make any difference."

He nodded his head in agreement. "You would always be the nurse, without the privileges of the true mother. In one way, it would be beneficial. You would know that in five years your obligation will end, and that you would be free to do what you wanted."

Obligations, she thought. That's what he thinks everyone feels about children. What a pity. "Would I ever see him again?"

"It's highly unlikely. After he's grown..," he shrugged, "...that would be up to him."

"You're offer is very..." her voice trailed off.

"It could be higher, if you wish to negotiate."

Oh, this man. His abruptness startled her. Embarrassed, she quickly responded, "Oh, no, that's not what I meant at all. I meant that you were being overly generous. You could have someone for a lot less."

"It's important," he assured her, "that you're happy during these years and know that you will be secure after it's over. Without financial pressure, you'll be able to give all your time to the baby." Bertrand smiled, feeling like he had explained everything that was necessary. He settled back in his chair and waited.

She saw his change of posture and realized what he was doing. He's waiting for my answer, she thought. "You want me to decide right now?"

"Time does seem imperative. When the child is ready to go home, it'll be necessary for you to go with him. And if you aren't interested, I have very little time to look for someone else."

"He's a beautiful baby," she said quietly.

Mr. Reed showed nothing.

"How can something so important be handled so quickly?" she asked.

"As you well know, Mrs. Wilcock's death changes all our plans."

"Yes," she answered. "I am well aware of this. It's one of the main reasons I'm even considering it." He's a beautiful, healthy baby, she thought.

"What name have you chosen for him?" she asked.

For the second time, he was brought up short. She could see that this question had never entered his mind.

He finally said, "A name?"

"He should have one!" she commented dryly. For that moment, she was not caring about his recent loss.

"Yes, of course! Susan...my wife, she liked the name Elliot. 'Elliot, with nothing in the middle,' she used to say."

"Nothing in the middle?" Ida asked.

"No middle name. She never liked them." Getting to his feet, as if turning away from his memories, he brought his attention back Ida Wilcock. "Well, what do you say to my offer?"

Suddenly, Ida knew. No one else was going to take this baby! How did she know? She wasn't sure. But it flooded her. With the Lord's help, for the next five years, she was going to be this little guy's mother! Rising, she extended her hand. Without hesitation, Bertrand shook it, and the agreement was put into effect.

# The First House

Elliot remained in the hospital five days. During that time, Ida received the completed papers from Bertrand Reed's attorney. Doing as he had suggested, she took the papers to a law office. She was nervous about leaving the contract there, so she asked if she could wait while it was being read. The firm did as she requested and charged her accordingly. She paid the three hundred dollars from her own pocket, with no intention of sending the bill to Mr. Reed. The attorney's report confirmed what Bertrand Reed had promised. The terms of the contract were binding, even to its inclusion in Bertrand Reed's will. Since Ida wasn't disturbed beforehand, she wasn't surprised or relieved with this information. She was only irritated that the lawyer had charged her so much.

Ida Wilcock never saw or heard from Bertrand Reed again.

Each month she received her money. In the fourth month of the first year, she received the title to her mortgage. Her home was hers, free and clear. And Mr. Reed had been right. What a difference it made in her life, being free from money worries. Sometimes, sitting alone as usual at the kitchen table, her mind would seem to almost go blank, because she had no worries. How many hours during the past twenty-five years, she wondered, had she spent sitting right there worrying about the future? Tears came when she realized how her own thoughts had robbed her of so much precious time she could have spent thinking of good things.

Ida found Elliot a pleasure to be around. She tried to remember that she was still a nurse, and this baby would soon enough be gone.

But through the process of daily living, those thoughts soon diminished, and her love for the baby continued to grow. His dark eyes began recognizing her, and the little mouth would form a smile.

She found herself thinking back to the raising of her own children. Had she been as attentive to them? Why had there been so much to do then, and now everything seemed so simple? She smiled to herself when she realized the truth. It had been her husband, God love him. He had been like another one of her kids. She laughed out loud when she realized this. Her laughter startled Elliot, and his expression made her laugh all the more. Then she realized he didn't know what to make of it, because he had never heard laughter before. Ida made sure that she laughed more often around the child. She made it a point, even though she had been used to living alone, that from now on she would talk and laugh out loud for her new houseguest.

From an early age, Elliot loved to hear Ida read. And he found the pictures in the books very exciting. He would make strange little noises and stare intently at colors and shapes. Ida wondered if he was seeing things that she didn't. When Ida would be more than ready to turn the page, to go on with the story, Elliot would place his little hand on the page, stopping her. And many times Ida would glance sideways and watch him, trying to read what was going on in this unique little mind. Of course, she would always see the same expression. He would be intently staring at the pictures, as if filling himself with the images. Only then would he lift his hand, giving her permission to turn the page.

Besides her enjoyment of reading to Elliot, Ida treated herself to a pleasure she never felt she could afford, since the death of her husband. Once again, she began having the daily paper delivered to her home. Each morning, she would seat herself at the kitchen table, coffee at hand, slip off the rubber band and read the paper, every section, while Elliot ate and scattered his breakfast on the floor all around his high chair.

One morning, as she unfolded it and began reading the front page, Elliot began to cry.

"What's the matter, Hon?" she asked, looking over to him. He stopped crying. She turned back to reading. He began to cry again.

She got up and checked his diaper. Dry. Besides, he had already stopped crying. She sat down and resumed reading. Once again, he started up. She turned and looked at him. He stopped. She turned back to her paper. He started. She looked at him again.

"You don't want me to read? Do you?"

Once more, he stopped crying and sat looking directly at Ida. She deliberately turned her chair slightly, so that she was now facing the high chair. Then, slowly she lifted the paper. Sure enough, he started again.

"Look," she said patiently, "all I'm doing is reading the paper. These are words that tell all about what's going on in the world." Then she dropped her eyes to the paper and began reading out loud. "...stepping up the offensive on traffic snarls plaguing Los Angeles County..."

Ida looked up at Elliot. He wasn't crying, but he was watching her. She continued to read aloud. "...The California Highway Patrol unveiled an ambitious six-month pilot program designed to alleviate congestion on the most troubled portions..." Ida glanced up from her paper. Elliot was eating once again, absorbed in the mess on his tray. She tried to resume reading silently, but Elliot would have none of it. He immediately began crying. Ida, laughing, retorted, "Alright, alright!" And once more, she began reading out loud. From that time on it became a daily routine, one that she learned to enjoy as much as he.

When Elliot was two and a half years old, Ida received a call from Mr. Reed's law firm. A woman was on the line. She asked how the child was. Was his health good? Was there anything that Mrs. Wilcock needed? When the woman had been told that everything was fine, she hung up. Ida cried for two days.

By the time Elliot was three-and-a-half, he was reading to Ida. Nothing difficult, but he certainly handled all the children's books she had purchased for him. When he turned four, she began taking him to the local bookstore. There, one large table in the front portion of the store, held the art and "coffee table" books. On his first visit, Elliot spent over two hours just looking at the pictures in various books. It was only when Ida's feet began aching from standing so long and turning pages for Elliot that she decided to take him home.

Before leaving, she mentioned to the clerk that there should be chairs for the customers, but he never felt the need to answer her.

At least once a week, Ida and the boy would walk to the bookstore. He never tired of it.

When he was four, she thought about putting him in a nursery school for a half day so that he could learn to play with other children. But she selfishly changed her mind, knowing that she would miss him too much.

* * *

Two months before Elliot's fifth birthday, at about three o'clock one morning, he came padding into Ida's bedroom. Silently, he stood watching her. Suddenly, she was awake.

"What is it, Elliot? Are you all right?"

Without a sound, he moved closer to the bed and touched her hand. "I think," he said softly, "that I will be going away."

"How do you know that?" She was wide-awake now.

"A man in a long black car will pick me up."

"How do you know this?" she asked, pulling him up beside her.

"I saw him," he said simply.

"Saw him? You mean outside? There's a car there now?"

"No," he said, laughing and thinking she was being funny. "I saw him in my room."

"Elliot, there's no one in your room."

"I know, but I saw him and the big black car too. Then I saw a lady wearing glasses, and she had black and white bandages around her head," he said, gesturing with his hands.

"Ah...you had a dream."

"Yes, a dream. You carried my suitcase in the dream." Elliot took her hand. "You cried in my dream."

She was near tears now. "I did?"

"But it's all right, because the lady with the glasses is going to be my friend."

"Did she tell you that?"

The boy paused at this question, thinking back. "No..., it was someone else, but I don't know who."

Ida looked down at this small boy beside her. Oh, how she loved him. And yet here he was, ready to go, expecting something new, knowing that everything was going to be fine. She gave him a big hug, and said, "Well, I'm sure glad about the lady with the glasses."

Elliot hugged her back and said, "I don't think you can go with me. Did you know that?"

Ida hugged him again. "Yes, Elliot, I know."

The tears came, but her crying was silent.

"And don't forget," she said softly, "Good friends always hug." How many times had she said that to him, reminding herself that the day was coming when she would lose him.

The morning before Elliot's fifth birthday, Ida and the boy were at their usual place having breakfast, when the phone rang. The call was from the law firm. It sounded like the same woman.

"Would it be acceptable if we picked up the boy on his birthday?" she asked. Ida responded that it would **not**, but that he would be ready the day after. Ida was granted the extra day and was told that the car would be there for him at eleven a.m.

Elliot's dream had been right. It was a long, black limo with a uniformed driver. Ida did carry Elliot's suitcase, and she did cry as he left her. Elliot, though, didn't ask the driver about the lady with the glasses. It was as if he knew that she wouldn't be in the car.

# The Second House

The driver was silent as he drove through the streets of the city. Elliot didn't mind, though, since he was busy looking outside. Ida hadn't owned a car, so this was a real treat for the boy. It was so quiet in there, and it didn't smell like the buses at all. The seats were soft with no cuts in them.

Soon they were on a freeway, and all the buildings were left behind. Green, fenced fields came alongside, some with animals grazing in them. Elliot couldn't contain himself.

"Horses! And, and over there are cows! Real cows! Look at all of them!" Elliot shouted out.

The driver glanced back at the boy, but said nothing. Miles further, they turned off the highway, crossed an overpass, and headed for a distant group of buildings. A brick wall surrounded the place. The limo slowed as it passed through a gate. Elliot's attention was drawn to a small brass plaque, embedded in one of the stone columns, containing a very ornate emblem. Below it read **St.Maurice Military Academy.** Elliot was too involved looking at the emblem to try to read the words underneath it. The limo drove slowly up the tree-lined driveway, stopping before a main building.

The driver carried Elliot's suitcase for him. He rang the front bell, which was beside two massive doors. Elliot was looking at the strange, winged figures carved on the door, when the door opened and a woman, with black and white bandages about her face and head, opened the door.

"Good afternoon, Sister," the driver said formally. "This is Mr. Elliot Reed." He handed the lady a large manila envelope.

The Sister looked down at Elliot and smiled. "Put his suitcase in the foyer, please. We've been expecting him." She stepped aside, making room for the driver. Then she held out her hand for Elliot to take. It was very white, and her nails had no red on them like Ida wore. Elliot took the fingers, finding them somewhat cold to the touch. They entered and stood to one side as the driver touched his hat.

"Thank you for bringing him," said the lady.

"You're welcome, Sister," the driver said, as he closed the door behind him.

"Well, Elliot Reed, welcome to your new home. We've been expecting you. I know that Mother Superior will want to see you right away." She opened another large door, took his hand once more, and led him through it. Elliot noticed that she seemed to float along instead of walk. He knew she wore black shoes because he could see the very tips of them under her long, black dress. Her fingers still felt a little cold.

Elliot was surprised at the size of the room they entered. It seemed to be bigger than Ida's whole house. And there were large rugs on the walls, and the windows had brightly colored pictures in them. Elliot had seen pictures like these in the books at the store. Oh, Ida would like to see these windows. They were so pretty with the light coming through them.

At the end of the large room was a small, delicate desk with a straight-backed chair behind it. In front of the desk were three rather large overstuffed, comfortable looking, chairs. The Sister led Elliot to one of them.

"You sit, and I'll let her know that you're here." Elliot watched as the lady floated toward another door and left the room.

After a moment, as he concentrated on it, Elliot heard voices. Not close, but far away. Behind where the glass windows were... they seemed to come from there. Somebody was shouting, and then there was some laughter. It sounded like boys to him.

The far door opened, and another lady, dressed like the first, entered and came toward the desk. This lady was bigger and much stronger looking than other one. She took big steps, and you could see all of her black shoes. For some unknown reason, Elliot felt he should stand when she came in. She had the manila envelope in her hand. "Hello, Elliot. I'm Mother Superior," she said as she seated herself behind the little desk. She opened the envelope, and as she read to herself, she off-handedly said, "How was your trip?"

"I saw some horses and some cows. They were all eating." He paused and thought about this for a moment. "Except for two cows! They were lying down, and one horse was biting his back."

Mother Superior was reading, not really listening to what the boy was saying. This rather strange folio was from a law office, explaining the history of Elliot Reed. Over a year ago, she had received correspondence from the same firm asking for admittance for Elliot upon his fifth birthday. Attached to the request had been a certified check for five thousand dollars. She had written back confirming that space would be available, and that they would accept the child at that time. She returned the check, telling the firm that they would pay at the time of the boy's entrance into the school.

So, as she had requested, there was a check for Elliot Reed's first year tuition in the large envelope. But there was also another check for one thousand dollars for "incidentals". Mother Superior had no idea what that meant.

She placed the envelope on the table and looked at the boy. His dark eyes were bright and without fear. He smiled at her. He's very open she thought.

"Well, young man, you are the youngest student we have."

"I'm five years old."

She couldn't help but smile. "Yes, I know. Just yesterday. Happy Birthday to you. Did you get presents?" she asked, trying to find out something about the lad.

"Yes," Elliot answered, "I got five of them."

"Oh? What were they?"

"Two books, a hug and a kiss, and this coat."

"That's a nice coat. What kind of books?"

"Picture books."

"Did you bring them with you?

"Yes. They're in my suitcase."

"Who gave you such nice presents?"

"Ida."

"Ida?"

"Yes." Elliot could tell that this lady didn't know Ida.

"Is there a lady here that dresses like you but wears glasses?" he asked abruptly.

"What? Why...yes," she answered, startled. "Many of our Sisters wear glasses. Why do you ask?"

"She's my new friend."

At that moment, the small, far door opened, and the Sister, who had greeted Elliot at the door, came gliding across the room. Elliot liked to watch her walk.

"Mother Superior, your meeting with Father Tinian is in three minutes," she said softly.

"Oh, yes. Thank you, Sister. Would you take Elliot to his dormitory and introduce him to Sister Mary?" She got up, came around her chair and stood before Elliot. Elliot stood once more.

"Welcome to St. Maurice's, Elliot. I believe that you are going to be a fine addition to our family." She patted Elliot on his cheek. Her fingers felt warm. As she left the room, she said, "He has two books in his suitcase. Make sure Sister Mary looks at them with him. We should see what kind of pictures Elliot likes."

Elliot and the floating Sister went through a door that was directly under the stained-glass windows. They entered a courtyard. The Sister, his suitcase in one hand and Elliot with the other, made her way around this large cement area. It was open to the sky, and the afternoon sun threw shadows across half the cement courtyard. Three structures, each with three floors, surrounded three sides of the area. The Sister and Elliot turned left, then climbed some stairs to the top level, and made their way down a corridor. On one side there were large dormitory rooms filled with well-made single beds. Elliot could see the beds through large windows. Everything looked the same. To the right, was a four-foot wall protecting the walkers from falling into the courtyard below. Elliot could not see over it.

They passed by the doors of the first room and entered the second. The Sister dropped Elliot's hand as they entered. He followed her past the line of beds to the rear of the dormitory room. Everything was white, white sheets, white covers and white pillows.

The Sister knocked on the door in the rear. It opened.

"Sister Mary, this is Elliot Reed."

"Hello, Elliot," Sister Mary said.

"Hello," Elliot replied. This lady had glasses, but it was not the right face. This was going to be where he was to sleep and still he had not found his friend. The floating Sister smiled at him and touched his face before making her way back to the hallway.

"Well, young man, we have been expecting you," said Sister Mary.

Elliot liked her face. She had pretty eyes and real dark eyebrows. She led him to a bed in the rear of the room, two beds from her door.

"I'll be right there," she said, pointing to her nearby door, "if you need me."

She was nice enough, but he could tell that her mind seemed to be on many things at the same time. She would say something to him, but never really hear what his answer was. When they looked at his picture books together, she really didn't care about pictures the way that Ida had. She never asked any questions or anything. While they were looking at his books, Elliot noticed that she moved her hands through her beads, over and over, the ones that were connected to a large black belt around her waist. He wondered what they were.

* * *

That evening, right after vespers, Mother Superior called a special meeting for the housemothers, the teachers and the nurse.

"Sisters," she began, "we have a very strange situation before us. I really should have called the meeting before vespers, because it certainly is going to call for prayer." She opened the manila folder before her.

"Let me read the letter that I received when Elliot Reed arrived today. He's five years old and came alone in a limousine."

She began reading. "Dear Mother Superior; This letter is to introduce you to Master Elliot Reed. We are sorry that we are not able to give you much history of this young man. He is five years old, without a mother or father. It is, at this time, our wish that he be educated, within your school, until the date of his high school graduation."

She paused, looking at her fellow Sisters.

"It is also the firm's wish," she continued, "that since you have children in your school who are not of the Catholic persuasion, that the above said, Elliot Reed, not be given any undue influences as far as religious affiliations are concerned. Attached are two checks: one for the first year's tuition, and the second for incidentals in the amount of one thousand dollars."

A small, little Sister with glasses couldn't help but laugh. "Incidentals! My! What is he expected to buy?" Her little face crinkled, seeing the humor in such a large amount of money for such a small boy.

The other Sisters seated around her seemed somewhat embarrassed by her impulsive outbreak. Some looked down at their hands, while others closed their eyes, as if trying to fend off her humor.

Only Mother Superior smiled, partially because she too saw some humor in it, but mostly because, through the years, she had learned to expect the unexpected from Sister Teresa.

"Yes," she said, "it does seem like a very large amount."

She looked down at the letter. "It's signed, William S. Bryant, Attorney at Law." There was a pause as Mother Superior placed the information back into the manila folder.

"Sister Mary, did you have a chance to look at the child's books he brought with him?"

"Yes, Mother Superior, but they're not children's books. One is a very expensive book about animals and birds and the other on graphics of the world."

"Graphics of the world. What's that?"

"It showed different forms of art work...photography, laser art, architecture, advertisements, and...things I had never seen before."

"And he liked it?" Mother Superior asked.

"He was quite taken with both books. He seemed quite excited to share all the pictures in the books."

"Did he say who gave them to him?"

"A person named Ida."

"The same thing he said to me. Not mother, but Ida," Mother Superior commented. "Well Sisters, we have a mysterious new boy, who likes strange books for a child his age, and might have been raised by a person named Ida. He has no father or mother and is being cared for by a law firm, which doesn't want the child 'persuaded'."

Mother Superior moved around the pew of the small chapel, as if preparing to leave, but then turned back to the seated Sisters.

"Though it certainly is not our policy to have favorites, in this instance, since he is the youngest student we have, we might all watch after him."

As she walked away, she wondered why she had said that. She knew it wasn't like her to say something without first weighing the consequences. Dear Lord, she thought, maybe in my old age I'm becoming more like Sister Teresa. That was a disturbing thought.

The following morning Elliot was taken across the school grounds to an area with small wooden buildings. He was led to the screen door of one and told to enter, which he did and stood just inside.

"Come over here," said the round-faced, little Sister Elizabeth. Then she did something that seemed very strange. She put something around his chest, read the markings on it, wrote something on a paper with a pencil, and then started to put the thing under his arm.

"Lift your arm," she said.

He did so. "What are you doing?" he asked.

"What?" she said loudly. "Speak up!"

His mouth was just a few inches from her head. "What are you doing?"

She paused and looked up from the thing. "I'm measuring you."

"What does that do?" he asked loudly.

"It shows me how big you are!" she said rather testily.

Elliot decided he shouldn't ask any more questions. Whatever the measuring was for, it didn't hurt.

When, it was over, and he went back outside, he saw that he was alone. The little building was a long way from the dorm area. He could look way over and see where the main office was, and then by looking way up there, to the top floor, he could see where he had slept his first night.

As he was looking...

**...a face flashed in his mind. It was a boy's face, one he had never seen before. He looked sick. He was sweating, and crying. His face was so skinny and sad-like...**

Elliot closed his eyes, seeing the face. He remembered "pictures" came into his mind like this before, but never of another person. The face disappeared suddenly when Elliot heard a voice behind him.

He turned quickly and saw a large, heavyset boy dressed in a khaki uniform. His stomach hung over his belt.

"Are you Reed?"

"Yes," Elliot answered.

"Yes, what?" the boy shouted, pointing to the two chevrons on his sleeve.

"What?" Elliot asked, wondering why the boy was pointing.

"Look, Reed. When you see a guy talking to you with these on his arm, you say, 'Sir.' You got me?"

Elliot wondered why the big boy's breath smelled so bad. "Yes, Sir," Elliot answered.

"O.K., then," he said, calming somewhat. "You're supposed to be at the infirmary."

"Yes, sir. What's that?"

"Holy cow! It's the hospital, dummy! It's the building right next to the tailor shop!"

Elliot wished he knew what this tailor shop was. He could only stand and wait for the next onslaught.

"Well?" the fat corporal said.

"I don't know where the tailor shop is."

"Are you trying to be a smart ass?"

"No, Sir."

"It's the building you just came out of! What did you do in there?"

"I got measured, Sir."

"Naturally! What the hell else would you do in a tailor shop! Now get your butt into the infirmary!"

Without hesitation, Elliot ran in the direction of the tailor shop. He turned to look, and the fat boy was following him. He ran around the corner into the building next to it, hoping that it was the infirmary.

Though it was the right building, it was the wrong entrance. Elliot closed the door behind him and peeked back through the thin curtains, watching for the fat boy. He didn't come. Elliot turned and looked at the room. It was small and had two beds. Someone was in one of the beds. Elliot saw strands of blondish hair sticking up from a pillow and when he stood up on tiptoe he could see that the boy was facing the other way. Then, as Elliot quietly tiptoed toward the other door, there was a cough and a slight moan. Elliot was unsure of what to do. He heard a weak, muffled cry. This stopped Elliot, and he turned and moved back to the bed. Placing his hands on the side of the bed, he lifted himself. The face of the boy in the bed was half-covered by the sheet.

Then his eyes opened, and Elliot knew. It was the boy who he had seen in his mind. He waited for him to say something, but the boy just stared. Elliot's arms tired, so he dropped from the bed. He waited a moment and then lifted himself again. He watched as the sick boy's eyes slowly closed and heard a shallow sigh escape from him. Elliot rested his weight on one elbow and touched the boy's face with a finger. The boy didn't move. Then Elliot saw a tear run down the bridge of his nose and onto the sheet. Elliot stroked the boy's face with his hand, just like Ida had done when he had an earache once. The boy's eyes didn't open again. Elliot dropped to the floor and walked to the door.

As soon as Elliot opened the door into the hallway of the infirmary, the Sister saw him.

"What are you doing in there?" Sister Sarah asked, heading right for him.

"I came from outside," Elliot answered.

"What? How? That door is never opened!" she said as she passed by him and entered the room with the sick boy. "You stay right there," she commanded, as she shut the door behind her.

Elliot did as he was told and stood like a statue in the hallway. He didn't have long to wait. The door opened, and she walked past him returning to her desk. "I would like to know who unlocked that door! Entirely against the rules!"

Once she sat, she noticed that the boy was still standing in the middle of the hallway. "You may move now. Come here." Elliot moved to the desk, wondering if she was going to be like the fat boy.

"Mr. Skinner is very sick. He's not supposed to have anyone in the room with him. You could get sick too."

"What's he got?" Elliot asked.

"Did you touch him?"

"Yes. On his head."

Hurriedly, she grabbed a folder from the top of her desk, quickly got to her feet, and took Elliot in tow, heading for the examination room. There, she washed his hands with a strong liquid soap and then did the same to her own. "He has a sickness called infectious hepatitis. Mr. Skinner doesn't seem to want to eat at all, and it leaves him open for all kinds of bad things," she said as she dried Elliot's hands thoroughly. Then she picked him up and sat him on a table in the center of the room.

"Will he get well?" Elliot asked.

She was surprised that a boy of his age cared about anyone but himself. "We hope so, and we're all praying for him."

She placed the folder on the same table, then opened a drawer and took out a stethoscope. "Take off your shirt." The lad did as he was told. She placed the stethoscope against his chest and listened. "Take a deep breath."

Elliot filled up, and held it. "Let it out," she said as she moved around behind him, placing the same device against his back. "Do it again." He took another deep breath and then another.

"I got measured," he said quickly.

"What?" the Sister asked, taking the instrument from her ears.

"I got measured, over at the Tailor Shop."

"Yes, all the new boys do," she said as she wrote something in the folder.

"Oh." He was glad to hear that he wasn't the only one. "Why?"

"How else would you get your uniforms?"

"I get uniforms?"

"Certainly! You're at St. Maurice's now."

He was silent, thinking about this. He was really happy about having a uniform to wear. "Will I get things on my sleeve?" He pointed to where the fat boy had pointed.

"My, no! You're way too little and don't know anything yet. Chevrons are for the bigger boys, who learn to be soldiers."

Elliot had to agree that the fat boy was much bigger than he. He was quiet while the Sister finished checking different parts of him, and he sat wondering what he must do to become a soldier. Elliot found his way back to his dorm.

It was filled with boys. They all wore uniforms. Elliot had looked for the fat boy, but decided he must sleep somewhere else. He noticed that the bigger boys weren't in this dorm; maybe they were downstairs or next-door. Two boys walked past him. They went over towards the large bathroom at the end of the dorm. When Elliot came back to the dorm after his physical, he had been told to stay in the dorm, but that he could look around. He'd gone into the bathroom. He had never seen such a big place. There was a whole row of stalls with a toilet in each one. And there were a lot of places to pee. Since he had peed in a bottle over at the infirmary, he didn't have to go.

Sister Sarah had told him that he was a healthy boy. He could only remember being sick once. He had told Sister Sarah about his earache and how Ida had put some warm stuff in there. He remembered he cried, while she had held him on her lap, but he didn't tell Sister Sarah that part. He wished he were with Ida now. He had looked everywhere he could for his new friend, but hadn't seen her. Mother Superior had been right. There were a lot of Sisters with glasses on.

"Are you all right, Elliot?"

Elliot turned where he was sitting on the bed. Sister Mary had come up behind him.

"Yes."

"How did your physical go?"

"She said I was healthy, and she thought I was going to be tall."

"Sister Sarah seems to know these things."

Elliot noticed that she was playing with her beads again. "What are those?" he asked, pointing.

Sister Mary felt as if she had been caught. For the past few months, she had realized that her rosary had become something more than counting her prayers when she would catch herself nervously fingering them. She didn't understand why she was doing this. She had been praying about it, but had received no answer.

"It's called a rosary, and we use it to count our prayers," she answered him.

He watched her as her hand dropped the beads. Her answer was strange to him. He wondered why she counted them. Ida had never said anything about this. He had said prayers at meal times and when he went to bed, but he never counted them.

"Oh," Elliot answered, deciding not to ask any more questions. Not until he found his friend.

"Dinner will be in one hour," she said as she moved toward the door of her room. Elliot liked to watch the Sisters move. They didn't hardly bounce at all.

* * *

Elliot's habit was to wake up early in the morning, when Ida and he would go for walks together, watching for birds and things. So, on Sunday morning, when Sister Mary came from her room to wake everybody up, Elliot was already awake, sitting up in bed and looking at one of his books. She looked at him, smiled, and then went down the aisles waking each boy.

Elliot brushed his teeth and changed his clothes, putting on a brand new pair of pants and a new shirt. Ida had bought all new clothes for his leaving. Even though he had everything new, he still wished he was like the other boys. They were dressing up in their best uniforms this morning. They even had coats with metal emblems in each lapel, the same emblem Elliot had seen on the front gate when he had entered the school. Each boy had a hat with the same emblem on the front, real hats, that had a leather strap around them and a dark brown bill in front. And everybody had really shiny shoes.

They went out to the outside corridor to line up; everybody looked like a soldier, with their khaki shirts and black ties. Elliot was at the very end of the line. He made the right face turn as well as he could and followed the rest of the boys down the stairs to the second level. The line moved slowly through two large doors, not too far from where Elliot had sat with the Mother Superior. When Elliot was about to enter, he noticed that the boys in front of him dipped their hand into a bowl that stood on a stand. Then, with whatever was on their fingers, they put a little bit on their forehead, then on their chest and then on each of their shoulders. Was he supposed to do that or did you have to have a uniform first? He wondered. He wished he could see what was in the bowl, but he was too short. Oh, if only he had his friend! There were so many questions to ask!

He passed by the bowl and saw that he was in a church. Not only was his Company there, but all the other boys too. The whole church was full, at least on the one side where all the uniformed students sat. The other side was sort of filled with Sisters and one heavy-set gray haired man with a red face. Elliot wondered who he was. He had on a uniform too.

Elliot found that he was seated in the very first row, right in front of a wooden fence. On the other side of the fence was a very strange and brightly colored area with covered tables, statues, a golden cup, a cross with Jesus on it, and a lot of different other things. After looking at everything, Elliot turned around and looked behind him. All the students were quiet and everybody had taken off their hat. Elliot turned and looked the other way, across the aisle, at all the Sisters. Some were kneeling, with their heads bowed, while others sat. They were all quiet too. Elliot wondered why the Sisters didn't sit up towards the front like he was. Most of them sat in the middle of the chapel. He saw the Sister who measured him. And there was Sister Sarah from the infirmary. Elliot began looking for Sister Mary. His eyes traveled up and down the rows. Then he came to a Sister who was looking right at him, and she was smiling!

It was her! It was his friend! There she was! He waved to her and smiled back. There she was, and she knew him too!

Sister Teresa had watched the children march into the chapel and sit in their places, just as she had watched for the past fifteen years.

How many new children had she seen come into the chapel for the first time? She had to smile when she saw little Elliot Reed walking behind the others. The thousand-dollar boy, she thought. She knew that the night before she shouldn't have laughed when Mother Superior had read the letter. She had asked the Lord to forgive her for her thoughtlessness. But how small he was, and how he noticed everything around him. She wondered if this was his first time in a church, and if he knew anything about the Lord? Probably not, if the request handed down from that law firm was any indication.

She watched as he turned and fearlessly looked at the rows of uniformed strangers who were now part of his new life. She wondered which group of students he would join. Would he be one of the many who listened to the teachings about Christ and then went about living their lives the way they wanted to? Or would he be one of the very few who would truly be blessed by being here? Quickly she said a prayer on his behalf. During it, she watched as he changed his position and began scrutinizing the Sisters.

There were certain Sisters, now watching him, who did not care to be stared at by the eyes of any little child. They felt the chapel to be a place of privacy. She could almost say with certainty that this would be the last time she would see his inquisitive little face turning during the Mass. She had to smile at his openness as his gaze met hers.

Then something he did startled her. He looked at her as though he suddenly recognized her! And even more than that, he seemed to be looking at her as if she too should know him. And now he was actually waving at her! Maybe his gaze wasn't directed at her at all. She turned quickly and looked behind her. No one else was paying attention; it had to be her!

She really didn't know what else to do, so she too raised her hand, ever so slightly, and returned his greeting. He continued to smile. And, for a brief moment, she had the feeling he was going to get up and come over to her. But then she saw the boy seated in back of Elliot tap him on the shoulder, and whisper something to him.

"Hey, you want to get in trouble? Turn around," the boy whispered to Elliot. He did as he was told.

But during the Mass, when the priest was reading from a big book, Elliot turned and looked at his friend. She had her eyes closed, and her mouth was moving. She must be praying, Elliot thought. Ida used to do that too.

After doing a lot of different things around the table on the other side of the fence, the man in the robes took hold of a golden pot-like thing that hung from three chains. Smoke came from inside of it. Elliot watched as the man swung it back and forth, and he said some words that Elliot didn't understand. He kept swinging it and saying words. The smoke had a really strange smell. At first, Elliot liked it, but then it got too strong. He couldn't seem to get away from that smell. He felt like he was going to be sick. If only the man would go swing it somewhere else or maybe stop...for a little while. Elliot had to get out.

He got up and ran down the aisle, his hand over his mouth. As he went by, one of the older boys laughed at him. Elliot wondered what he was doing that was funny.

He made it to the corridor, then he threw up. A Sister came out of the church and took him back to his dormitory. She seemed mad at him for what he did, even though she didn't say anything. She told him to go sit on his bed and wait for the rest of the boys to come back. Right after she left, Sister Mary came into the dormitory. He watched as she came to his bed and sat down beside him.

"Do you feel better now?"

"The smoke made me sick."

"I know," she said, as she took his hand. "We don't use incense for every service. This was special."

"What was the smoke for?" he asked.

"It's an offering to God."

Elliot watched her face, wondering if he should ask her. Even though she took his hand, he felt she really didn't want to.

"What is it?" she asked, seeing his dark eyes watching her intently.

"The Sister with glasses. She sat in the row in front of you."

"Yes?"

"What's her name?"

"Well, let's see, who was there? There were four Sisters in front of me. There was Sister Florence first. She doesn't wear glasses. Sister Angela, no glasses. And there was Sister Teresa, and she wears glasses. Next to her was Sister Constance, who wears glasses too. Which one do you mean?"

Sister Mary watched as Elliot closed his eyes. He seemed to be going back over what he had seen in church.

"She was the little one, I think."

"That would be Sister Teresa." What could he ever want with her, she thought.

"Does she take care of little boys like you do?"

"No, she teaches at the school."

"Will I go there?"

"Yes, but not to her class. She teaches one class above you."

"Oh," Elliot said, trying not to cry. How was he going to be with his friend?

Sister Mary could see the disappointment on his face. She wondered what his thoughts were, to make him feel that way. Well, one thing she had learned, don't ask too many questions of the boys. They'll tell you what they want you to know. The rest had best be left alone.

"Are you hungry?" she asked. "The other boys are having breakfast."

He took her hand and went with her. He was hungry.

* * *

The classrooms were in the rear portion of the school, next to the playing field. The younger boys had to climb metal stairs to the second floor of the building. Elliot's company split up into the four groups, each with its own classroom. Being last in line, Elliot followed the boy in front of him and entered the last classroom. Each boy stood beside a desk. Elliot stood next to the door, not exactly sure what to do. He watched as the Sister stood up from behind her desk and said, "Be seated." Everybody sat.

The Sister looked at Elliot, started to say something then looked at the classroom. There were no empty desks. Her eyes moved immediately to the fourth desk in the second row. There, sat a blond haired boy, with his head lowered.

"Alfie, weren't you told to go to Sister Teresa's room today?"

He didn't answer.

"Alfie, please stand."

He stood. All the boys around him were smiling, and one even laughed out loud.

"That's enough now," the Sister said. Everybody was looking at Alfie. He looked down at his shoes.

"Well, Alfie?"

"I like it here, Sister," the boy mumbled.

"I couldn't hear you, Alfie. Please, speak up."

"Couldn't I stay in here? I like it where I am. An' I don't read so good."

"Alfie, you <u>can</u> do the work. We've already talked about this before."

Alfie mumbled again. "George says it's real hard."

"George said what?"

"He said it was hard. And that Sister Teresa was real tough."

"Alfie, you're six and a half, and you are certainly ready for bigger and better things. Get your pencil box and go see Sister Teresa. Her students love her."

"Not George," Alfie mumbled, as he lifted his desktop and fumbled through the desk.

"What?" said Sister Beatrice, hearing exactly what he had said.

"Nothing," the boy answered, as he stood up, holding his pencil box. He shuffled his feet but didn't move.

"Well?" the Sister said.

He was near tears and his lower lip trembled as he spoke.

"I can't do it, and I know it. George showed me his book, and I can't do it." Alfie did his best to hold back the tears.

From where he was still standing by the door, Elliot said, "I'll go."

"What?" the Sister responded.

"I'd like to go with Sister Teresa."

This was turning out to be great fun for the class. They all laughed.

"Now, class!" Sister Beatrice said sharply. They quieted immediately.

"Elliot, you are too young. And besides, you have to know how to read before you can move to the next class."

"I know how."

The class couldn't help it. They laughed again. Even Sister Beatrice had to smile.

"Really?" she said to Elliot, not unkindly. "Do you read words or sentences?"

"Books. I read books," Elliot said brightly.

This was too much for both Sister Beatrice and the class. Everybody laughed. Such a courageous little boy, the Sister thought, so small and yet so sure of himself. She really couldn't remember something as special as this.

"That's enough class." Sister Beatrice noticed that Alfie had once again sat down, and wasn't laughing with the rest of the children. Maybe she had made a mistake about him.

"Boys, that's enough," she said as she moved around to the back of her desk. Well, she thought, one thing at time. First, she would handle the new boy. She opened the top drawer and brought out a copy of the first reader. She walked over and handed it to Elliot.

"Do you think that you could read this book?"

Elliot took the book and looked at the cover. He had never seen it before. He opened it and turned the first few pages. This is a very easy book, he thought. It was about a boy and his dog, but the pictures weren't very good.

"Yes, I can read this." He quickly read the only sentence on each page, but he thought the story a little dumb.

Sister Beatrice was surprised, as were the boys in the class. She knew that he could handle anything that the rest of the class was now doing.

"Very well, Elliot. You really can read." She went to the desk and brought out another book, much more difficult. This was one that Sister Teresa was using in her class.

"What about this one?"

Elliot took the book and opened it. This one was much more interesting, and the pictures were quite good.

"This has nice pictures. I like the polar bear."

He turned back to the first page. "It's called, 'Animals from the Snow'." He turned to the second page and began to read. Though he was somewhat slower in some spots, he read very well. Not only did he read, but also the Sister could tell that the boy retained what he was reading. She stopped him as he turned the next page.

"Where did you learn to read, Elliot?"

"Ida taught me."

"Ida? Was she your teacher?"

Elliot had never really thought about who Ida was to him. She just was. "She was my friend," he answered.

"The boys in Sister Teresa's room are older than you. Some of them are even eight. Do you think that would bother you?"

Elliot could only think about being with his friend. "No, I don't think so."

"If it does, will you promise to do something for me?"

"What?"

"Will you tell Sister Teresa if there are things you don't like or understand? Will you promise to do that?"

Elliot knew he would do that, no matter what. "Yes, I promise."

Sister Beatrice reached into the bottom drawer of her desk and brought out a brand new pencil box. She handed it to Elliot as she took the reader from him.

"This is for you, Elliot. Each new student gets a pencil box, and it's yours to keep. Whenever you move up in classes, you'll take this with you."

She turned to the class as she took Elliot's other hand. "Class, I'm going to take Elliot next door. I expect you to be quiet while I'm gone. You may talk to your neighbor, but stay in your seats. And no shouting!" With that she led Elliot from the room.

As they stood at the door of the next classroom, Elliot watched as she softly knocked on the door. She partially opened it. Elliot could hear Sister Teresa talking to her class, but she stopped as the door opened. Elliot's stomach felt funny as he waited to meet his friend.

Sister Teresa peered over her little glasses and saw Sister Beatrice. She smiled, came out the door and joined them in the hallway.

"I'm sorry to bother you, Sister," she said softly, "but there's a problem with Alfie moving. He's very unsure of himself and asked to stay. Then, Elliot said he would like to come into your class."

Sister Teresa was surprised as she felt little fingers take her hand. She looked down and saw Elliot looking up at her. He was smiling. She wrapped her fingers around his.

"I can read," Elliot offered.

"You can?" Sister Teresa said, as she smiled.

"He could even read, 'Animals in the Snow'," Sister Beatrice offered.

"In that case, he should certainly be in here with us."

"I have to be," Elliot said, looking up at his new friend.

The two Sisters glanced at each other as Sister Beatrice left, each wondering what the youngster meant. Sister Beatrice paused before returning to her classroom.

"Elliot, do you remember seeing me in church yesterday?"

"Yes," the boy answered. He was so glad to be with her.

"Do you remember waving to me?"

"And you waved to me", he answered with a smile.

"That's right; I did. But I was very surprised when you waved. Why did you do that?"

"Because."

How many times had she heard the same answer from young children? 'Because' seemed to be a sufficient answer for almost any question asked. She was almost sure her next question would receive the same answer.

"Because why?"

"Because I was looking for you."

"Looking for me?" she replied, surprised. How could that be, she thought. Of course, there was one possibility. "You mean someone told you what I looked like?"

Elliot had never really thought of it in that way, but she was right, someone had told him what she looked like. "Yes, someone told me."

"Who?" she asked.

"I don't know," he answered, smiling up at her. He was so glad to find his friend. Now she could answer all the questions he had.

There were other questions Sister Teresa wanted to ask this friendly little boy, but she could hear commotion in the classroom. Taking his hand, she entered, already knowing where Elliot would sit. Instead of in the back, where all the new students started, she would place him in the front row near the window. He was too short for the back.

In the first hour Sister Teresa discovered that Elliot was a good reader, listened very well, and watched every move she made. It was almost disconcerting, the way he looked at her. Every time their eyes would meet, he would smile. And for some reason, she felt obligated to return his smiles. She found herself wanting his attention to irritate her, but something within her kept saying that it was necessary for the boy to be behaving the way he was. She knew there were things she didn't understand.

When the bell for lunch sounded, there was a flurry of activity as the boys put their books and pencil boxes away. Then they stood. Elliot did the same. When the room had cleared and boys had marched by rows from the class, Sister Teresa looked up from her desk to see Elliot seated once again. They were alone in the room. The other boy's footsteps echoed down the metal stairs.

"It's time for lunch, Elliot," she said.

"Can I eat with you?"

"With me? Why would you want to do that?"

"Because you're my friend," he said.

"I am?" she answered with surprise. She had heard five-year-olds say some pretty surprising things before, but nothing like this.

"Ida said that friends always had lunch together."

"Who is Ida?"

"She was my friend before you."

"Oh. Did she bring you to St. Maurice's?"

"No, a man in a big, black car did. Past horses and cows."

What was she to do with this strange little boy? Mother Superior had made reference to how he was to be treated. Of course, Sister Teresa had no idea it would be up to her, to see that he was treated properly.

"You know, if we stay here much longer, we're both going to miss lunch."

But the young boy just sat there with his hands folded on the desktop.

"In this school," she continued, "the teachers eat in one place and the cadets in another."

"Where do you eat?" he asked.

"We have a dining room near where the cadets eat."

"Can I go there too?"

Well, she thought, he certainly isn't one to give up easily. She finished cleaning the top of her desk and stood up. Elliot stood too. She went to where he was, stood in front of him, and then knelt so that she was at eye level with him. Elliot smiled. Ida used to do this too. She would get small, like him.

"How do you know that I'm supposed to be your friend, why not Sister Beatrice or Sister Mary in your dormitory?"

"The dream showed you." Elliot replied

Sister Teresa dropped back on her heels. So that's why the strange acknowledgement happened in the chapel! That's why he's so sure.

A dream! How many dreams had she had in the past? How many times had she thought about them, wondering what they might mean? And how many times had she stopped herself from thinking or acting upon them? She remembered, as a novice nun, how she had wanted to talk about her dreams, but her superiors had been unwilling. Though it hadn't been said directly to her, she was given the impression that the power of Satan could be the cause of some dreams. And if that were the case, how would one tell the difference between the good ones and the evil ones? So, she had been obedient to her superiors. And now, a dream from a small boy!

"You saw me in your dream?" she asked.

"Yes, and the man with the long black car. I thought you had bandages around your head."

"You had never seen a nun before?"

"A what?"

"A person like me. You have never seen one of us before?"

"No."

"In the dream, did I tell you I was going to be your friend?"

"No, it was someone else."

"Who?"

"I don't know."

"But you believe the dream, don't you?"

Elliot was surprised at her question. Such a question had never entered his mind. What did she mean? What was she saying?

"What?" he answered.

Sister Teresa could see by the look in his eyes that her question was foreign. She should have known that such a question was not part of this child's makeup. There was no doubt in his mind about the dream, nor had there ever been. It was a foolish question, one that should never have been asked. A Scripture came to her mind as she took the hand of her new friend: "Let the little children come to me and do not hinder them, for the kingdom of heaven belongs to such as these."

"Never mind," she answered. "Why don't we go see what we're having for lunch?"

Since it was Monday, cream of chicken was being served. Sister Teresa could smell it as she opened the door to the Sister's dining room. As always, whenever someone was late to a meal, everyone turned to look and see who was opening the door. Sister Teresa had promised herself that she would not laugh or even smile at any of the expressions that would certainly be on their faces. So she did the best she could not to look at all. She was sorry, however, to see Sister Florence drop her bread, and Sister Beatrice stop with her fork in her mouth. Sister Teresa couldn't bring herself to look at the head of the far table, where Mother Superior would certainly be watching as the Sisters shifted slightly so that the two latecomers could sit together.

Oh dear, Sister Teresa thought, Elliot is too short for the table. His eyes barely reached the edge of it. But, without hesitation, he shifted his weight slightly and somehow ended up on his knees so that he was tall enough. What a smart boy, she thought as she took Elliot's hand and said a prayer of thanksgiving for both of them. Elliot closed his eyes too, while someone set a plate before him. He could smell the food on it. Oh, he was hungry.

* * *

That evening Mother Superior met privately with Sister Teresa. It was decided that, for the time being, Sister Teresa would have lunch with young Mr. Reed in her classroom. A bag lunch would be provided, just as for Sister Sarah in the Infirmary. Mother Superior made it clear that she expected Sister Teresa to let her know as soon as she felt it was appropriate to go back to their regular arrangements. Sister Teresa readily agreed, not really knowing what it would be like to have lunch everyday with a five-year-old boy. She didn't tell Mother Superior about the child's dream. She really didn't know Mother Superior's thoughts on that subject, but in the fifteen years she had been at St. Maurice's, she had never heard dreams discussed.

Two nights after her meeting with Mother Superior, Sister Teresa had the following dream.

**She stood near a very narrow bridge that swung high above a dark ocean. Each end of the bridge was connected to a cliff. Down below she could hear the waves of a dark waters breaking against rocks on the shoreline. She felt as though it was just the beginning of a new day, with the early morning sun reflecting off grayish clouds. As she waited to see the sun, she heard a voice at the other end of the bridge. And as the shadows disappeared from the far cliff, she could see that it was Elliot. He was calling to her, but she could see he would not move onto the bridge. She knew that she had to cross to him. As she took her first step onto the bridge, she was fearful because the bridge at its center became somewhat narrower. Again, Elliot called to her, and she took another step. She felt the bridge begin to sway. She took a tighter grip on the ropes, caught her breath, took another step, and felt the violent swaying of the bridge.**

She woke with a start. She glanced at the clock. It was five-thirty. Good, she thought as she got out of bed, it's a good time to get up.

She looked out the window and across the lawn towards the front of the school. She could make out the silhouette of the trees in the early morning grayness and was reminded of her dream. She felt a constriction in her throat, tenseness in her stomach, and tears came into her eyes. Is this because of the dream?

Without thinking, she looked back at the darkened room, to the spot at the end of her bed, the place where she always went for her closet prayers. She knelt in that familiar spot, crossed herself, and as was her habit, she spoke out loud.

"Heavenly Father, I thank you for your love and your guidance in my life. I praise your Holy Name and thank you for your blessed son, Jesus, my Lord and Savior. May his precious Spirit guide me in all that I do." She paused, wondering what the correct words should be for the guidance she now needed. Usually when she thought such a thing as "correct words", she would reprimand herself for not just saying what she wanted to say and be done with it. But now, she knew she was on unfamiliar ground. She knew she was coming back to an area of experience that she had given up years ago. Dreams!

"I don't know what to do, Lord."

Immediately, a thought flooded her mind: **Yes, you do. You know exactly what to do.**

"I do?" she said. "What do I know to do?"

And she waited.

Her mind was quiet. No illuminating thought came. She waited. As time passed, her mind drifted to the Scriptures, and she thought about a scripture she often found diverting and peaceful. The night of Jesus' death, when He was in the upper room, and comforting His disciples, He told them that He was going to prepare a place for them, so that they could be where He was. She always found comfort in this thought; her mind would try to visualize what the heavenly city would look like, and what it would be like to be there with Him. It was her favorite diversion.

**"What else did I say?"** This thought startled her because she knew that she would not ask that question of herself. **"What else did I say?"** She stared at her hands in the morning light, wondering what He meant? She got quickly to her feet and went to her small desk. On top of it was her Bible. She opened to the Gospel of John and turned to the fourteenth chapter. Her eyes fell on the words:

"If you love Me, you will obey what I command."

Her thoughts automatically went to a verse in the fifteenth chapter. She didn't have to look this one up:

"This is my commandment that you love
one another as I have loved you."

"You want me to love the boy!" she said out loud. She knew that this was the correct answer, but she felt embarrassed as she said it. Her heart didn't want to admit it, but she had the feeling that the Lord was asking more of her than she had given in the past. Suddenly, she questioned her past fifteen years of service. Had she not given as much of herself as she was capable? Tears filled her eyes. She knew that there had been a bridge between each boy and her, and she had been afraid to cross it. There were needs that these boys had that went beyond just teaching them to write, to spell, and the basic principles of mathematics. She had taken the easy road; she was sure of that. Carefully, she had stayed within the guidelines set down for her. In fact she had even been grateful at times because of the protection that these "rules" had given, keeping her from never having to cross that swaying bridge. She began crying softly, while seated at her little writing table.

* * *

The nurse, Sister Sarah, was pleased at the recovery of Felix Skinner. His stay in the infirmary was two weeks shorter than she had expected. While he was gathering up his clothes, she instructed him to eat properly and do whatever he had to do to keep from getting sick. His large eyes looked up at her, but she wasn't sure whether he even cared about eating. In all her years of taking care of young children, Mr. Skinner was the saddest looking boy she had ever treated. When she saw him, she was always reminded of the pictures of the children standing behind barbed wire in concentration camps. His body was so thin, and there was always a feeling of hopelessness about him. In the year that he had been at St. Maurice's, she had given him three physical examinations, always hoping to find something definite that would help her to understand why he looked as he did, but nothing ever showed up. On the charts, he seemed to be healthy, but healthy or not, no seven-year-old boy should look or act like he did.

She patted him on the head and sent him out the door. As she watched him walk across the parade ground, she crossed herself and asked the Lord to look after the little mite.

Elliot had thought the empty bed, two down and across the aisle, might be for another new boy. He was surprised when he came back from class one day, and there was the sick boy, sitting on the bed. Elliot recognized him immediately. What had Sister Sarah called him? Skinner. His name was Skinner. Elliot smiled as he went by, but Skinner didn't notice him. Elliot decided to go back and say hello.

"Hi," Elliot said.

Felix slowly looked up and stared at the dark-haired kid in front of him. He didn't recognize him.

"Hello," he answered. He looked at the kid again. There was something about him that looked familiar, but he didn't know what. Besides, he didn't even care. He looked up again. The kid just kept smiling and looking at him. "What is it?" Skinner said tiredly.

"I saw you in the infirmary," Elliot said.

"When?" Skinner asked.

Elliot didn't understand time. "Sometime."

"What?" Skinner squinted at him.

"I saw you when you were sick. You opened your eyes."

"Oh," Skinner said, as he looked back at his hands like he had been doing before the little kid started talking to him.

Elliot wondered why Skinner just sat there not really doing anything. "My name is Elliot." He waited for an answer. None came. He turned and walked back to his bed.

At dinnertime, Elliot tried to sit next to Skinner but another boy pushed in front of him, so he ended up across the table. He watched Skinner as he ate. Or, what was more like it, he watched him as he hardly ate at all. Sister Sarah was right, Elliot thought, Skinner did not eat enough. He would get sick again. Elliot noticed that he ate his dessert first, then a little potatoes, but everything else he left on his plate.

Skinner noticed Elliot watching him. "What's the matter?" he asked abruptly.

"Sister Sarah said you didn't eat enough, and that's why you get sick." Elliot noticed that the other boys at the table looked up as he said this. Skinner noticed this too.

"So?" Skinner countered. "What, are you going to do, tell her?"

"No, I won't do that. But you're supposed to eat good."

Skinner glared at him for a moment, then looked back down at his food. He hated meat; he hated vegetables, and all this stuff on his plate. He wished this kid would shut up. He didn't even like the kind of bread they had tonight!

Then Skinner got a surprise. He watched as the little guy scooted his dessert over in front of him.

"What are you doin'?"

"You like the Jell-O."

"Yeah, so?"

"You can have mine," Elliot said simply.

"What for?"

"So you won't get sick."

Skinner looked at the dessert, then back to the kid. "You better not leave it there or I'm gonna eat it," Skinner warned him. The other boys had stopped eating and were watching with interest. Nobody gave up a dessert, nobody. Skinner took the dessert and started to eat it. "Boy, you are really dumb. You didn't think I'd do it, did you?"

Elliot wondered why he wouldn't eat the rest of the food; it tasted real good to him.

* * *

Elliot stood before Sister Agatha, then turned and looked into the mirror. Oh, how he loved his uniform. He touched the metal emblems on his collars and then moved closer to the mirror and stared at the reflection of them. Sister Sarah had to smile at the enthusiasm Elliot showed.

"I'll have your other pants ready in two days."

"I get more?"

"Yes. They wear out faster than your coat."

"Oh," he said, now taking off his hat and inspecting it.

"Does the hat hurt your head?"

"Oh, no. I like it!" he said as he quickly placed it back on his head. "Will I get a sword when I get bigger?" He had seen a high school boy, Adjutant Finney, marching the cadets on the parade grounds.

"I thought you wanted chevrons on your sleeve," Sister Agatha said.

"I like the sword, and the thing you carry it in."

"The scabbard," she said, amused at the ambition of this little one. "That's what the Captain carries. Do you know what you have to do to become the Captain?"

"Get big," he said quickly, knowing this answer to be true.

Sister Agatha laughed and sat down next to him. "That's true, but it takes much more than that. You have to be very smart, get good grades, be a strong leader, and be able to stay out of trouble. Can you do all those things?"

"What is 'be a strong leader'?" As he was asking this, as was his habit, he took the Sister's hand. She was surprised, but pleased.

"Well, you have to be looked up to by the rest of the cadets. They must be willing to follow you, and do the things that you ask of them. And you must tell them the right things and not be afraid to follow the rules."

Elliot's dark eyes watched her steadily while he listened closely to every word she said. He thought about what she was saying.

"I think I can do that. Ida said she thought I was smart."

"Sister Teresa thinks you're smart too," Sister Agatha said, although she knew she was not supposed to pass on what other Sisters said about cadets. Oh, well, she thought, the friendliness of this little guy makes one do things they usually wouldn't.

Elliot smiled and said, "Then I have to get good grades and get big. I think I can do it."

Sister Agatha laughed and said, "I think you can too!"

*　*　*

Felix Skinner was surprised when he saw little Elliot Reed in his class. He noticed that Sister Teresa had put him up in front. Maybe Elliot was a midget and really older than all of them. And even though she had put him next to the window, Skinner noticed that he didn't look out of it like most of the guys did. This new kid watched Sister Teresa and always did his homework. Skinner thought Elliot Reed is a jerk. He still gave up his desserts and then acted like he didn't care. The rest of the guys at the table thought he was nuts. He had heard them talking about Reed in the dorm. They were right though, this Reed was crazy.

When the class was leaving for lunch, Skinner noticed that Reed stayed in his seat. Why? What was he doing in there? And then Skinner saw that it happened everyday. The guy never ate lunch with the rest of them.

Skinner really didn't want to talk to him, but he wanted to know what was going on. So one night before 'lights out,' he walked over to Reed's bed. Reed smiled up at him. The dope was always smiling.

"How old are you?"

"Five."

Well, he wasn't a midget. "How come you don't eat lunch with us?" Skinner asked quickly. He didn't like starting conversations.

"I eat with Sister Teresa. We have a paper bag lunch.

"How come?"

"She's my friend, and I'm not supposed to eat with the rest of the Sisters."

Skinner considered this for a moment. "What's in the paper bags?"

"Sandwiches, apples, and stuff like that," Elliot answered.

Skinner didn't know what else to ask, so he turned and went back to his bed. He wondered what Elliot meant about Sister Teresa being his friend. She was a Sister, how could she be his friend? What a dope.

* * *

Sister Teresa had decided not to tell Elliot about her dream. But she did make one change immediately. She decided that from now on she would look forward to these lunch meetings with Elliot. She would no longer be concerned about what they might talk about or if she could spend a whole hour with a five year old or any other such thing. She decided she would find enjoyment in it no matter what. In her prayers, she always asked the Lord to bless these lunch times. Seating themselves and preparing to enjoy their lunches this day, Sister Teresa prayed as usual. Then they both opened their bags.

"Skinner talked to me last night," Elliot said while unwrapping his sandwich.

"He did?" Sister Teresa asked, truly surprised. Skinner only talked when talked to. "What did he say?"

"He asked me where I eat lunch."

Now why would Felix Skinner care about that, she wondered? "And what did you say to him?"

"I told him I eat with you, and we have paper bag lunches. And then he asked what was in them. And I said sandwiches, apples and stuff like that. Then he walked away."

Felix Skinner is one strange young boy, Sister Teresa thought. He has been here a year and nobody seems to be his friend. My, I'm starting to think like Elliot, she thought, what with his idea of friendships. She smiled to herself.

"I think he's supposed to be my friend too," Elliot said quietly.

Sister Teresa felt her arms turn to "goose flesh". "Why did you say that?"

"I saw his face."

"In a dream?"

"No. I was standing out on the cement, after I got measured."

"What did you see?"

"Just his face. He was real sick, and he was crying.

Just the way he was in his bed."

"What do you mean, just the way he was in his bed."

"I went into the wrong door, and I saw him in his bed. I went up to him, and he opened his eyes. He was just like the picture in my head."

"You mean you saw him in your mind before you saw him in his bed?"

Elliot nodded his head affirmatively and kept eating his sandwich. Sister Teresa couldn't eat. She was sure something wonderful was going on, and she was part of it. But what was it? This little boy in front of her had dreams and visions! Suddenly she wanted to cry again. The same feeling she had when she was in her room flooded over her. She had no idea what was bringing this on, but that the tears just wanted to come. She excused herself and went into the deserted hallway. There, she cried like a child.

Somehow, she knew God was doing something special and that He was giving her the privilege of being part of it. Then, in her tears, something unexpected happened.

Reflecting back eight years, while in a local bookstore searching for books about vegetable gardening, she had seen a paperback book of the life of Martin Luther. Without thinking, she had picked it up and read the front and back covers. Then it had struck her as to what she was doing. She quickly replaced the book in the shelf, thinking how fortunate it was that she was alone. Twenty minutes went by as she browsed the store. But she had ended up standing in front of the paperback section, still looking at the spine of that book. She knew it was the only copy they had. What difference that made, she had no idea. She found herself reaching out and picking the book from its place.

If the cashier had found any humor in a Catholic nun purchasing a copy of Luther's life, he had given no indication. She had quickly stuffed the little brown package into her habit and left the store. The idea of growing a small vegetable garden had left her mind for good.

She had read the book late at night. In three days she had finished it. She found she had something in common with Mr. Luther. He too had been dissatisfied with his spiritual walk, but because of outside pressures, he had been forced to find his way into the Word of God. For over a month these thoughts had kept disturbing Sister Teresa's daily prayers and her time of teaching. She knew that the near-cloistered life she led would not allow the circumstances to change as they had with Mr. Luther. Things could go on just the way they were until she died and most probably would. And yet, like Luther, she desperately desired more than she had now. But, when trying to determine what this hunger might be, she had found no answer.

Early one morning, while in that drowsy state between being asleep and awake, a plan came to her mind. She too, like Luther, would read the Bible. And at the same time, in her prayers, would ask God for guidance and for that something more. Something that would fulfill this hunger she couldn't express. Though this plan had made little sense to her, she had decided to leave logical thought behind her and just trust that God, through His mercy, would answer even prayers that could not be voiced.

She had begun with the first book of the New Testament, Matthew. She had read slowly and carefully. She had only read a little early each morning, so as not to take away from her regular duties. It had taken weeks before she finished the four Gospels. After each book, she would contemplate what she had read and each morning before her reading, she would pray to God...for this 'something'.

She had been carrying out her plan for five months and was in the second chapter of the Book of Acts, reading about the day of Pentecost. She had read about the tongues of fire and the violent blowing wind. She moved on to the speech that Peter made to the crowd. Then something happened; Sister Teresa had actually felt as if she were one of the large crowd who was listening to Peter. His words gained new reality, as if pointed towards her.

> *"Therefore let all Israel be assured of this: God has made this Jesus, whom you crucified, both Lord and Christ." When the people heard this, they were cut to the heart and said to Peter and the other apostles, "Brothers, what shall we do?"*

Sister Teresa had found herself saying out loud, with all the emotion that must have taken place two thousand years ago, "Brothers, what shall I do?"

*Peter replied, "Repent and be baptized, every one of you, in the name of Jesus Christ so that your sins may be forgiven. And you will receive the gift of the Holy Spirit."*

As she had read these words, she had fallen to the floor of her small room and heard herself cry out, "Oh, God I do repent in the name of Jesus, and I ask that my sins be forgiven!" She had felt as if her heart was about to break. Then, something had flooded her. She had felt a warmth and a sense of well being so strong, so soothing, that it took her breath away.

As she had gasped in surprise, she had opened her mouth to speak, and a strange language had come from her. She spoke it, but she did not understand it. She spoke it again. And again. Then she had let herself go, and the language had flooded from her. Oh, what a wonder it had been! Though she hadn't known what she said, she had no longer cared. The peace and the reassurance that she had received were beyond her comprehension.

She had continued to speak and weep, missing both prayer and breakfast time.

She had told no one about her rebirth and infilling, about the wonderful miracle that had taken place within her. She wasn't exactly sure why secrecy was important, but she felt that it was best to be quiet about it.

Even so, the other Sisters knew that she had changed. Sister Teresa, at times, smiled for no apparent reason or she had even been known to laugh during times that should have been serious. Some of the Sisters had even commented on Sister Teresa's looks, how they had changed. They weren't exactly sure of how, but she certainly looked different to them. Whatever the changes were with Sister Teresa, many of the Sisters decided that they weren't for the best, what with her seeming rather aloof. Sometimes, she would even leave the grounds, going into town for whatever reason. She always got permission, but still, none of the other Sisters ever went into town alone.

Sometime after her experience, Sister Teresa was not exactly sure when, she had stopped using the language of tongues. And she wasn't sure of the reason. She had thought about it, wondering why she would give up something that had given her so much pleasure, so much assurance. Whatever the reason, she had certainly stopped using it. But now, in the hallway of the school, as she knelt and cried, she let her language return. Oh, how good it felt, how right to talk to God and not have to think or worry about what was being said! Oh, how she had missed it!

She hadn't seen Elliot as he stuck his head out of the classroom and looked down the hall. Nor did she hear him as he walked up to her and stood watching. She did feel the little hand as it touched her shoulder. Startled, she saw Elliot standing in front of her. His dark eyes were concerned but there was no fear in them. "Are you alright?" he asked.

"Yes," she answered softly. "I'm just fine." Taking the little boy into her arms, she gave him a big hug. It was the first time she had ever hugged a cadet. She felt his little arms hug her back, and then he said, "That's what friends do. They hug!"

She couldn't help but laugh. For some reason, she had never heard anything sweeter or funnier. She couldn't stop laughing. Elliot soon joined her, and they both laughed and laughed and laughed.

* * *

Sister Teresa and Elliot decided together that Felix Skinner should be watched after. Elliot told her how he didn't eat anything but desserts and potatoes. Sister Teresa put him high upon her prayer list and confided in Sister Sarah, because she knew the concern she had for Skinner.

One evening after dinner, when all the boys were at their beds, Elliot noticed Skinner looking over at him. But when Elliot returned the look, Skinner would glance away. Elliot caught him again. If fact, every time that Elliot looked up from his book, Skinner would be looking over at him. Elliot went over and stood before his bed. Skinner was looking at his thin hands.

"How come you wouldn't eat my dessert tonight?" Elliot asked. He stood there a long time. Maybe Skinner wasn't going to answer him.

"What did you have in your bag?" Skinner asked, still looking down at his hands.

"At lunch?"

"With Sister Teresa," Skinner snapped.

Elliot had to think because he really didn't care so much about the food as he did being with his friend. "Ahh, I had a meat loaf sandwich, a banana and two cookies."

"Could I come too?"

Skinner's question had come quickly, and he did not make any eye contact with Elliot. Elliot really didn't know what to say.

Skinner glanced at him. "Well, can I?"

"I don't know. I think I have to ask."

Sister Teresa had been surprised at Elliot's request. Her first thought was to say no, but she hesitated. Why had she and Sister Sarah been praying for the Skinner boy? They had been asking God to make a change in the boy's life. Well, here it was. How could she say no? Since she wasn't going to say no, what was the best way to handle it? She certainly couldn't take the responsibility of making such a decision. It would have to go through Mother Superior. And how would she react to another person involved in the luncheon? Would she stop it because it was becoming too complicated? Sister Teresa didn't want that to happen.

"What do you think Elliot?" Sister Teresa asked.

"It would be good," he answered.

"Why?"

"Because."

Sometime Sister Teresa thought she would never learn.

"Let me find out if it will be alright. Let's not say anything until I find out." Elliot nodded his head as he took another bite from his sandwich.

Sister Teresa decided to tell Sister Sarah about Felix Skinner's request. She broke out in a smile. "Perfect," she said to Sister Teresa. "Just perfect!"

Sister Teresa was not sure she saw the perfection in it.

"How do we know if Mother Superior will allow it?" Sister Teresa added, as she watched the face of the nurse. It seemed strange how little she knew about Sister Sarah. After fifteen years, she had no idea what her strengths and weaknesses might be.

"Mother Superior just might, if you could get Mister Skinner to agree to something first."

"What's that?" asked Sister Teresa.

"He must promise to eat all of what he gets in his paper bag, no matter what."

Sister Teresa saw the merit to it immediately. "She wouldn't turn it down, not if she saw the benefit to his health, would she?"

"And at the same time," Sister Sarah added, "we'll have Mister Skinner making a responsible move. He has to make up his own mind to eat."

Sister Teresa smiled broadly at the way Sister Sarah's mind worked. "You should be in politics Sister."

"You mean we aren't?" Sister Sarah answered with a straight face. Both Sisters laughed as they went to see Mother Superior about their plan.

They had been right. She agreed immediately, but Mister Skinner had to agree too. It was planned that Sister Teresa would talk to Mister Skinner after the rest of the class had left for lunch.

In the morning, before the cadets entered the classroom, three bagged lunches were placed in the lower drawer of Sister Teresa's desk. There were no markings on the bags, and the contents were identical.

As the class stood for the lunch break, Sister Teresa, instead of staying at her desk as was her usual way, moved next to the door through which the cadets would be leaving.

"Alright," she said. With this command, the students, by rows, moved passed her, each wondering why she was at the door. As Felix went by, she took his thin arm and moved him beside her. They waited there until all the boys had left. Then Sister Teresa moved back to her desk and sat.

"Come and sit, Felix," she said.

Felix started back to his desk in the middle of the room. "No, not back there, sit next to Elliot." Felix did as he was told. Sister Teresa waited until Felix settled and looked up at her.

"Elliot has told me that you would like to eat lunch with us. Is that right?"

Skinner only paused for a moment. "Yes, Sister."

"I talked to Sister Sarah about you. She thought it would be a good idea too, but she said that you would have to promise to do something."

"What?"

Sister Teresa brought out the three lunches and placed them on the front of her desk.

"Then we went to Mother Superior, and she agreed too."

Sister Teresa pointed to one of the brown bags. "You have to promise, no matter what is in here, that you'll eat all of it. If you won't promise, you'll have to go with the other boys."

Skinner looked at the bags, then back to Sister Teresa.

"Are they all the same?" he asked cunningly.

Sister had a difficult time not smiling. "Yes. All the bags are the same. And Felix, you have to do it everyday. You'll have to eat all of it...every single day, just the way we do."

"I don't like crusts," he said softly.

"You will now," she answered evenly, "every bit of them."

Skinner glanced at Elliot and saw that he was looking directly at him, as if he too were waiting for his answer.

"O.K.!" he said to Sister Teresa. "I promise."

With that, Elliot came forward, took his lunch, and returned to his seat. Felix watched, and then went up to the desk. He looked at the two bags, and then at Sister Teresa.

"It's your choice," she said, smiling at this strange little boy who was taking the first step out of his shell.

After making his selection, he walked slowly back to the desk and opened his sack. He looked in it and then looked over at Elliot, who had already taken his sandwich out, but was waiting for the blessing to be given. Felix took his out too, unwrapped it, and waited with Elliot. Sister Teresa said the blessing, and then they ate, except Felix. He looked at his sandwich for what seemed a long time. So long in fact that Elliot had stopped eating and was watching to see if Skinner was going to do it. Finally, having made up his mind, Felix picked up his sandwich. Holding it lightly in both hands, he slowly turned it as he ate all the crust from the sandwich. Once he had a mouthful, he chewed.

Sister Teresa paid close attention to her own food, so that she wouldn't laugh, but Elliot did no such thing. He laughed immediately, and then decided on the same plan of attack for the rest of his sandwich. The boys looked at each other with their mouths full of crust. Sister Teresa thought she saw a smile on Felix's face.

*  *  *

One night, when Elliot was eight and a half years old, he dreamt:

> **Father Tinian was saying Mass in an open field, which was covered with thick, green grass. There was no altar, no sacraments, but Elliot could see Father making the same movements he made in church. Between Elliot and Father Tinian was a rectangular hole in the ground. Elliot wanted to look into it, but wasn't able. He felt as though he were seated, like in church, where he could watch but not participate. Father Tinian moved to the hole and made movements as though sprinkling holy water into it.**
>
> **From over the grassy hill, behind Father Tinian, a funeral procession appeared. All were dressed in black, except Sister Teresa, who was in a bright, multi-colored habit. She walked beside a tall, blond, middle-aged woman and was talking happily with her. Behind them, walked a large, gray-haired man with wooden crutches. And floating in the air behind him, in a clear plastic casket, was the body of Gordon Grayland, the fat young man who had yelled at Elliot to go to the infirmary. He was clothed in his St. Maurice's dress uniform. Behind the casket were a large number of people, all dressed in black.**
>
> **The casket floated over the grave and slowly disappeared into the ground. As it moved downwards, some of**

**the older boys from the Academy went to present arms, giving a last salute to their friend. As Elliot was watching Father Tinian mouthing words over the grave, he saw the soul of Gordon coming up and out of the open grave. Gordon's eyes were open, and if he had wanted to, he could have turned his head to look at the mourners. But his attention was focused on something straight upward. It was a bright light, and, smiling, he disappeared towards it.**

**Elliot noticed that only Sister Teresa saw this; the rest of the people were busy mourning. Sister Teresa became so excited that she jumped from the seat next to the blond lady, began clapping and lifting her arms skyward. No one paid any attention to the Sister; they were too busy being mournful.**

Elliot woke with a start. He was wide-awake, blinking in the semi-darkness. He thought about his dream, not exactly sure what to do about it. Lifting up on an elbow, he looked over at Skinner's bed. Then he got up and quietly walked over to his sleeping friend.

"Hey, Skinner," he whispered. Skinner didn't move until he touched him.

"Huh? What?"

"I had a dream," Elliot said.

"What about?" he said sleepily, he was always glad to see his friend.

"About Grayland," Elliot said.

"His parents took him away somewhere," Skinner said.

"I know. He was really sick so they took him away. But let me tell you my dream."

Then, quietly, Elliot whispered out the dream, making sure he remembered all of it. Skinner found the whole thing fascinating.

He stared at Elliot when he finished and then finally said, "Wow! What does all that mean?"

Elliot knew he couldn't hold this in, and they were best friends now. "He's going to die."

"He is?"

Elliot thought about what he had just said, then added, "In fact he might already be dead."

"Wow! How do you know?"

"I'm not sure," Elliot replied.

"Maybe that's not what the dream means," Skinner said.

"It does," Elliot said quietly.

Skinner believed him. "Wow!"

The next day, Elliot told the dream to Sister Teresa, exactly as he had told Skinner. She listened intently and then was silent for a long moment. Finally, she glanced at Skinner, then back to Elliot. The two boys were inseparable now, both good students, and growing at a furious rate. Though they had left her class over a year ago, the special lunches still continued. None of the three had wanted them to stop.

"Did you know that Gordon is very sick?" she asked the boys. They both nodded in agreement. "He's so sick that after he left the school, the doctors put him in a special hospital." The boys didn't know this. She leaned forward and looked directly at Elliot, "Do you think Gordon is going to die?"

"Yes," Elliot replied.

"Tell me what the dream means," she said.

"I don't know all of it, only that he's going to die, and that you're supposed to go to the..."

"Funeral," Skinner said, helping his friend with a word he was not used to saying.

"Yes, funeral," Elliot repeated. "I think the tall, blond lady is his mother. You're supposed to be with her."

Sister Teresa glanced at a certain desk in the third row, near the back. She remembered Gordon very well. He hadn't come into her class until he was nearly eight. He had been a very slow learner, and the kids had made fun of him. It hadn't taken long before he started acting up in class, trying, through humorous antics, to win some friends. The only thing accomplished by this behavior was it irritated her.

One day she had gotten so upset with Gordon that she kept him after class. She remembered that she had purposely continued correcting papers while he sat and thought about what she was going to do to him. When she finally looked up, something happened within her. She saw him for what he really was, a very unhappy, friendless, fat child. Her heart went out to him, and she knew she wasn't going to punish him.

She remembered that she had called him up to the front of the row to sit in the seat that Skinner was sitting in now, and they had talked for over an hour. She had asked about his family, about what he liked and disliked, and then as she had gently questioned him, he tearfully told her that he didn't have any friends. At that moment, she had told him that there was Someone who wanted to be his friend, who would never let him down. She remembered the look that had come across his face, when he had asked her who it was. He had said he needed a friend like that. But when she had told him about Jesus, he had answered in dismay, "But He died!

"Only for three days," she'd answered. And then she had told him the plan of salvation. Oh, how that young child listened. She knew without a doubt that it was God's time for him.

"You mean He really likes me?" Gordon asked as she finished.

"Yes. He knows how lonely you are."

"He does? Would He help me to find some friends?"

"I think He will. Why don't we ask Him?" She had taken hold of his chubby hands, and the two of them had prayed together. She remembered so clearly how Gordon had opened his heart to his new friend and Savior, how the tears had come to the lad as he asked his Savior for help.

"Yes," she said quietly to Elliot. "I'll be sure to go to the funeral, and I'll talk to the tall, blond lady, just like your dream showed."

She included Skinner in her glances, making sure that he felt part of the plan. "It might be wise not to mention this to anyone else. I'm afraid they wouldn't understand."

The boys agreed.

Three days later the school was informed that Gordon Grayland had died. The time of the funeral was set, and a color and honor guard was selected from the student body. Father Tinian made sure that Gordon's best friends were picked as the casket bearers.

Mass was said at St. Maurice's chapel, with the immediate family and the student body in attendance. His family sat in the front rows, in front of the Sisters. Skinner was the first to see the tall blond lady enter. He nudged Elliot. Elliot glanced across the aisle and caught Sister Teresa's eye. She, too, had seen the tall lady and watched her enter, leaning on a gray haired man who was limping.

Strange, Sister Teresa thought; he isn't on crutches. She wondered if he might have a wooden leg. It was a terrible time for it, but she had to suppress a smile. Sometimes the symbolism in dreams was so clever it made her laugh. She knew without any hesitation that God had a marvelous sense of humor, and she loved Him all the more for it.

She watched as the man and woman walked towards the first pew. Yes, this was undoubtedly Gordon's mother. She wondered why, during so many years, she had never met Mrs. Grayland? The woman was having a terrible time. It was all she could do to hold herself together as her husband walked her to their seats. But then, as she sat there, her shoulders gave way. She seemed to crumble into silent crying. The man stiffly put his arm around her, doing what little he could to comfort her.

Since she had heard about Gordon's death, Sister Teresa had been praying for a graceful meeting with Mrs. Grayland. She had already asked Mother Superior for permission to attend the grave-side service. Usually, the Sisters would attend only the Mass and not accompany the family to the gravesite. Mother Superior had been surprised at the request.

"Did you know him well?" she had asked.

"Yes. We had some long talks when he was in my class."

"Oh, I'm glad. What was he like?"

"At that time, lonely."

"Really? He always seemed so gregarious," she said, as she continued working at her desk. She looked up at Sister Teresa for a moment. "I think it might be very nice if you went along with the boys."

"I thought I might say hello to Mrs. Grayland, if the opportunity called for it."

"Oh, do you know her?"

Sister Teresa knew she was taking a chance. The tall, blond lady might not even be the mother. “No, but I thought a few words about her son might help her.”

For the first time Mother Superior gave Sister Teresa her full attention. In fact, the Sister could not remember the last time the Mother had looked at her so closely. “Is there something I should know?” the large woman asked bluntly.

“No, but there were some nice moments that her son and I shared. Maybe knowing about them will help her.” Sister Teresa hoped that she wouldn’t be asked what these moments had been.

“I’m glad you thought of it. Gordon was her only child.”

At the end of the Mass, Sister Teresa stood and moved into the aisle. She waited as the Grayland’s approached where she was standing.

“May I help?” asked Sister Teresa when Mr. Grayland approached.

There was a look of gratitude in the eyes of the tall, elegant man. “Thank you,” he said.

He moved to the other side of his wife, and Sister Teresa put her arm around the woman’s waist. When their eyes met, Sister Teresa was shocked. There was more than grief in this woman’s face. She had the look of a frightened animal! It was as though she were ready to panic, to run away. And her body was rigid.

Sister Teresa took hold of her hand and whispered, “It’s alright now. I’m with you, and I’ll stay as long as you need me.” She was shocked at her own words. Where did they come from? Why in the world did she think she would make any difference in what this woman felt? Then the woman relaxed some and even returned pressure to Sister Teresa’s hand.

They walked from the chapel.

As soon as they reached the outside area, Mr. Grayland turned and went back into the chapel to lead an older woman from the pew. Sister Teresa, not knowing what else to do, lead Mrs. Grayland down the outside corridor and into the main lobby. The limousines and the school buses were waiting on the long driveway out front. Gordon was being buried in the family plot at Larchmont Cemetery, some thirty miles from the school.

"Would you rather wait in the lobby or in the car?" Sister asked her.

"The car, please," Mrs. Grayland answered.

Sister Teresa walked her to the limo directly behind the hearse and opened the door for her. As Mrs. Grayland got in, she looked up at the Sister, reaching out for her hand.

"Please," she implored. Sister Teresa got in beside her, and Mrs. Grayland closed the door. Even though the day was cloudless, the car's tinted glass made it dark inside. They were alone in the limousine. Mrs. Grayland took the Sister's hand again.

"I hope you don't mind."

"No, not at all," Sister answered. Sister Teresa cupped her other hand over the woman's. As she did this, a shocking realization flooded her: **This woman was an adulteress and has already planned her suicide**. In that instant, somehow, Sister Teresa knew startling and hidden things about the woman! She also knew that this knowledge was true. Simultaneously, as this realization came to her, she remembered having read in the Scriptures how Peter had miraculously known the heart of Ananais! But what a frightening thing to know! What was she supposed to do with such dangerous knowledge?

She said a short silent prayer, and then looked at the face of the woman. Mrs. Grayland was certainly past her youth, but still very attractive. She wore rather heavy makeup, as though trying to hide the years, and yet her skin was still healthy and had few wrinkles.

"Mrs. Grayland, I would like to ask you a question about your son. Would that be alright?"

"Yes. What is it?"

"Where do you think he is now?"

"Why, he...he must be, ah, in heaven...or maybe in purgatory, waiting...maybe."

"He's in heaven, Mrs. Grayland," Sister Teresa assured his mother.

The Sister felt something unique taking place within her; some inner strength she'd never felt before was there to guide her words. And, oh, how calm she felt.

Mrs. Grayland was searching the Sister's face. "How can you be sure?" she asked. There was a bittersweet quality in her voice. Her faithlessness was suddenly in the open. A visible hardness was in her eyes. "Nobody knows for sure where they go, do they?"

"I'm sure of where your son is. I know for sure."

Mrs. Grayland withdrew her hand and had turned, staring out the window. Sister Teresa could sense that Mrs. Grayland, though she might continue to listen, was not going to let these words change her mind about such things.

"Mrs. Grayland, I know the truth about your son. Just as I know that you have been involved in adultery and have already planned your suicide."

The woman turned back suddenly, shocked. Sister Teresa's immediate thought was that this must be the same look that had been on the faces of Ananias and Sapphira just before they died. It was a mixture of anguish and fear, terror and dread, washing across Mrs. Grayland's face.

"How do you know that?" she snapped.

"I don't know how, but it's true, isn't it?"

"Nobody knows that!" she cried out.

"God does," Sister answered calmly.

Mrs. Grayland blinked, then blinked again. Her mouth opened to speak, then closed. Her hands flew up as if checking to see if her mouth were open, they darted back to her lap. Sister Teresa once again took both of the woman's hands in hers.

"God wants you to know that He knows everything about you," Sister Teresa continued softly. "He wants you to know that your son is with Him now, and that he will be there forever."

Mrs. Grayland's large eyes were wide as she listened to Sister Teresa. It was as though these were the first words she'd ever heard.

"He is, isn't he? He really is," Mrs. Grayland declared. Hope was in her voice.

"Yes! And the Lord wants you to be there too."

"Me?" A look of dismay came over her tear streaked cheeks and running eye shadow face. "But you know about me! I've...I've done things I can't even talk about. I can't even think about them without feeling sick."

Now her tears were for herself, the terrible shame she had been feeling for the past two years.

Sister Teresa saw the young pallbearers bringing the casket from the rear of the chapel. She knew she and Mrs. Grayland didn't have time to finish their talk. She touched Mrs. Grayland's face, causing her to look up at her.

"The people are coming now."

Mrs. Grayland looked up quickly, started to reach into her purse for her make-up mirror, and then suddenly decided she didn't care what she looked like.

"Don't go. Stay here with me. I have to talk...to find out more. Please."

Sister Teresa turned and looked through the back window. She saw Mr. Grayland helping his mother into the limousine behind them. She watched as he closed the door. Then he looked in their direction and began to make his way slowly towards the car.

"Your husband's coming."

When Sister Teresa looked back to Mrs. Grayland, she saw the woman break once again. Fresh tears coursed down her cheeks.

"I blamed him for everything. He had his leg removed..."

She stopped talking as he opened the door. Sister Teresa began to move over, making room for Mr. Grayland beside his wife.

"Oh, Sister. Please, stay where you are," the tall man said. "This will be fine," he assured her as he drew down one of the small jump seats and with some difficulty, slowly sat down.

Mrs. Grayland had taken Sister Teresa's hand, drawing her back to her side. "I need you here," she said rather strangely.

Then the driver shut the door of the limo, and the three of them sat in the semi-darkness. Mrs. Grayland watched as the young cadets placed the remains of her son in the back of the hearse.

"Robert?" she said, still watching the casket slide forward.

"Yes?" he responded, watching her tears as they mixed with her mascara.

"I'm sorry for the things I've done to you."

She's never said anything like this before, Robert thought, and he really didn't understand what was happening. He looked from her to the little Sister sitting next to her. She looked so small sitting there next to his strikingly beautiful wife. What's happened between these two? "Loretta, what do you mean?"

The hearse moved out in front of them, and their limo followed. But, at this moment, the body of the boy has been forgotten.

"I mean, that I've blamed you for things I just couldn't handle," his wife answered. "I've stayed out of your bed...because you lost your leg to cancer. I've been afraid to touch you. I'm sorry."

"It's alright," he said uncomfortably.

"No it isn't," she responded softly. "It's never been right to hurt you." She paused, looking down at her hands as they grasped the little Sister.

"When you got sick and thought you were going to die, I didn't help you. You told me your fears, and I...I was only afraid of what was going to happen to me. I didn't want to comfort you. I didn't want to hold you, to take care of you."

"Oh, Loretta..." was all the man could say. Sister Teresa could see that he was near tears.

"I can't remember the last time I told you that I loved you," his wife said ever so softly. "Can you?"

For the first time she looked at him. "Oh, Robert, I'm so sorry. I do love you. I love you more now than I ever have. Please forgive me for the things I've done to you."

Sister Teresa didn't really know what to do. Everything was becoming so personal, and here she was...stuck! Lord, she thought, why do You want me here? This seems to be a scene that only You should see and hear.

"I found out something from..." Mrs. Grayland looked quickly at the Sister. "I don't even know your name."

"It's Teresa," the Sister said quickly.

"I found out from Sister Teresa that God cares about us."

"God?" the surprised Mr. Grayland said.

"She told me things about myself that nobody else knows, things that I would never talk about. And Robert, she knows that Gordon is in heaven."

The surprised man opened his mouth to speak, but found he didn't know what he should say. He really didn't understand anything that was happening. "I'm sorry," he said. "I don't know what to say."

"And you shouldn't," Sister Teresa said. "It's your wife. She's learned something wonderful. In time, it will become clearer for you, Mr. Grayland. I told her about your son, so that her heart would be at peace. She's right though, I am sure of what I have said."

Mr. Grayland believed her. There was something very powerful about this little lady. When she talked, he wanted to listen. He somehow knew that she knew things he couldn't fathom. He watched as she moved over and patted the seat where she had been sitting.

"Please, Mr. Grayland, sit close to her. You two need each other now. Besides, that little seat was just made for me."

Mr. Grayland moved slowly over to the back seat. Sister Teresa watched as Loretta Grayland reached to help her husband. As Sister Teresa settled in the smaller seat, she saw Mrs. Grayland gently kiss her husband's cheek. Oh, this is the way funerals should be, the Sister thought! How her heart sang out to God for letting her be part of such a wonderful, wonderful miracle!

* * *

Four years have passed.

**As Sister Teresa stood on the cement of the dormitories outside corridor, she wondered why her bare feet weren't cold. It was nighttime, and it seemed to be foggy. Or was it? She looked down at her feet. She could not feel the polished cement. What does this mean, she thought? And what was she doing outside at this time of night, without shoes? She started to look at her body, to see how she was dressed, when suddenly she discovered that she was in the cement courtyard below. She looked around. Everywhere she looked around the school there was grayness. She shuddered involuntarily. Someone was behind her! Quickly, she turned and looked. She could see no one through the gloom. She felt as though she wanted to**

**run...to get away from this baleful grayness that seemed to be turning to darkness. She turned again, putting her hands before her as protection against an onslaught she felt was coming. But there was no one. Nothing there! She was terribly frightened. She cried out for help. Her voice began as a scream, but came out only a frail whisper that barely left her lips. She tried to pray, but her hands would not come together as was her practice, nor could she close her mouth. And she was much too terrified to close her eyes.**

**She heard something in the distance. Was it thunder? No. Though it rumbled, it had an eerie, human quality to it. Then she knew. It was laughter, a venomous laughter, so malignant, so noxious, as to make her flesh crawl. An oppressive fear forced her to her knees, and as she fell, she found that she was naked. The rumbling, pernicious voice laughed all the more as she tried to hide herself in the terrible darkness that now covered the school.**

Sister Teresa woke with a scream. She found herself clutching her arms, as if protecting herself from anyone seeing her breasts, while her legs were drawn up to her stomach. She began to weep. The fear from the dream had filled every pore of her body. The memory of the ominous darkness had made its way into her body, as if to give the dream a deep reality. Then, from within, she knew that a spiritual darkness was upon St. Maurice.

She got up from her bed and looked at the little clock on the nightstand, 3:00 a.m. She grasped the clock and turned off the alarm, all the time crying uncontrollably. She collapsed by the foot of the bed and wept all the more. Her anguished prayer was spoken simply: “I don’t know what to do, Lord. I’m frightened, and I know that there is something terribly wrong at this school. I thank You for what You have shown me, Lord.”

Even at that very moment, as she was thanking Him, another thought occurred telling her it was not important, and that it was, in fact, not real at all, but just a ridiculous dream. But, overcoming this thought, she continued praying.

"I know Satan is here somewhere in our school, and he is laughing at us! I thank You for showing me this, Lord." As she spoke these words, they struck hard at her sense of what was real. Had she, in the past, really believed there was a Satan? Had she read it in the Bible, but never really believed it? Or had she believed that because of the work she did and the place where she lived, that Satan would never be able to enter? She wrestled with these thoughts, finally she came to the conclusion she had never taken the Deceiver, the Liar, seriously.

"Oh, dear God," she cried out, "forgive my sin of unbelief!" She felt as though her walk had been a sham, a pious amble through a field of clover! How can one have a belief in God without believing that Satan exists also? What a foolish woman of God she was! As she began to rebuke herself, a word of knowledge came to her mind:

**"He has been here for a long time."**

And then directly after, a word of wisdom followed:

**"You cannot stand alone."**

"Stand? How do I do that?" she said aloud. And just as quickly, her mind recalled the scripture: *"Therefore put on the full armor of God, so that when the day of evil comes, you may be able to stand your ground, and after you have done everything, to stand."* There was silence as her mind raced along, flitting from one scattered thought to another, skipping about the information she had just received.

"If Satan has been here a long time, what do I do?" She knew as she spoke that she had already been told what she needed to do. "Who do I get to help me? Who will believe me?"

She prayed fervently for guidance that morning. Who should she ask? Who would stand with her? She received no answers, but she resolved to keep asking.

As Sister Teresa sat at breakfast she glanced at the faces of the other Sisters, knowing that for them everything was just the same. Nothing had changed from last night as far as they were concerned. It was only within her! And what was she supposed to do with it? Everything was different, and yet nothing had changed! She wanted to climb up on the table and shout at them. To tell them that they were all in desperate trouble! Instead, she looked down at her food.

She had no appetite. She wanted desperately to talk. She wanted to tell people things; make a plan of some sort! She wanted to do something! But what? She felt an irritation she'd never felt before, and it surprised her. Was she angry? If so, with who? She didn't want the thought to come, but she wondered if she was angry with God.

At that, she felt the blood flush her cheeks that she would even think such a thing! What gall, she thought. What nerve! She quickly asked His forgiveness. She was being a ninny! She had been given information of something that was going on at the school, and it was her job to...to what? Certainly God wanted her to do more than just sit here and fret!

Everyone was minding their own business, eating their food, and lost in their own thoughts, except for Sister Sarah. She had been watching Sister Teresa and wondering what was going on in the little Sister's mind. She wasn't eating, and she seemed to be battling with something. This was not the first morning that Sister Sarah had watched her.

Five years before, when Sister Teresa had taken such an interest in Mr. Skinner's health, Sister Sarah had been taken with her. She, Sister Sarah, had thought that Sister Teresa, more than all the other teachers, seemed to care about the overall welfare of the boys. Sister Teresa had been the only one who took the time to come to the infirmary and ask about the health of her students. If there had been matters needing prayer, they would do it together, right on the spot. And the way the little Sister prayed! No "Hail Mary's" or "Our Father's." No, that wasn't her way. She got right in and asked the Father for everything she needed.

Sometimes it made Sarah giddy just listening to her. Once she even laughed out loud when Sister Teresa asked Jesus to shake a certain boy by the seat of his pants, so that he would wake-up about himself! Sister Teresa had heard the laughter and had joined with her. And, beside that, Sister Teresa was the only teacher who ever asked her opinion about the cadet's welfare.

After breakfast, Sister Sarah decided to wait outside the dining room until Sister Teresa came out. It was Saturday—no school—and the infirmary was empty, praise the Lord!

"Sister Teresa?" Sister Sarah said softly as she fell in step beside her. She startled Sister Teresa, who jumped slightly as she looked up at the tall nurse.

"Oh, Sister Sarah," she laughed nervously. "I'm sorry. I'm afraid my mind was somewhere else."

"I thought that you might like to talk," the tall Sister said as they walked toward the lawn area.

Sister Teresa glanced up quickly. Why did she ask, she wondered? She wasn't sure what to say in return. Should she confide in her? She certainly needed to talk to someone. But there was a hesitation, a momentary pause, within her about sharing this terrible dream. Then again, she had been told that she could not "stand alone".

"Did I look like I needed someone to talk to?" she asked with a smile.

"Well, I did notice you during breakfast. It's not like you to not eat your meal." Both of the Sisters laughed. Maybe I should find out how she feels about dreams, Sister Teresa thought.

"What do you think about children and their dreams?" Sister Teresa ventured. She watched Sister Sarah's face as they walked slowly through the garden area.

"Dreams? Well, they certainly have a great many of them when they're sick. I've always felt that fevers had a lot to do with it."

It sounded as though she cared nothing about dreams. The hesitation inside her became stronger. "Do you remember your dreams?" she casually asked.

"I used to, but not much anymore. When I first entered The Order, I remember I had dreams almost every night."

"So did I," Sister Teresa answered. "Did you talk about them to anyone?"

Sister Sarah laughed. "My, no. I can just imagine what the Reverend Mother would have said." There was a moment of silence as the two women walked together.

"Some of the feverish children used to tell me their dreams when they'd wake in the middle of the night. I never could make heads nor tails of them."

Sister Teresa's heart felt heavy as they continued their walk. She changed the subject from dreams to some trivial incident concerning a cadet, and then finally said her goodbyes. She spent the rest of her free time that day in prayer and Bible reading.

After a week of prayer and keeping to herself as much as possible, Sister Teresa concluded two things: First, there was a war to be fought, and without prayer the battle would be lost, although she still had no idea what the battle might be. And, secondly, since she could not stand alone on this matter dealing directly with the school, then Mother Superior must be told. She knew this dream was important enough that it must be brought before the entire parish. She made an appointment to see the Mother Superior.

Standing outside the Mother Superior's office, which was directly connected to the large receiving room in the main building, Sister Teresa wiped her hands together. When she was nervous, her hands perspired. Sometimes she would joke to herself about this strange characteristic, telling herself that she was part canine but not today. She knocked.

"Come in," she heard through the door. She entered. Mother Superior was watering two plants that were on a table behind her desk.

"Sit down, Sister. I'll be right with you."

Sister Teresa thought about the Mother Superior who had preceded this one. She had a large office that overlooked the front lawn with plenty of windows and sunlight for all kinds of plants. This office had no windows, and the plants were weak-leafed and had a sick-green color. Sister Teresa had always wondered why she had moved into this small place. It probably had something to do with holiness.

Mother Superior finished her watering and placed the watering can on the bottom shelf of a bookcase. Then she sat at her desk. "Now, what would you like to talk about?"

Sister Teresa had made up her mind that she would be direct and to the point. "A week ago, I had a dream."

"A dream?"

"Yes. I know that usually dreams are not thought to be important, but I believe that some dreams should not be ignored."

There was a slight pause before Mother Superior answered. "And you had one of these?"

"Yes," Sister Teresa answered evenly. It's strange, she thought, how uncomfortable I always feel around this woman. Mother Superior didn't have to do anything, but that's the way it always turned out. Maybe it was because the woman never let anyone know what she was thinking. She never let anyone inside.

"I believe it is important for you to hear."

"Very well," Mother Superior said as she took her ring of keys from her waist belt and laid them on the desk in front of her.

Sister Teresa felt like getting up and running. She looked down at her hands for a brief moment, gathered herself, asked Jesus to guide her words and moved slightly forward in her chair.

"I found myself walking on the upper corridor, outside the dorm. It was nighttime. I wondered why I was out there without any shoes on and why my feet weren't cold. As I looked up from my feet, I found myself to be in the middle of the parade grounds." She closed her eyes to better recall what had happened.

"And then I knew that it wasn't night, as I had thought. It was daytime, but there was something, a foggy grayness, something sinister around me. I felt there was someone, something...behind me. It frightened me, and I quickly turned. Then I thought I felt someone from the other direction. I turned again. But I saw no one. The grayness, the thickness, was getting heavier...deeper. I was so frightened I cried out for help. But when the words left my mouth, they were no more than a whisper."

Sister Teresa felt the sweat break out on her palms. Without thinking, she wiped them quickly on her habit. She opened her eyes and looked directly into the eyes of Mother Superior.

"Then, I heard a low rumbling sound, much like thunder in the distance. But it had a quality about it that made my skin crawl. It was...like laughter, ugly, terrible, mean laughter. It frightened me so that I began to weep. My tears seemed to cause the laughter to grow more hideous, more obscene. I tried to pray, but I couldn't close my mouth. I couldn't even get my hands together. I looked for a way out, a way to safety. And there was none. This darkness covered the entire school. Everywhere I looked, grayness and a terrible heaviness. I became so frightened I fell to the ground. I thought I would faint. As I touched the cement, I discovered that I was naked. And when I tried to cover myself with my arms, the laughter became uglier and more evil."

She was feeling lightheaded, so she leaned back in the chair. "Then I woke," she said softly.

Mother Superior's expression was the same as when Sister Teresa had begun. There was a long silence.

"Why do you tell me this dream?"

"Because, its interpretation has to do with St.Maurice's."

"What do you mean?"

"There's more to the story. I think it will make things clearer."

Once again, she moved forward in her chair, as if hoping that this act of urgency would help Mother Superior understand.

"I got up from bed. I couldn't stop crying. It was as if that evil voice had followed me into reality. Every nerve in my body felt the ugliness, and I went immediately into prayer. I was so frightened I could only pray through my tears." She knew she had to say what had come next, but she didn't want to.

"I knew when I woke, who the laughter came from. There was no doubt in my mind."

She was hoping the Mother Superior would respond; maybe ask a question or two. But it was as if the woman had turned to stone. She just sat there, expressionless, impassive, almost as if a part of her had left the room. Oh, my Lord, Sister Teresa thought, what have I gotten myself into? She knew, however, that she had to go on.

"I knew it was Satan. I knew that for some purpose his darkness had enveloped the school."

There was still no movement from Mother Superior. Sister Teresa decided to push on, to finish as quickly as possible. She certainly had to tell it all, no matter what the consequences.

"Afterwards, during my prayer, 'a word' came to me." She wondered if Mother Superior understood what this meant.

Sister Teresa continued, "First it said, **'He has been here for a long time.'** And then the inner voice said, **'You cannot stand alone.'** At first, I didn't understand what this meant, but I do now. The Lord expects us to do warfare against Satan, because our school is in trouble. And he expects all of us to become prayer warriors and stand together in the battle." There, she had finished.

Mother Superior drew in a deep breath, as if for the past few minutes she had been holding everything out. "Sister Teresa," she finally said. Then, she stopped, as if deciding to take another conversational tact. She began again.

"Sister Teresa, this was only a dream."

"But God uses dreams to reach people," Sister Teresa responded.

Mother Superior paused. Then she reached for her keys and grasped them in her hand. Is she getting ready to leave, Sister Teresa thought? Is the meeting over?

"Are you saying that your dream was from God?" Mother Superior questioned.

"Yes, Sister," Teresa answered without hesitation. "I wouldn't bother you if I didn't."

"And why would He select you?"

"I've thought about that. And I believe there are two reasons. First, He knows I believe that **HE** is the **ONE** that gives dreams. And, secondly, He has prepared my faith in this area."

"What does that mean, exactly?"

"For the past seven years I have been writing down my dreams, asking the Holy Spirit for interpretation and doing the best I can to follow His wishes."

"You write them down?"

"Yes, in a journal." She would not tell the Mother Superior that a five-year-old boy had given her the courage to do this.

"And this dream was different from the others," Sister Teresa continued. "The dreams I've had in the past seemed to be for my personal use, to help me grow, to show me little things about my cadets, simple things to help. But with this dream, I know I'm supposed to be the messenger. We're supposed to gather together. This is a dream for all of us."

Sister Teresa thought she saw a tiny twitch around the jaw line of Mother Superior's face.

"And you are saying that Satan is here in this school with us?" the large woman asked.

"I think God is saying that we're under attack, and we have been for some time."

"In what way?"

"I don't know exactly. I believe that He'll tell us during our prayers and our fasting."

As Mother Superior paused, Sister Teresa was aware that she had never seen this woman so careful in selecting her words. Each question was preceded by a pause somewhat longer than usual. Everything seemed to be askew, as if there was more going on than Sister Teresa realized.

"And what would you have me do in this?" Mother Superior asked.

"I was hoping you would allow me to tell the dream to the Sisters, and you would lead us in this battle."

"And when would we do this?"

"As soon as possible and for as long as necessary."

"You mean that we should set aside our daily prayers and our daily routine?"

"Yes, as long as it doesn't interfere with the life of the cadets." She paused and tried to collect her thoughts. "I'm sorry, Mother Superior. Maybe I haven't made myself clear about this. I think that there is a terrible urgency. I believe that the dream shows that."

"Yes, the dream," Mother Superior answered curtly. "All these changes would be based on...a dream."

Sister Teresa felt like reminding her that because of a dream Joseph saved the baby Jesus from certain death. And what if Joseph had been filled with unbelief about his dream? What would have happened to our Savior before his time? She wanted to shout this or anything else that might make this enigmatic woman forget about her daily prayers and routines! What good had the prayers and routine been doing in the past, since Satan was at work right here! Right now! But she said nothing.

Oh, Lord, forgive me for my thoughts, she prayed as Mother Superior stood. The meeting was over. Sister Teresa felt sick to her stomach.

"I'll have to think about this," Mother Superior said as she reattached her keys to her waist belt. Sister Teresa would never know, but the inside of Mother Superior's hand was punctured from holding the keys too tightly during their conversation. Mother Superior gave no hint but could feel the moisture of the small amount of blood that was not yet congealed.

"May I talk to you about this again?" Sister Teresa asked, having resigned herself.

"I will talk to you when the time is right," Mother Superior responded, as she went to the door. She opened it for the little nun and watched as the Sister made her way across the large, empty waiting room to the door of the dormitories.

Mother Superior opened her large hand and looked at the small puncture. It was strange that she had not felt the pain. She took out a handkerchief from her pocket and wiped away the blood. She reminded herself to wash it thoroughly when she got to her room.

How strange Sister Teresa was becoming, keeping a journal of all the mish-mash that went on inside of that mind of hers! And now Satan was at the school! Oh, dear Lord, am I supposed to be the keeper of Sisters-gone-mad? Weren't two hundred and twelve male cadets enough? As far as she was concerned, the subject of dreams would never be mentioned again. If Sister Teresa did insist upon pursuing the subject, she would let the Diocese handle it. Maybe they would find a transfer in order.

*     *     *

Some friendships are almost impossible to explain, such as the one between David and Jonathan in the Bible. Their loyalty, their accord, seems to spring directly from the kindred spirits of the partakers. Unspoiled by ambition, undaunted by differences in personalities, not debased by perversion, these unique fellowships persevere through everything. So it was with Elliot Reed and Felix Skinner.

When Felix awoke in the mornings, the first thing he would do would be to look two rows over at Elliot's bed, (the two of them had changed dorms when Elliot was ten) and there his friend would be, already awake. And as was Elliot's habit, he would be reading some book. Felix would sleepily look in his direction. Elliot would glance up from his book, acknowledging his friend with a smile and a wave. Felix used to wonder how Elliot could always wake up so early. His friend didn't have a clock, and yet he was always the first one up. But after a few years of seeing this, Felix just took it for granted that Reed would always be awake when he awoke.

The companions always spent breakfast eating and not talking. Skinner was no longer picky about food. In fact, sometimes he ate more than Reed. In the classroom, Skinner had long since picked up his friend's habits of attention and studiousness. Since he was older than Reed, he felt compelled to at least keep up with him in the classroom.

When they had been younger, Reed always wanted to discuss things the teacher had talked about in class. Most of the time Skinner hadn't paid close enough attention to talk about it, which embarrassed him when his friend would enigmatically smile at him and slowly shake his head.

One day, being overly embarrassed and irritated, Skinner had asked him, "Why do you always shake your head at me when I don't know somethin'?"

Elliot had shot a question back at him. "Why don't you listen in class?"

"Why should I?" he had answered without thinking.

"How are we supposed to talk about things, if we don't listen?" Elliot had retorted.

"But I don't care about those things!" Skinner said emphatically. Then, once again Elliot had looked at him with that smile and given him that same old shake-of-the-head.

"There! You did it again!" Skinner shouted at him.

"How do you know if you don't care about something, if you don't know what it is?" Elliot challenged, looking at him evenly.

"What?" Skinner shot back lamely. He had felt trapped and dumb. He understood exactly what Reed had said, and he didn't have an answer for it.

Elliot had stared at him for a moment then begun to walk away. "You know what I mean. I think you're really smart, and you don't want yourself to know about it."

"Now what does that mean?" Skinner yelled after him.

He had only stayed mad at Reed for a few hours, but had brooded over his friend's words for several days. He had decided he'd give it a try and listen in class, so the next time Reed wanted to talk about something, he'd know what to say.

And it worked! They began talking about all sorts of things. Skinner had found he was interested in a lot of things he'd never thought about before. Although he became an "A" student, and the teachers treated him differently, he told Reed he didn't care about such things. After Skinner's remark, Reed smiled that smile again and shook his head the way that annoyed Skinner.

In sports, it was a different matter. Skinner not only didn't care about athletics, he didn't have any aptitude. In the beginning, he'd tried to keep up with Reed.

When Reed was eight, and Skinner was nine, Reed became interested in baseball. Picking up a glove and a ball one day, Elliot threw the ball up in the air. Running underneath it, he caught it. Skinner decided to try it too. Putting on the glove, he'd also thrown the ball in the air. At least, he thought it was going in the air. The ball landed about ten yards to his right. He and Reed looked at the ball, surprised.

"Try it again," Reed encouraged.

Felix did, but the ball had slipped off the tips of his fingers and landed behind him. Skinner looked quickly at Reed, to see if he was laughing. He wasn't.

"Let me throw it up for you," Reed said.

"O.K. Throw it high," Skinner answered. Reed threw the ball up, and Skinner positioned himself. It missed the glove and hit him on the shoulder. "Ow!" Skinner cried out.

Other sports went the same way. Swimming, which Reed loved and was very good at, petrified Skinner. Even before attempting it, he knew that he would sink like a rock. He was right! That's exactly what happened. Two dog paddles from the side of the pool, and he was on the way to the bottom. He was the only boy in the school that couldn't float, even though he had one hand holding the side. Everything sank except his hand.

The difference in their physical abilities made no difference in their friendship. At first, Skinner showed concern about losing his friend and once more being alone. In team sports, a lot of attention was given to Elliot when the guys were choosing up teams, but

Skinner soon found out, things like that didn't matter for him. Elliot would finish winning the game and still spend his free time with his friend.

This friendship was not one-sided. Elliot's needs were also great, though based differently. He needed Skinner as he needed Sister Teresa and, before that, Ida. They were his friends, and he needed close friends as much as he needed food and sleep. Though he very seldom talked about the importance of them, he thought about them often and thanked God regularly for them. Yet, such a tender and wholesome friendship is liable to be grievously misinterpreted.

* * *

Ralph Purdon, an overly curious boy when in the showers with the other boys, had been approached when he was twelve. Though he certainly hadn't been aware of it, it was carefully planned. He had been swimming in the pool, later than usual because two of the older boys asked if he would like to play tag. Since he felt it a privilege to be with high schoolers, he jumped at the chance.

Just the three of them were in the pool, a privilege Ralph didn't know was possible, because it was after swim hours. The game they were playing was simple and was a favorite at the school. The one who was "it" had to touch someone under water, below the waist, before he can stop being "it".

Ralph was a good, fast swimmer and a quick diver. He was soon being tagged and tagging in return. Then, when he was at the shallow end, hiding near the steps, he noticed the other two in the center of the pool at the deep end. He swam underwater towards them; he saw that one of the guys had pulled the other's bathing suit down to around his knees. When Ralph came up for air, he noticed they were both laughing. Quickly, he went under again and saw the first boy touching the other guy's genitals, and both of them kicking off their trunks. Both suits floated to the bottom of the pool, and the two guys were holding each other, touching and rubbing. Both had erections.

Ralph found himself getting excited. He couldn't stop watching them. He'd never seen anything like this before. He didn't even want to come up for air, but had to. Then, as he went under again, he saw that it was all over. The two high schoolers were at the bottom of the pool, putting on their swimming trunks. When they came up, they swam to the edge of the pool and got out. Ralph did the same. During the entire time, they never looked at him and acted as if they'd been alone in the pool.

As they were leaving the pool area, on the way to the showers, one of the boys put his arm lightly around Ralph's shoulder and asked if he was all right. Ralph said he was. And that was all there was to it.

After showering, as they were leaving, the one who had invited Ralph in the first place asked if he would like to play tag again sometime. Ralph answered that he would and asked when they would do it. The high schooler only smiled and waved goodbye.

As the days passed, Ralph kept thinking about what he had seen in the pool; he could hardly wait to be asked again. A week passed before they approached Ralph. This time, they allowed him to participate with them. It was at that time, in the pool and afterwards on a locker room bench, that Ralph Purdom became a willing member of a very secretive alliance called "The Group".

It was three years later when the older Group members told Ralph how closely he had been scrutinized before being asked that first time to "play" tag. They told him exactly how and why he was chosen. They watched him as he was showering, to see if he was interested in "what the older boys had". Ralph laughed when they told him this, readily admitting that he had enjoyed looking. They also told him of the many off-handed questions they had asked about what he liked and disliked about his family and what kind of friends he preferred. He had also been told secrets and then tested by other Group members to see if he would divulge what he knew. When Ralph thought back on these things, he could see how careful and thorough The Group had been.

So when The Group found out they could trust him, and he seemed to have the correct personality traits, they had taken a vote and asked him to play tag. Ralph's first partner, the one in the pool and later in the locker room, was the high-schooler who had brought his name up to the rest of The Group at the very beginning. He was given the exciting privilege of "Initiation".

The swimming pool hadn't been the only place used for testing young recruits. One evening, when Dale Barkley was thirteen, he was alone and crying, thinking himself hidden over by the handball courts. He'd only been in the school a few weeks and felt so lonely. Sometimes, he just couldn't stand being by himself, and he really didn't know how to make friends. He remembered feeling lonely at home but never like this. So when it got so bad he couldn't take it anymore, he would find a place to be alone, and he would cry.

It was during one of these times, alone crying and not aware he was being watched, that an older boy, a high-schooler, had come up to him and asked what was wrong. At first, Dale hadn't told him, but he found the high-schooler so nice, not like the other older cadets, that he'd decided to talk. The older boy seemed to really care. He listened and even told Dale that he knew how he felt, because he used to feel the same way. The older boy also told him it was all right to cry, and that if he liked, he would be his friend. The high-schooler boy put his arms around him and let him cry. Dale felt a wonderful stirring and felt love at that very moment.

A few days later, Dale was asked by his new friend to meet him at the rest room near the gym. Dale could hardly wait. When Dale went through his Initiation, he had been unaware that another member of The Group had been outside, watching out for them and protecting their privacy. After that day, Dale no longer felt alone.

Another cadet, Freddie Strikler, selected at thirteen, had been pushed while playing basketball one Saturday afternoon during free time. He bruised his leg against the wall and had difficulty walking. One of the high-schoolers, the one who had asked him to play, suggested a rubdown for the leg instead of going to the infirmary. Freddie agreed. Using an oily liniment while on a bench in the locker room, the high schooler helped Freddie find his way into The Group. Freddie hadn't been told until a year later that he was pushed purposely, and that the doors of the locker room were guarded during his Initiation.

With Aubrey Forrester, it had been different. When he came to the school at age thirteen, he was looking for such a gathering as The Group. His mother found him in the shower with his stepfather, firmly lathering each other. This was her third husband. After a terrible battle, which Aubrey really enjoyed watching, his mother divorced his stepfather and sent her son to St.Maurice's.

Needless to say, she had not divulged her son's sexual history, nor had the school deemed it necessary to ask about such things. In some vague way, Mrs. Forrester had hoped that this wonderful school would be able to change these perverted habits of her young son.

Leslie Marner, the final member of The Group, was the most delicate of the troupe. Even when he was little, he liked playing with dolls and being involved in the same activities his mother did like cooking, cleaning house and even acting as his mother when she would verbally strike out at his father. Not once did he take sides with his father against his mother. When she would take her son into her confidence about her troubles, they would become his troubles.

It was no wonder he was so hurt when she had decided to put him in the St.Maurice Academy. She had given him no explanation. One day, she had just packed up some clothes, put him in the car, and drove him there. Of course, through the years, she had visited him every Sunday afternoon, taking him to the movies and out to dinner, but it hadn't been the same.

He had been enrolled over a year before she told him that his father had suddenly left home, and she didn't even know where he had gone. Then, as she had done so many times before, she confided that she really didn't care, and she was better off alone. Leslie remembered that he hadn't felt the sympathy for her like before. In fact, when he got back to the dorm that night, he decided he really didn't care about her anymore and was glad he was at St. Maurice's with some real friends. He had nestled his head on his pillow and thought about his father being gone. He cried. And, oh, how he wished Ralph Purdom had been in bed beside him, so he could tell him about the loss of his father.

The Group was always kept small, and only one or two boys of twelve and thirteen were selected each year as "newcomers". All the rest were high schoolers, usually in the same dorm. As the years passed and the seniors graduated, the "newcomers" became high schoolers. The strongest and the smartest one of them would then become the leader. When he was a senior, Ralph Purdom was it. He was the perfect choice, a company commander, number one swimmer on the team, and the head lifeguard at the pool. Because of the authority entrusted to him, he had the freedom needed to lead The Group.

The Group was smaller than it had been previously, with only four members left under Ralph. Though this number was very safe, as far as detection was concerned, Ralph and the other high schoolers wanted some younger recruits, who always brought a great deal of excitement and were such fun to teach. Ralph, especially, was finding that the older he got the more specific his appetites grew, and it was the younger boys who excited him the most. Very seldom, in his fantasies, did he even think of one of the present Group members, who he could have anytime, but always of a younger boy who he was "Initiating".

Besides - the other four boys in The Group were after Ralph Purdom about making the decisions of whom they should invite. All had to agree on who they were going to test, and since Ralph wasn't getting around to making a decision, the others were getting impatient. Dale and Aubrey, both juniors, suggested three different boys. They didn't care which one was chosen, as long as it got done. Freddie, though, was so involved with Ralph, that he didn't care who was chosen or when they got around to it. Leslie didn't like the number "five", because someone was always left out.

Very seldom did more than two "get together" because of the fear of being caught. Sometimes a ménage a'trois would take place, but it didn't happen often because of the increased danger. Only once had all five, late at night, left their dorm and met in the laundry room, spending three naked hours together. Since they were almost caught when someone stopped outside the door of the laundry room, it was decided that no matter how much they all liked it; they would never to do it again.

Ralph decided on a meeting. He checked out a basketball and went to one of the outside courts. Dale met him, and they began to shoot baskets. The other three one at a time, to make it appear as if by chance, joined them. They had been taught caution and believed in it.

Leslie was the next to show up. He despised all games and didn't even pretend to enjoy them. Yet, because of The Group, he came with his tennis shoes on and faked playing as best he could. Leslie had been the last one initiated two years before.

"Who have you got in mind?", Freddie asked Ralph, while he was trying a long shot. He made it. He turned and looked at The Group.

"Reed," Ralph finally declared.

"Elliot Reed?" Dale asked.

"Oh, my God, he's beautiful!" Leslie said.

Ralph paused, letting the name settle into the minds of his friends. "What do you think, Freddie?"

"I agree with Leslie. He's really pretty. What "proof" do you have?"

"O.K.," Ralph said, "let's look at him. First he's got just one friend, and as far as I know, that's the only one he's ever had."

"That's right," Aubrey said quickly. "You never see him with anyone else." He wanted to keep on the good side of Ralph, as well as to have Reed.

"Reed is certainly friendly enough," Dale pointed out. "Anytime you say anything to him he smiles."

Freddie was direct in his questioning. "Do you think he and Skinner are 'playing'?"

Ralph answered that question with a question. "What do you think?" He let that sink in for a moment. "Just think about those two guys."

The Group members each pictured Elliot and his friend in their mind and thought about their own feelings for a young boy like him.

Ralph continued. "Have you ever seen the way they look at each other? I've watched them in the dining hall. You can see it on their faces." He paused, knowing that they all had to agree before a newcomer could be tested. However, he omitted telling the others that for the past few weeks he had been fantasizing about Reed.

As he had thought about Elliot, he had also remembered how years ago he had fantasized and brought to mind over and over what had happened in the pool with two high schoolers. He had remembered elaborating and recreating the actions to include himself in the underwater fondling. Even before that encounter in the pool, through his thinking, Ralph had given himself over to this way of life. Unimpeded by any thought of morality, he had already decided which road he wanted. Ralph Purdom had already played a hundred games of tag in the pool, before anyone even asked him.

Now, he had been preparing himself for this special newcomer. Each night, alone with his thoughts, a new set of games had been devised. In his bed before going to sleep, Ralph would picture Elliot Reed. He saw Reed naked many times in the shower at the pool, and he knew exactly what his beautiful body looked like. All the things that he liked to do with The Group, he did with Elliot Reed in his mind, there in the dark in his bed.

"What about the lunches the two of them have with Sister Teresa?" Leslie asked. "Haven't they been doing that for years?"

"She's not a priest. I doubt if they confess anything to her," Dale commented dryly.

"Besides," Aubrey Forrester said quickly, "who'd suspect you if you spent your lunch time with some saintly old lady for years." He hated anybody who had anything to do with religion. "It's a perfect cover-up."

"I thought about that too," Ralph lied, "and I think Aubrey is right. You know how smart Reed is. It fits."

Ralph waited. Finally, Leslie said, "Why don't we take a vote. I'm sick of playing catch with this dumb ball!"

They all looked at each other and finally agreed to vote. Aubrey was the first to speak. "I say, yes!"

Then all the rest of The Group gave their approval.

"It's settled," Ralph said. "Now all we have to do is work up a plan."

"He's good at sports, all of them," Freddie Strikler commented.

"He swims like a fish," Dale added.

Ralph was getting exactly what he had planned. "What about tag then, with all of us?"

"I don't like to swim," Leslie pouted.

"You can watch the door then Leslie," Dale said. "Ralph's right. I've seen him playing tag with the young kids. He'll go for that."

Ralph looked over The Group before saying, "All agreed?" Leslie watched everyone as they nodded in agreement, then everyone turned to him.

"Oh, all right! But you have to promise to tell me everything that happens. You can't leave out one tiny little detail. Promise?"

* * *

Mr. Weston was the swimming instructor at the school, but was only there part time. He left at three in the afternoon, and all swimming after that was watched over by the high school lifeguards. Four of them had been trained in Red Cross lifeguard techniques, and they reported to Ralph Purdom. Swimming stopped at four-thirty, with dinner an hour later.

The Group planned on playing their game of tag at four-thirty on Tuesday, because Elliot and his age group had the pool until that time. It was a little after four when Dale Barkley came in, waved at Ralph and dove in. Dale paid no attention to the younger kids, nor did they to him. A few minutes later, Freddie came in and dove in the deepest part. He began doing laps the short length. Aubrey Forrester was the last to enter. He tested the water with his foot, then walked around and got in the shallow end. He knew how to swim, but today he only floated lazily.

Ralph blew the four-thirty whistle. All fifteen of the twelve and thirteen year olds quickly got out of the pool. They knew that if they were slow, they would be kept out for a whole week. Ralph had stationed himself between the pool and the door to the showers. Elliot was the third boy to the door.

"Hey, Reed, you're getting pretty fast with your swimming."

Elliot was surprised that Ralph Purdom had talked to him. He was the number-two man on the swimming team and a high schooler.

"Thanks," Elliot said quietly.

"Think you're fast enough to play some tag with high-schoolers?" Ralph questioned. His smile was open and friendly. The other three high schoolers paid no attention to what was going on, but swam in different portions of the pool.

"I don't know," Elliot answered. He had wondered how fast he would have to be to play against the bigger guys.

"Would you like to give it a try?" Ralph asked.

All the other young boys were in the shower by this time, and it would take them about ten minutes to be dressed and ready to leave.

"Now?" Elliot asked. "Isn't the pool closed?"

"Not if I don't want it to be," answered Ralph jokingly. "Sometimes we like to hang around and play some good hard tag." He watched the face of the youngster. "It's O.K. for you to stay. You won't get into any trouble, cause I'm the boss."

Elliot thought it might be fun. He wanted to see if he could keep up with good swimmers, and Ralph was the lieutenant-in-charge.

"All right," Elliot answered.

"Great," Ralph said, as he removed the whistle from around his neck. "Let's do it!" He dropped the whistle and dove in the deep water. He was a powerful swimmer and was in the center of the pool in a moment.

"All right," he shouted. "I'm 'it', but it'll be the last time!"

Elliot dove into the shallow end and stayed under water, moving to the stair area. It was his plan to try to hide there. It usually worked with the younger kids, but not with the high schoolers, he soon found out. Before he knew it, Ralph had touched his leg, and he was "it."

Swimming quickly, Elliot caught and touched Freddie Strikler. And so the game went for about fifteen minutes. It was Freddie Stickler and Dale Barkley who dropped their bathing trunks first. Elliot didn't notice them at first, but soon saw the trucks floating to the bottom. When he looked to the left and saw two bodies close together and touching each other, he was surprised at what he saw. They weren't supposed to be doing that, he thought. He came quickly to the surface and discovered who the two were. He looked for Ralph and saw him surface on the other side of the pool.

"They aren't supposed to do that!" Elliot yelled to Ralph. All four of the boys had surfaced and heard Elliot.

"Do what?" Ralph called back.

"They have their bathing suits off and were touching each other," Elliot answered, believing that Ralph Purdom didn't know what was happening.

Ralph knew as soon as he heard the words that he made a mistake in his choice. As he watched Elliot's face, he could see that it showed no desire or excitement, only disapproval. Elliot was not going for it.

When Ralph didn't answer immediately, Reed swam to the edge of the pool and climbed out. He headed for the locker room. All four of The Group had the same thought at the same time. This kid could ruin everything. Freddie and Dale dove to the bottom to get their trunks. Ralph and Aubrey got out and followed Reed into the locker room.

"Don't let him get his clothes," Ralph whispered to Aubrey as they entered the locker room. Reed had taken a towel from the shelf and was drying. Aubrey went and stood in front of Reed's locker. Ralph watched the youngster as he dried. Elliot still had on his trunks.

Ralph knew he should be scared; but he felt excited. Yes, here I am, he thought, everything's blowing up in my face and yet I'm very, very excited. His mind was alert. He looked over at Aubrey, who had a strange, excited look about him, not at all what one might expect when everything was about ready to explode.

Freddie and Dale entered the locker room. As Ralph motioned to them, they seated themselves on a bench.

"What exactly did you see?" Ralph asked.

"I already told you," Reed answered apprehensively.

"Tell me again."

"They had their trunks off and were touching each other."

"Where exactly?"

"They were touching each other's penis."

"And that's bad?"

Elliot stared at him for a moment. "Yes. It's wrong."

"Were they hard?"

Elliot didn't like this kind of questioning. He was getting nervous. All four of the high schoolers were watching him, and he didn't know exactly what to do. He wanted to get his clothes, but Forrester was standing in front of his locker.

"I asked you a question?" Ralph said evenly.

"Yes, sir," Reed said. "They were hard." He moved to his locker. "I'd like to get my clothes."

"And you've never had one?"

"What do you mean?" Elliot asked.

"You know what I mean. Answer the question."

"Yes, when I wake up. Sometimes, when I dream, I wake up with one."

All four of the boys laughed. Ralph didn't seem to be worried at all. The other three boys relaxed.

"With dreams, huh? What about with Skinner?" Ralph demanded.

"What do you mean?"

"You two are good friends, aren't you?"

"Yes."

"Do you love him?"

"Yes."

"Well?"

"I love him because he's my friend. I don't touch his penis. That has nothing to do with friendship."

"How do you know if you've never tried it?"

Elliot looked at the large high schooler. He was feeling nervous and wanted to get out of there. "Could I get my clothes, please?"

Purdom had moved nearer to him. "I asked you a question."

"I don't have to try something I know is wrong. It's a sin."

Aubrey spoke up for the first time. "What the hell do you know about sin? You aren't even Catholic."

"It's O.K., Aubrey," Ralph said evenly. "Move out of the way and let him get dressed."

Aubrey took a quick, surprised glance at Ralph, and then moved to one side. There was an expectant silence as Elliot opened his locker door. He took out his clothes and shoes, and put them on the bench. The boys watched as Reed pulled off his trunks. Reed reached for his underwear, but Ralph put his foot on the bench, holding down his shorts, then nodded to Aubrey, who quickly reached down and snatched up Reed's swimming trunks, throwing them on top of the lockers. Dale and Freddie got up from the far bench and moved behind Ralph. All four of the boys stood looking at the naked body of Reed.

"We were hoping we could all become friends," Ralph said.

"Give me my underwear," Elliot entreated. He was frightened now and near tears.

"At least you should try something before you start telling us what sinners we are," Ralph said as he reached out and stroked the arm of the frightened, younger boy.

Reed moved backwards and knocked his hand away. He backed into Aubrey, who greedily grabbed the smooth flesh of Reed's buttocks. Elliot twisted away and jumped over the bench. Before he could run, Dale and Freddie grabbed his arms and pinned him against the lockers.

"What do you think we ought to do with this guy?" Ralph asked, already knowing what he was going to do.

Elliot heard a locker open and shut, but he couldn't see what was happening, because they were forcing his head against the lockers. He was crying now and unable to move.

"You're the boss, Ralph," Aubrey said.

"I'm afraid Reed might talk about what he saw in the pool. Maybe he might even talk to Father Tinian or to Sister Teresa. What do you guys think?"

"I think you're right," Freddie Stickler said. He watched as Ralph took a jar of Vaseline from his locker. He knew exactly what was going to happen. "I think maybe we should teach him how to be friendly."

Ralph was standing directly behind Reed now and whispered in his ear, "Then again, who would believe you, four high schoolers against one twelve year old? Four trusted high schoolers, who have rank in the school. Besides, if you were to say anything, something might happen to your skinny friend. You wouldn't want anything to happen to Skinner would you? He could even fall from the second or third story of the dorms. It could happen! Do you know that, my beautiful friend?"

Ralph felt as though he was in a trance, both the things he was saying and what he was feeling. He'd never been as excited as he was at this moment. The power he felt was extraordinary. As he placed a piece of wide tape over Reed's mouth, he saw tears coming from the boy's beautiful eyes. This only increased the desire he felt.

"Bring him over to the bench," Ralph said, as he removed his own trunks. As the other boys held the sobbing Elliot in place, Ralph slowly sodomized him, so not to damage.

It didn't take long. When Ralph finished, the boys took Elliot into the shower and left him curled up in the corner while they satisfied each other, then showered. Elliot kept his eyes closed and faced the wall, not moving until the last shower had been turned off, and the boys were dressed and ready to leave. Then on the way out, Ralph turned and said, "You have ten minutes to get out of here. And remember, nobody will believe you."

Elliot remained still until he heard the four of them leave the building.

He slowly rolled over and got to his feet. His mind seemed almost to be blank; no thoughts, either good or bad, seemed to be there. He turned on the shower, putting both hands on the tile wall because he felt so weak. As the cold water hit his body he knew that he was going to be sick. Moving to the center of the shower room, where the drain was, he threw up. It drove him to his knees. He retched deeply again, then slowly righted himself. He stood and turned on the hot water. He soaped himself, wondering if he was bleeding. He was afraid to touch himself, to find out, for fear of hurting all the more. He carefully cleaned himself, then turned off the shower and dressed.

He didn't want to go to dinner, but he knew if he didn't, the Sisters would ask questions. He couldn't hurry, even though he was already a few minutes late. Everybody looked at him when he came in, but he didn't care. He went to his place next to his friend Skinner and sat down. Reed didn't look at him. He knew that he should, because he always did, but he couldn't. He felt ashamed. He wanted to cry again, but he knew he didn't dare. He tried to eat, but the food wouldn't get past his throat. Finally he just sat and waited for the meal to be over, trying to keep his mind a blank.

Skinner knew there was something wrong as soon as Reed had come through the door. First of all, he was never late anywhere. Never! And second, he looked all white-like, with no color in his face. Also, he moved slower than usual. And finally, he made no eye contact before he sat down. Something was very wrong, but Skinner kept quiet while they were at dinner.

Five or six times during the meal, Elliot could feel Skinner watching him. What was he going to say to his friend when they got outside? Skinner was smart, and Elliott knew that he wasn't hiding things very well from him. People who didn't know him, or didn't care, wouldn't know anything was different – but Skinner would know. What should he say to him? Whatever it was going to be, Elliott knew that it would have to be a lie. He would never tell his friend what happened in that locker room. He would die before he would tell. He was ashamed, and he felt so unclean. But I can't keep thinking like this, he thought. He knew, if he did, he would start to crying again.

It was the first question Skinner put to him when they left the dining hall.

"What's wrong with you?" he said quickly. Elliott saw the concern on his face. That made him want to cry too.

"I had a real bad fall in the shower. I thought it broke my back, I hit so hard."

"Holly cow! Maybe we should go see Sister Sarah."

No, I'll be all right. I just need some rest...some sleep."

"Your face looks kinda white. Are you sure we shouldn't go over and see her?"

"I'm sure. I'll be alright tomorrow."

They walked back to the dorm in silence. Elliott went to bed early that night and pretended to be asleep. He had never felt so miserable in his life. He wondered if he would ever feel clean again.

*  *  *

On Wednesday, Elliott decided not to attend the usual lunch with Sister Teresa. He used the lie about his back as the excuse and asked Skinner to tell her. He just couldn't face her now. After lunch, when

Skinner saw him at class, he told him that Sister Teresa was worried for him, and that he should go to the infirmary. He didn't go.

The next day he begged off from lunch again, and Skinner went alone. This time, Sister Teresa sent a message that if he didn't come to lunch the next day, she was going to make him go to the nurse. He knew that he had to meet with Sister Teresa, but he wanted to do it alone.

The next morning, when Skinner woke up, Elliott was standing at the side of his bed.

"I have to see Sister Teresa today," Elliott said.

"You'd better or she'll be coming after you," Felix answered sleepily. Last night, I was thinking that maybe you should see her alone."

"That's what I was going to ask you, if you'd mind?"

"Well, now you don't have to ask," Skinner said through a yawn. "Tell her, I'll see her Monday."

At noon, Elliott knocked and stuck his head in the door. Sister Teresa looked over her glasses at him, as she always did when he was any distance away.

"Come in here and let me look at you."

Elliott went to stand in front of her desk. Skinner was right, thought Sister Teresa. There is something wrong with Elliott.

"Where's Felix?" she asked.

"He'll see you Monday."

"Well, tell me what happened," she said as she gestured towards his desk. As he went to sit down, she got up, followed him, and sat at the desk next to him.

He began the same story he had told Skinner. Though she listened to his words, something more important was happening. Suddenly she knew that she was supposed to touch him. She waited until he finished the story, then reached out and gently took his hand. She saw his throat tighten, as if tears were about to come. He turned his head and looked out the window.

This boy has been hurt in his spirit, not in the flesh, she thought. How could a fall cause something like that? She decided not to question his story. He needed a friend now, not an inquisitor.

"I think it's time I tell you some important things," she said, waiting for him to look at her. "I want to tell you something that no one else knows."

"When I was about to take my vows as a nun, there was one something that almost stopped me. I knew that I could never have my own child. Then a question came into my mind, who was more important God or a child?"

She smiled and gently shrugged her shoulders. "When I answered that question, I took my vows. But just because God was first, doesn't mean that I didn't miss having a child. Though I made my choice, and I'm not sorry, I still felt..."

Elliott saw tears come into her eyes, and she smiled almost shyly at him. "Then something happened that I never expected. God answered my heart's desire. A five-year-old boy came to this school and told me he had seen me in a dream, and that I was supposed to be his friend. He wouldn't take 'no' for an answer. Well, he became more than that to me. He became the child I never had. I knew that I felt the same love a mother feels for her own child. And now I know that until I die, I'll always feel that way about you."

Elliott knew that he couldn't answer her from his heart. If he did, he'd fall apart. That could not be. Nobody would ever know about what had happened. He continued looking out the window as he said, "I feel that way about you too. I've always known that you loved me. And I know that you understand me and expect me to become a man."

He kept staring blankly out the window.

What a strange thing to say, thought Sister Teresa. She understood she was being told something, but she was not exactly sure what it was. This was the first time Elliott had ever been obscure. One thing she did know – he didn't want to be questioned.

"There's something else I want to tell you. Do you know what the name Elliott means?", she asked.

Elliott finally turned from the window and looked at her. There were tears in his eyes. He shook his head. "No," he answered.

"I looked it up when you were about seven. It's the English version of a Hebrew word. It means, 'Jehovah is my God.'"

Oh, no. Elliott thought. New tears came into the boy's eyes. "It does? What's the Hebrew word?"

"Elijah," she said with a smile.

"We've read about him," Elliott answered, blinking away his tears.

"I know we have. What do you remember?"

"He was a prophet, and people were chasing him."

She was surprised at what he remembered about Elijah. Most would remember how he stopped the rain in Israel for two-and-a-half years through prayer.

"That's right," Sister Teresa said, going along with his thoughts. "The king's wife, Jezebel, had promised to have him killed."

Elliott was quiet for a moment, remembering the story. "I remember that Elijah felt so alone that he wanted to die."

"But was he really alone?"

Elliott was motionless. Then, quietly he said, "No. God spoke to him"

Sister Teresa wondered what was going on inside the boy's head. What was all this meaning to him? "Do you remember what God said to him?" she asked.

"No." Elliott answered.

"Well, in so many words, He told him he wasn't alone, and He still had work for him to do."

"I remember now. Then Elijah went and did what he was told."

"That's right. And it was a long, hard walk across the Damascus Desert." She paused and prayed to herself. Lord, I have no idea what's going on here. I just ask your guidance for this boy in all that he does. Whatever has happened, help him and give him strength, Your strength.

"Do we all have to cross deserts?" he asked.

She paused before answering, knowing he was talking about himself. "If we're trying to do the will of God, yes!"

"Why? Why do we have to go through them?"

"Because in the desert, that's where we have to look for God's help and have faith what He'll do for us."

Elliott hated this desert and was so ashamed that he hadn't even talked to God about it.

Sister Teresa stood, wanting to pray for this son of hers, but she no longer wanted to be quiet about it – no more closet prayers for this boy! She felt a deep desire to try new things! Like the things she had read about in the Bible but never tried, like "the laying on of hands." For some reason she felt a deep irritation. No! It was more than irritation. It was anger! With a quick motion, she placed both her small hands on top of Elliott's head.

"Lord, I bring my son before you. In the blessed name of Jesus, I ask for Your help, Lord God, oh mighty Jehovah. I know that Elliott loves You, and he wants to abide in Your love. In the name of Your son, Jesus Christ, I forbid the devil to be here! Get out! Now! In the name of Jesus, out!"

She found that her voice was raised in anger, and she was shaking. Then she noticed that Elliott was shaken too, and tears were running down his face. She wasn't sure what she had done, but she trusted in God that this violent prayer had been answered.

Elliott slept in peace that night. Inside, he felt whole again, not the same, but whole.

As the days went by, he knew that from now on he would be more careful about the people he trusted. He also started finding out the best ways of protecting himself against any kind of evil that would come against him. Spiritually, he began praying more earnestly, asking God for his protection, just as he had heard Sister Teresa. Physically, he began a strict program of weight training and running. He finally found a use for the thousand dollars that had been on the books for these many years. With Sister Teresa's help, he got permission to go into town once a week for lessons in self-defense.

Ralph and the rest of the Group were expecting the worst for the first few days. They made sure they stayed away from one another, waiting to see whether they were going to be found out. After the third day, Ralph felt the danger had passed. Reed wasn't going to say anything. Ralph knew that from now on they would have to be much more careful in selecting recruits. And they were, yet that same year two thirteen olds were selected and fit in just fine. The year after that, after Ralph had graduated, three more initiates were selected. And so it continued. No one ever mentioned the rape. It was as if it had never happened.

* * *

Over the years, Father Tinian had received three written reports about Sister Teresa. None had been good. But then again, none had been bad enough to have her stand before him for a reprimand. Now, she was asking for a meeting. She had quietly spoken to him after mass, and he gave her an appointment for the following day. When he returned to his office, he had looked through her records and found that she had been at St. Maurice's for sixteen years. Before that, she had been at an out-of-state parochial school. While at that school, she had asked for a transfer, and received it with an exemplary recommendation.

Sixteen years, he thought. He hadn't remembered when she came to the school. It seemed strange, since he always extended an invitation to any new sister to come to his office, so they could get acquainted. As far as he could remember, he had never done that for Sister Teresa. He opened the door between his office and the small sitting room where Sister Teresa was waiting. Though there were two chairs there, she was standing.

"Please, Sister, have a seat," he said.

Sister Teresa returned his smile as she walked past him into the office. He seemed friendly enough, she thought.

Father Tinian had decided that since he had not greeted her properly sixteen years before, he would do so now.

"Would you like coffee, Sister? It's only that instant stuff, but it's nice to talk over."

Sister Teresa couldn't help but smile. She had never heard a beverage given such a position. Though she really didn't care that much for coffee, she said yes. She watched as the priest poured hot water into two cups and added a spoonful of coffee to each. He looked at her questioningly.

"No, I just take mine black," she said with a quick smile.

His large brown hands made the cup look small. She wondered if his people were from Spain.

"I looked at your records and found that you've been here for sixteen years. Do you know, I can't remember you ever coming into my office before today."

"That's right. I've never been here," she answered.

"Really? Usually, when a Sister first comes to the school, I make sure to greet her."

"I believe that you were on a holiday when I came. I remember, because I always wanted to see the place where you had gone."

Smiling, Father Tinian asked, "Where had I gone?"

"Hawaii."

He remembered immediately. "Of course! I was there playing golf. I looked forward to that week for six years. Oh, what a time! I still think of it."

"Did you get to the Island of Molokai?" she asked. She was enjoying his openness and energy.

"No. I spent my time on Maui," he answered. He looked at the woman for a long moment. "Interested in Father Damian are you?"

"Yes. I would like to see the colony, to see where they did their work."

"There are no more lepers now."

"I know. But I've read about him, and the Sisters that took up the work after his death."

"A courageous time," he said softly.

"Yes. God blessed them."

This little nun surprised Father Tinian. The reports gave no indication of her adventurous nature.

"I'm glad you came in to see me. We're only sixteen years late, that's all," he laughed. "What would you like to talk about?"

Well, here it is, she thought. The chances are that Mother Superior never talked to him about their conversation concerning her dream. Besides, that was a year ago, and the dream she wanted to talk about to Father Tinian now was entirely different.

"I've had a dream," she said.

"Ah!" he answered quickly. "Do you need help with its interpretation?"

"What?" she responded, pleasantly shocked.

Father Tinian misinterpreted the look that had come onto her face. "Oh, I'm sorry. Have I misunderstood?"

"Oh. No! That's exactly why I've come. Are you saying that you believe in the importance of dreams?"

"Oh, yes," he said with a quick laugh. "I learned their importance the hard way."

"What do you mean?" she asked quickly.

Father Tinian wasn't sure how much he should say about this subject. It had been years since he even talked about it. "Let me ask you a question in return. How important is the subject to you?"

"Very...please, I would appreciate hearing anything you have to say."

Still he hesitated. "Are any other Sisters involved with this subject?"

She understood exactly what he was asking. "As far as I know," she answered emphatically, "there are no others remotely interested in dreams. Whatever you say will not leave this room."

Father Tinian was relieved to see that she didn't mince words; she was quite direct.

"Not many people within the church are interested in dreams," Father Tinian began. "Some of the secular world has renewed their interest, but not the church. We're nothing like the church of history. For the first five hundred years after the Resurrection of our Lord, the Church fathers governed their lives and their churches through their dreams. They would even gather together and discuss them, making sure of their interpretations!"

He stopped himself, took a drink of his coffee and smiled at her. "Even though that's another story, what I was coming to is this. There is no training for priests on the subject of dreams any longer."

Sister watched him change to a more comfortable position in his chair and then smiled.

"When I was a young priest, my heritage was very important to me. I came from a minority in East Los Angeles. As a small boy, when my grandfather was very old, he would tell me stories about our family's history, fascinating stories. During his mother's time, a Mandan Indian came down to Mexico. Do you know anything about American Indians?"

"No," she answered, but she certainly was interested. She felt like crying; she was so happy to hear someone talk about the things that were important to her.

"I didn't either, but it fascinated me. My great grandmother married an American Indian, which meant that it was part of my heritage! No other kid in my neighborhood had an American Indian in their family." He paused and then laughed.

"In my last year of seminary, I asked permission to be placed on an Indian Reservation. Two weeks after graduation, I was sent to a small church on a Reservation in Wyoming. I was the junior priest to a man in his seventies, who had lost most of his hearing. There were sixty-four Shoshones families and forty-two Arapahos in our congregation."

He laughed again and then took another sip.

"It's been such a long time since I've thought about this... And I've never talked about it to anyone. When I look back on it, I can't help but laugh." He smiled broadly and continued. "I had been there for three days. I was twenty-four years old at the time. Our rectory only had one room, and I had a small desk in the corner. Father was at his desk asleep, something he usually did in the afternoons. The door opened, and in walked a Shoshone Indian who was about thirty years old. He was a big, strong-faced fellow in Levi's and a work shirt. I said hello to him, and he nodded back. He looked over at the priest and then turned to me."

"He began telling me a story, which lasted for about three or four minutes. I listened carefully and quickly knew that this was the strangest story I had ever heard. I knew the man was crazy and was wondering how I could get out of the room without being killed. When the Indian finished his story and said, 'That was my dream. What do you think?'" Father Tinian threw his head back and laughed. Sister Teresa laughed with him, finding the situation as humorous as he did.

"What did you do?" she asked.

"I didn't have to do anything. He must have known how ignorant I was, when he saw me sitting there with my mouth open.

He just turned and walked out the door!" The Father and Sister laughed together again.

"I told the old priest about the Indian's dream. He just nodded knowingly and said, 'Good. That's very good.' Later, he told me that interpretation of dreams was a way of life with the Indian, and they didn't separate their sleep-time from their awake-time. The old Father taught me a great deal during the next five years, and I studied what few books there were on the subject."

"How did you come to be here?" she asked, without thinking. She noticed Father Tinian flinch ever so slightly. "I'm sorry, Father, I shouldn't ask such a question."

"No, no. It's O.K." he said with a comforting gesture. "Do you remember The Little Big Horn incident?"

"The one with General Custer?"

"No," he said with a laugh. "But it took place at the same location. It was nineteen years ago. A group of Indians had a run-in with Federal Marshals over land rights. Two Indians were killed. I was there at the time and unfortunately my picture got in the newspapers. The Diocese didn't like that sort of publicity. Three weeks later, I was sent here."

"Were the Indians from your Reservation?"

"No. I'm afraid not. I went as moral support. There were other priests and pastors up there too. I think I was picked out because I was Mexican, and at the time, rather vocal about my Indian heritage."

"And here you are."

"And until now, I've kept my mouth shut," he laughed. Father Tinian noticed that the little nun seemed apprehensive. Whatever was involved with her dream, it must be very important to her.

"Why don't we talk about you now? Tell me about this dream of yours."

For the first time, she felt calm, and she knew that she did not have to be cautious about her words. But before beginning, she reached into her pocket and drew out a folded, letter-sized paper, which she handed to him.

"I've written down the dream," she said. "I read where that was an important thing to do."

He smiled and took the sheet, which was filled with writing on both sides.

"That's right," he answered. "It helps bring back all the small details and gives a clearer understanding for future dreams." He placed the paper on his desk, then got up and came to sit in the chair facing Sister Teresa.

That's kind of him, she thought. Now the room became very informal and relaxed her even more.

"Please, tell me," he said.

"The dream happened three nights ago. **In it, I woke up startled. There was a loud knocking at the door to my room. It was nighttime. Sleeping in the same room, on a little cot near my window, was Elliot Reed."**

"The boy in our school?"

**"Yes. The knocking had awakened him too. He got up and was looking at me. Then the loud knocking happened again. This time, even louder. Outside the door, a voice that I thought I recognized, shouted, 'Come out, come out, son of our people!'**

**It frightened me. I wasn't sure why I was afraid, but I didn't want to open the door. Again, the Bam! Bam! Bam! And again the male voice called, 'Come out! Son of our people! Come out!'**

**I knew I had to open the door. So I got up, and Elliot followed behind me to the door. I opened it."**

She paused and wiped her hands on her habit.

**"When I opened it, it wasn't the normal hallway by my room that I saw. It was a large, brightly lit open area, filled with our high school boys in uniforms. In front of them, with a mask on, was...you."**

"Me?" Father Tinian said.

"Yes, that's why I felt I had to come and see you."

"Well, you were right. What happened then?"

**"You took off the mask and said the same words again, 'Come out! Come out!' you said. And then all the boys in back of you began to chant the same words over and over again. And then you put the mask back on and reached your hands out for Elliot."**

"Did I try to come into your room?"

She thought for a moment. **"No, you just beckoned and kept chanting over and over again, 'Come out, come out.'"**

"Then what happened?" he asked.

**"Elliot came out from behind me and walked over to you. He did hesitate two or three times, but he went. Then you grabbed**

**him by the wrists and quickly took him over to the crowd of boys. It was as if you were afraid of him coming back to me,"** Sister Teresa said, hesitantly.

"Is that all?" Father Tinian asked.

"No," she answered slowly. **"Then I felt so alone I started to cry. And the door to my room swung shut.** Then I woke up."

"Is there anything else?" he asked.

"Oh, yes. As I started writing down my dream, I remembered that all the boys were dressed in their parade uniforms and had scabbards at their sides. Then, slowly, as I pictured them in my mind, I could recall some of their faces. They were ex-adjutants from the school."

"And what about the boys you didn't recognize?"

"I had a feeling they were the adjutant captains before my time here."

He nodded his head, thinking about what she was telling him.

"You're probably right," he reflected. "If you were to look in the old school yearbooks, you would most likely find them."

"I did, and they were," she responded with a smile.

"Good for you," he said. Leaning forward, he continued. "Did you know that in certain tribes, the word 'mask' and the word 'spirit' were the same?"

"Really?" she said, excitedly.

"Whenever they wanted to portray the spirit, they wore the mask or they talked about the mask."

"Then my dream is showing me something that deals with the spiritual?"

"Yes," he answered. "Most assuredly."

"I don't think I understand."

He smiled and responded gently, "That's exactly why you had the dream, so you would understand."

He paused and thought for a moment. "Let me tell you something. Maybe this will help you understand. This Elliot Reed...is he very special to you?"

"Yes."

"So much that you love him like a son?"

"Yes, that's right."

"Then this all makes sense," Father Tinian continued without hesitating.

"It does?"

"How old is Reed?"

"Fourteen."

"And where are his parents?"

"He has none as far as we know."

"This is extraordinary," he said, humbly shaking his head. "In olden times, in American Indian and African tribes, every young man was 'called out' through a ritual. It was a special occasion when he was between twelve and fourteen, and would leave his mother's hut or tepee to join the men of the tribe. It was necessary that a spiritual and physical separation take place between the mother and son. In Hebrew tradition, the same thing happens with the bar mitzvah, which is a time of shouldering responsibility and religious duty. The boy had to have an awakening, a new birth as a man. The father of the boy plays a central role of the boy's crossing into manhood."

Father Tinian paused, looking kindly at Sister Teresa. "Now <u>your</u> boy is being called out."

"Amazing," she answered. "What does this mean as far as Elliot is concerned?"

With a smile, Father Tinian teased, "Ah, spoken as a true mother." He watched as Sister Teresa flushed slightly, then he continued on a more serious note. "Well, if I'm interpreting this dream properly, it looks as though Colonel Whitcome will have to become part of this."

This startled Sister Teresa.

"Oh, thank you Lord. There's something else in the dream I forgot to tell you," she said hurriedly. Getting quickly to her feet, she went to his desk and got the paper with the dream written on it. Turning it over, she read for a moment, then said, "Look at this in the third paragraph." She handed it to him.

Father Tinian read out loud, **"Amongst the cadets, I would see a face, as if it were hiding in the crowd. I would see it for a moment then it would disappear and then reappear. It was the face of Colonel Whitcome!"**

Father Tinian chuckled.

"What is it?" she questioned.

"It fits the Colonel, that's all. He's such a recluse. One **is** never really sure if he's even at the school anymore. When was the last time you saw our Colonel?" he asked with a grin.

She thought about that for a moment. "Well, I'm not quite sure, exactly."

Father Tinian laughed, "See what I mean?" Getting up from the chair, he made his way to the desk. "It looks like the dream is saying that we should prepare Mr. Elliot Reed for the job of Adjutant Captain. Don't you agree?"

"Yes. That's what I thought it meant."

"Well, it's Colonel Whitcome's job to select the Adjutant Captains."

"Has he made his selection for next year?" Sister Teresa asked.

"I don't know. We usually discuss it at the end of the school year. Why do you ask?"

"Because Ray Alexander was one of the boys in the dream."

Father Tinian thought about this. "And he'll be a senior next year, won't he?"

"Yes," Sister Teresa answered.

"Was there anyone else in the dream who is still at the school?"

"No," she answered, "Just Cadet Alexander."

The Father pondered this. "Elliot's just a sophomore now. Are you saying he's supposed to become Adjutant Captain after Alexander?"

"If we are willing to go by the dream, it seems possible."

"The school has never had an eleventh grader as the Adjutant Captain...only seniors", he mused. "This certainly would cause troubles among the seniors." He thought about it for a moment.

"But, then again, anytime you follow a dream, the old ways are usually broken down, and new things have to be tried."

He looked at Sister Teresa for a moment, while making a decision. "Let's keep this dream to ourselves until I talk to Colonel Whitcome."

"Yes, of course", she answered. "I would like to thank you for listening to me and for caring about ...these things."

Father Tinian smiled at her and then stood up. She followed suit.

"I really didn't get to finish my story about the Reservation", he said as he walked her to the door. "A month before I was transferred from the Reservation, that same Indian, who had told me his dream five years before, came and shook my hand. We had become friends, and I asked him what the occasion was? He said to me, 'You will be leaving soon, and I wanted to be the first to say goodbye.' The night before, in a dream, he had seen me leaving the Reservation. To him, it had already happened."

Sister Teresa left his office knowing that she was no longer alone. She hurried back to her room, wanting to pray for the meeting between Father Tinian and the Colonel.

Father Tinian remained standing by his closed door, shaking his head over the little Sister. No wonder Mother Superior was writing reports about her saying this woman is a mystic and believes in direct revelation from God! It looked like things were picking up at the old school. As far as the Colonel is concerned, the Father thought, he wouldn't be told about the dream. One thing Colonel Whitcome didn't have was a spiritual ear. No. He would have to be handled differently.

* * *

Colonel Harold Whitcome's past, as well as the history of his father and grandfather, was the U.S. Army. His grandfather, Franklin Whitcome, had been a colonel in the infantry and had been decorated for valor in the First World War. Harold's father, Franklin Junior, was a highly respected Brigadier General, noted for his tactics in light artillery. In fact, Harold had been born at Fort Bennings while his father was a young captain being taught his trade. The name Harold had been selected because of Franklin Junior's love of poetry. One of his favorite poems had been <u>Harold the Dauntless</u> by Sir Walter Scott:

> 'The bickering lightning, nor the rock of
> turret to the earthquake's shock, could
> Harold's courage quell.'

In a sense, Harold had lived up to his name. He had been courageous, even to a fault. Whether it had been in time of war or peace, Major Whitcome had the courage to live by what he believed. His sense of right and wrong, taught him at a very early age, was always being enforced. He felt that he should not submit to change, which he believed would be weakness in his character, but he also had the inexplicable desire to lead other people towards <u>his</u> views. This indefinable urge had certainly proved correct when it had come to leading his men into combat. Harold's war record and his capacity to bring his men back alive, was beyond reproach.

But, in areas of relationships, such as marriage, working with other officers, and the strategy of everyday living his dogmatic beliefs had not been received as he had wished. In fact, in many instances, his convictions brought on disputes that were never fully resolved. This had always surprised him. In recollection, he found that he had lost most of these private wars, and that many of them were still vivid in his memory. Yet, the victories he won on the battlefields had long since faded to shadows, and he certainly would never admit to anyone that he was still aware of memories too painful to muster up.

When his father died, leaving a rather sizable library of military tactics, poetry and literature to him, Harold found that he really didn't care much for any of them. He sometimes wondered why he kept the lot. Despite these feeling, no matter where he was transferred, he would always pack them carefully in fifteen wooden crates and have them shipped to his new post. Once billeted, he would make sure they were dusted and placed in their proper shelf-order. Twice, he had to have shelving built to specification because none had been available. Though it had been costly, he didn't question doing it.

All this had taken place before his retirement. Once out of the army and on his own for the first time, he had felt fortunate to find a position at St. Maurice's. His duties were simple, seeing that all cadets received military training, no matter what their age. His title, as in the U.S. Army, was Colonel.

Harold never had any children. He had been married once, but his wife had only stayed a few years. After that, he kept mostly to himself, surprised at how long he had been saddened by his divorce.

When things really got bad, he would get drunk and find a whore, but still felt rotten the next day. After a time, he gave up nights with the prostitutes, but continued to use the bottle. As he was nearing his fifties, his liver started acting up and the doctor told him it was 'dying time', if he didn't change his nightly habits.

At St. Maurice's, he had been given his own secluded small house, separated from the Sisters and cadets. He found it to his liking. It even included a small study with plenty of room for his father's books. After his bout with his liver ailment, Harold found that he spent much of his free time in the study and that his attitude towards his father's books had changed. They had turned out to be his best friends, his only friends in fact. Aside from constant back pain, he was in good health for being fifty-nine years old. He felt mostly satisfied with his solitary life.

That night, after Sister Teresa's meeting with Father Tinian, the Colonel received a phone call, an unexpected irritation. He looked at the clock; it was nearly seven. "Hello", he answered curtly.

"Colonel, this is Tinian. I hope I'm not disturbing you?"

He hadn't received many calls from Father Tinian before. "Not at all," he answered.

"I was wondering...instead of waiting until the end of the term, if we could have our meeting sooner?"

Harold wondered what had happened. It was not like the school to change any of its habits. Though it concerned him, he certainly wouldn't ask. "It would be just fine with me. When would be a good time for you?"

"How about making it Tuesday at two?" Father Tinian asked. He could never read anything behind Tinian's words.

"That would be just fine. See you then." They hung up.

Tuesday! Today was Friday. He had to wait the whole weekend, and then some. What could it be? In the fourteen years he'd been here, Father Tinian had never asked for a special meeting. Many times the Sisters would ask because of deportment problems with the cadets, but never Tinian. Come to think of it, since he had turned down an invitation for golf a few years ago, he hadn't heard from Tinian. Damn, now he wouldn't be able to concentrate on his reading at all! Whether he liked it or not, Father Tinian was the boss. And he couldn't forget it.

The first part of the meeting went as usual. The Colonel talked about how the year was going and how the cadets were doing; the meeting was rather dull and uneventful. There must be something in the works though, the Colonel thought. Then came "the pause" when both men knew the regular business was over. Tinian smiled, then bent and rummaged around in one of the bottom drawers of his desk.

The colonel shifted his gaze to the view out the office window, which looked over the huge lawn in front of the school. It was so peaceful. He was always surprised at the number of birds that populated the area. At his small house, he only had five or six birds that came to his door regularly. He enjoyed feeding and watching them.

"You like this view, don't you?" Father Tinian asked, as he took some manila folders from the drawer.

"Yes," the Colonel answered, somewhat embarrassed at being caught. "It's quite peaceful."

"I hope you don't mind coming in early. I know you didn't have time to do your written report, but there are a couple of new things I'd like to discuss."

"I don't mind at all," the Colonel answered.

"First," Tinian said as he opened the top folder, "I'd like you to see these."

He took four or five opened letters, with their envelopes attached, and handed them to the Colonel.

As the Colonel browsed them, he saw they were from parents, and that they were thank you letters about their sons and their school achievements. All were very complimentary to the school and the military program. His name was mentioned in them. They thanked the school for having such a fine officer to guide the boys. He looked at the names of the boys but couldn't recognize any of them. He knew very few of the lads by name.

"Well, these are very nice," he said to Father Tinian.

"I thought you might appreciate them. I know we did. And I'd like you to know that Mother Superior also has the highest regard for your work here."

"Very kind of her."

Father Tinian opened the next folder and looked in it. "I was reading over your report from last year and happened to notice a paragraph that must have escaped me when I read it before."

"Oh, what was that?"

"Where you talk about the need for a more in depth training for the boys who are given authority."

He began reading out loud. "'Sometimes, because of the short amount of training time which is given to the officers, certain areas of discipline and practice fall short.' Do you remember writing this?"

"Yes," The Colonel replied, wishing he had reread his copy of last year's report.

"Do you still feel that way?" the Father asked.

"Oh, yes. I think it is a yearly problem. It seems that we just get them so they conduct themselves like officers, then they graduate."

Father Tinian looked down at the report again. "I don't know how I could have missed this. It seems like something we should have dealt with earlier. Don't you agree?"

"Though it certainly is an important problem, there doesn't seem to be any answer for it."

"What if we started earlier?"

"Earlier?"

"Yes. What if you selected from the eleventh graders, instead of seniors for instance? Would that work?" He could see that the idea surprised the Colonel.

"Well, that would give us two years, if we selected properly," he said thoughtfully.

"Do you think it would be worth a test?"

"Yes. It might be just the thing."

"I know that this coming year is too quick to start such a program, but..." Tinian paused a moment for a dramatic emphasis. "Have you already chosen the Adjutant Captain for next year?"

"Yes. I've selected Ray Alexander."

"Excellent choice, excellent," Tinian said with a smile. He had just gotten verification of the dream. Thank you, Lord, thank you, he thought.

"Well," Father Tinian said, "I am certainly not against trying a new plan, if you think it might help the school."

"I think we'll see more stability within the ranks, when the authority doesn't change so quickly."

"Very good," Father Tinian continued. "Do you think there will be any negative feelings from the seniors, if you pick a lower classman?"

"We train these young men to take orders. Their feelings will have to be of secondary importance."

He must have been tough to be under when he was in the Army, the priest thought. "A good point, Colonel. That's the way it is in the Army, isn't it?

"Yes, and as it should be, the man best suited for the Job gets it."

"Very good then! Year after next, we can look for a Junior Adjutant Captain. We'll try a new way! What we'll do to this end is to make sure that you get all the grades and reports of the top juniors for next year. Let's hope that we'll have a good selection. Is there anything else we can do to help?"

"No," the Colonel answered, "if you will just show me the records of the boys with the highest grade point averages and best deportment, I think I can take it from there."

"Excellent," Father Tinian said, then pausing before continuing. "But wait...there may be one more point. I hope I'm not over-stepping my boundaries, but since we're dealing with boys who are somewhat younger, it might be advantageous for you to spend a little more time with the ones in your selection." He thought he saw the Colonel flinch, but he couldn't be sure.

Tinian pressed further. "I know that the younger age might be a stumbling block for Mother Superior, but once I tell her that you are going to spend more time with the candidates, making sure that they have the maturity to handle the pressure of authority, it will set her mind at rest. She trusts your judgment."

"Making sure the lad is mature is important," mused the Colonel, weighing the amount of time he would have to spend. His only thought was that it would only have to be done every two years, instead of one. Even though he felt the scale was tipped in his favor, he still asked, "Maybe you could amplify this idea of spending more time?"

"Well, I'm not exactly sure. Maybe some social time with the boys, some fireside chats as a group. That way you might be able to see which of the boys are looked up to by the others. I have no doubt there must be a stand-out leader among the best students."

The Colonel had to admit this wasn't a bad idea and that he should have thought of it years ago. In the past, the only way he had selected the Adjutant Captain was to take the largest and best-mannered boy who was qualified. Then, after-the-fact, so to speak, he got to know the boy. He didn't like to admit it, but he had been disappointed with some of his choices.

"I see what you mean," the Colonel answered. "Let the best of them select their own leader."

"Yes, that's it. It might work, don't you think?" Father Tinian asked while standing.

"Yes, it might at that," the Colonel answered, as he slowly got up from his chair.

The two men shook hands. It was the first time the school had ever used one of the Colonel's ideas. He felt rather good as he left the priest's office.

Before the meeting with the Colonel, Father Tinian had looked closely at Elliot Reed's records. His grades were as high as you could get them, and his deportment reports were above reproach. Through the years, only accolades had come from his teachers. There was one problem, however. He was not a Catholic. The school had never had an Adjutant Captain who was not a Catholic. He wondered why Sister Teresa hadn't mentioned this. However, Father Tinian thought, smiling slightly, the dream didn't take this into account either.

* * *

In the middle of Elliot's sophomore year, Colonel Whitcome received five manila folders from Mother Superior. On the outside of the first folder, attached with a paper clip, was an envelope. Inside was the following note: **I will pray for your selection and for this new direction.** A scrawled, M.S. was the signature below it.

The Colonel stood by the small desk in his study as he read the one line. Even if she hadn't signed it, he would have known it was from Mother Superior, because it seemed so laconic. She had always been a mystery to him, never saying enough to really tell you what she thought or what she wanted. And yet as he thought about it, he smiled. Mother Superior was not the only one; all women mystified him, from his mother to his ex-wife. Whereas those two had talked so much they made him crazy, this nun said just enough to keep him off-guard and ill-at-ease.

He groaned. He would have liked to sit while he looked over the records of these cadets, but his lower back was giving him trouble again. He found it better to stand, placing his hands on the desk so that he could transfer a portion of his weight to his arms, as he moved from one leg to the other. He found this helped to relieve the pain.

The first two records showed boys who had very good grades, and the usual amount of small, unimportant indiscretions reported through the years. As usual, the notes from the disgruntled teachers stopped as the cadets matured. These were the same kind of reports that the Colonel had been seeing for years, bright kids with the usual amount of "snakes and snails, and puppy-dog tails" thrown in.

Yet, the third folder was different. Even before he opened it, he knew it was unique. It was slightly heavier and thicker than the others. This cadet's name was Elliot Reed. As usual, the Colonel could not put a face with the name. By the size of the folder, he could tell this lad had been at the school for sometime. As he opened it and scanned each sheet, it became apparent that this cadet had not gone through one grade without his teacher giving him at least one note of commendation! Not even one semester had passed without some kind of positive acknowledgment! This is impossible, Harold thought. Nobody could get along with some of the nuns who teach in this school! There are at least two "Captain Blyths" and one "Mad Hatter" who teach here!

He hurriedly went back through the commendations, looking at the names of the nuns who sent them in. Yes, he thought, even the monsters of the classroom had given this cadet letters of approval! He had never seen anything like this. And the lad's grades couldn't get any better. There was even a letter from the swimming coach mentioning Elliot Reed's capacity for workouts! The Colonel would have laughed if his back hadn't hurt so much. Was there anything this boy couldn't do?

Since everything was filed in chronological order, Reed's early history was tucked against the back of the folder. It was there that Harold noticed two things that made him pause. First, the lad had no parents. He had been sent to the school by a law firm. The Colonel wondered what the consequences of this might be, and what the lawyers had done with the kid for the first five years.

Then, he noted the boy's religious affiliation stated, "none". Since Reed wasn't a Catholic, why had he received this boy's folder at all? Colonel Whitcome knew without a shadow of a doubt that if he had not been a Catholic, he would never have gotten the Commandant job. And now he received this? Once again he glanced at the note from Mother Superior. 'I will pray for your selection and for this new direction.'

"Now what the hell is she saying?" he said out loud. Just how new of a direction did they want the school to take? The more he thought about it, the more definite he was that this was not a mistake. He knew that Father Tinian and Mother Superior had gone over each of these records thoroughly, as they did each year. They would never miss something as important as the boy's religion.

All right, he thought, since this must be the case, it meant that they had sent Reed's file on purpose. Were they telling him that it was all right to select somebody outside the faith, to select on ability alone? He did remember in his conversation with Father Tinian, that when he mentioned the U.S. Army's way of having the right man for the right job, the priest had not seemed opposed to such an idea. Shifting his weight and giving a sigh, he set Elliot Reed's file aside and looked at the last two folders. They were about the same as the first two cadets, good, but nothing like Reed's.

He certainly wanted to meet this Elliot Reed, but at the moment the only thing he could think about was his debilitated back. He groaned and slowly lowered himself to the floor in front of the small heater. Stretching himself out as best he could, he thought what it would be like to have a healthy liver so that he could get numb-drunk.

From the floor by the heater, where he remained during these terrible struggles with his back, he had studied the cadets' five records thoroughly. It took three days before the pain had subsided enough that the Colonel could leave his apartment. On Thursday, two days before the Christmas vacation was to begin, he stood on the steps overlooking the parade grounds. He watched the Battalion go through dress rehearsal for the Christmas break. This Saturday all the parents would be present under the canopies, listening to the marching band and watching the cadets going through their drills, waiting to take their boys home for two weeks.

But this day, the Colonel would see an improper line within one of the companies from time to time, yet on the whole they looked fairly good. The Colonel glanced at the marching band, seeing they were as slipshod as ever, never being able to maneuver properly while playing their instruments, but he was doing his best not to be irritated over this. In fact, he had been trying to think of it as a source of amusement. Once, two or three years ago, a young lad had mishandled a drumstick, which had flown into the seated crowd of adults, landing in the lap of someone's grandmother. Everybody had laughed over that one. What made the mishap even funnier was that the young drummer became so flustered he stepped out of ranks and stood waiting for the old lady to hand him back his stick. She was so startled; she sat looking down at the strange wooden thing, not knowing where it had come from. From that time on, the Colonel had tried to become more philosophical about the soldiering of young musicians.

On this cool afternoon, the Commandant concentrated on watching Company B. This group held the sophomores, including all five of the cadets whose records were on his desk. Elliot Reed was easy to find because he was the Sergeant at Arms, marching in front and to the right of the first line of the company. Ahead of Reed, company center and three paces in front, was Archie Reynolds, a senior and the B Company Commander. He carried a saber and barked out the drill commands.

Whitcome watched Reed closely. He gauged that he was slightly less than six feet, but still growing. When the Colonel had first looked at him, he thought him skinny. But as he watched Reed's movements to commands, he began to see that the lad was in extraordinary shape. The colonel was reminded of a group of young marines who had covered his flank on a skirmish years before. They had looked like this Reed. After that battle, when his men and the marines were relaxing together, one of the marines had taken his shirt off and poured water over himself. He had looked like a chiseled piece of granite.

This fifteen-year-old boy reminded him of that man. He marched like an athlete, no wasted movement and no bravado, just a smooth directness as he followed every command. The Colonel could find no faults with this cadet's abilities on the drill field. In fact the longer he watched, the more graceful he seemed to be. Well, I'll be damned, the Colonel thought, I'd give him a written commendation too! He smiled and painfully walked to his office.

That afternoon, Lieutenant Archie Reynolds was called into the Colonel's office. The young lieutenant stood at attention, wondering what he was doing here. Had he done something wrong?

"At ease," the Colonel said. Archie went to parade rest. The Colonel held out a sheet of paper. Archie took it and read it. There were five names on it, all from his company.

"What we talk about now is confidential, understand?"

"Yes, Sir."

"What do those five cadets have in common?"

"Well, they're all sophomores, and they're the best brains in the company."

"When you selected Reed for Sergeant of Arms, were any of the other names in the running?"

"No, Sir."

"And why was that?"

"There's something he's got, and they don't."

"Such as?"

"Well, for one thing, nobody messes with him, Sir."

"You mean he's tough in a fight?"

"Well, not really, Sir. As far as I know, he's never had one."

"Then how would they know?"

"He studied some sort of Karate."

"Where does he do this Karate?"

"Sister Teresa takes him into town on Saturdays, but it's more than that, Colonel."

"What do you mean?"

"Well, it's the way he does lots of things. He rope climbs faster than anybody ever has. He does as many chin-ups as he wants, and the last one is as fast as the first one. He can swim thirty laps and still look strong." The young Lieutenant paused and thought for a moment. "I've seen him get out of the pool and go run five miles. Not a jog, Sir, a run. Nobody messes with him, Sir, not even the seniors."

"How is he at taking orders?"

"No problems, Sir. He doesn't cause any trouble. In fact, he..."

"Yes?"

"He never crabs about anything. And he helps the other guys."

"What do you mean?"

"Well, some of the guys aren't too smart, and he helps them. And they know they can always count on him."

The Colonel paused in his questioning. He was beginning to think that this was being made up, as if there was a Hollywood script being read. No fifteen-year-old boy acts like this. "This Reed, what are his negative characteristics?"

Archie thought about this for a moment. "Well, Sir, some of the guys think he's weird. They don't like being around him.

"Why's that?"

"They say he can see things in them. They don't like him looking at them. They say he's got strange eyes."

"I don't think I follow you."

"It's hard to explain, Sir", Archie said, pausing to think of a better example. "Like, one morning I woke up at five thirty. Reed's bed was empty. The light was on in the locker room. He was in there, already dressed, reading. I said to him, 'What the hell are you doing up so early?' He smiled at me, and waved his book."

"What was he reading?""

"Something about Romans."

"Romans?"

"Yes, Sir, the outside of the book said, `Book of Romans'. I guess what I'm saying, Sir, is he doesn't act like the other guys."

"He makes people nervous?"

Archie thought about this for a moment. "Yes, Sir, that's about it. Before he waved that book at me, the way he looked at me..." Archie stopped, and smiled. "Yes, Sir, he makes you a little nervous when he looks at you."

"If you had to select a Sergeant of Arms from that list, who would it be?"

"Besides Reed?"

"Yes." The Colonel watched as the cadet looked over the list.

"Well, I guess it could be Kirby or maybe Gardner, Sir."

"You don't sound too sure."

"No, Sir. I've got the one I want, whether he makes us nervous or not."

The Colonel smiled. "I see. Well, you'll be able to keep him."

As the Colonel reached out and Archie handed back the paper with the names, the Colonel said, "Just a reminder, Lieutenant, this conversation goes no further."

Archie came to attention, saluted and said, "Yes, Sir."

The Colonel returned the salute. Archie about-faced and left the office. The Colonel slowly got to his feet. His back was throbbing, and he had a headache from it.

* * *

Elliot Reed would meet Colonel Whitcome even before the Colonel expected it. During the Christmas holidays, when most of the boys had gone home, Elliot had a dream about Colonel Whitcome:

**The Colonel seemed to be in some kind of a prison filled with books. At least there were bars over the windows and heavy locks on the one door in the room. But then again, there was a nice rug on the floor and a small heater. Next to the heater, lying on the floor was Colonel Whitcome. He was wrapped in heavy, rusty chains. As Elliot moved closer**

**to him, he saw that the chains were connected together by locks, large old rusty ones with corroded keyholes.**

**"Where are the keys to these locks?" Elliot asked him. There was no answer. Then Elliot noticed that the Colonel's ears had mufflers over them and that the mufflers were old and had somehow grown to become part of the ears. Elliot knew that he could not remove them. He looked closely at Colonel Whitcome's face and saw that the man was blind with a dark film covering his eyes. Elliot touched the membrane. It was like thick leather, rough to the touch.**

**During all of this, the Colonel didn't move. It was as if he didn't know that someone was with him. Suddenly, Elliot felt so much compassion for him that he started to cry. As his tears fell, Elliot knew that they would do nothing to help free him.**

**He stopped crying and out of frustration, grabbed hold of one of the large locks. He yanked on it, but it did not yield. As he continued to hold the lock, however, it began to disappear within his hand! Then the chains near the lock started to fade from view. Elliot grabbed another lock, and it too disappeared.**

**As Elliot released the last chain from the body of the Colonel, Elliot awoke.**

Abruptly, he sat up in the near-empty dormitory. The inside of his hands felt strange. He tried to look at them but it was too dark. He touched his palm with a finger. It felt sort of warm and slippery. He rubbed his palms together. Yes, they both felt that way.

Sister Teresa wanted to hear Elliot's dream, but she stopped him as he began. "Elliot, I want you to do something for me."

"What?"

"I want you to tell your dream to Father Tinian." This was the first time Sister Teresa had not been receptive to him. He wondered why. He wanted to ask her what was the problem? Why she didn't want to listen? "I think you'll be surprised", she continued, seeing the look of confusion on his face. "Father knows a great deal about dream interpretation. And I know that he wants to help." This was very difficult for her. She wanted to explain everything to him, but she knew it was not her place.

"All right, if you want me to I will," he finally answered. "You're not mad at me are you?"

"No, I'm not mad. I just know that Father Tinian wants to know more about you. And besides, he's a nice guy." She smiled and folded her hands in her lap. She really wanted to hug Elliot, but those days were gone.

Father Tinian liked the boy as soon as he came into his office. He wasn't really sure why, but maybe it was the boy's openness or the calm way he held himself. As the lad entered the room, Father Tinian tried to remember the last time a cadet had asked for a personal appointment. He couldn't remember one. Most of the cadets he heard through the mesh at confession but he never had a chance to meet any of them. Since this boy wasn't Catholic and had never been to confession, they had never said a word to each other. In the back of this thought, Father Tinian knew that it should not be this way.

"Have a seat," the priest said easily. The lad sat. "What would you like to talk about?"

"I had a dream, and Sister Teresa told me to come to you."

"Ah, a dream", he said as he tried to measure the boy's intent. Had Sister Teresa told him about their meeting? No, he doubted it. "I hear you two are good friends."

"Yes, since I came to the school."

He certainly wasn't nervous about this meeting, Father Tinian thought. He sat erect and calmly looked back at him.

"Do you remember many of your dreams?" the priest asked.

"I seem to remember the important ones," Elliot answered straightforwardly.

"Well, let's hear this one," the priest said as he brought a small writing pad out from his desk. As the boy began, he started to take notes, but then thought better of it and concentrated on listening. The amount of detail the lad recounted was amazing.

"...as I saw the last of the locks and chains disappear, I woke up." Elliot glanced down at his hands, but for some reason he didn't feel comfortable telling the priest about the moisture that had come to his palms.

"You're right," the priest said, "it is an important dream. Tell me what you think of it?"

"As I left the dream, I thought there was a chance that he was still locked up, even though all the chains were gone."

"Were you still in the dream when you thought this?"

"I'm not sure, maybe somewhere in between. But I think the Colonel might have put those chains on himself."

This startled Father Tinian. Where did this insight come from? This boy was only fifteen years old!

"What do you think the chains represent?"

"I thought about that. If I put myself in his place, if I were blind and deaf, I might not want to move."

"Too frightened?"

"Yes, plus I wouldn't know where to move to or what to do."

"Yes, I see what you mean," Father Tinian answered.

Elliot paused, and then said, "And the chains and locks were very old."

"He's been carrying them for a long time," Father Tinian added.

"Yes," the boy said quietly, with a look of anguish on his face. He was very near tears.

Father Tinian was not quite sure what he should say. Was he here just to listen, he asked himself or should he give advice? This boy was going through something that the Father didn't entirely understand. He decided to be direct and say what he was thinking. "What do you think you should do?"

"I think I'm supposed to meet with him."

If the situation hadn't been so serious, Father Tinian would have laughed. He knew the Colonel well enough to know the outcome of such a meeting. But then again, what of this dream? What if the boy was right? The lad was serious enough about this to come to his office about it. Besides, it wasn't difficult to see that the boy was carrying some form of a burden for the stiff-necked old soldier. The Colonel had become a recluse. Even Mother Superior had been commenting about how solitary the old veteran had become. If Father Tinian remembered correctly, she had used the word "hermit."

"Have you ever met the Colonel?" Tinian asked.

"No, Father."

"He's not an easy man to talk to."

Elliot Reed smiled for the first time. "Everybody in the school is afraid of him."

"What about you?"

"Yes, me too," Elliot said with a laugh. Father Tinian laughed with him.

"Why don't I set up a meeting for you. This would be a good time, what with everyone gone for the holidays."

"Could I meet him at his house?"

"Really? Why there?"

"I think I'm supposed to be in that room with all the books."

Father Tinian paused. "What if the books and the room are symbolic?"

"They might be, but I don't think so. I think the room is real."

Well, there you have it, Father Tinian thought. Now he understood why this boy and Sister Teresa were such fiends. They both felt they knew exactly what was going on in the spiritual realm, just like the Indians. When they knew something, they knew it! "This is a tall order," the Father reported. "Do you know that in all the time I've known him, I've never been inside his house?"

Since Elliot didn't really know what to say, he said nothing. But he did know that Sister Teresa was right. Father Tinian was a nice guy, and by the sound of it, he was the only one who would be able to set up the meeting.

"If I do set it up, what are you going to do?"

"I don't know. I hope I'll know when I get there."

* * *

Colonel Whitcome always looked forward to the holiday break. It used to be that he would get into his car and head for different places, usually somewhere in the Arizona desert, where there was some warmth. But for the past few years, because of his back, he had stayed in his small home, thankful for the solitude. When he had received the call from Father Tinian, he had a difficult time being civil. He thought, how much am I supposed to give to this damn job? He had listened as the priest had actually asked if a cadet could meet him in his home! Who said that priests didn't have guts! But he had held his temper, composed himself, and answered as calmly as he could that he had an office for such meetings.

"I'm sorry I have to tell you this, because we wanted to keep it as a surprise," Father Tinian said.

"What's that?" the Colonel asked, falling into the priest's trap.

"We thought it might be nice if we painted and laid a new carpet in your office. I'm sorry; we should have asked first, but we already have the painters down there." It had been that morning, in fact, that Father Tinian had called them off another job.

"Oh!" the Colonel said lamely. Now what can I possibly say, he thought. He had wanted the place fixed up.

"Besides, the cadet who wants to meet with you is Elliot Reed."

The Colonel paused. "He asked to meet with me?"

"Yes. Did you read his records?"

"Yes!"

"Interesting, aren't they?"

"Yes." The Colonel really didn't want to discuss his feelings about the records with anybody. This was his decision to make. "Did the Cadet say why he wanted the meeting?" the Colonel asked.

"Not exactly, but there seemed to be some urgency about it."

"You mean he wants to meet right away?"

"Oh, yes."

The Colonel knew he was stuck. Besides, he really wanted to meet with this young man. Maybe he could kill two birds with one stone. "All right then, what about this evening, say, right after supper."

"I'll send him over", the priest replied. The Colonel gave a gruff goodbye and hung up. "Gotcha, you old grouch!" Father Tinian said out loud in his office. It was going to cost him about five hundred dollars for the Colonel's office renewal, but it was worth every penny!

Elliot dressed his very best, making sure his uniform was in order and that his shoes were flawless. He wished Skinner was there to take a look at the back of him, but he'd gone to visit his mom. Elliot liked Skinner's mom and prayed often for her. She worked hard to keep her son in the school. Skinner's dad was dead, and he was her only child.

Elliot didn't eat much during supper, because he was much too nervous. He tried to think about what he was going to say or what he might do, but nothing came to mind. Had he made a mistake? No. He knew that he was supposed to meet with the Colonel. He pushed the dessert away and looked around.

There were only eight or ten boys in the dining room. Each sat in his usual place, making the emptiness even more apparent. All the others in the room were younger than he and were paying attention to their own plates. Elliot closed his eyes and prayed. "Father, would you help me do the right thing with the Colonel? I don't know what I'm supposed to do, and I feel real nervous about it." He paused and listened. Nothing! Silence! "He's a grump, Lord. That's what everybody tells me."

**Don't listen**, something said within him.

"What?" he said out loud. Then again, **don't listen.**

Elliot opened his eyes and looked down at his plate and smiled. He understood.

Getting up from the table, he cleared his dishes and went outside. Turning away from the dorms, he headed across the parade grounds, past the infirmary and the tailor shop, then onto a path that went through a tall hedge. In front of him was a lawn with a single large tree, and on the other side of it, a small house. Behind it was a single garage.

It was dark now, and a light shone from one of the rooms in the house. Elliot went to the front door and rang the doorbell. He heard it buzz inside. He waited, but nothing happened. He wondered if he should ring again, but then thought better of it. He would wait.

Harold moved as fast as he could, but every step was painful. He neglected to turn on the porch light before opening the door. The cadet saluted him in the dark.

"Come in. Come in," the Colonel said curtly.

Elliot entered, taking off his cap as he did. He quickly tucked the cap in his belt. He came to attention.

And as was his habit, the Colonel looked the cadet over, noticing everything in one glance. He found no fault with him.

"Thank you for seeing me, Sir."

The Colonel had been correct about his height, slightly less than six feet. He stood before the lad and waited. He had found through the years that you could tell a great deal about a man by just waiting him out. Silence was a powerful tool. The boy's eyes did not waver. It only took a half a minute before the Colonel realized that the B Company commander's words were quite true. This Reed had a strange way about him. But it was more than his eyes. It seemed to embrace his entire presence. As the Colonel broke his gaze and moved to the side, the cadet's eyes stayed straight ahead.

"What's so urgent, cadet?"

"Excuse me, Sir, but do you have a room with shelves filled with books, and a little heater on the floor?"

Though surprised by the question, the Colonel knew there would be a sensible answer to it. "Are you in the habit of looking in my windows, Cadet?"

"No, Sir. I've never been to your house before."

He believed him. "Then who told you about that room?"

"No one, sir."

The Colonel moved in front of him again and looked directly into the boy's eyes. "If you've never been here before, and nobody told you, then how did you know?"

"With your permission, Sir, would it be all right if we talked in that room?"

This boy certainly is strange, the Colonel thought. "Why is that necessary?"

"I'm not quite sure, Sir, but I feel it is necessary."

The Colonel peered closely at the lad for a moment, then decided to go along with his request. Besides, his curiosity was up. "Very well, follow me." He slowly made his way toward his study.

As Elliot had been standing under the gaze of the Colonel, he had again begun feeling that strange moisture in his palms. As he turned and followed the colonel, he looked at his hands. They were reddish-looking and felt wet.

The Colonel led him down a short hallway, opened a door and entered before him. As soon as Elliot entered, he knew that this was the room in the dream. Things were slightly different, but this was the place. A sofa, unseen in the dream because that had been Elliot's vantage point, was against the far wall. In the center of the room, facing the bookshelves was a large, overstuffed leather chair. He had seen a portion of that chair in the dream. To the right and slightly in front, was the heater. It was not the same shape as the one in the dream, but it was a heater. To the left of the chair was a large goose-neck lamp. In front of the bookshelves was a portable wooden stair with two steps. The bookshelves went nearly to the ceiling. To the right of them was a desk and chair.

The Colonel watched him as he looked around his room. Elliot smiled at him.

"Now, what's this all about?" the colonel asked.

"I'm not really sure myself, Sir. Would it be all right if I asked you a question?"

"Is that why you requested this meeting, to ask me a question?"

Elliot thought about this for a moment. "Yes, Sir, in a sense. Yes, it is."

"Then ask your question."

"Do you ever lie down on the floor in front of that heater?"

"What?"

"On your back."

What the hell is this, blackmail, the Colonel thought? "I don't see what this has to do with you, Cadet."

"It really doesn't, Sir. I don't exactly know why I'm here, but I know I'm supposed to be. The only way I can find out why is to ask questions."

There was a pause.

"Are you waiting for an answer to your question?" The Colonel really didn't want his personal business known by anyone.

"If you don't mind, Sir." As Elliot was saying this, a strange vision came into his mind.

**The Colonel, naked to the waist, was laughing and jumping up and down. He was clapping his hands, just like a kid would do.**

Elliot wondered what this meant.

"I think it's time you answered a question from me, before I consider answering yours," the irritated Colonel stated.

"Yes, Sir?"

"How do you know these things?"

"I saw you laying on your back, right here," he said as he pointed down to the spot, "in a dream."

The Colonel blinked, opened his mouth, and then shut it. "You saw me in a dream?"

"Yes, Sir. That's why I'm here."

"What was I doing on the floor?"

"Nothing, sir. You were just lying there." Elliot decided against telling him how bound up he had appeared.

"A dream?" the Colonel said again.

"Yes, Sir."

"I've never heard of such a thing."

"Yes, sir," Elliot said, agreeing with the Colonel.

"And you think this means something?"

"Yes, Sir."

"What?"

"I don't know, Sir. That's why I thought it might be good to ask questions."

I certainly stepped into that one, the Colonel thought. This is one strange kid. No wonder nobody wants to mess with him. "All right, yes, I do lie on the floor from time to time."

"Why do you do that, Sir?"

"I do that because I have back problems, from time to time," he answered caustically. Lately, most of the time, he thought to himself.

Elliot suddenly understood his vision and what he was supposed to do. "You're not supposed to have a bad back, Sir," he said.

"What?"

"I mean, you don't have to have it."

"What the hell are you talking about?"

"I know why I'm here and what I'm supposed to do."

"What's that?"

Elliot hesitated for a moment, and then decided to push on.

"If you'll take off your shirt and lie on the floor, I'll show you, sir."

"Show me what?"

"How to get rid of your sore back."

"My back is not sore; it is damaged! The doctor's say it may be beyond repair even with surgery!

"I'm sorry, Sir. I used the wrong word. I'll show you how to get rid of your damaged back."

"What will you do?"

"I'll put my palms on your back."

"What will that do?"

"I'm not sure."

"What do you mean, you're not sure?"

"I've never done this before."

"Then how do you know it will do anything?"

"We won't know anything until we try."

The Colonel stared at the youth. "This is ridiculous!"

"I don't think so, Sir," Elliot said patiently.

"Why do I have to take my shirt off?"

"That's the way it was shown to me, Sir."

The Colonel found himself disconcerted at the thought of obeying this cadet, but his back was a continuous painful reminder that he should be willing to try anything. Abruptly, he loosened his tie, threw it on the chair, and unbuttoned his shirt. Taking it off, he draped it over the same chair. He stood in his undershirt. "This too?" he questioned sharply.

"Yes, Sir."

He sighed and started to lift his undershirt with both hands. A sharp pain prevented him. "Uhhh...," came from his lips. His legs almost gave way. "Oh, God," he whispered.

Elliot moved forward and helped him remove the garment. Slowly, Colonel Whitcome lowered himself to the floor. If he hadn't been in such pain, he would have been terribly embarrassed.

"What part of your back hurts?" Elliot asked.

As the Colonel looked up into the concerned face of the boy, the difference in rank left the old officer's mind. Here he was, looking into the face of a fifteen-year-old boy and hoping this lad wasn't completely crazy. At the same time, he knew he could no longer pretend his pain was manageable. Tears came into his eyes. "It feels like the whole spine area," he groaned. "Oh, I...I can't even move to show you. Oh, God."

"That's all right. Don't talk now," Elliot said gently. "I want you to close your eyes."

Harold blinked once and then did as he was told.

"I'm going to place my hands on your back. I just want you to try to relax as much as you can. Like in the dream, you don't have to do anything."

Elliot placed the palms of his hands along the Colonel's spine. Then Elliot closed his eyes and began pressing softly on the spine area. As he did this, he recalled the vision of the Colonel jumping up in the air and clapping. Elliot smiled as he slowly moved his hands down the man's back.

Harold shuttered slightly and gasped.

Keeping his eyes closed, Elliot continued visualizing the happy, clapping man. Then he said, "Thank you, Father." He smiled. "Yes, Father, we thank you.

Elliot heard the Colonel crying. Opening his eyes, Elliot saw the Colonel's tears trickling onto the floor. Then, a moment later, the Colonel's entire body was shaking with the crying. Elliot watched, concerned, not exactly sure what was going on. Then the Colonel turned his head slightly and smiled through his tears at a puzzled Elliot.

Elliot looked at his palms. His hands were back to normal and the moisture was gone. Then something really strange happened. The Colonel, while still seeming to cry, began giggling. At least that's what it sounded like to Elliot. Yes, there, he did it again! It was a giggle. Then, it turned into a short laugh. "What's going on?" the Colonel asked. But, unable to contain himself, he began laughing harder.

Then Elliot, surprised, felt a giggle come from inside of him. Then he too began laughing with the Colonel. Then, as they looked at one another, they laughed all the harder. They laughed until they could laugh no more.

"What did you do to me, boy?" he finally asked.

"I don't know," Elliot replied.

"You don't know?"

"No, Sir. I think Jesus did it."

There was silence for a moment. Then the Colonel said softly, "Jesus did it." Then the man was crying again. As Elliot watched, a loving sadness welled up in him, and he joined the Colonel as they cried together. Neither of them were embarrassed for themselves or by the other. After they stopped, there was another period of silence.

"Oh, I feel so good," the Colonel said, "but I'm afraid to move."

"You don't have to be, Sir. You can walk now. You can even clap your hands and jump up and down, if you want."

"I...I can?" Elliot could see that this struck the Colonel as funny. The Colonel began laughing again. "There's ...there's nothing I'd like better than to clap my hands and jump up and down!" the Colonel exclaimed through his glee. Elliot found this one of the funniest things he had ever heard, and he too started all over again. Finally, the laughter slowed down and ended.

"Oh, I'm exhausted," the Colonel, said happily.

"Do you want to get up?" Elliot asked, getting to his feet.

"Why not. Let's give it a try."

The Colonel's first movement was slow and tentative as he reached his arms forward. There was no pain. Then he got up on his hands and knees. He felt fine. Slowly, he stood all the way up. He felt good. He stretched his arms as far above his head as he could reach. Looking at Elliot, he smiled. Then his eyes filled with tears, and he slowly shook his head.

"I haven't been able to do that for twenty years."

Elliot smiled back at him. "God did good."

More tears came to the old warhorse's eyes, and he laughed. "Yes! Yes, He did."

* * *

The next morning, after Mass, Father Tinian was surprised to see the Colonel in his waiting room. "Well, what a nice surprise. Come on in."

The Colonel was smiling. He nodded and followed the priest into the office.

"Would you like some coffee?" the priest asked.

"I sure would," the Colonel replied, grinning. Father Tinian glanced quickly at him and found himself smiling back. The Colonel seated himself in the chair across from the desk.

"What's happened to you?"

"That's why I'm here. I woke up this morning and knew I had to come and tell you."

Tinian brought the coffee to him, sitting in the chair next to him. "Well, I'm glad you did." Watching the Colonel drink from the cup, he continued, "You look different somehow."

"I am different. I've never felt like this in my life. Did you know I've had a bad back?"

"Yes," the Father answered.

"You did?"

"Some days you look like you could barely move.

"Well, for the last two years, it was so bad I could hardly move." He smiled, set his coffee cup on the desk, and stood up. "Look at this," he said as he bent and touched near his toes. From there he reached up and stretched, then squatted into a deep knee bend. Then he sat and smiled at the startled priest.

"What happened?"

"It was Elliot Reed," the Colonel said quickly. "He came over, said he had seen me in a dream. Told me to take off my shirt and lay on the floor!" The Colonel laughed.

"And you did it?" the priest asked, intrigued.

"There's something about that boy that makes you believe what he says to you."

"I know exactly what you mean. Then what did he do?"

"He put his hands on my back. They were barely touching me. I'm not sure how long they were on me, when all of a sudden my back felt real warm, and it started to tingle. Then the tingling went everywhere in my body, right to the top of my head."

"A healing," the priest said quietly, "a miracle."

The Colonel looked at him and swallowed back tears. "That's what I had, isn't it?"

"Yes, God touched you."

"That's what Elliot said. He said he didn't do anything; it was Jesus." The two men looked at each other and smiled.

The Colonel moved forward slightly in his chair. "Though I wanted you to know about my back, there's something else I have to tell you. You might say this is a confession. Is it all right, here in the office?"

"Confession is good anywhere."

The Colonel smiled at this as he drank a little coffee.

"When I was about seven, I ran away from home. I don't remember why, but I made a sandwich, put it in a bag, and left by the front door. I can't remember where my mother was, but nobody stopped me. I had walked five or six blocks, when I noticed a large black man behind me. He had on a light colored suit, a dark tie and shiny black shoes. I remember mostly his shoes, because he soon caught up with me and was walking right beside me. I looked up and saw that he was looking down at me. He was smiling. He walked beside me for about a block and never said a word. I walked a little faster, and so did he. I stopped. So did he. I started to cry. He knelt down and patted my shoulder. Then he asked me where I was going."

"I told him the truth. I was too afraid to lie. He looked at me for a moment, lead me over to the curb, and we both sat down. He told me a story about when Jesus was a young boy, and how his parents where so worried when they couldn't find him. He told me the whole story, how Jesus was in the temple where he was supposed to be, doing the Father's work.

"Then the black man asked me a question. 'Is that where you're going? Do you know what God wants you to do?' I told him, no, I didn't know where I was going. Then he talked about Jesus and what he did, what his job was, and how much he liked little kids." The Colonel hesitated and looked into his cup. Then the man walked me back to my house." He paused and smiled at the priest.

"Did you ever find out who the black man was?" Father Tinian asked.

"Yes. He was a Protestant Chaplin. He knew my father and had seen me around. You see, I lived on a military base, and it would have been impossible for me to really run away. They would have never let me out the gate."

Both the men smiled at this, and then sat in silence.

"When I was in so much pain on that floor, and Elliot put his hands on me, the pain went away, and do you know what was the first thought that came into my mind?"

"What?"

"That black preacher and our time together. It came to my mind, and I remembered the whole story. And I remembered that after I got home, for the next few weeks, how I thought a lot about Jesus and what the black man told me. But then I stopped thinking about Him and finally forgot the whole situation. This morning, for the first time since I was a kid, I got up and prayed. I thanked Him for what He did for me, and asked Him to forgive me for not remembering Him."

He looked directly at the priest. "I've never been to confession here because I never believed that Jesus cared what any of us did." The tears came again, but the Colonel didn't care. "I know now that he cared about me all these years."

"You know what the boy said to me about you?" Father Tinian asked.

"No."

"He said, 'I think I'm supposed to go and see the Colonel." Father Tinian paused and touched the other man's arm. "I have a confession to make to you, Harold. I almost told him no, that it wouldn't do any good, that you would never listen. I'm sorry."

"Well, you should have been right. I still can't believe what that boy had me do! When I was flat on my stomach, without a shirt on, I was saying to myself, 'I've finally gone crazy!'"

With a straight face, Father Tinian said, "Do you think this will color your decision as to who you'll name as your Adjutant Captain?"

Both men burst out in laughter. Then the Colonel replied, "You know what else went through my mind?"

"What?"

"In both cases, I was helped by people who didn't even know me."

The priest thought about this for a moment. "Though I don't like to admit it, neither one of them were Catholics, either."

* * *

Elliot, at the end of his sophomore year, was called into Colonel Whitcomb's office. The cadet stood at attention before the Colonel's desk.

"At ease," the seated Colonel said. Elliot went to parade rest. "We're going to try something new next year, Cadet Reed. We've decided to select a cadet from the junior class and promote him to Adjutant Captain. In this way, we will be able to have a longer period of time to train our officers."

It seemed as if the Colonel was waiting for a response from him. "Yes, Sir," Elliot said quickly.

"We've selected you."

Elliot wasn't prepared for the abruptness of the announcement. Though he had been working towards the goal of Adjutant Captain for his senior year, this stopped him short.

The Colonel was looking at him, waiting for a response, but Elliot didn't know what to say, but finally, "I'm just a Sergeant of Arms, sir."

"I know that."

"It seems a long step up, Sir."

"It is," the Colonel said quietly. "I have no doubt you can handle such a step or I would not have recommended you for the command."

"Thank you for that, Sir," Elliot said, hesitating. "Do I have the right to a personal decision on such a matter or is this a command?"

"It is up to you to decide," the Colonel said, hiding the irritation he felt.

"Is it against military protocol to ask for time before giving you my answer?"

"Not at all," replied the Colonel evenly.

"There's one more thing, Sir. May I speak directly, Sir."

Oh, this boy is unnerving, the Colonel thought. "You may say what you like."

"I appreciate your confidence in me, Sir. I've been dreaming about being the Adjutant Captain since I came to St. Maurice. My reason for asking for time is to make sure I'm ready for such a responsibility. There's something I have to do first."

What could that be, the Colonel asked himself. No other cadet had ever asked for something like this. "Take care of what you have to do and get back to me then."

"Thank you, Sir. May I speak of this to two other people?"

"To cadets?"

"To one cadet and one nun, Sir."

"Very well, but make sure the cadet understands that your conversation with him is to go no further. If it does, I will hold you responsible."

"Yes, Sir," he said as he saluted. The Colonel returned it. Elliot about-faced and left the office.

* * *

Felix Skinner was waiting for Elliot near the playing field. "What did he want?"

"Let's take a walk." Elliot turned him, and they headed for the parade grounds. The field behind them was filled with kids playing games. "He wants me to become the Adjutant Captain."

"Why would they tell you now? That doesn't make much sense."

"He wants me to take over next year."

"How can you do that? You'll only be a junior."

"That's what they want. They want me to be Adjutant for two years."

"Holy Cow!"

"Yeah."

"There's going to be some pissed-off seniors."

Elliot hadn't really thought about that, but he knew he could handle whatever came. He looked at his friend's face. "What about you? What do you think about me doing it?"

"Me? What difference does that make?" Skinner said. "You've been thinking about this since we've known each other. You got the job and that's it."

"I didn't give him my answer yet."

"What? Why not?"

"Two reasons. The first one is you. You've been a corporal for seven years."

"Are you gonna start that crap again?"

"They've asked you to be a sergeant five times, and you've turned them down every time."

"So?"

"So, it's got to stop.

"What do you mean?"

"If I become Adjutant, you have to agree to take on whatever authority I give to you."

"Why?"

"Because you'd be good at it, and there are a lot of kids who need your guidance."

"You're like a broken record!"

Elliot was silent. He had learned through the years that it was sometimes best to let his friend stew, so they walked while Felix dealt with his irritation. "I don't see what one's got to do with the other," Felix fumed. Elliot said nothing. Felix stewed some more.

"Are you trying to tell me that if I don't do what you want, you won't take the job?" Skinner challenged. Elliot just walked along beside him, not even looking at his friend.

"You wouldn't do that!" Skinner insisted. "You want this command too much!" Still no words from his friend. Skinner was becoming more agitated. "You really piss me off! You know I don't like telling anybody what to do! It's none of my business!"

"Is that your answer?" Elliot asked quietly.

"And what if it is?" Skinner shot back. "Would you still take the command?"

"No."

"Oh, for cryin'..." Felix wanted to cuss but he knew what Elliot thought about that. "You're always trying to change me?"

"That's because you're a hermit, and you're not supposed to be."

"How do you know?" Felix asked without thinking. Then quickly he added, "No, don't tell me. I take that question back." They continued walking in silence, with Felix's slender body jerking this way and that. He never could hide it when he was irritated, his body spoke for him.

"What kind of a command?" Felix finally asked.

"Whatever it is, will you do it?"

"You mean you aren't going to tell me what my job will be?"

"Not until I'm the Adjutant."

"What if I don't like it?"

"You don't like anything at first."

Felix thought about this. "That's true. What if I don't like it after a while?"

"Then we'll talk about it."

"I've heard that before."

"Well?"

"All right: I'll do it! I don't like it, but I'll do it!"

His body was very animated now, a foot stomp here and a raised arm there, and then a double-shrug of the shoulders. And all the while there was muttering going on about freedom of choice, and the pressures of friendship.

* * *

Sister Teresa went to open the door of her classroom at the end of the day. She was surprised to see Elliot waiting in the hallway. He waved at her. She smiled and motioned for him to come in. As he entered, all the youngsters standing next to their desks watched as Elliot came to stand beside the little sister. Every eye in the room was on him.

"All right class. By rows," she said quietly. As they marched out the classroom door, past her and the high schooler, she noticed there was a difference in how they carried themselves.

When the last cadet had left, after sneaking a quick glance at Elliot as he shut the door behind him, Sister Teresa chuckled, "They were showing off for you. Usually they shuffle, not march."

"They look so small."

"No, you're just too tall," she said brightly, looking up at him. He laughed, then went and twisted into his old desk. He looked funny sitting in it, and Sister Teresa laughed. He laughed with her. They quieted, and he looked out the window at the playing field, finally turning back to her.

"The Colonel has asked me to be Adjutant next year."

"Good. Exactly as it should be."

"You're not surprised it's a year early?"

"You're supposed to be the Adjutant when you're a junior. Father Tinian and I discussed it last year."

"You know for sure?"

"Yes. There are no doubts."

Elliot looked at her for a long moment, and then nodded his head. "All right. I wanted to check with you. I'm afraid the Colonel wasn't too happy when I asked for some time before giving him my answer."

"He's an army man. He expects to be minded," she said, and then added, "So will you soon."

"I'd better go give him my answer."

"I heard about his healing."

"Who told you?"

"Father Tinian."

"How did he find out?"

"The Colonel went to his office the next morning and told him all about it. He's a changed man. Did you know that?"

"No."

"Father Tinian says they're becoming good friends, and that the Colonel is growing close to the Lord."

"That's good to hear," Elliot said. "Do you think he was ever married?"

"Why, I don't know. I don't know anything about the man's past."

Smiling, Elliot asked, "Do you think he'd get mad if I asked him?"

"Well, it is a personal question," she replied. "How important is it to you?"

"Pretty important, I think."

"Well, you helped the Lord do something nice to him, maybe he'll return the favor."

"Maybe."

She gathered up her student's papers, and the two of them walked from the room.

*  *  *

The Colonel had left his office. Elliot started to go back to the dorm, to wait until tomorrow to tell the Colonel his answer, but then thought better of it. He walked over to the Colonel's house and rang the buzzer. It didn't take the Colonel long to get to the door.

"Ah, Cadet Reed," he said, "come in."

"I hope you don't mind, Sir. I didn't want to wait until morning."

"It's all right, come into the study." Elliot followed him. The Colonel went directly to his desk, took some sheets of paper from the top of it, and placed them in the top drawer.

Elliot thought he might have been writing a letter.

"Well, young man, have a seat." Elliot sat on the sofa.

The Colonel stayed at the desk. "What's your decision."

"I would very much like the command, Sir."

"Good."

"I was wondering, Sir. Next year, how will you select the officers for each company?"

"I won't. You will. You'll receive a file of each student worthy of promotion. It will contain his grades and his deportment reports. I'll be here to help, but the selections will be yours. After all, they'll be your lieutenants.

"I see, Sir," Elliot answered. "Would it be possible to ask for someone's file, if you don't receive it?"

"Did you have someone in mind?"

"Yes, sir. He has excellent grades but he has turned down promotions for the past few years. They might have given up on him."

"And you haven't?"

"No, Sir."

"His name?"

"Felix Skinner."

The Colonel wrote the name down on his calendar. "I'll take care of it."

"Thank you, Sir."

"Is there anything else?"

"Yes, Sir." He looked at the Colonel, then at the wall of books. "You've been all over the world haven't you, Sir?"

"Most places, yes."

"Have you read all these books?"

"Yes."

"I've never been over three miles from this school. I've read most of the books in the library, but..."

The Colonel had been in the school library. It was filled with books on doctrine and the history of the church. The titles had bored him so much he hadn't even taken one from the shelves. It was certainly a place for priests and nuns, not for cadets. "You say you've read most of them?"

"Yes, Sir, but there's a lot of them in Greek and Latin."

Though he didn't say it, the Colonel wished he knew what that boy had learned from those books. Now, he wanted to go back into that library himself.

"What is it you want?"

"Would you mind if I read some of your books?

Harold had always been cautious about giving liberties to people. If they wanted to get closer to him or become part of his life, he was normally very reticent. Now, he found it easy to ignore that part of him.

"What interests you?"

"Well, Sir, for the past year or so, I've had an interest in females."

"What?" the surprised Colonel said.

"I mean, girls my own age. But the problem has been, who could I ask?"

"Well, I don't have any books on that subject."

"Oh, that's too bad. And we don't have any classes about them here either."

"That's for sure," the Colonel laughed.

"There might be another way, if you wouldn't mind," Elliot continued.

"What do you mean?"

"You could tell me about them."

"Me?"

"Yes, Sir. It doesn't seem right to ask Father Tinian."

"Well, I don't know if I'm the right one either."

"Have you been married, Sir?

What a time to ask such a question, Harold thought. Since his healing, he had been thinking about his ex-wife. In fact his thoughts had been going back through their marriage together, piecing things, finding out how big of a fool he had been.

"Yes, I was, for a few years."

"What was it like?"

He had to smile at such an open question. "What was it like?" he mused, wondering what he should say. "Well, it was certainly different from living alone. You always had to think about the other person. Every decision had to include her."

"Was that hard to do?"

"It was for me. I think I could do it better now, but then I didn't know how. I married when I was thirty. It seemed I should have been mature enough, but I wasn't." It surprised him how easily he could talk about this. And he didn't mind taking responsibility for his failure. He knew he had been at fault.

"What would you do differently?"

"Well, first of all, I'd include her in everything I did." He smiled at the boy and continued. "That's all she really wanted. She didn't like being alone, and she wanted to feel like she belonged."

"Yes, that would be important, wouldn't it?"

"I think, when you are really close together, nothing else matters." He looked at the lad, and then said quietly, "Just between you and me, I really screwed up. She was twenty-three years old, and just as pretty as you could want. She loved me. She even loved the Army because I was in it!" He laughed, and Elliot joined him.

A few moments of silence followed. The Colonel had grown quiet. Then looked at Elliot and shrugged his shoulders. Elliot knew that this was not easy for the Colonel. There were so many questions he wanted to ask, so much he wanted to know, but he could see that the Colonel had said enough. Elliot got up from the couch and walked to the bookshelves.

"There are so many to choose from," he said.

"Go to the shelf to your right." the Colonel directed. "Now on the second shelf from the top, about the fourth or fifth book. It's called, Jane Eyre."

Elliot reached up and took it from the shelf.

"Start with that one," the colonel continued. "That row and the one below it are fiction."

*    *    *

The summer went by quickly for Elliot. There was a great deal of spare time, and he used it to read, to continue his workouts, and to talk to the Colonel. The Colonel had taken to long walks around the playing field every day, and Elliot would pass him as he ran. He could see that the man was losing some of his paunch, and that his stride had quickened through the summer weeks.

One day, Elliot slowed in his run to walk beside the Colonel. "Your pace has picked up, Sir."

"I'm working towards beating you in a race," the Colonel said dryly.

Elliot laughed and then saw the Colonel smile. "How long before you'll be ready, Sir?"

"If it goes the way I've planned, sometime within the next year or two."

"I'll look forward to it," Elliot responded. He was quiet for a few steps and added, "I'd like to appoint a senior for the Commander of Company A."

"What's your thinking on it?"

"Since it will be my first year in that dorm, and the seniors and juniors will be together, I thought it would cool some tempers if I selected a senior."

"Do you think he would take orders from you, since he is older?"

"I would hope he would, Sir."

"Who do you have in mind?"

"Bill Dante."

The Colonel glanced at Elliot. That's a gutsy move, he thought. He didn't doubt that Elliot knew Dante would have been selected as the next Adjutant, if a senior had been selected.

"He certainly has the capabilities," the Colonel answered.

"Yes, Sir."

"When he returns to school, would you like me to talk to him first?"

"If you don't mind, I think I'd better handle it."

"Not at all. You're in command."

Elliot was quiet for a moment while they walked, then added. "Thank you for the use of your library during the summer."

"I expect you to use it just as much when school starts up. Any time you want."

"Thank you, Sir. I was hoping you wouldn't mind."

The Colonel looked at him and smiled, "Do you think you'll need books on self defense?"

"I've been taking care of that for a few years now," Elliot replied.

"You and Sister Teresa?"

"Yes, Sir. She takes me into town on Saturdays."

"I heard. Does she take lessons too?" the Colonel asked with a slight smile.

"She doesn't even like to watch. Too barbaric, she says."

"Well, sometimes the people we have to deal with are barbaric," the Colonel said knowingly.

"Yes, Sir," Elliot said, as he picked up his pace and continued his run.

* * *

Bill Dante returned to St. Maurice's two days early because he was sure the Colonel would be calling him into his office. He had prepared for this day, making sure that he followed all the rules and regulations of the school. He had worked hard at leadership, taking each promotion seriously and never jeopardizing the position given to him. He had held leadership positions in sports, and as far as he knew, he was respected by both the cadets and the Sisters.

He was summoned, and when he entered the Colonel's office he found Elliot Reed sitting at the desk of the Adjutant Captain. The Colonel was not in the room.

"Why the hell are you sitting there?" Dante asked.

"I've been given the command."

"What?"

"The school decided they wanted an Adjutant who could command for two years instead of just one."

"What is this crap?" Dante exploded. "When was this decided?"

"I'm not sure exactly when, but I do know that it was decided without my approval." He didn't know Dante well. He had played sports against him but had never really gotten to know him. Older cadets never had much to do with a lower classmen.

"Why isn't the Colonel here to tell me this?"

"I asked permission to see you alone. I felt it was my job, since we might be working together this year."

"Working together? You're a junior!"

Elliot ignored the outburst. "I want you to command Company A."

Dante checked what certainly was going to be a quick, angry retort, and thought about what the junior was offering…a smart move. Without a senior in charge of the seniors, he'd have a hell of a time getting things done. And how else would he do it, except through a senior A Company commander?

"You're trying to cover your ass. Without a senior, you'd have a hell of a time getting things done."

"You've missed the main point."

"What do you mean?"

"I asked you because you deserve it."

"I deserve more than that!"

"I know you do, but this is the best I can offer you."

"I don't think it's enough."

Elliot looked at him for a long moment without answering. He couldn't blame Dante for not being able to hold down his pride.

"Would you do something for me?" Elliot continued.

"What?" Dante answered, not really believing that this kid would ask something of him.

"I'd like you to think about taking the command."

"I don't have to think about anything."

"Yes, you do. First, if you don't do it, someone else will take it. Second, your anger is going to wear off and what then? You're a leader, not a follower. Do you want to stay angry all year while some other cadet tells you what to do?"

"I don't have to listen to this crap."

Elliot got up from his seat. "Yes, you do."

Dante was about his same size, but had twenty pounds on him:

"Whether you like it or not, I'm the Adjutant, so I'm your Commander." He went to stand directly in front of Bill Dante.

Dante was discovering something unexpected about Reed. This lower classman didn't seem angry, and Dante felt that Reed wasn't afraid of him at all. He wondered what would happen if he took a swing at him. Well, Reed was certainly giving him an open invitation, standing right in front of him. But the longer Dante looked at him, the more he decided against it.

"I hope that we can work this out so that your last year will be a good one for you," Reed stated. "You've been a credit to the school, and you're a fine leader. I don't think you want this to change after all this time."

He means all he's was saying, Dante thought. He isn't pulling any crap, and he really cares about what happens to me!

Suddenly, Dante felt a little stupid. If he were in Reed's place, could he have handled this situation the same way? No, he didn't think so. Reed would have been out on his ass, and he would have had an enemy all the rest of the year.

"Would you take a day and think about it?" Elliot asked.

"All right."

"Good. I look forward to hearing from you."

Bill Dante turned and left without a salute. Elliot didn't mind. At least, he didn't have to fight him.

* * *

While working at his summer job at home, Felix Skinner had wondered about the command waiting for him. Reed and he had talked over the phone every couple of weeks, checking up on each other, but Reed would never tell him what he had in mind. It got to be a joke after a while, with Reed finally telling him that he was going to be the first cadet to make janitor.

When Felix returned, he found he did not have a bed in the Company A dorm. He also found that there was a message that he was expected to report to the Colonel's office upon his arrival.

He changed into his dress uniform, leaving his luggage in the locker room of his old Company B dorm. Then after checking himself carefully in the mirror, he headed to the Colonel's office. He knocked on the door.

"Come in."

It was Elliot's voice. Skinner entered smiling, but when he saw that the Colonel was also in the room, he lost his smile and saluted. "Corporal Skinner reporting as ordered, Sir."

The Colonel returned the salute, then said, "At ease, Cadet. I understand that you and the Adjutant captain are acquainted."

"Yes, sir."

"He'll give you your orders."

Skinner made a turn, moved three steps and stood before his friend's desk. He saluted. He wanted to smile, but held it in.

"Sir."

"At ease, Corporal," Elliot said as he returned the salute. He too had a hard time not showing his gladness at seeing his friend. He watched as Skinner went to parade rest.

"Have you already found out that you don't have a bed in Company A?"

"Yes, Sir."

"You'll find your place up in Company E."

Oh, my God, he's given me the Pee Legs, Felix thought. He can't do that! I hate little kids! They're a pain in the ass!

"Yes, sir," Felix answered. He could feel the Colonel's eyes on him. He wondered if his face was red or blue? Were his eyes bulging?

"You know my thoughts about how important the first year or two are for the little cadets," Elliot continued. "Naturally, we wanted someone who had been through what they were going to go through. Since we were both raised here, and I needed someone I could trust to care for them, you were selected."

Care for them? Felix thought. I don't want to care for the little buggers! Some of them are still wetting the bed! I thought we were friends? "Yes, Sir."

"We'll have our first Commanders' meeting this coming Monday. That will give you a few days to get acquainted," Elliot said, looking down at a sheet in front of him. "You'll have forty-two first and second graders this semester."

Felix wanted to scream, but could only say, "Yes, Sir."

"Sister Agnes is the dorm Sister. She's new this year, and I know that she will look forward to your knowledge and help."

"A new house mother?"

"Yes. Is that a problem?"

"No, Sir, just a surprise. So many things happening at once." Skinner hoped Elliot would get his meaning.

"That's true," Elliot said, fully understanding what Felix was saying, "but it's nothing you can't handle."

Felix was concentrating on not grinding his teeth. "I'll do what I can, Sir."

"Thank you, Lieutenant."

He was being dismissed, and he hadn't been able to say a word! He saluted, made an about-face, and walked towards the door.

Elliot smiled as he watched his friend leave the office.

Only he could have seen the slight twitch in Skinner's arm, then a little side movement with his knee, and even that big hitch with the shoulder.

"Seems like a good soldier," the Colonel said as he went back to the work on his desk.

"Yes, Sir, he is," Elliot replied with a grin. He just wished he could see and hear Skinner as he made his way to Company E.

Everybody in Company B watched Skinner as he picked up his suitcases from the locker room. He was muttering to himself, his arms flinging this way and that, and his legs twitching to and fro. They laughed out loud when they heard him give what sounded like a mournful howl as he walked down the hall.

Skinner climbed the stairs to the top level. He couldn't remember being up here since he was seven years old. E Company, or the "pee-legs" as they were so unaffectionately known, had their own dorm on the very top floor. No other company was even on the same floor with them! Nobody wants to be around the little buggers, he thought. When he reached the top of the stairs, he peered down the hallway. He could hear the little monsters but couldn't see any of them. He took a deep breath and walked toward his doom.

As he entered the large room with the small beds, the noise immediately began to diminish. Each young cadet, as they saw this tall, angry-looking high-schooler staring at them, became silent and afraid to even move. The silence became so noticeable that the young lads who were in the bathroom and the locker room stuck their heads into the dorm to see what was going on. They too became like statues.

Felix Skinner had his first taste of power. He was surprised by it, but at the same time savored it. He chewed on it and found it to his liking. Maybe these little buggers could be controlled, he thought, as he walked in a few paces, keeping his same countenance. Slowly, for effect, he looked over the lot of them. As he was doing this, the door to the Sister's quarters opened and a face peered out at him. It was the face of an angel.

It was Felix's turn to go into a trance. The face of this exotic creature was framed in a Sister's habit. He felt that this must be some kind of a strange hoax being played on him. He had seen many Sisters, but none had ever looked like this. Then the beautiful creature smiled at him.

He smiled back. He felt his shoulder twitch. Oh, please Lord, he thought, not now. No strange movements from this body of mine that I can't control.

The vision came out from behind the door and made its way toward him. She was slightly taller than average and moved just like all angels move.

"I'm Sister Agnes," she said.

"Really?" he answered dumbly.

She laughed and replied, "Yes, really."

Felix felt sweat break out on him, and he quickly tried to cover his tracks.

"I'm sorry...sure, you must be. Who else would you be?" Holy cow, he thought. Holy cow!

"I'm Felix Skinner. I'll be the Commander for Company E this year." Then he added quickly, "and maybe next year."

The vision was smiling and looking at all the silent cadets. "Well, I'm certainly glad you're here. I see now what it takes to keep order."

Felix decided to take charge right away. "All right, Gentleman, go to your own beds!"

The scramble was on. Little bodies moved in every direction at once. It seemed as though no one was near his own bed. Then something strange happened within Felix as he watched them. The memories of his own actions at this age flooded through him. And he knew that, once again, Elliot Reed had been right in his assessment of him. Felix Skinner felt his heart go out to these scrambling little guys, as they were in the act of doing the best they could to please this big high schooler.

* * *

The news of Elliot Reed's appointment as Adjutant spread quickly through the returning student body. The new seniors were angry that one of them had not been selected, while the new juniors, just appointed to Dorm A, were very quiet, not wanting to offend the seniors. The seniors had expected Bill Dante to be selected. There was no question in their minds that he was the deserving senior. And who was this junior, anyway? What the hell right did he have to be Adjutant?

A group of Bill Dante's friends moved toward him right away. As they huddled around him, angrily voicing their objections to what had taken place, they found Dante was strangely composed as if he'd accepted what had been done to him. The huddle broke up, as does a tornado when it loses its violent wind, and Dante's friends felt cheated and wondered why he hadn't risen to the same heights of indignation as they had.

Dante was surprised at his own attitude when his friends approached him, but it didn't take long for him to understand he had already made up his mind about the command of Company A. He was going to take it. Reed had been right about him. He certainly didn't want to take orders from somebody else. As his friends gathered around to sympathized with him, another thought came to him; he wasn't going to start out his last year by bad mouthing this new Adjutant. He knew that the Colonel had made this decision and if there were any problems, he would back Reed, not him.

Watching his friends walk back to their own beds, he knew he had been fortunate in the Colonel's office. Reed let him blow off steam and still gave him a chance for the job. He got up and went to the office.

* * *

Sister Elizabeth, from the tailoring house, was looking through the side window and saw Elliot Reed coming across the parade grounds. She smiled as she watched him carrying his dress uniform. She knew she would have six rush jobs, what with tailoring for the new Adjutant and five new company commanders. Elliot knocked before entering.

"Come in."

Smiling, he handed the old nun his uniform.

"What am I supposed to do with this?" she asked without a smile.

Elliot answered her, also without a smile. "I am no longer a Sergeant Major."

"So what are you now?"

"They've decided to make me a private."

"They've caught onto you, yes?"

"Yes. I thought you should be the first to know."

She laughed. He always said something to make her laugh.

"Do you remember when you were five, the first time you came to me? She had told him this story many times.

"What happened?" he asked.

"At first, you wanted to be a Corporal. But then you saw the sword of the Adjutant and you asked me what it would take to become Adjutant?"

"What did you tell me?"

"I told you how difficult it would be, and what you would have to do. You listened closely. You weighed everything I said very seriously, then you looked up at me and said, 'I think I can do it'."

Elliot looked down at the seated woman. She looked tired and maybe not too well. "I have a question to ask you," he said kindly.

"What would that be?" answered Sister Elizabeth.

"During the years, when you were sewing all my uniforms, did you pray for me?"

She regarded his face and saw that he was serious about the question. "Yes," she answered truthfully, "I have plenty of time for such things."

"Thank you," he said quietly, "for everything you've done for me."

She was embarrassed. "It's my job. Go away now or I'll make you a corporal."

He paused for a moment, but he could see that she was not going to look up from her work. He wished he had remembered to pray for her. He hadn't. He gently patted her shoulder, shutting the door quietly behind him. Sister Elizabeth watched him walk down the path and onto the parade grounds. She cried softly as she attempted to go back to her work.

The following Saturday morning Elliot Reed stood before Colonel Whitcome on the parade grounds. The entire school was in dress uniform, watching as Elliot attached his scabbard to his waist belt. Then, receiving the sword from the Colonel, he drew it to the present-arms position, signifying his acceptance of the command. The Colonel acknowledged with a return salute.

As the Colonel moved away from the small table that held five more scabbards, plus five ornately etched swords, the crowd of parents and onlookers applauded. Elliot Reed moved forward, taking the Colonel's place. He paused, then barked out:

"Lieutenant William Dante, front and center!"

From the ranks of Company A, Dante smartly moved forward, made a right turn and ended up in front of Elliot. Dante went through the same procedure with his sword as Elliot had, then smartly moved to his new position in front of A Company. Once again the crowd acknowledged his achievement. And so, each of the five companies received their new commanders. The last to be called was Company E.

"Lieutenant Felix Skinner, front and center!" the new Adjutant commanded. Leaving the ranks of Company B, Skinner also moved smartly forward and stood before his friend. As Elliot moved forward and handed the scabbard to Felix, he heard a very faint, "Holy Cow, look at us now."

Then as Elliot handed him the sword, he said as a returned murmur, "Don't cut yourself."

Elliot watched as Skinner brought the sword to the position of present-arms. After Elliot's salute, he turned and marched to the front of Company E.

One of his six year olds, in the last line of his company, started to clap. His company was too little to carry rifles as the other companies did. Everybody in the stands laughed, and then joined in the clapping. Mrs. Skinner, in the middle of the second row, was crying. She had never been more proud of her son. She only wished his father could have been alive to see this with her.

* * *

The images were so strong, so vibrant, so charged with energy that even in his dreaming Elliot felt his body reacting. And yet the scene was so simple, seemingly so innocent and almost pastoral in its setting.

> **Elliot was looking out at the playing field. The grass was uncommonly green without all the bare spots it normally had from overuse. In the center of the field, really too far away to see clearly, stood a little girl. She looked about twelve, maybe, and her dress seemed to be torn. Her head was bowed, and it looked as though she might be crying. As Elliot started to move out onto the field to get a closer look, the ground moved under his feet. He jumped back, off the dark, green grass. He looked down. Now the earth was still. Could it have been his imagination? Cautiously he tried again. As soon as he had both of his feet planted on the grass, his feet felt the movement again. It was as if something alive was right under the surface of the earth. He quickly jumped back off. It was too unnerving.**
>
> **He looked out at the girl. Had she moved? She seemed somewhat closer. She had short brown hair and was swaying from side to side. She glanced up and then looked down again. She was crying, and half of her face was terribly scarred.**

Elliot was immediately awake, fully alert. The face of the crying girl had looked familiar. He closed his eyes and brought the figure back to mind. Once again, he watched as she lifted her head. The scars on her face were deep, with the sunlight hitting the moisture of the tears as they ran through the darkened, disfigured skin.

As she dropped her head again, Elliot felt another strange sensation. Startled, he opened his eyes and quickly came up on one elbow. He was sure that he was being watched! It was three o'clock in the morning. Everyone in Company A was sleeping. So then, slowly, he settled back in his bed.

"Lord, what is this all about?" he said in a soft voice.

Then once again he closed his eyes and brought up the first image of the playing field and the girl. As he had done with so many of his dreams before, he attempted to go through it entirely, memorizing every detail in his conscious mind.

But then, in the middle of it, he was startled to find that he knew he was being watched! It must be within the dream, he thought. I'm being watched in the dream. As I'm looking at the girl, someone is watching me! More than anything else, this mystified Elliot. Was there really someone else in his dream, or was this strange happening some sort of symbolism?

The one thing Elliot was sure of was that he had no idea what this dream was about. And, what about the little girl? Why did she look familiar; he didn't know any girls. Then, as he fell asleep, he said, "Lord, help me to know what you want me to know."

* * *

It was Friday afternoon, and Colonel Whitcome entered his office at three. He was a little earlier than usual because this was his golf day with Father Tinian, and they had gotten an earlier tee time. Elliot looked at the clock as he entered.

"Afternoon, Sir."

"Hello, Elliot."

"How did you do?"

"That priest is uncanny around the greens. He beat me by seven strokes."

"That's better, though. Last week is was ten strokes."

"True, true," the Colonel replied as he looked over the top of his desk. No business had come in to concern him, as far as he could tell. He could play golf every day, and it wouldn't make any difference.

"Father Tinian told me something interesting today," Colonel Whitcomb mentioned. "He said that about forty percent of the student body has fallen in love with Sister Agnes."

Elliot laughed. "She's very beautiful. There's talk about her in every dorm."

"How's Lieutenant Skinner handling it?"

"He's very protective of her. Anytime he comes around the other cadets, they make sure they don't talk about her."

Now it was the Colonel's time to laugh. "He's smitten too." He looked over at Elliot, busy at his desk. Then he asked, "What about you?"

Elliot looked up at him and saw the questioning look on his face. "Is this the way a father would question his son about a girl?"

The Colonel thought about it for a moment. "Exactly. This is what it would be like." Elliot didn't answer. "So?" the Colonel queried.

"I think she's very beautiful, but she belongs to God. I want one of my own."

The Colonel couldn't help but laugh. "Don't let the ladies hear you say that. They'll think you're a chauvinist."

"Why?"

"You can't own one."

Elliot thought about this for a long moment. "God says we're supposed to."

"He does? Where does He say that?"

"He says that the husband's body doesn't belong to him alone, but also to the wife. And he says the same about her. It's not hers alone, but the husband's too."

"Really? Where does it say that?"

"In the first book to the Corinthians, chapter seven."

The Colonel thought about this. "You mean the wife is not supposed to say no?"

"Neither is the husband," Elliot answered. "God says we're supposed to become one flesh. You have to have one of your own to do that. That's what I want."

What was the name of that Book in the Bible? The Colonel quickly marked it down on a piece of paper. This made up his mind; he was going to have to read that Book!

* * *

Elliot was in his third mile around the track when a momentary vision of the little girl in his dream flashed in his mind. He slowed.

It repeated itself. He stopped, breathing deeply, and concentrated on the feeling going through him. As the flash-visions continued, he felt, the same strange sensation he had had four nights ago, that he was being watched.

As he wiped his face with a small towel he carried at his waist, the vision occurred again and once again the strange sensation followed. While drying his face, he scanned over the field. There were cadets over the whole area, enjoying their Friday afternoon free time. Nobody seemed to be paying any attention to Elliot; each group of boys was caught up in their own activity.

But as Elliot turned to look at the vacant baseball diamond, at the far end of the field, he saw a lone cadet standing near the latrine. He seemed to be watching Elliot. Not stopping to look, Elliot kept turning his head. Once his back was turned to the cadet, he placed the towel back into his waistband and stretched. Then he slowly went into a waist bend for limbering. As his head neared his knees he could see the cadet. He still seemed to be watching Elliot.

What was Duane Curtland doing out there by himself Elliot wondered? Coming out of his stretch, Elliot started into an easy jog. When he got to the far end of the track, he left it and continued to jog towards Duane. Duane immediately disappeared into the bathroom. Elliot went to the door of the building, where he stopped and listened. He heard rustling of clothing, but no voices. He entered.

It might have been pure reflex on Elliot's part, but he was beginning to dodge even before he saw the fist coming. He moved sideways, receiving the blow on the side of the head and was knocked against the wall. He saw a flash of a naked torso, part of a buttocks and a leg. Balancing him against the wall, he leg-kicked. He caught the hip area but knew he didn't have the leverage to do real damage.

Another fist caught him in the rib area from the side. As he was hit, he grabbed the wrist and turned it quickly. He heard a scream and kicked toward the noise. He hit Curtland in the stomach, sending him crashing against a metal partition that enclosed the toilets.

Elliot came up quickly, but felt another blow to his neck area just below the ear. There was just a dull pain, as the adrenaline beat through him. He rolled over the cement and came up with both arms protecting his face and throat area. Looking between his hands, he saw the furious face of Arnold Larson. Just as Larson's naked foot was coming in, Elliot ducked, grabbed it and twisted. Larson lost his balance and tried grabbing hold of a urinal. Arnold slipped further, and Elliot delivered a heel to his side, just above the waist. This kick had the correct leverage and force. The big senior let out a scream and grabbed hold of his ribs.

"You son-of-a-bitch!" he yelled out in pain. He tried to get up, struggling to land another fist on Elliot's face. Elliot aimed a deliberate blow with the stiffened heel of his hand to the Larson's cheekbone, knocking his head against the urinal. Larson lost consciousness. Elliot turned quickly, knowing that someone, besides these two, was in the room. He kicked open the door to the far toilet. On the floor, huddled as far back as he could get, was a thin little twelve-year-old named Ernest Harper. He was naked, and his clothes were underneath him. He was crying. At that moment, Elliot knew why the face of the little girl in the dream had looked so familiar. It was Harper's face. Immediately, Elliot's attitude relaxed, and he looked away from the frightened, naked boy.

"Put your clothes on Harper," Elliot said evenly.

Shutting the door to the toilet, he looked over at the figure of Duane Curtland. He didn't look hurt, but he hadn't moved from the position where he had landed from Elliot's kick. His face was against the cement and his eyes were closed.

"Curtland, get up," Elliot commanded. Slowly, the lookout got to his feet, but his eyes were still toward the ground.

"Go outside and wait for me there."

The lad did as he was told. Larson was coming around. "Are you getting dressed, Harper?" Elliot asked over the partition.

"Yes, Sir," came the weak, frightened voice from the toilet.

Larson opened his eyes and saw the Adjutant standing a few feet away. Larson felt the back of his head, then looked at Reed again. He wished he had a gun. He would kill him.

"Get your clothes on and come outside," Elliot said as he started to leave the rest room. He paused and then once more looked to Larson. "And don't say a word to Harper." Larson didn't answer. "Is that understood?" Elliot said softly, moving a step closer to the big senior.

"Yes."

"Yes, what?" Elliot asked. The two young men looked at each other, then finally the naked senior said, "Yes, Sir." Elliot went outside.

Duane Curtland was leaning against the rest room. He looked like he was going to be sick. He was shaking and tears were running down his cheeks. Elliot looked quickly about, seeing if any of the other cadets on the field had taken notice of the way Curtland was acting. They were too far away and nobody was paying any attention.

"Curtland, I want you to stop crying and go to my office. And say nothing to anyone. Move!!" Curtland did as he was told.

Ernest Harper came from the restroom and stood looking at the ground. He had on shorts and a tee shirt.

"Lift your head up, walk normally, and go to my office. Do you understand?" Elliot said softly.

He was still crying. "Yes, sir."

"You have to stop crying, now. That's an order."

The thin boy caught his breath once, then again, and brought his tears under control.

"Move."

Elliot watched the small boy walk across the field, while he waited for Larson. A few moments passed, and Larson came out, glaring at Elliot. A bruise was already showing on the side of his face. It might spread to become a black eye. Elliot could feel the fury that was in the large cadet. He saw the muscles in Larson's neck bunch up as he glowered at him.

"If you're thinking about starting again out here in front of the other cadets, don't," Elliot said without looking at him.

"Why don't you kiss my ass?"

Elliot turned and smiled at the sullen face in front of him. "I don't want anyone else to know what was going on in there. Do you?" All Elliot received from his question was a hateful stare.

"Larson, you just do as I tell you. Walk slowly over to my office, take a chair, and don't say a word to your two friends. They'll be in there with you." He waited for an answer but didn't get one. "Did you understand my command?"

"Go to hell."

Elliot paused, deliberating what he should do. Then, he turned and faced Larson. "This is the last time I'm talking to you. You either carry out my order or I'll make it so you can't. If what you want is force, I'll put you down where they have to come and get you in a stretcher. Make up your mind now!"

The pain was beginning to throb in Arnold's cheek. He could feel the swelling, even though he hadn't touched it. He wasn't very good with pain, and there was a good chance that Reed might be able to carry out his threat. He turned and began walking toward the Colonel's office. Elliot walked behind him for a short way.

"When anybody asks you about the black eye you're getting, you'll tell them you fell." With that, Elliot began jogging back to the track. He ran half way around, finishing in front of the gym.

As he hurriedly showered, the memories of what had happened when he was twelve years old flooded back. Little Ernest Harper, laying on that floor weeping, had reminded him, though he doubted if Harper had been raped. No, most probably that had not been the case. As he let the cold water beat on his flesh, he asked the Lord to give him wisdom and patience with this terrible mess.

Since it was Friday, and the Colonel and Father Tinian were playing golf, Elliot knew the office would be empty. When he walked into it all three of the cadets were there. They stood when he entered. Elliot sat at his desk. There was a long silence as he measured each cadet. Larson was angry, still filled with fury. Curtland looked very nervous and jumpy. Ernest Harper was still in tears, completely exhausted, almost ready to fall.

"Larson, you and Harper wait outside," Elliot directed.

Both cadets started to move toward the door. Elliot stopped them with his words. "When being dismissed, what is the correct procedure?" Ernest saluted immediately, but Larson still held back. Elliot waited until he finally saluted. Then the cadets moved outside.

"Curtland, move forward."

Curtland took three steps to the desk and saluted. Elliot returned it, but did not tell the cadet to go to rest.

"How long have you been involved with The Group?" Elliot asked. Curtland hesitated, afraid to talk about his past.

"Would you rather talk to Father Tinian and Mother Superior?"

"No, Sir."

"Then talk to me."

"I was approached three years ago," Curtland said, trying to hold back the sobs he felt coming.

"Who approached you?"

"He's gone now, Sir."

"Who approached you?"

"Dale Barkley."

Elliot remembered him well. He had been the one who held his arms under the bench, while Purdom...

"And what about the twelve-year-old outside? When was he approached?"

"Maybe you should ask Larson, Sir.""

"I'm asking you. I want you to answer all my questions."

"This was his second time."

Elliot got up from his chair and walked over to the lad. His body was sweating, and he smelled bad. "Look at me."

Curtland turned his head and looked into the Adjutant's eyes.

"It's all over in this school. This is the end of it. But it can end in one of two ways. Either I know all there is to know or the school authorities will know about it, which means that your mother and father will know too."

Curtland was too nervous to keep his eyes on the Adjutant.

"Look at me!" Elliot continued. Curtland turned back to him, but there were tears in his eyes.

"In the eyes of this school, what you have been doing is a sin. It means immediate dismissal. Did you know that?"

"Yes, Sir."

"And your parents, how would they feel?"

"Terrible, Sir. They don't know this about me."

Elliot looked at him for another long moment and went back to his chair. He sat and watched as tears ran down the shaken cadet's face. Elliot hoped he had prepared him for the next questions.

"How many more are involved?"

Fear came onto the cadet's face. "Sir, I can't do that."

"Do what?"

"Tell you who the others are."

So there were others. Elliot thought as much, but he had to be sure. "I didn't ask you their names. I asked you how many more were involved?"

"Four, Sir."

"Is Larson the leader?" Elliot knew this question was tough on Curtland. Elliot knew that if Larson was the leader, he was certainly big enough and tough enough to frighten the lad.

"Curtland," Elliot continued, "if Larson is the leader, when I get through with him, he won't be leading anybody anywhere, except maybe himself out of this school. Now, answer my question."

"Yes, Sir, he is."

"Very well, that's all for now. Wait outside."

As he turned to leave, Elliot said, "Send Larson in."

When Larson entered the room he left the door open. Elliot could feel the hateful spirit of the cadet as he approached the desk. There was no remorse or fear in this one. Elliot knew this would have to change or none of these cadets would be able to stay in the school.

"You left the door open. Close it."

The large cadet went back and closed it. There was a foolish arrogance about him as he approached the desk.

"Is this the way you approach all your problems?" Elliot asked.

"What?"

"By acting tough, by giving off this tough crap like you don't even care."

Larson looked straight at him, but said nothing.

"Well, it's not going to work. Step back four paces."

Larson was surprised, but did as he was told. Elliot got up from his desk, moved around it and came to stand in front of him.

"I'm standing in front of you so that any time you're tempted, feel free..." Elliot said. "But just remember, you'll pay for anything you try." He paused to let the challenge sink in. "I've known about the group for sometime."

This certainly wasn't a lie.

"I know that you recruit youngsters, and that you're the leader." Elliot waited for an answer but received none. "I also know that if you aren't willing to make some changes, you'll be out of the school." Once again, he waited.

"What kind of changes, Sir?"

"Your group, it's all over. This is your last year here, and you have to stop what you've been doing. No more recruiting, no more sexual acts. And that's not all. I want you, right now, to tell the other four to come and see me, one at a time."

"What other four?"

"If I have to go get them, then you're out of the school. And so are they. Your only chance to graduate from here is to do as you're told." He waited. "Well?"

"This is none of your business."

When Elliot heard this, something happened within the Adjutant. He moved a step closer, and his eyes became cold. Anger spread through him. "Oh, it's my business, all right. And I'm very close to showing you just how much it is my business. Don't tempt me."

Larson could sense new fury from within Reed. He could even see it in his eyes.

"Larson...are you willing to do as you're told or are you going to jeopardize all the rest of them?

Larson was feeling something coming against him that frightened him. He had the feeling that he would like to move to the other side of the room but knew he still might not be safe. He wasn't going to fight the Adjutant.

"I'll tell them, one at a time."

"And when you do, that will be the last time you will talk to any of them this year. Is that understood?"

"Yes, Sir." Larson could see beads of sweat on the Adjutant's forehead.

"Are any of the four youngsters, like Ernest Harper?"

"Yes, Sir. One's from Company C."

"I want to see him first." Elliot paused and looked into the cadet's eyes. He could see that the arrogance was gone.

"Tell them nothing. Say nothing except that I want to see them." He waited for the answer.

"Yes, Sir."

"And one other thing. If you think that Curtland said something to hurt you, if you retaliate, I'll come after you. There will be no reprisals against him or anyone else."

"Yes, Sir."

"I'll want to see you in two weeks."

"See me?"

"That's right, in two weeks. We'll talk. I'll ask questions, and you'll answer them." Larson started to say something, but saluted instead.

"Send the other two in."

"Yes, Sir." Larson exited, closing the door behind him.

Elliot had a moment to pull himself together. He was shaking. He hadn't known he could be so angry. He took two deep breaths as the door opened, and the two cadets entered. He sat behind his desk, as they marched to it and stopped.

"Private Harper, what you did is against the laws of this school. Are you aware of that?

"Yes, Sir."

"Are you also aware that your act was against God's laws?"

The young lad was dismayed, not knowing what to say.

"Wel l?"

"No, Sir, I wasn't. I don't know God's law."

"Then you'll learn them. You'll report here next Friday at two p.m. with a Bible. Do you understand?"

"A Bible? I don't own one, Sir."'

"Ask Sister Teresa if you can borrow one."

"Yes, Sir."

"And Private, you are ordered to never speak another word to Corporal Larson or to Corporal Curtland. Is that understood?"

"Yes, Sir."

"If either one of them try to speak to you, you will report to me immediately.

"Yes, Sir."

"And one last point. You'll never talk about what has happened today to anyone!"

"Yes, Sir."

"Then the matter is closed."

Harper was amazed. "You mean you aren't going to tell my parents?"

"The matter is closed. Go back to your dorm."

He was crying as he saluted and left the office. Curtland had tears in his eyes, but he stood at attention and waited.

Elliot looked a long moment at Curtland. "Larson is calling in the other four. I will meet with each one." He paused. "You will no longer have any close friends in this school. You won't be allowed to talk to any of these cadets again. You'll have to find new friends. Is this understood?"

"Yes, Sir."

"Are you willing to do this?"

"Yes, Sir."

"If you have troubles with this, this office is open to you."

Duane Curtland didn't understand. "What, Sir?"

"If you need to talk, I'm here as a friend."

There was a knock at the door. Curtland opened his mouth to speak, but then thought better of it. He saluted. Elliot returned his salute, and Curtland turned to leave. As Curtland opened the door, Bobby Brolin stared at him. Curtland paid no attention, but held the door until the small lad walked past him. Then he closed it behind him.

Brolin's heart felt as though it was going to go through his chest. He looked over and saw the Adjutant looking at him. He quickly went to stand before the desk and saluted. The Adjutant returned his salute.

"Look at me," the Adjutant ordered.

Bobby obeyed. His whole body felt clammy, and his stomach began to turn. He constricted his throat so as not to throw up.

"Are you going to be sick?"

"Yes, Sir."

Elliot pointed to the door to the Colonel's bathroom. Cadet Brolin ran to it. He just made it. Elliot heard him lose his half-digested lunch, then flush the toilet. After a moment he returned. He looked pale as he stood there. Elliot saw that he was even smaller than Ernest Harper.

"Sit in the chair," Elliot directed.

The lad did so. He had a chill, and his small body shook like a little dog.

"Do you know why you're here?"

"Yes, Sir, we've been caught."

"How long have you been part of this?"

"Three months, sir. I've been with them six times. I couldn't stop."

"Well, you've stopped now."

"Oh, yes, Sir."

"What would your parents think?"

"My dad left. It's only my mom. She..." holding back tears, "she wouldn't understand at all." Elliot was sorry he had asked that. He could tell he needn't threaten this one.

"I'm ordering you not to be with any of then again. You are not allowed to say one word to them as long as you are in this school."

"Yes, Sir."

"Do you believe in God?"

The question surprised him. "Why, yes, Sir, I think so?"

"Were you aware that you were breaking His law when you did what you did?"

"I felt awful guilty, but I didn't know why."

"Next Friday, I want you here at two-thirty, with a Bible."

"Yes, Sir, but I don't have a Bible."

"Ask Sister Teresa for one and be here."

"Yes, Sir."

"You know that you can't talk to anyone about this?"

"Yes, Sir. I don't want to."

"I want you to report to me if any of the group tries to talk to you."

"Yes, Sir."

"Are you feeling strong enough to walk?"

"Yes, Sir." Elliot sent him out of the office.

The other three came, one at a time. Each cadet was frightened and surprised that the Mother Superior was not going to be told.

Strange, Elliot thought, after he had seen them all, they all seem to be the same kind of boys. They were all quiet ones, none of them dumb, and all really lonely, looking for friends.

Three days later, Sister Teresa motioned to him after school. "How many Bibles should I have available?"

"Two should be enough," Elliot answered.

"Two?" she said quietly, "I've already handed out three."

"Three?" Elliot said, surprised. But she was already moving down the hall and away from him. He looked after her and wondered what was going on.

That next Friday, Ernest Harper showed up with his Bible. As they were beginning to look at some passages, there was a knock on the door.

"Come in," Elliot said.

The door opened and Duane Curtland stuck his head in. "I've got a Bible too. Can I come in too?" And so it became a class of two. But then Bobby Brolin showed up twenty minutes late, so it became a class of three.

During the seventh week of the class, Ernest and Bobby received Jesus Christ as their Savior. Duane Curtland watched as the two younger guys said they needed Jesus to help them not to be lonely, and to be there for them when they needed help. He got a little embarrassed when Bobby started crying and the Adjutant put his arm around the boy, consoling him. It wasn't five minutes later that both Bobby and Ernest were laughing like crazy; really happy about what was happening.

Duane Curtland thought often about that day. Sometimes, during the night, he would talk to Jesus too, asking him to help when he got lonely and started thinking about what he had been doing for the past three years. Many times he thought about God, and those kinds of things. He found himself thinking less and less about his past life, and more about the things the small class talked about on Fridays. Then, over the months, he started looking forward to the classes. They lasted the whole year, until summer. He watched as Ernest and Bobby became good friends. From time to time, he prayed to Jesus that he too would be lucky like they were. But he did feel fortunate about his talks with the Adjutant. Sometimes, on weekends, when the Adjutant had time, Duane would go see him, and they would have long talks about Jesus and His disciples. The Adjutant would tell him a lot about the miracles, and about the life of Peter and Paul;

things Duane didn't know anything about. Besides, he liked to hear Reed talk about them. Sometimes he felt like the Adjutant had been right there with Jesus and the disciples. Duane wondered how the Adjutant remembered all those things about such a long time ago. Some of the guys in his dorm said he was just kissin' ass, but he didn't care. What the hell did they know?

Arnold Larson never changed inside. Elliot knew this, but from time to time would still send for the large senior, always hoping that the ice might melt. It never did. Larson hated him and certainly never trusted him. Even so, as far as Elliot knew, Larson carried out his orders. Even at graduation, the senior never said a word to Elliot. He received his diploma, saluted, left the stage and never acknowledged the Adjutant at all. He left the school without saying goodbye to anyone. Elliot saw him walking behind his mother and some of her friends.

* * *

The summer months were good for Elliot. The Colonel and Father Tinian invited him to join them at golf. He found the game much more difficult than it looked, so he caddied for both of them. He learned about the use of clubs, the etiquette of the game and came to like the game enough to start practicing while they played. He even took some lessons from one of the young pros at the club. The Colonel told him that his progress was excellent, and that they wanted him to start playing with them. They made plans for the first week in August.

The school was very quiet, with only six cadets there for the summer. The main dining room was closed, and the boys ate in the small room next to the kitchen. Elliot had doubled up on his workout time, and also had plenty of hours for the Colonel's library. Sister Teresa had gone east to visit her only brother. She returned in the second week of July. The day after she returned, she made it a point to go down to Elliot's office for a visit. He saw her through his window as she walked along the path toward his office. He was at his front door before she got there.

"How is your brother?" he asked with a warm smile. He always had an urge to hug this little nun, but he always thought better of it.

"I just can't understand it. He seems to be getting older and older." They both laughed as they entered his office.

"Do you know that this is the first time you've been in my office?"

"I do. I thought I would give you the first year without butting in."

She's in rare form, he thought. It was certainly not like her to come down here. He wondered what was on her mind. She sat, and he pulled up a chair across from her.

"This is a nice surprise," he said.

"And how is the Colonel these days?"

"Very well. Father Tinian and he are teaching me golf."

"Are you hooked?"

Elliot laughed. "I'm afraid so. It's a very difficult game."

She paused for a moment, looking intently at him. "You do like difficult things, don't you?"

Well, something is up, he thought. "Sometimes, yes. It keeps things from getting dull."

She smiled, but it was not difficult to see that her intentions were serious. "Has anything happened to you lately? Any dreams, visions, anything like that?"

"No, not lately. Things have been quiet."

She nodded her head as if on another thought, then said, "I may be wrong, but I think you will be leaving here soon."

"St. Maurice?

"Yes."

"Before I graduate?"

"Yes, very soon. I was unsure about telling you this, but then I thought, if I'm wrong, so what, what's the harm."

"What happened?"

"Two weeks ago, you started coming into my mind. You wouldn't go away." She couldn't sit still, so she stood and paced as he had seen her do so many times in her classroom.

"I started praying for you. I asked the Lord to protect you from sickness and danger." She shrugged. "Nothing. And you were still heavy on my heart. I asked the Lord if you were in some sort of trouble. No answer. So I started praying about you for the coming year, about your position as Adjutant."

She looked at her young friend for a long moment, before she shook her head. "It was like I was in a desert. Nothing came of my prayers for you, and yet you kept coming into my thoughts.

"Then three days ago, I said, 'Lord, you'll have to tell me what you want me to know about Elliot. And then I heard, "He's leaving."

"Wow," Elliot said softly. "I wonder where I'm going?" He thought for a moment, and then mused quietly, "There has been something strange that I really never thought about it, until now."

"What's that?" she asked as she sat again.

"Usually, I pre-plan everything. In the mornings I'll wake up and take notes of my thoughts for the coming week or sometimes even a month or two. And here it is just over a month before school starts, and I haven't thought about the new semester at all. I should have planned about a new commander for A Company, but I haven't. That's not like me."

"We don't have a lot of info to go on, do we?" she said with a smile.

"No, but I have to agree with you, something might be up."

* * *

On the second of August, during an unexpected summer storm, Mr. Bertrand Reed, age 62, the Chairman of the Board of Reed Industries, was killed in a freak accident. While riding in the rear of his limousine, the auto skidded from the road and hit a utility pole. Mr. Reed, who was not wearing his safety belt, was thrown forward, breaking his neck on the wet bar. His chauffeur received a broken wrist.

The law firm of Armbruster, Byrant, McCavy and Carruthers heard about the accident four hours later and began moving as quickly as possible. Bill Bryant called Mrs. Harriet Reed Swindale, acknowledging his sorrow over the loss of her brother.

"I think you know how close I was to your brother, and what a shock this is to our entire firm."

She certainly did know how close Bill Bryant was to her brother. She hadn't heard from this man for fifteen years. "Thank you, Bill. It was certainly a shock to all of us too."

"I know that this isn't the correct time to discuss his affairs," the lawyer said sympathetically, "but since your capacity with the corporation has now changed drastically, there is an immediacy."

"Yes, of course. The funeral will be on Wednesday."

"Would Thursday be too soon, then?" he asked.

"Should the entire family be there?"

"It would be best. I know your aunt is mentioned, and the rest of your family should know where they stand as far as their position within the Corporation."

"Yes, of course. What time would you like us there?"

"I would be happy to come out to your home, if it would be more convenient."

"No, that's quite alright. Would ten o'clock be suitable?"

"That would be fine, Mrs. Swindale," he said, then started to thank her.

"Good," she interrupted, and the phone went dead.

Bill Bryant looked at the phone, slowly putting it down in its cradle. What was it about this woman he didn't like? She always seemed polite, but then again... He remembered getting a note from her fifteen years previously. A simple note saying that the Swindale family was changing law firms and that the new firm would be contacting his office. And that was it. He had never heard from her again. Later Bryant had learned that she and Bertrand had a falling out. What the trouble had been, he never found out, but then again, he had never asked. It probably had something to do with her husband, Graham Swindale, since he had left Reed Industries about that same time. Bryant, through the years, was very aware that Bertrand Reed never again mentioned his sister's name. Well, Bryant thought, this is a hundred thousand dollar a year fee, and this woman is now the major stockholder. After all, she would be paying almost half of his annual salary. He buzzed for his secretary. Everything had to be just right for the Thursday meeting.

The Swindale limo had five people in it on Thursday morning.

"I don't see why I have to go to this damn meeting!" Tina Swindale finally said. She had a terrible night, and now was expected to sit on one of the jump seats in the back of the limo. "I've got absolutely nothing to do with the company, and I'm not feeling very well this morning." She didn't look at the back seat, where she usually sat. That's where her mother and father now sat, with her crazy great Aunt Elsie between them. Her brother was sitting on the jump seat by the opposite window, listening to his crappy music on a Walkman.

"Watch your language, young lady," her mother said smoothly.

Tina looked sideways at her mother. What a pain-in-the-ass she could be, she thought. "My language really doesn't seem to be the point. The point is...what am I doing here?"

Her mother looked out the window, no longer thinking about her daughter. She felt her new blue dress pressing against her sides. It was a perfect fit. After she had worked out in the weight room and taken a hot, tingling shower this morning, she had slipped the dress over her head, knowing immediately that she had worked herself into it. This was a 7-8 size she had bought at a specialty store. Fifty-one years old, and she was the same size now as she had been at twenty! She had done it! It had taken three years of hard work, but she had done it! She had even been able to firm up her large breasts somewhat.

And now, almost like it was a gift for losing the weight, she was about to receive a huge company. How big, she really didn't know, but it would provide more money than she could spend in a lifetime. She smiled to herself. Money. Money. She wanted to laugh out loud but didn't. She wished that she had someone to share this with, someone who really cared about her family the way she did.

Her husband, she remembered, when he had heard of Bertrand's death, had actually been sorry about it. My God, what an attitude! The man was ruined because of her brother's take-over, and he's sorry to hear about his death!

Harriet noticed that her son had taken the Walkman from his ears and was exchanging a tape from the pockets of his coat.

"Arnold, I want you to leave that contraption in the car when we go up to the offices."

"Why?" the seventeen-year-old said sullenly. "I don't even know why I'm even here. Why did I have to come along?"

Oh, God, these children, Harriet thought. She sometimes wished she never had them. She decided to ignore her young son's questions.

He put the earphones back on his head, and everyone sat in silence once more.

"Who's going to be at the meeting?" Elsie Reed Tidwell asked Harriet.

"Bill Bryant, Aunt Elsie, Bill Bryant," Harriet said too loudly.

Elsie had to smile as she heard the answer. Not that there was anything special in Bill Bryant, but it was the way her niece always answered her. Harriet would respond just a little louder than necessary, and almost always repeat things at least twice, sometimes even three times. She must think I'm hard of hearing and that I'm forgetful, Elsie thought.

But she was neither. She had been living in the Swindale house for five years, and Harriet had always treated her this same way. Maybe that's why she very seldom talks to me, Elsie mused. She must feel uncomfortable being around a handicapped person. The thought struck her as funny, and she laughed out loud.

Both Harriet and Graham glanced quickly at the woman sitting between them, and their eyes met. Harriet looked hastily back out the window while Graham's look lingered on her.

She's lost more weight, he thought. She looks good. He wondered why she was doing it; he knew it certainly wasn't for him. Usually he slept in their library. They hadn't made love in… he really wasn't sure how long it had been. He did remember that she hadn't reached a climax for years, and he felt crummy, even when he did. This wasn't the first time he felt their lovemaking didn't make any difference. He left their bed quietly and made his way to the library, feeling the same sadness he had felt before making love to his wife. They didn't discuss it at the time, in fact they never did.

He looked at her new blue dress. Strange, he thought, she could lose so much weight, and her breasts stayed big. How the hell did that happen?

"Are you O.K., Elsie?" Graham asked Harriet's aunt.

"Oh, yes, I'm fine," she answered. "You know, I remember Bill Bryant when he was the newest lawyer in the firm. My husband said he would be the head of it someday."

Her husband, Harriet's father's brother, had been dead for fifteen years. "Well, your husband knew what he was talking about," Graham responded.

"Yes, he did," she answered, "about many things." Then she was silent.

Graham smiled down at the old lady. She was seventy-five, still had a good mind, and had lived with them for the past five years. Thank God she did, Graham thought. Without her money, we would not have been able to keep up the estate or get the rest of the crap the family likes to have. And the strange thing is it was the old lady's idea. One day, when all our savings had been used up, and we were in a terrible argument about selling the place, she called on us. Charles drove her up in the old Rolls Royce, and she asked if she might talk with both of us. She told us that she would like to sell her estate and come live with us. She had no other family, and she was lonely and tired of being in that big place all by herself.

Graham remembered that he had a difficult time holding back the tears. He remembered that somehow this little woman had known that he and his family were in the process of falling apart. And then she showed up, and for some reason he didn't understand, he knew that this old lady loved him! Through the years, he wondered why she did. And when Elsie had moved in, she took over the expense of the entire estate. What the family had wanted, they had gotten. She had held nothing back, nor had she ever complained.

As he now looked at her frail little body seated next to him, a feeling of love and gratitude welled up within him. He took her hand and held it. My God, he complained to himself, why don't I at least go visit her once in a while? She lives in my house, and I only see her at suppertime!

Harriet noticed the handholding. She had seen her husband do kind things to Elsie before. She remembered when he used to do that sort of thing for her too. The Limo pulled up to the law offices.

Bill Bryant made certain he was out in the waiting room when the family arrived. After formally greeting the three adults, he turned to Tina Swindale. He had first met the daughter when she was about five; she's turned out to be a beautiful girl, the lawyer thought. About nineteen, he imagined. But, as he shook her hand and tried to make light conversation, he decided he liked her better when she was five. He greeted the son last. Arnold managed to shake hands with all the indifference that a seventeen-year-old could muster.

"Thank you all for coming," he said. Taking Mrs. Tidwell's arm, he escorted them through the heavy doors and down the long carpeted hallway to his corner office.

"How have you been, Bill?" Elsie asked.

"Just fine," Mrs. Tidwell," he answered with a smile. He had always appreciated her husband. Years ago, they had belonged to the same club.

"You can still call me Elsie. My husband had a high regard for you. He said that someday you would be the head of this firm."

"Why, thank you, Elsie. I felt the same way about your husband," he smiled. "And the years have shown that he knew what he was talking about."

As the secretary opened the door for them, they entered his office. "Would anybody like coffee or a soft drink?" the secretary asked.

"I'll take coffee, black," Graham Swindale said, seating himself in one of the chairs in front of the desk. Elsie Tidwell made her way to a seat near the window. She disliked these kinds of meetings, especially when it looked like her niece was going to be in charge. The children sat in the plush leather sofa against the wall.

Harriet smiled to herself as she took the other large chair facing the desk. She wondered if Bill Bryant had thought about her taking Reed Industries away from his law firm? If he did, they were of his own making. And yet, at the same time, she knew that it would not be to her liking to set his mind at rest. What about the past fifteen years? Should she just forget about them? After her note to him, did he ever try to get in touch with her? Not a word from him. Well, this little secret would be hers. She would keep the man on pins and needles even though she would never leave the firm. She knew that for the past twenty-five years, it had been William Bryant who had guided her brother through many difficult times, helping him to become one of the most successful men in the industry. If this hadn't been so, her brother would have gotten rid of him long ago. So she found herself only half listening as the reading of the will took place. Instead, she thought about her history with this firm.

Then she noticed that, with the exception of her husband, the rest of her family was more interested in the view out the window or in their hair or clothing, or anything else but the boring words pouring from the mouth of the white-headed, old lawyer.

Suddenly Harriet was very alert, but not quite sure what she had heard.

"Would you repeat that, please," she said.

"Certainly," Bryant responded, wishing he could see their faces as he reread the paragraph.

"The stipulations concerning Elliot Reed and this law firm will continue to be fulfilled. This agreement has priority over all transfers of monies given to the beneficiaries."

Harriet glanced at her husband, then back to Bryant. "Who is Elliot Reed?" she asked.

"Your brother's son," Bryant answered. He noticed that this had gotten everyone's attention; all were now staring at him.

"His son?" Graham asked.

"By whom?" Harriet asked sharply.

"His wife, Mary Reed," Bryant answered quietly.

"Bertrand said the baby died at birth!" Harriet snapped.

"I knew he didn't," Elsie said with a smile. "When Bertrand told me, I knew he lied."

"Why would he do that?" Harriet asked, looking at her.

"Because he didn't like any of us, and he didn't trust us," Elsie answered.

Byrant decided to continue before the family got embroiled in a fight. "Elliot Reed has been in a military academy for the past twelve years. For the first five years, a nurse raised him within her own home."

"You mean Bertrand didn't raise him?" Harriet asked, her voice rising.

"No. He never saw the child, only at his birth."

"That sounds like him!" she said, openly angry. "And what were the stipulations made with your firm?"

"That in the case of the death of Bertrand Reed, Reed Industries would continue supplying funds for the lad."

"Until when?" Harriet asked. She seemed to become angrier with each of her questions.

"Through his years of education, as far as he wanted to go. If college, then even to a doctorate, if he wished."

"What other financial arrangements were made for him?"

Bryant could almost feel Harriet Swindales anger. "None. Only to help him as much as possible during his education."

"Bertrand didn't want him in his business?" she demanded.

Aunt Elsie laughed at this and shook her head. "He never wanted any of us in your father's and my husband's business!" She smiled at Harriet. "He trusted no one!"

"All right, Auntie," Harriet said, still angry at the truth of what her brother had done. She would admit readily that she didn't care a damn about his son, but it just galled her that he had held so much contempt for her that he hadn't even told her the child had lived.

"Why did he send him to a military school? He didn't care anything about the Army," Graham interjected.

"If I remember correctly," Bryant answered, "I think he mentioned that his wife's brother went there years ago."

"Doesn't that seem like a strange reason?" Graham asked.

"Not in the situation Bertrand was in," Bryant responded. "He felt he had to act quickly. From what I remember, he said the whole idea came to him while he was in the hospital, just after he learned of his wife's death."

"Far out," Arnold said, "I got a cousin who's in the military."

"Arnold, that's enough," Harriet snapped. There was a moment of silence as the family digested what had just transpired. Tina, smiling openly, found the whole situation very amusing. Anything that screwed up her family, she was all for it.

"Did Bertrand want this young man to complete his high school education at this school?" Harriet asked.

"Yes, that was the plan," Bryant said.

"Since Bertrand is dead, who has jurisdiction over the boy?" Harriet asked. She thought she already knew the answer, but she wanted to make sure.

"Since Mary's brother died, and she has no other living relatives, you would be his guardian until his eighteenth birthday."

"He was born two weeks before I had Arnold," Harriet said. Unexpectedly, her thoughts flashed to the fear that Mary's death had put a hex on her, and how she had made sure she went to the church before going to the hospital to give birth to Arnold. She remembered having two contractions while in the confessional.

"Yes, he's the same age as Arnold."

"Far out," Arnold said.

"And what does this school cost a year?" Harriet asked.

Bryant looked down at his notes. "Last year, it was seventeen thousand, six hundred dollars."

"Have you sent the check for this coming year?"

"No. It goes out the third week of this month."

"Then don't send it," she said quietly.

Bryant knew he had to be careful. "Very well. What did you have in mind, as far as his finishing high school?"

"My daughter went through public school, and my boy goes there now. I don't see why he can't do the same. Seventeen thousand a year for a high school education is ridiculous."

This woman is unbelievable, Bryant thought. She has just been handed control of millions, and she's concerned about a few thousand! "I'll see to it immediately," he answered, keeping his face emotionless. "Then the boy will be living with you this coming year?"

"We'll find room for him," she replied. She stopped and thought about what she had just said. "What kind of a boy is he?"

Bryant, amused, hoped she had just taken in a homicidal maniac. But he said, "I'm sorry, the firm was told not to interfere unless the school made a call to us. We never heard from them."

* * *

Two days later St.Maurice's received a certified letter informing them that Elliot Reed's tuition would not be forthcoming. Mother Superior went directly to Father Tinian, who in turn called the Colonel. The three met.

In a very short time, with all of them feeling exactly the same about the situation, it was agreed that the school would pay the last year's tuition for Elliot. This option had always been open to Father Tinian, but he had never found cause to use it. Calling Elliot to his office, Father Tinian asked him to enter and sit.

"Elliot, we have just received word from the law firm that has been handling your finances that they will not be paying for your last year."

Sister Teresa had been right, Elliot thought. "I wonder where I'll be going next?" he said to the three of them.

There was a moment of silence as the three looked at Elliot, wondering how such a question came out of the information he was just given? He didn't seem to be surprised at all.

"We hope that you will be right here," Father Tinian replied kindly. "St. Maurice's will take care of your costs."

Elliot looked first at Father Tinian, then at the Colonel. "I don't think I'm supposed to stay."

"What do you mean?" the Colonel asked abruptly. He was so shocked it just came out. "Excuse me, Father", he said quickly to Tinian.

"It's all right, Harold, I was going to ask the same question."

"If I did leave, where would I go?" Elliot asked.

The three adults looked at each other. It was obvious that they had no idea. Mother Superior moved slightly in her chair, "I think I should call the law firm."

"Yes, Mother Superior, please do," Father Tinian said. She left the office.

"Could you explain to us what you meant?" the Colonel asked again.

"Sister Teresa told me a week ago that she thought I might be leaving."

"But we just told you, you don't have to," the Colonel said a little testily. He liked this boy and didn't want him to leave.

"I know, Sir, but maybe I'm supposed to."

The Colonel started to say something but looked at Father Tinian instead. The Father was smiling.

"Did she have a dream, Elliot?" the Father asked.

"No, Father, she got it through prayer."

"What did she hear?"

"Just that I would be leaving very soon."

The Colonel didn't understand what was going on, but he could tell that the two of them understood each other. As difficult as it was for him, he decided to keep quiet.

The three waited silently until Mother Superior came back. It was only a minute, but it seemed a great deal longer. She sat before she talked. "I spoke to a Mr. William Bryant. He said that Elliot has an aunt, and that he would be spending his last year of high school with her and her family. I also asked if the firm or the aunt would have any objections to Elliot staying his last year here, if we deferred the costs. He said he didn't think so, that it would be up to Elliot."

Now all three looked at the boy. "It's up to you, Elliot. You're welcome to stay, but you don't have to," Father Tinian said.

Elliot smiled at Father Tinian and quoted a scripture, "Listen to counsel and accept instruction, and in the end you will be wise."

Both Tinian and Mother Superior smiled and nodded their heads. Once again the Colonel was wise enough to keep quiet.

"Yes, of course," Father Tinian said. Then, after a long pause, he continued, "Many are the plans of man's heart...even a priest's...but it is the Lord's counsel that stands."

Elliot thought about the scripture just given to him. "I think I have to accept Sister Teresa's words to me as from the Lord." He smiled as he continued, "Besides, I have a family now. I would like to meet them."

"When would you like to leave?" Father Tinian asked, understanding how the young man felt.

"In a few days," Elliot answered. "Mother Superior, could you find out where I'm supposed to go?"

"The law firm is sending the information. Mr. Bryant said it should be here tomorrow."

"Thank you." The boy paused and looked at the three people before him. "It's going to be difficult to say goodbye. You have been my only family."

Much to everyone's surprise, it was Mother Superior who spoke first. "You were one of the few boys in the history of this school, who came here having no one in the outside world. At first, that made you special to all the nuns here, including myself." As she stood, Elliot stood. She cleared her throat, ever so slightly, before she continued. "And as the years passed, that never changed. I know I speak for every nun you ever dealt with when I tell you how good it has been having you in our school."

She moved over in front of Elliot, patting his cheek and taking both of his hands in hers. "May God's blessing be with you wherever you go."

"Thank you, Mother Superior," Elliot said, gently squeezing her hands in return, "Thank you for watching out after me all these years."

"It was a pleasure," she said, as she ever so slightly nodded her head at Father Tinian, seeking permission to leave the room. He nodded in return, and she turned and moved quickly from the room.

"Well, well," Father Tinian said, "Wasn't that something?"

"It was nice of her," Elliot said, "I think it's going to be difficult to leave. I remember leaving somewhere once before, but it was so long ago."

"You were little then," Father Tinian said, "five years old."

"It's strange. I've been trying to remember about her lately, but only her name came to me, Ida. That's all I remember," Elliot said. Then he added, "I wonder, would it be all right if I left the school for a few hours?"

"What do you need?" Father Tinian asked.

"I would like to go visit Felix Skinner before I leave."

"Where does he live?" the priest asked.

"In a little town about fifty miles north of here."

"How would you get there?" the Colonel broke in.

"I thought I would take a bus."

"Nonsense, I'll take you," the Colonel said.

"He and his mother work during the day. We wouldn't get back until late," Elliott said, concerned about the Colonel's sleep.

"I'm a big boy," the colonel quipped, "I can stay out past sunset. Do you have his address?" the Colonel asked, already thinking about logistics.

"Yes, Sir."

"Good. We'll leave about four-thirty this afternoon. That should be about right."

"Yes, Sir. Thank you, Colonel"

Father Tinian couldn't help but laugh at his brusque friend. Finally the Colonel laughed back, then Elliot followed suit.

The afternoon was hot, and the Colonel took off his uniform jacket. He was sweating slightly under his arms. Elliot hadn't worn a jacket, just his khaki shirt with the tie. He read the map and guided the Colonel. As they left the city, the Colonel decided against the freeways, saying that he never liked them. They drove through some small towns, then farmlands. The next town they came to was where Mrs. Skinner lived. They turned onto his street right at six-thirty.

"There, Sir, up ahead on the right. That's the address."

The Colonel pulled up and shut off the motor. He kept his old car in top condition with a lot of wax on the body. He looked at the little house.

"There's a car in the driveway," the Colonel said.

"I think that's Mrs. Skinner's," Elliot replied. The Colonel sat looking at the house. "Shall we go in, Sir?" Elliot asked.

"What? Why, yes, I thought maybe...I could wait out here, but that wouldn't seem correct, would it?"

"No, Sir," Elliot agreed. It was too hot, and he didn't want him sitting out here. Elliot thought he might feel that he had to hurry. The Colonel got out of the car and put on his jacket. He placed his hat under his arm and walked in step with Elliot to the front door. He cleared his throat as he rang the bell.

They heard someone running through the house, and then Felix opened the door. He saw the Colonel first. His mouth fell open; he blinked and then saw Elliot, "Holy cow! Wow! Hello, Sir."

"Hello, Lieutenant", the Colonel said rather uncomfortably. Skinner was dressed in Levi's and an old tee shirt with a hole over his left shoulder.

Felix didn't know what to say to Elliot. "Hi, Ell- ahh, Adjutant." He still hadn't invited them in.

"Hi, Felix," Elliot said with a big smile. "Do you think we might come in?"

"Oh, sure. Holy cow, I'm sorry, Sir. Come right in." He moved out of the way, and the Colonel came in first.

Standing on the other side of the room, in an apron, holding a drying cloth and a plate was a woman. As soon as she saw who it was, she broke into a smile.

"Colonel Whitcome, what a nice surprise. Hello, Elliot! Oh, my, this is such a surprise!"

"I hope it's not too much of a surprise. We tried to call before we left, but no one was here," the Colonel explained apologetically.

"Yes, Felix and I work until five-thirty. It's so nice to have you here. Is everything all right?" The Colonel looked to Elliot to answer this.

"Oh, yes, ma'am, everything is fine. I needed to talk to Felix, and the Colonel thought there might be a chance I'd get lost if I took a bus," Elliot said with a smile.

"Nonsense," the Colonel said. "I knew for sure he would get lost."

It took just a moment for Felix and Mrs. Skinner to understand that the Colonel was joking, and then they laughed. There was an uncomfortable moment, with no one sure of what to say.

"I wonder, Mrs. Skinner, would it be all right if Felix and I took a walk for awhile?" Elliot asked.

"Of course. Colonel, would you like a cup of coffee while you wait?"

"Thank you, ma'am, that would be nice. I see that you're drying dishes."

"Why, yes."

"Well, I know how to do that too."

She smiled as the Colonel came to help her. The boys turned and went out onto the porch.

"What's up, Elliot? Why'd you come way out here?"

"Let's take a walk," Elliot said, as he began down the steps.

Felix watched him for a long moment before he followed him. He fell into step beside him.

"There's been a change."

"What do you mean?"

"I'm going to be leaving the school in a couple of days."

"You mean you're leaving for good?"

"Yes."

"Why would you do that?"

"There's been a thing about money. Besides, I've found out I have an aunt. I'll be staying with her and her family."

"Where does she live?"

"I don't know yet. The law firm is sending the address where I'm supposed to go." Elliot had made up his mind that it was best not to tell Felix that he could have chosen to stay if he wanted to but chose not to stay.

There was another long pause, and then Felix said, "This is really lousy."

"We've been together for such a long time. I don't know what I'm going to do without you," Elliot said quietly.

"Yeah, I feel the same way," Felix replied. "And I'm so lousy at making new friends."

"You won't have time for new friends, not with those 'little buggers' of yours."

"That's true." Another pause.

"When will you be leaving?"

"It looks like a couple of days."

There was quiet as the two friends walked along the empty street. Then Felix said, "I pulled a 'you' the other night."

"What do you mean?"

"I had a dream. I dreamt you and me were playing handball together. I was serving. I waited for the ball but you never returned it. I turned around to see what was wrong, and you were gone. I couldn't find you."

"Felix...

"Yeah?"

"You know...you are the best friend anyone could ask for right."

"So are you, Elliot. I...I don't know what I'd have been without you."

"Twelve years is a long time. We were lucky."

"That's the truth. We'll always remember these times, won't we?"

"There's no way we can forget," Elliot said with tears in his eyes. The boys walked along together, not knowing what more to say. They just enjoyed each other's company.

* * *

The first few miles of the ride back to St. Maurice's were quiet. Elliot's sadness covered him like a blanket. The Colonel could feel it all over the lad. He'd have to do the talking. "Did you know that Mrs. Skinner's husband was an Army man?"

"Yes, Sir."

"He lost his life in combat."

"Yes, Sir. He died when Felix was four." The Colonel drove on, still thinking over his time with Mrs. Skinner.

"Her mother named her Amelia, after Amelia Earhart. Did you know that?"

Yes, Sir. If she would have been a boy, they would have named her Frank, because her dad liked Frank Capra movies."

"Is that right? She didn't tell me that one," the Colonel responded.

"She probably would if you had more time."

The Colonel glanced at Elliot, then back at the road. "You seem to know a lot about the family."

"Yes, Sir, I know everything about them."

The Colonel was a little hesitant about his next question, but he had to know. "She's a nice looking woman. Do you know why she never married again?"

"Yes, Sir." Elliot looked over at the Colonel, who was suddenly concentrating on the road a little too much.

"Is it a secret?" the Colonel asked.

"No, Sir. She told Felix she would only remarry if she found a Catholic man who really loved the Lord."

"That's what she told her son?"

"Yes, Sir."

The colonel thought about this. Now he could feel Elliot's eyes on him. "What is it?"

"Nothing, Sir. I was just wondering if you told her about your back?"

"Yes, I mentioned it."

"Did you tell her who healed you?"

"If I remember correctly, I did mention the Lord."

"Did Mrs. Skinner seem pleased?"

"Why, yes, she seemed so, if I remember correctly."

* * *

The law firm arranged for a cab to pick up Elliot and take him to the airport. He had already said his goodbyes to Father Tinian and all the Sisters. Now, he was sitting in the large waiting room with his one suitcase beside his chair. Across from him, waiting with him, was Sister Teresa. He was in his dress uniform, with his Captain bars on the shoulders.

What a difference from the first time I saw him, when he had thrown up during Mass, Sister Teresa thought. And yet there was something about him that had not changed, but had stayed youthful. She knew it had to do with his spirit. It was the same to her. The same spirit that took her hand in the hallway of the school, years ago, when Elliot was looking for his friend, was the same spirit that was smiling at her now.

"Do you have your airplane ticket?"

"Yes, Mother Superior gave me everything I need."

"Good."

"It's only five hundred miles, maybe I can come back after graduation."

"That would be nice, but you don't have to look back. That's what's important. We'll love you and pray for you, no matter where you are."

"I know, Sister, I know.

"These are the things you have to do." She leaned forward in her usual manner, when what she was about to say was important. "You must keep on the full armor of God, don't forget his Word and keep listening for His voice."

"I will, Sister. You keep praying for me. If you get any words for me, call or write."

The chimes to the front door rang. Elliot took his one suitcase in one hand and the Sister's hand in the other. "I don't know how to thank you."

"Good. Later, I'll meet you in heaven and we'll discuss it."

He smiled, kissed her cheek and opened the door. The cab was waiting.

# The Third House

"Charles, maybe you should make a little sign with his name on it."

"I don't think that will be necessary, Mrs. Elsie."

"How will you know him?"

Charles, their chauffer, already had the front door of the Rolls Royce half-opened. "If he has spent most of his life in a military academy, I won't have any trouble at all."

Elsie, in the back seat, smiled, and agreed. "Oh, yes. He probably will stand out somewhat."

"Yes, ma'am," Charles said, as he lifted himself out of the car.

Once on the sidewalk, he pulled down his suit coat, adjusted his tie, bent over slightly and smiled at Elsie in the back seat, then walked into the airport terminal.

Elsie smiled back and watched him disappear through the glass doors. She always liked to watch Charles walk. He carried himself with all the elegance of a corporate executive and that's why she dressed him like one. It pleased her that he most probably looked as good as any man in the airport. She smiled serenely and turned her attention to people leaving and entering. She enjoyed watching people.

Charles waited to the side of the gate, away from the main crowd of greeters. As Elliot Reed came down the walkway from the airplane, Charles knew him. Though he was still in his school uniform, Charles felt he would have known the boy if he had been in a bathing suit. There was little doubt that he was a Reed, and

Charles was immediately reminded of Susan Rydell Reed, the boy's mother.

How many times had Charles seen Susan drive up to Mrs. Elsie's estate to visit? Each time she came, Charles would wash her car, checking the oil level and the pressure in the tires. Even though he knew that Bertrand took good care of his wife and her Mercedes, he still wanted to do something for her, because Susan had befriended Mrs. Elsie.

"Mr. Elliot Reed?"

Elliot glanced quickly towards the voice and smiled. "Yes."

"Good afternoon, Sir. My name is Charles. Mrs. Elsie Tidwell is here to pick you up."

"I don't take a cab, then?"

"No, Sir. Plans have been changed."

"Who is Mrs. Tidwell?"

"She's your great aunt, Sir. She thought it would be nice if you drove to your new home with someone from the family."

"Well, thank you. That's much better than a cab."

"Yes, Sir. Do you have your luggage claim tickets?"

"Yes," Elliot answered as he produced one ticket from inside his hat. "I only have one suitcase."

Elliot saw that Charles had his hand out. He wondered why. "Do you want the ticket?"

"Yes, Sir. I'll get your bag for you."

Elliot looked at the tall slender man, with the white hair and the perfectly fitted suit. "Why would you want to do that, Sir?"

"Mister Reed, I'm Mrs. Elsie's chauffeur," Charles said in a pleasant tone, unashamed of what he did.

"You are?" Elliot responded, surprised. "I saw chauffeurs at a funeral once, and they all had on uniforms."

"They did not work for Mrs. Elsie," Charles said, still waiting for the ticket.

"Would you mind if I helped you with it?" Elliot asked. "It's pretty heavy, and I'm used to it."

"As you wish," Charles replied. Since Charles had hit his sixties, he didn't look forward to carrying heavy things. "This way, Sir, to the luggage area."

Charles opened the trunk of the Rolls Royce, and Elliot lifted and placed the suitcase inside the trunk. It doesn't look heavy, Charles thought, at least not the way this lad handles it. He noticed how careful Elliot was not to mar the trunk's carpeted flooring. Charles opened the back door and announced, "Mrs. Elsie, may I introduce you to your great nephew, Elliot Reed."

As Elliot removed his hat and entered the Rolls Royce, he saw seated on the far side of the automobile, a little, old lady with an afghan thrown over her legs. She was smiling and had her bird-like hand poised to be shaken. He gently took it.

When Elsie saw the lad, she too was immediately reminded of Susan Reed. Though he was darkly handsome, as his father had been, he had the warm eyes and full mouth of his mother. His brown eyes were smiling at her as he continued holding her hand.

"Thank you for coming to get me."

"I wouldn't have missed it. You're family. Someone had to be here to meet you."

He gently let go of her hand, and they smiled at each other. Charles got behind the wheel.

"Charles said that you are my great aunt."

"That's right. I'm your grandfather's only sister, Elsie Reed Tidwell. Years ago, when my brother came home one weekend from college, he brought a friend, Joseph Tidwell, with him. I met them at the door and fell in love. My husband and your grandfather created Reed Industries, with God's help."

"How long did you know your husband before you married him?" Elliot asked.

The question startled Elsie. If anything, she thought the lad might ask about Reed Industries. But no, he asked about something important.

"My father made me wait one year, but I would have married Joseph that night!"

"You loved him right away?"

"No, not really. It didn't happen until dinner." They both laughed at this, unaware of Charles as he laughed too.

"What happened?" Elliot asked.

"We couldn't take our eyes off of each other," she replied. "I was seventeen years old and had never even thought about falling in love. I think at the time I was going to be a nurse, or a movie star, something like that. But at dinner that night, I knew exactly what I wanted to do. I wanted to be with Joseph Tidwell. Nothing else even mattered." She was silent for a moment.

"He's gone now?" Elliot asked.

"Yes, he died a long time ago, fifteen years. We had forty-two years together." She looked at the lad next to her. "Your grandfather died four days after my Joseph's funeral. But, even before that, your father had taken charge of the company."

"My father, what was his name?" Elliot asked quietly.

"Bertrand Reed."

"I thought maybe my mother's name might be Ida."

"No, it was Susan Rydell Reed."

"Yes, that's what Charles told me. Then who was Ida?"

"I don't know," Elsie answered. She watched the boy as he looked out of the window. What kind of a life had he had without a family, she wondered. How much did he dislike the lot of them for not being with him during these important years?

"We didn't know about you until last week," Elsie said.

"I don't understand."

"Your mother died right after you were born. Your father told the family that you had died at the same time."

"Why would he do that?"

"No one really knows, but he didn't like this family much."

But then, as she thought about what she had just said, she added, "That's not true. He didn't like his family at all. After the death of Susan and the lie about you, he had nothing to do with any of us. He lived alone, traveled continuously, with all of his time going into Reed Industries."

"He didn't want a baby without his wife," Elliot said bluntly.

"Yes, that's about it. He...he was a very private man. Even as a boy, he stayed by himself. But when he met Susan, it was as if he'd always been waiting for her. When she died he went back to what he had been."

"By what you said, he seems to have done the right thing."

"What do you mean?"

Elliot smiled. "He wanted to be alone and didn't want friends. I don't think I could have stood not having a friend. I've always had a friend."

Elsie smiled back at him. "Good for you! I feel exactly the same way. Maybe you and I will be friends."

"And Charles too!" Elliot replied, glancing toward the front seat.

Elsie already knew that she was this boy's friend. As she and Charles laughed, she took the lad's hand and held it as tightly as she could.

As the stately old Rolls drove up the driveway to the Swindale Estate, Elliot was taken with its size and beauty. Green lawns and shrubbery surrounded the sprawling two-storied mansion. To the side of the huge house, nestled in a group of large trees, was a five-car garage with apartments above it. As they drove in, a large new Lincoln Continental (with the driver's door open) stood running in front of the house.

"It looks as though Mrs. Swindale is leaving," Charles said to the rear seat.

At that moment, Harriet Swindale came from the house, and then saw the Rolls. She stopped, unsure of what to do, and then took a look, trying to see in the back seat of the car. Though she could not tell who was in it, she could see someone. As she walked toward the car, Charles got out and opened the rear door. Elliot opened the other door, got out, and moved to the driver's side and smiled at Harriet.

"Hello, ma'am," he said.

Charles helped Elsie from the car, and she stood looking at her surprised niece. "Harriet, may I introduce Elliot Reed, your nephew."

My God, Harriet thought, he's better looking than Bertrand was! "Hello, young man," she said with a slight smile.

"Elliot," Elsie said, relishing the awkwardness she saw Harriet going through, "This is your aunt, Harriet Reed Swindale."

"I would like to thank you for taking me in," Elliot said, unsure if he should put his hand out to a lady. "Mrs. Tidwell has told me what a surprise I was."

"Yes... Well, it's nice to have you here. I'm sorry my son Arnold isn't here to greet you...someone your own age. I think he's staying over at a friend's house...somewhere. I'm not sure when he'll be home."

Elliot didn't know what he was expected to say, so he said nothing.

"I'm sorry I have to leave," Harriet said, "but it's an appointment I've had for quite some time. As far as a place for you to stay... there is an apartment next to Charles's. It needs a little cleaning, hasn't been used for some time..."

"That will be fine, Mrs. Swindale, just fine. Thank you very much," Elliot replied.

"Charles will show you, and I'll see you when I get back," Harriet said, as she glanced quickly at Elsie. Elsie was more interested in looking up at the house.

Why the hell didn't Elsie tell me she was going to pick the boy up, Harriet thought. She nodded at the smiling boy and went to her car. She could have easily cancelled her beauty appointment, but what good would that do? She put the car in gear and moved past the Rolls. Elsie smiled at her and waved. Harriet ignored her.

"May I help you to your room?" Charles asked Mrs. Elsie.

"No, Charles, I feel just fine. That staircase is the only exercise I get. Why don't you take Elliot to see his place?"

"Thank you again for picking me up," Elliot said to her. Then, coming closer asked her quietly, "Who is that girl watching us from the upstairs window?"

Elsie answered without looking at the upstairs window again, "That, my great nephew, is your beautiful cousin, Tina Swindale. Usually she has no interest in what I do, so she must be looking down here to see you."

With that, Elsie turned and walked towards the house. Charles was holding the car door open for Elliot to get in the back seat, but the boy asked, "Could I sit in front with you?"

Charles smiled and nodded. He watched as the lad ran quickly to the other side and hopped in beside him. Elliot closed the door gently, as he'd seen Charles do at the airport.

"Do you know how to drive?" Charles asked.

"No, Sir. They never taught that at school."

Charles pulled the Rolls up in front of the garages and stopped.

Elliot had seen something that interested him, so he got quickly out, moved to the front of the car and looked over the hedges at the back lawn.

Charles moved to the trunk of the car and, without thinking, tried to lift Elliot's large suitcase. It wouldn't even budge.

"What have you got in here?" Charles called out, laughing.

"I'm sorry," Elliot said, hurrying to the back of the car. "The Colonel gave me some books to take with me."

Charles watched as the lad, seemingly with little effort, lifted the suitcase from the trunk. He stood holding it, waiting for Charles to lead the way. They climbed the stairs to the apartments.

"That sure is a beautiful swimming pool," Elliot said.

"Do you like to swim?" Charles asked.

"Yes, Sir. Everyday."

"Good. The Swindales certainly won't mind. They'd like somebody to get some use out of it."

"Do you swim?" Elliot asked.

"Only out of fear," the chauffeur replied. He pointed at the first apartment and said, "This first one is mine, and, walking on, "this one is yours."

He held up a key in his hand. "I'm afraid one key opens both apartments."

"I won't need a key," Elliot said with a laugh, as he moved his suitcase into the darkness of the shaded room. Charles turned on the light.

The small living room was being used as a storage area and was filled with old pieces of furniture piled on top of each other. There were two sofas, parts of beds, bookshelves, upright lamps and mattresses leaning against the far wall. The two men stood there, looking at the dusty mess.

"As you can see, Mrs. Swindale does not like to throw things away," Charles said, trying to keep the irritation out of his voice.

"Isn't that lucky!" Elliot said excitedly. "You mean this is all going to be mine?"

"Yes. You like it?"

"Like it? It's fantastic! And look at all this stuff! All I have to do is clean it and put everything where it should be, and I'll have my own room!"

"I'm afraid the bedroom and kitchen look about the same."

"You mean there's more?"

"What? Yes, of course. You can't be expected to live in one room."

"This is like a little house! I'll bet it's almost as big as the Colonel's!" With that, Elliot took off his coat, then tie and shirt. He was ready to start.

"What should I do with the stuff I don't need?"

"There's a rather large storage area behind the garages. I'll open it for you."

"What about a broom and a mop, stuff like that?"

"I've got everything you need. I'll put it on the porch."

"Great. Thank you, Sir. This is going to be wonderful!" Elliot said as he walked through all the dusty stuff, inspecting each item. "I've never had my own place before. And look at what I get! This is just fantastic!"

Charles shook his head in amazement, knowing that the lad would never believe that Harriet Swindale had put him out there as a form of chastisement, a way of making sure that the lad knew his place. There were plenty of unused bedrooms within the main house. Charles smiled, wondering what Mrs. Swindale would think if she knew how her plan had backfired.

After Charles left to get what the boy needed, Elliot selected all the pieces he wanted to keep, and then started hauling all the rest down to the storage area. He found more pieces to select from the bedroom, and the kitchen was full of pots and pans, silverware, and all the stuff he would need to set up his own house.

First, Elliot moved everything out of the bedroom and cleaned the floors and the walls. He wanted to get this room finished before it got dark. He had just moved his bed into place when there was a knock at his door. It was Charles.

"Mrs. Elsie wanted to know what clothing you have?"

"Well, I have my uniforms and my sweats for my workouts."

The lad had taken off his shirts and was standing before Charles. Because of the closeness of the small apartment and the difficulty of his labor, sweat covered Elliot's muscular shoulders and chest. Though Charles certainly did not want to blatantly stare, as far as he could tell it looked as if this lad's perfectly proportioned body had no fat at all! Not an ounce! No wonder he could lift that suitcase with ease.

Recovering his thoughts, Charles continued, "That's what Mrs. Elsie and I thought. You need clothes. What styles do you like?"

"Style? I don't know. I've never owned any, except when I was little."

"Yes, of course. That was a foolish question," Charles said as he thought about the problem he had just brought up. Then he smiled and said, "Maybe it's not such a problem after all. Why don't you get cleaned up, and we'll take a ride. It's Friday afternoon, and I think I know where we should go."

"Yes, Sir. I'll be right down."

They parked near the Galleria Mall. Though there was an entrance for valet parking, Charles would never use it. He allowed no one to drive the Rolls but himself.

"Have you ever been in a mall?" Charles asked as they walked towards one of the entrances.

"No, Sir."

"It's something like going into a wild animal reserve," he said, opening the glass door.

It did take Elliot by surprise. His attention was immediately drawn to a huge fountain that shot water over two stories in the air. His eyes continued up, and he saw that the three-storied building had a glass roof. Within this huge edifice were all kinds of small stores, selling almost anything you could want. The building was filled with people, mostly young. Charles led him to an empty bench that was centrally located, and they sat to watch the people walking by.

"When you see some clothing you like," Charles stated, "let me know."

Since it was summer, many of the younger people were in short pants and tee shirts. Some of the guys with their girlfriends were dressed in Levis, while others had on white duck pants and well-ironed dress shirts.

"I like the way he looks," Elliot commented, pointing to a tall young man wearing white ducks and a short-sleeved sport shirt.

"Me too," Charles replied. Getting up, he went over to the lad, who was talking to a pretty young girl. "Excuse me, young man."

"Yeah?" the young man responded.

"Would you mind telling me where you buy your clothes?"

"At George's on the second level. I work there."

"Are you working tonight?"

"Yes, Sir. I'm on my break."

"When will you be through with your break?"

"In about ten minutes."

"Thank you."

Charles walked back to the bench and sat. "He buys his clothes at George's on the second level. We'll go see him in about ten minutes." Charles noticed that Elliot was still watching the couple.

"She's pretty, isn't she?" Elliot seemed to be asking Charles a question.

"She most certainly is," Charles answered. Elliot continued watching the couple until they walked off. Then, he once more joined Charles in looking for clothing.

A noisy gang of teenage boys entered the mall. They were dressed in sloppy, ill-fitting and torn clothing. Some of them had strange haircuts and a couple of the boys had pierced ears. Most of them were smoking. Elliot glanced at them once and then turned his attention away from the group. Their clothes did not interest him at all. But Charles kept watching them until they were near the bench.

Elliot heard one of the boys say, "Hi, Charles. What are you doing here?"

Looking up, Elliot saw a slender young man with long straggly brown hair standing in front of him. His left ear was pierced with four or five rings, his eyes looked glassy, and he didn't seem stable on his feet. He was smoking a cigarette, and his two fingers were yellow from the nicotine tar.

"Hello, Arnold. This is your cousin, Elliot Reed. Elliot, this is Arnold Swindale," Charles said. Elliot noticed curtness in Charles's tone, the kind used by Colonel Whitcome when he was displeased.

Elliot stood, and the two boys shook hands. "Hello, Arnold."

"Oh, hi, Elliot."

Someone in his crowd spoke up, "Hey, what kind of a uniform is that?"

Elliot looked at the person who asked the question. From the smirk on the guy's face, it was apparent he really didn't want an answer, so Elliot ignored him.

"When did you get here?" Arnold slurred. Elliot could smell liquor on him.

"This morning," Elliot answered. He saw Arnold take a quick glance at the seated Charles. He seemed nervous around him. "Hey, nice meeting you. See you later, huh?"

"Sure," Elliot answered, "see you later."

The gang walked off as one of them said something about Elliot's uniform, causing them all, except Arnold, to laugh.

Elliot sat down next to Charles. There was a moment of silence.

"What did you think of your cousin?" Charles asked.

"He looks unhappy. And his friends do too."

Charles thought about this. Unhappy? Well, that's certainly true. In fact, in the past five years, since Charles and Mrs. Elsie had been at the house, Charles couldn't remember the last time he had heard Arnold laugh. Elliot was right.

"His mother's worried about him," Charles said.

Elliot was silent for a moment and then said, "What about his father?"

"I don't even think they see each other much. Mr. Swindale stays in the library most of the time." He thought about this for a moment, and then added, "The more I think of it, they don't talk to each other even when they're together. At least, I can't remember them talking much about anything, even when I've driven them places."

"Does Arnold use narcotics?"

Charles nodded, "His family thinks he started when he was a sophomore."

Elliot sighed, but said nothing else. The two of them looked at more "walking" clothing for a few minutes, then went up to George's on the second floor.

The tall young salesman's name was Lance. Elliot tried on the duck pants. They had white, black and light beige. Elliot liked the white and beige. Charles bought four pair of each. (He would have purchased more, but that was all they had in a size twenty-nine inch waist.) Lance found tapered shirts for him that would fit over his forty-three inch chest. Charles selected a dozen of these, different colors and designs, making sure that they went properly with the pants. Underwear, socks, belts and two pair of soft calfskin leather shoes were also selected.

After Charles had wandered off, looking for a light jacket, Elliot said to Lance, "Would you mind if I asked a personal question?"

"What's that?"

"Was that your girlfriend you were talking to?"

"When?"

"When Charles asked you where you bought your clothes."

The boy thought for a moment, then laughed. "No, that's my sister. She's still in high school."

"What school does she go to?" Elliot asked.

Lance looked a long moment at Elliot then smiled. You weren't thinking of trying to hit on her, were you?"

Slightly offended, Elliot answered quickly, "I would never hit her."

Lance gave him another look, then laughed. "She goes to Laurelwood High. Her name is Rachel Davis, O.K.?"

"Yes, O.K.," Elliot answered. Elliot wondered what high school **he** would be going to?

Then Lance said something strange to him. "But I'll guarantee you, you'll strike out. They all do."

Elliot started to ask him what he meant, but Charles came back carrying two windbreakers. Elliot liked them both, so Charles bought them. Lance had never had a better sale or a bigger commission check than this week, more money for college.

Elliot waited until they were back in the Rolls before he asked the question. "What high school will I be going to?"

"The one in our area is called Laurelwood. You'll be a classmate of Arnold's, if his grades are up from summer school."

"Summer school?"

"That's the place you go if you have a difficult time passing your regular school year."

"Oh."

Because of the hour, they stopped at a fast food place and went inside to eat dinner. Elliot didn't think much of the food. He very seldom ate beef, and the place didn't have vegetables and fruits. He took a couple of bites, then stopped.

"Do you always eat your meals out?" Elliot asked, as he looked down at the mound of French fries.

Charles smiled and shook his head. "No, usually I eat at home. I cook my own food."

"Cooking, is it hard to learn?"

"It depends. What do you like to eat?"

"Vegetables and fruits mostly. Sometimes chicken and fish."

"I would have bet on it."

"What do you mean?"

"The way you look. Who taught you to eat like that? Was it the school?"

"No, it was mostly Daniel?"

"Daniel who?"

"From the Old Testament, the Book of Daniel." He thought for a moment, then added, "And Jesus too. He ate the same type foods as Daniel, but probably more fish. High in protein, low fat."

"You learned to eat from the Bible?"

"Sure."

"How do you know what they ate was correct?"

"Because Daniel was better nourished than the young men who ate the royal foods."

"What were the royal foods?"

"Rich and greasy, probably a lot like this stuff."

Charles looked down at his food, then at the smiling Elliot. "Very well," Charles said, "I'll teach you how to cook, and you might be able to teach me better eating habits."

"It's a deal," Elliot said, as he pushed his plate away. He didn't even like the smell of it.

Elliot woke a little after five. Since Charles had given him permission to use the pool, he reached into his suitcase and brought out his trunks. He slipped them on. It was still dark as he turned on the light in the bathroom, got a towel and made his way quietly down the stairs.

There was just enough early morning light for him to see as he jumped a small hedge, walked across the back lawn, and stood by the pool. Slight twists of steam were rising off the water. A heated pool, Elliot noticed. Elliot touched the water with his foot, a little too warm for his taste but not too bad. He dove in at the deep end, silently entering the water, then swam the length of the pool underwater. Coming up at the shallow end, he turned, pushed off and started a slow, four-kick crawl.

While he was under the dark water, he had gauged the pool to be five meters or so shorter than the one at St. Maurice's. He decided to do sixty-five laps instead of fifty. He felt his back muscles begin to loosen and stretch as he reached through the smooth surface of the water. He would pick up his pace after thirty laps.

Tina Swindale had slipped into the house a little after five, silently made her way up the staircase and into her room. As was her habit, after a long date, she turned on the shower, standing under the powerful stream of hot water. She liked her European showerhead, because she could adjust a needle-like spray that almost hurt her skin when it hit. She stood still, letting the water pelt her back. After five minutes or so, she turned and did the same to her front.

She thought about Alex. He'd be going back to college in a few weeks, back to football and all the things he did to stay in shape! Good God, what a bore! When she had told him she wouldn't be going back this year, that she was bored with school and everything that went on there, he took it personally. She smiled. He took everything she did as personal. If she looked at him too long, he wondered why. When she didn't look at him often enough, he wondered about that too. She knew him and used him, depending upon her moods. Sometimes she felt as though she really loved him. At other times, she knew that she never had. How long had she known him? Since the first grade, when his father had become the president of his company and had moved into the neighborhood, that's how long it had been. That long ago, it's no wonder she was bored. She sighed and decided to let the water hit on her back again. She felt her lids beginning to close slightly. Her arms were feeling heavy. She was about ready for bed, nodding toward sleepiness.

What was she thinking about? Oh, yes, Alex. He wanted to marry her. Since she didn't have any interest in school, he had asked her why they shouldn't marry now. Why, in God's name, she thought, would she ever want to do that? Since she was bored now, what would she be like married to him?

She smiled when she thought about how many times through the years she use to break up with the huge bear. Whenever she found a new boy that caught her attention, she would start a fight, crying, and leave Alex, making him feel like it was his fault. After she tired of the new boy, she would find a way to "get Alex back". My God, she thought, I'm even bored and disgusted with those games! She turned off the water and dried herself.

She hadn't told her mother yet about not planning to return to college. She wondered why not? She didn't think her mother would care. And if she did, what would her mother do about it? Nothing, except go into one of her pouts, believing that this simple manipulation would always get what she wanted. But Tina knew the game too and would ask her what the matter was? Then her mother would tell her how disappointed she was that she didn't have the maturity to follow through with her education. Tina would act as though every word was important, listening for just the right time to say she was sorry and then apologizing at just the right moment. Then, after a week or so it would all be forgotten, and Tina could do whatever she wanted.

Even getting her way was becoming a bore. She looked at her beautiful figure in the full-length mirror. She was even bored with looking at herself. She went into her bedroom, put on her nightgown and opened the rear window slightly. She disliked the air conditioning.

As she started to leave the window, she heard a strange noise. She stopped, listened, but was not able to place it. She moved closer and put her ear to the screen. It sounded to her like someone was in the pool. She went over and shut off the light in her room, then opened her window all the way.

Yes, it was someone in the pool! Was it Arnold and his idiot friends? No, it couldn't be, she thought, there wasn't enough noise. Besides, their mother had told him that if he ever brought his friends back here, he could leave with them for good.

Tina listened closely and tried to see in the early morning light. Yes, someone was swimming all right. She could make out a figure going back and forth. Nobody she knew could swim like that, except for Alex, and he'd gone home. Besides, she knew that he would never do anything without permission.

She put on a robe, went out into the hall and then quietly down the back stairway. She opened the door and cautiously made her way onto the patio. She knew how far she could walk before being seen by someone in the pool. She stopped. The light was better now. If she moved just a few more feet, she would be able to see the pool.

She became aware that the swimmer had stopped. There was silence. She froze, not knowing what to do. She listened intently but heard nothing. Slowly, she took a step forward, then another, then one more. When she took the last step, she saw Elliot Reed, towel in hand, watching her!

"Hello," he said.

Tina didn't know what to say.

"Did I wake you?" he asked. "I'm Elliot Reed. I moved in yesterday."

The boy was built so well, Tina had a difficult time looking only at his eyes. Good Lord, she thought, I have to say something! "I know who you are," she said a little too sharply. "I just didn't know who was using the pool."

"I'm sorry; I should have let someone know. And I'm sorry I woke you."

Tina wished she would have had been wearing one of her bathing suits, because then she would feel on a more equal footing. Let him see how disconcerting **her** body could be! Without another word, she turned and walked back through the patio and up to her room.

Elliot watched her as she left; thinking that he had better do his running first from now on, then swim when it was a little later in the day. He went back to his apartment, changed, and decided on a ten mile run.

There were very few cars on the tree-lined streets as he left the estate. About a mile from the house, Elliot found a park area with what looked like a wide running path. As he went along this path, at a turn he suddenly came upon two women riding horses. Startled, one of the horses shied. The woman rider skillfully brought the animal under control. Elliot moved to one side and stood still.

"This is not a jogging path, young man."

"Sorry, ma'am," Elliot answered quickly. He walked out of the park area, shaking his head. He certainly wasn't making many friends on his first morning.

When he got to the street, he once again began to run, picking up his speed. He noticed that the neighborhood had begun to change drastically. The houses were smaller and the streets had cars parked along the curbs instead of on the properties. It was still early enough that traffic was not a problem.

At about five miles out, as he was approaching an intersection. He decided to turn and make his way back. As he did, he noticed that across the street, on the far corner, was a little church. For some reason he stopped and looked at it. It wasn't in very good shape; the small white fence surrounding it was partially broken down. The grass in the lawn was dry and tall. It wasn't difficult to see that the place was not in use.

Elliot jogged across the street and stood in front of the little building. He looked down at the lawn and saw where a sign had been. The two posts that had held it had been broken off. The gate in the little fence was open and pulled loose from its top hinge.

He walked to the front porch and tried the door. It was locked. He went to a dusty window to the side of the door and looked in. The room was dark and unkempt. All the pews were there, and a small pulpit was visible at the far end of the little church. Above it, attached to the wall, was an empty cross. The church hadn't been used for a long time.

Elliot walked down the steps from the little church, wondering why he was so interested in it. Even as he began to jog back to the house, he turned and looked back. Strange, he thought. But then, he concentrated on his running and picked up his speed, moving quickly through the neighborhood.

When he got back to the garages and climbed the stairs, Charles stuck his head out of his apartment door.

"Good morning, Elliot."

"Good morning, Sir."

"Are you hungry?"

"Yes, Sir, I am."

"Good. Mrs. Elsie would like you to join her for breakfast."

"Yes, Sir."

"Eight o'clock?"

"Yes, Sir." Then Elliot added, "Would it be possible to get some paint?"

"Certainly! Look in the small shed, in the back. There are all kinds of paints and brushes in there."

Elliot showered and dressed in one of his new outfits. He looked at himself in one of the still dusty mirrors and laughed. He really looked funny in this outfit. He felt like he was looking at a stranger. And the outfit felt strange too. It was so light he felt like he didn't have any clothes on at all.

Only after he got to the back of the house did he wish that he had asked Charles exactly where he was supposed to go to meet Mrs. Tidwell for breakfast. He opened one of the back doors to the huge house.

"Hello?" he said. No answer. "Hello!" he said a little louder.

This room must be the laundry room. There were washing machines, dryers, a couple of ironing boards, and shelves full of sheets and stuff.

Suddenly, the door at the other end of the room opened and a black lady was looking at him.

"Hello," Elliot said, "I'm Elliot Reed, and I'm supposed to meet Mrs. Tidwell for breakfast."

The black face looked at him for a moment longer, then said, "Well, you got the right house, but the wrong room."

She opened the door, and Elliot could see the rest of her and part of the kitchen. She was a short, powerful-looking woman dressed as a cook.

"Come on, honey, I'll lead the way. It took me three days before I stopped getting lost around here."

She led him through a very large kitchen with two separate breakfast nooks, which were empty, around a corner and into a massive dining room. Mrs. Elsie was seated alone at long table.

"I found this young man in the laundry room. Do you want him?"

"I most certainly do, Marny," Elsie said with a smile.

"He's all yours," the black lady said. Turning to Elliot, she asked, "And what would you like to eat this morning?"

"Whole grain cereal, if you have it and fruit."

She looked him over. "How much fruit?"

Elliot smiled and said, "I like fruit."

"And fruit likes you," she said, as she disappeared into the kitchen.

Elsie laughed and pointed toward the chair next to her. Elliot sat down.

"That Marny says what she wants, and she can cook everything."

"I wanted to thank you for the clothes, Mrs. Tidwell."

"You're more than welcome. But you must call me Elsie or at least Aunt Elsie."

"All right, I'd like to call you Aunt Elsie."

Marny returned carrying a large bowl filled with cereal. In her other hand she held an ornate porcelain pitcher half filled with milk.

"You can start with this, Mister Elliot. I'm still shaking the trees for the fruit." Then, she was gone.

Elliot poured a little milk and bowed his head in prayer. Elsie watched and smiled. As he began to eat, she said, "I want you to have a house phone in your apartment, just like Charles."

Elliot started to speak, but she held up her frail hand. "You eat, I'll talk. Usually I eat alone, so this is a treat. And I also want you to have more clothes than you have. Summer won't last forever, so you'll need warmer things. Will you do that with Charles? Just nod, don't talk."

Elliot smiled and nodded affirmatively.

Elsie took a sip of her coffee, before continuing, "Charles said that you didn't know how to drive. I suggested we send you to some driving school, but he wouldn't hear of it. He said <u>he</u> would teach you, which is quite extraordinary. It certainly isn't like him to want to help young people. Usually, he just scares them away he's so reserved. So, he wants to teach you to drive. Is that all right with you?"

Elliot nodded yes again.

"Good. I want you to know that if you want to swim in the pool in the early morning, it is all right. You certainly didn't make much noise, and you did not wake Tina up. That I know for sure. Besides, I'm glad to see someone getting some use out of all that warm water."

She paused and thought for a moment. "You haven't seen the house yet, have you?"

"No, ma'am."

"Well, maybe this afternoon, after Graham is up, you can take a walk around and look at it."

Harriet entered the room through the main doors from the hallway. Elliot stood as she entered. She went to sit in her regular seat, at the head of the table.

"Good morning, Harriet," Elsie said, "how was your workout?"

"I've decided to change, a light breakfast, then my workout. Good morning, Elliot. Please, be seated."

"Good morning, ma'am," Elliot answered. "Where do you work out, Mrs. Swindale?"

"I have a room that I turned into a small gym," Harriet answered.

"Small?" Elsie said. Turning to Elliot, she continued, "She turned the old billiard room into a wonderful place. She took a room that nobody used anymore and turned it into one that's made a new woman out of her."

"Aunt Elsie, please," Harriet said, slightly embarrassed, even though she was proud of what she had done.

She rang the small silver bell. Marny, carrying Elliot's fruit came through the kitchen door.

"Good morning, Mrs. Harriet," Marny said as she placed the extra large bowl of cut, mixed fruit in front of Elliot.

"Good morning, Marny," Harriet replied. She looked at the bowl of fruit, then at Elliot. "I think I'll have the same, but a much smaller portion."

"Yes, ma'am," Marny said. "Would you like coffee or tea?"

"Neither, I think. Maybe some mineral water."

"Yes, ma'am," Marny said as she disappeared back into the kitchen.

Elsie was still thinking about what her niece had done. Besides, she enjoyed telling good things about people. "How long have you been using your workout room?" Elsie said, wanting to pick up the conversation again.

"Aunt Elsie, Elliot's not interested in this," Harriet said. She had tried to get her husband and her son interested in the gym but neither one had cared.

"Oh, yes I am, ma'am," Elliot said quickly. "I'd like to hear about it."

"How long, Harriet?" asked Elsie, not giving up.

"It's been nearly three years," Harriet answered.

"And what was your dress size when you started?" Elsie persisted.

Harriet was so embarrassed she had to laugh. "Aunt Elsie, this is ridiculous!"

"No, it isn't! Now what was it?"

"It was a twelve."

"And what is it now?" Aunt Elsie asked.

"It's a seven."

"Thirty-five pounds, she's lost!" Elsie said to Elliot. "From a size twelve to a seven!"

"Wow," Elliot said, really meaning it, "You must have worked really hard."

"I did." she said, smiling. "The first two or three months I had to crawl around the house, I was so sore."

Elliot laughed and said, "I know what you mean. I was the same way at school. If I didn't keep at it, I get sore right away."

"Did they have a workout room at the school?" Harriet asked.

"No, ma'am. But they had a set of weights and some old dumb-bells around. And we set up a pulley system against the inside wall of the basketball gym."

"To work on the back?" Harriet asked.

Elliot smiled, "Yes, ma'am, that's right. We had a hundred and forty pounds on it, but we kept breaking the ropes. Suddenly, we'd find ourselves flying across the gym with a handle in your hand."

Harriet had to laugh. Elsie was pleased to see that Harriet had someone who cared about the same things she cared about. "You should see this place, Elliot," Elsie said, "It's really something special."

Marny entered with Harriet's fruit and glass of mineral water, which she set before her. "Thank you, Marny," Harriet said.

"Yes, ma'am," she answered. Then, speaking to Elliot, "Do you want toast or anything with that fruit, young man?"

"That would be nice. Thank you," Elliot answered.

"Wheat, right?" Marny questioned.

"Yes, please," he answered.

"And no butter?" Marny said.

"Yes," Elliot laughed. "How did you know that?"

"Now, two of you eat the same," Marny said as she left the room.

Smiling, Harriet said, "For the past two years, I've been eating the same way." Taking a bite of her fruit, she asked Elliot, "Would you like to see the workout room?"

"Yes, ma'am, I sure would," he answered.

This would be the first time she had ever shown the room to anybody who really seemed to care, and she found herself looking forward to it. "Why don't we look at the room after breakfast," she said, as she took a sip of mineral water.

The workout room was at the north end of the ground floor. Elliot followed Harriet down the hall, amazed at the size of the house. It seemed to be as large as the whole main building at school.

"My father and his partner, Elsie's husband Joe, loved to play Snooker," Harriet said, as she led him down the long hallway.

"What's Snooker?" Elliot asked.

"It's an English billiard game played on an extra large table. Anytime the two of them wanted to unwind, they would come in here," she said as she opened the door.

Elliot realized immediately that this was a place that most people who were involved in weight training only dreamt about. The large room had at least a dozen different machines, all brightly chromed, as were the weights that were attached to them. The wall to Elliot's right had a mirror that ran from floor to ceiling. All the machines faced that wall.

The far wall, the one near the back yard, had been reconstructed in glass and contained sliding glass doors. Beyond the doors was an enclosed patio area, protected by trellises, which were covered by flowering vines. The patio area contained a small rockfish pond with a waterfall cascading into it. Three lounge chairs and a small table finished the beautiful setting.

Harriet watched the boy's face. She could see how he was taken aback. His eyes kept going from the machines to the beautiful setting outside, as though he couldn't make up his mind, which he liked looking at the most.

"This is...the most amazing place I've ever seen," he finally said.

Harriet could tell that he meant it. She smiled and watched as he walked up to one of the machines.

"Did you design this place?" he asked.

"Yes," she said. "Then after the place was built, I had an expert come in and tell me what equipment I needed."

"Do you use all of the machines?" Elliot asked, wondering what they all did.

"Most of them," she answered, "but some are for power lifting... for men."

"Oh, does your husband work out with you?"

"No, he doesn't like this sort of thing...no interest."

Elliot felt that he should change the subject. "There are so many machines."

"Yes," she laughed, "that's what I thought when I first started, but each one works a different set of muscles within the body. For instance, the one you have your hand on works the front of the thighs, the upper leg."

"That means, that when you get on a machine, you know exactly what's being worked. No guesswork?" Elliot asked.

"Exactly. Once you learn how to work the machine properly, you know exactly what it's doing for you."

"So you can tell where you're weak, right away."

Harriet laughed. "I was weak everywhere when I started. Would you like to try it?" she asked, without even thinking.

"Yes, please."

Elliot took off his shoes and sat on the device. "What do I do?"

"First, we have to adjust the seat for you."

Elliot got up, and she changed the position of the seat. He sat down again, and she looked it over. "Wrap the front of your ankle under the padded area below."

Elliot looked down and saw where she was pointing. He did as he was told.

"Now," she said, "just lift your feet forward."

He did it. His legs came up with ease. Harriet laughed.

"Oh, I forgot to change the weights. You're just lifting what I do." She added forty more pounds. "Now try it," she said.

He did, and his feet went forward without any effort. She looked at the boy and then back at the weights.

"Maybe I'll add some more," she said as she slid the pin forward and added another forty pounds. "Alright, now try it."

Once again, Elliot lifted his feet, still without much effort. "Oh, that's better," he said with a smile. "Maybe just a little bit more."

Good Lord, Harriet thought as she added another twenty pounds, this boy's a gorilla! She watched him as he lifted one hundred and fifty pounds! The muscles in his upper thighs looked as though they were going to break right through his trousers!

"This is great!" she heard him say as he lifted the weight over and over again. "How many should I do?" he asked, smiling as he worked.

"A dozen per set," she replied. She could only stand and watch in amazement as he finished the first set with very little visible discomfort.

"Wow," he exclaimed, "that's fantastic! It really burns."

"That's the way it's supposed to feel. Now wait a few minutes and do another set. Then you would move on to the next exercise. You would work the lower portion one day, then the torso the next."

Elliot only hoped that she would let him work out in this place. He smiled and rested as his aunt showed him which of the other machines were for the legs.

An hour later, Elliot left, after having worked his legs and trying some of the other machines. Though Mrs. Swindale had not asked him back, she did tell him that dinner was served at six. He thanked her for the workout and once again, for his apartment, then left.

He walked down the hall, through the dining room and into the kitchen where Marny was stringing beans.

"Did you have enough to eat at breakfast?" she asked.

"Yes, ma'am. Thanks."

"My name is Marny. Everybody calls me that. Would you?"

"Yes, Marny."

"Good. You want to take some fruit with you?" She watched the boy pause. "Look in the big refrigerator," she continued, "down at the bottom. And over on the sink are plums and apricots. Take some over to that apartment of yours."

As Elliot picked up a handful he said, "Thanks, Marny."

"You're welcome. Use that door over there," she said, pointing. "Are you going to be here for dinner?"

"I think Mrs. Swindale is expecting me."

"So is your Aunt Elsie. You be here. What do you want for dinner? More fruit?"

Elliot laughed. "I like any kind of vegetable and fish too."

"How do you like your vegetables cooked?"

"Still crunchy," he answered.

"That doesn't surprise me. You want your fish raw?"

Elliot laughed and replied, "No, I like it cooked."

"Well, my, my," she said as she smiled at him. "Goodbye, youngster, goodbye."

"Thanks, Marny." And he was gone.

Marny shook her head and smiled. She liked the boy. Would wonders never cease?

Elliot had the woodwork of his kitchen half painted when he heard the screen on the front door bang. He looked out. It was Arnold Swindale. He was dressed, as Elliot had seen him last night.

"Hi," he said.

"Hi," Elliot said in return.

"Lookin' good," Arnold said as he looked around the partially cleaned apartment. "Would you mind if I used one of your couches to sit?"

"Help yourself," Elliot said, still holding the brush. "I'm going to be doing some painting in here."

"That's cool," Arnold answered, "We can talk right through the wall."

Elliot continued to paint for a minute and then looked into the living room. Arnold was sound asleep, with one leg draped to the floor. Elliot walked over to him, straightened him out and threw a blanket over him. Arnold smelled bad.

Elliot continued painting throughout the rest of the day. At five in the afternoon, there was a knock on the screen.

"Elliot?"

"Yes, Sir?" Elliot said, as he walked from the kitchen.

Charles was looking through the screen. "Mrs. Elsie asked me to tell you that dinner was at six."

"Thank you, Sir. Could you come in for a minute?"

"Certainly." The chauffeur, attired immaculately as always, entered and saw the sleeping Arnold on the sofa. "Ah, the wayward child," he said without smiling.

"What should I do with him?"

"Is he drunk?"

"I don't think so, but he smells like he has been."

"Why don't we leave him here until you go to supper. I'll make sure he's taken care of."

"Will you need help?"

"I don't think so. I think it best handled while the rest of the family is occupied with eating."

Though Elliot got to the kitchen a little before six, Marny told him to wait before he entered the dining room. She said the others were always late.

He sat in the kitchen and watched her work. She had a large kettle of something steaming on the stove, and she was slicing tomatoes for the six salads she was preparing.

"You said you liked all sorts of vegetables?"

"Yes, ma'am," he answered. "What's in the pot?" he asked. The smell was wonderful.

"That's a bouillabaisse, young man, with crab, shrimp, lobster, fish and oysters. I mix them all with vegetables and herbs. It tastes better than it smells."

Elliot was salivating. All the work he'd done had made him ravenous, and he had finished off the fruit Marny had given him before noon.

"Thanks for the extra fruit this morning, Marny. It really hit the spot."

"You're welcome, child. Gorillas need to eat often."

Marny had stopped what she was doing and was listening. She nodded to herself, then said to Elliot, "They're in there now. You go on now, around that way to the hall," she said, pointing, "and then come in the proper doors, like the family. I don't want them thinking you're part of the help."

"I don't mind," he said.

"I know you don't, child. That's why I don't want you to."

Elliot wasn't exactly sure of what she meant by that, but he did as he was told. Going through the hallway, he slid open the main doors to the dining room.

"Ah, Elliot," Elsie said quickly, "come in, come in." The chair next to her was vacant. It was the same one he sat on that morning. Harriet Swindale was at the far end, with Tina seated across from Elliot's place. Elliot saw who must be his uncle at the other end of the table.

As he was about to sit, Harriet said, "Graham, this is your nephew, Elliot Reed."

Elliot moved to the far end of the table as the man stood and offered his hand. They shook as Elliot said, "It's nice meeting you, Sir." His uncle's hand felt moist, almost slippery.

"Hello, Elliot, I'm Graham Swindale. It's nice having you in our home."

"Thank you, Sir, for having me here."

Elliot moved to his seat next to Aunt Elsie and sat.

"Have you met everyone?" Graham asked.

"We haven't been formally introduced," Tina said.

Elliot looked at her. She was beautiful, just as Aunt Elsie had said. Her blond hair was pulled back from her face and her dark green eyes were startling. Her lips were full and soft looking.

Harriet said, "Elliot, this is my daughter, Tina."

"Hello," Elliot said. He watched as she glanced at him briefly, then looked away as she said, "It's nice having you here, Elliot."

Then Elliot heard his uncle say, "What bedroom have you given him?"

Elliot noticed Tina begin to smile as she glanced up at him.

"I thought he might enjoy it more if he were on his own. I suggested the apartment next to Charles," Harriet replied as she rang the silver bell.

Elliot watched his uncle as he took his napkin from the silver holder and placed the smooth linen on his lap. His hands shook. Elliot wondered what was wrong with him.

"How does that suit you, Elliot?" Mr. Swindale asked.

"What, Sir?" Elliot asked, missing the question.

Wouldn't you know it, Graham thought, this boy is just like my son, Arnold. He doesn't listen either.

"Does the idea of the apartment suit you?" Graham repeated.

"Oh, yes, Sir, just fine. I've never had a place all to myself. And the apartment is just the right size."

Marny entered with five salads, placing them before each of the family. Elliot's salad had more tomatoes and celery than the rest of them.

"I'm glad you like it," Graham continued. Then, as he looked at the empty chair, he inquired, "Has anyone seen Arnold?"

He looked at his wife, but she had already picked up her fork and resisted looking toward him.

"He wasn't at dinner last night either," Graham announced to everyone at the table.

"Or the night before that," Tina said.

"Well, has anybody heard from him?" his father asked.

Elliot waited, but he could see that he was the only one who knew where Arnold was. "He was asleep up at my place, when I left him. Charles was going to see him to his room."

"At your place? How long has he been there?" Harriet asked.

"I think it was since about one this afternoon."

Marny bumped the swinging door open with her hip. She was carrying a large tureen of her bouillabaisse, which she set in the center of the table.

"Who told Arnold where you were?" Harriet asked Elliot.

"I don't know. He just showed up at the screen door."

"I told him," Marny interjected. "I fed him a sandwich, and then he wanted to know where to find his cousin. That boy looked terrible, but he said he was alright."

The family was quiet as she returned to the kitchen. She came back immediately, carrying a large bowl of steamed vegetables setting them near Elliot's side of the table.

"Did you make the garlic bread with the bouillabaisse?" Tina asked.

"Yes, honey, it's coming. And I made a special zucchini bread that my mamma used to make."

"Zucchini bread?" Tina said petulantly. "It sounds terrible."

"My mamma said it was the healthiest bread in the world for you. Keeps everything moving proper like." With that, Marny was gone.

"Whatever made her fix something like that?" Harriet asked.

As the family began to eat, Aunt Elsie interrupted. "Elliot, will you say grace?"

Everybody stopped and looked at Elliot. He had not picked up any silverware yet, and he had his hands folded in front of him.

"I've never said the blessing out loud before," he replied to his great aunt.

"I'd like to hear it," the old woman said. "My father used to say it."

Elliot closed his eyes. The rest of the family followed suit.

"Father, we thank you for this food. We ask a blessing upon the cook, Marny, and her family. Thank you for this time when this family joins together to eat your food, Lord. We thank you for all you give us, in Jesus' name."

During the meal, Elliot really enjoyed the zucchini bread. Elsie and he were the only ones who ate it. His Uncle and Aunt tried a little piece but returned to the French bread. Tina wouldn't even try it. Elliot found the bouillabaisse delicious. He wondered if three helpings would be too many. He didn't want to make a pig of himself, but he had them anyway.

The vegetables were cooked just right; Marny had put herbs on them that brought out the different flavors. Aunt Elsie was right; Marny was a great cook. Tina commented on the vegetables, saying they were not cooked enough, but everyone else ate them without comment.

During the meal a silence came over the table and the Swindales ate their meal without conversation. It was almost as if there should have been a plaque on the wall stating, "No Talking While Eating". But the silence didn't bother Elliot since St. Maurice's had followed the same policy, "Eat, don't talk".

After the meal, when Elliot had said goodnight to Mr. and Mrs. Swindale, Aunt Elsie asked if he would walk her to her rooms. As Elsie took his arm, Harriet said, "If you would like to learn the rest of the machines, Elliot, I begin my workout at nine in the morning."

"Thank you, Mrs. Swindale. I'll be there," Elliot replied as he and Aunt Elsie left the room.

Tina waited until the door had shut behind them. "What was that about?" she asked, turning to her mother.

"He was interested in the weight room. He worked out a little this morning."

Tina looked closely at her mother, "What's with that kid?"

"What do you mean?"

"Aunt Elsie is treating him like a son, and you're working out with him."

"So?" Harriet asked. "The boy is really interested in working out."

Tina looked at her mother, deciding against saying anything further. She glanced at her father, but as usual, he didn't seem interested in what was being said. He was nibbling at his food, not really eating much. She got up from the table.

"Why don't you work out with us?" Harriet asked.

"It's boring."

"Not when you look in the mirror and see the results," Harriet answered.

"My mirror looks fine," her daughter said as she left the room.

"You won't be nineteen forever," Harriet muttered to herself. Then she looked at the other end of the table.

"Graham, maybe you should have a talk with Arnold. I've asked him over and over again to be here for supper."

"I think you're right. It's time I talked to him," Graham responded.

Harriet watched her husband as he once again went back to pecking at his food. How many times had she asked him to talk to their son? He always said he would but never did.

When Elliot and Aunt Elsie stopped to rest on the landing of the staircase, Elsie said, "When we went to see Bill Bryant, your dad's lawyer... when we found out about you, Bill told me that you weren't a Catholic."

"That's right," Elliot answered.

"I know why your dad did that, why he told the school not to convert you."

"Why?"

"When he was young, in his teens, he used to say to me, 'A man should be able to make up his own mind about everything, even his own religion'."

Elliot thought about that. "I agree with him," he said finally.

Elsie laughed and said, "I thought you would."

As they started up the remainder of the stairs, the old lady continued, "Does that mean you won't be going to church now?"

"No," Elliot responded quickly, "but I would like to find a church where I understood the words."

Elsie nodded, amused. "I always felt that our family liked not being able to understand. Then we didn't have to get involved."

"Do Mr. and Mrs. Swindale go to church?"

"Yes, but they go to late Mass. He's not good about getting up early."

Elliot thought for a moment. "What does Mr. Swindale do?"

"You mean for a job?"

"Yes, ma'am."

"Graham's a writer," she replied. After thinking about it for a moment, she added, "Yes, he says he's a writer. Until five years ago, Graham was the president of Reed Industries, with your father as chairman of the board. Bertrand got him out."

"Why did he do that?"

"I guess he felt Graham wasn't doing the job. Bertrand took over as both chairman and president. He must have been right in doing it. In the past five years, he added millions to the company."

"Does Mr. Swindale drink?"

"It shows doesn't it?" she answered. Elliot kept silent.

"Yes," Elsie continued, "he drinks, and that was probably one of the reasons he was pushed out. But whatever the cause, Harriet never forgave your father." Elsie stopped on a stair, looked down to make sure no one was listening, then continued. "Strange, when Harriet was little, all she could talk about was her brother Bertrand this, Bertrand that. She wanted to be with him all of the time. When he went away to college, she cried for hours. He had to call her every night. Whenever he would come home, she seemed to come alive. But all that changed." Elsie leaned on Elliot's arm, and they walked the rest of the way to her room. "I think Harriet expected to marry someone like your father," she said, as Elliot opened the door for her. She motioned for him to enter too and shut the door behind them.

"When your father married Susan, Harriet didn't even want to go to the wedding."

"Wasn't she already married to Uncle Graham?"

"Yes, for four years."

"I don't understand."

"By that time, she had found out that Graham wasn't like she thought he should be."

"That he wasn't like my father?"

Then Elliot's great aunt smiled mysteriously at him and said, "You see, Harriet ignored Bertrand's dark side, never wanted to see <u>all</u> of her brother. Everybody has a dark side. Did you know that?"

Elliot nodded in agreement and said, "`Sinful from the time our mother's conceived us."

"Yes! That's the truth! Harriet still doesn't know that!" Elsie said excitedly. "How did you know?"

"David. That's what David said."

"David who?"

"King David...from the Bible. After he committed adultery with Bathsheba, he found out what sinner's we all are."

"Well, he was certainly right!" she said as she patted her nephew's hand. "Where did he say that...in the Bible?"

Elliot could see that she was getting tired. He led her over to her chair by the window. "In the fifty-first psalm," Elliot said as he seated her.

"That's a good thing to know, young man," she remarked. "When you understand that, you don't have to get surprised by what people do. Hmmm... Fifty-first psalm."

Elliot nodded in agreement, then asked, "Is there anything I can get you before I go?"

"You've already given me that, a chance to talk."

"We'll do it again," Elliot replied.

"Good night, young man," she said. "I hope you find a church." She had already planned on adding that to her prayer list.

Once downstairs, Elliot went to the kitchen, planning on going through the back yard to the garages. Marny was cutting some homemade bread, and Arnold was sitting at the breakfast nook in the corner. He looked better now, having showered and changed clothes.

"Hey, Elliot, what's happening?" he said with a wave.

"Hi, Arnold," Elliot answered. "How are you feeling?"

"Better. Sleep sure helps. I really had three wild days. Party, party, party."

Marny placed a filled plate in front of him, with a glass of milk. Arnold didn't take time to say thank you, but just went right into the top sandwich. As Marny walked back to the sink, she rolled her eyes, letting it be known to Elliot what she thought about Arnold's parties.

"Hey," he said with a mouthful, "all we got is three more weeks before the grind starts. Got to get the most out of it. Isn't that right?" he asked Elliot.

"What grind?"

"School, man! P..r..i..s..o..n!"

Elliot found the boy strange, not only in his choice of words, but also in the way he moved. It was as though all of his movements had been practiced. Nothing seemed spontaneous, or relaxed, even though that was probably what Arnold was trying to produce.

"Hey, you want to go out tonight?" Arnold continued.

"No, I don't think so."

"You got a car?"

"No, I don't drive."

"Really? Why the hell not?"

"I never needed to go anywhere."

Arnold thought about that for a moment. "Hey, that's right. You've been in the same place your whole life! Jesus, that's too much."

Elliot winced at the way Arnold used the Lord's name. Though he had heard it vilified many times at the school, there was something different about the way his cousin did it. Elliot turned and went over to Marny.

"Thanks for the dinner, Marny. Aunt Elsie said you were a great cook. That's the best meal I've ever had."

"Watch out, youngster. I'll make you fat."

"You could do it, too," he retorted with a laugh. With that, he said goodnight to both of them and left by the back door.

Arnold watched him through the window. "Man, that guy is weird. I mean, weird."

Marny listened to Arnold. She finally realized, that in part, she agreed with him. Elliot was weird! He didn't act like any seventeen-year-old boy she had ever met! She laughed out loud, and said to Arnold, "You know, you're right. That boy is weird!"

Arnold smiled and said, "Right on!" It was the first time Marny had ever agreed with anything he had to say.

Tina woke early, much too early for her. She tried to go back to sleep, but she couldn't. She stretched and yawned, thinking how she never really liked Sundays because there was nothing to do. Mother had suggested that they go shopping together this afternoon. Maybe that would be a good time to tell her about not going back to college. Throwing the covers off, she got up and looked out of the window. Another nice day, maybe she would drive over to her friend Donna's house. Her parents were away on vacation...

Then Tina saw Elliot Reed going toward the pool. He was wearing his swimming trunks and had a towel over his shoulders. Oh my God, she thought, look at him!

He put the towel on the lawn, then went over to the deep end and tested the water with his foot. He stepped back and did some stretching with his arms over his head as far as he could. Tina caught her breath. He was beautiful! She had always thought that Alex was well built, but this boy. Oh, God, was he something!

During his stretching exercises, he spread his legs apart and bent forward, grabbing his ankles. It looked as though his back might just pop. She watched as he came out of his bend and moved to the side of the pool and drove in. There was just the slightest ripple where he entered the water. She watched as he swam underwater, coming up at the shallow end. Then he pushed off and began swimming laps, just as he had the other morning.

Tina hurriedly put on her makeup, slipped into a bathing suit, one that brought men to their knees, checked herself in the mirror, and headed for the pool. She had suddenly decided that today was a good day to work on her tan.

Elliot didn't notice her until she was already at the side of the pool, seated in a lounge chair. He was only on his twenty-fifth lap and as he made his turn, he saw her. She was reading a magazine. He stopped his swim, thinking that he should at least be polite.

"Good morning," he said.

She looked up from her reading and smiled. "Hello. How's the water?"

"It's a little warm, but good."

He watched as she got up from the chair and made her way to the side of the pool. Suddenly, Elliot knew that he shouldn't be watching his cousin. She was beautiful, and the bathing suit she had on was much too revealing. He felt a slight tightness in his stomach as she bent over in front of him and touched the water with her hand.

He pushed off the bottom and started swimming again. He knew that whatever she was doing, she was doing on purpose, for some reason she was showing herself off to him. He knew she didn't care anything about the temperature of the water.

He increased his kick and surged forward, putting all his effort and concentration into the water. He continued lap after lap, not looking at her, closing his eyes as he turned his head for breathing. Though he didn't want it, the image of her striking figure came into his mind. For the first time, he was sorry that he retained images so well.

Tina stood at the edge of the pool, watching him cut through the water. She noticed that he would not look at her. She smiled, as she thought to herself; "What do you know? I'm not bored anymore." She left the pool and went up to her room.

A rather unusual thought went through her mind. Elliot and she were first cousins. If they slept together, it would be incest. The thought stopped her. She stood still before her mirror, looking at herself, finding that the idea excited her. She didn't try to reject the notion, but mused over it. She began contemplating what it might be like. And what made it all the more tempting to think about was, she knew he was a virgin. About this she was sure. She began feeling a little giddy. Ummm, this was much better than boredom!

Elliot made sure that he completed his swimming long before eight. He wanted to be sure that he wasn't late for the workout with Mrs. Swindale. He went back to his apartment, changed into his old workout shorts and a sweatshirt with the sleeves cut off at the shoulders. He ran into the main house and saw that the kitchen was empty. He helped himself to a few pieces of fruit and some cereal.

He was waiting by the door to the workout room when Harriet came down the hallway. She was dressed in another pretty sweat outfit.

"Good morning, Elliot."

"Good morning, ma'am."

"I saw you in the pool this morning. You must get up quite early."

"Yes, ma'am. I like the early mornings."

He opened the door for her, and they went in the workout room.

"I like to use the bicycle first. A good warm up," Harriet said. "How many laps do you do in the pool?"

"Sixty-five," Elliot said as he looked at the pull machine designed for the back area. He had never seen such beautiful machines.

"Sixty-five?" she exclaimed.

"Yes, ma'am."

"And you still feel like working out?"

"I've been swimming that distance since I was twelve. You get used to it." He turned and looked at her. "Would it be all right if I used this one? It's for the arms and back, right?"

"Yes," she replied. "You sit on the bench and draw the bar down behind your neck. It mainly works the shoulders and the back."

Elliot went behind the machines and checked the weight that was on it. Fifty pounds. That was a lot for a woman as small as his aunt.

"Do you work with fifty pounds?" he asked.

"Yes."

"That's a lot. You're strong."

"I'm getting there," she answered, pleased at the complement.

Elliot moved the metal peg to one hundred and thirty pounds. He sat down and took hold of the chrome bar over his head. Slowly and evenly, he pulled down until the bar was directly behind his neck. Slowly he let the bar go back to its original position. Harriet marveled at his strength.

The two of them worked out for over an hour. Harriet showed him how to work each machine and watched as he used each machine aggressively. She found that she liked having someone to work with, even though they didn't talk much.

When he was about halfway through his workout, Harriet noticed he took off his sweatshirt. She slowly closed her eyes, knowing that looking at a body that beautiful had to be a sin. She set in her mind that in the future, she would get used to this. That's all there was to it!

That afternoon, while Elliot was writing a note to Sister Teresa, Charles showed up at his door. Both of his arms were filled with bags of groceries.

"Hello, hello," he greeted through the screen.

Elliot went quickly to the door and opened it for him. Charles came in and headed for the kitchen. Elliot followed.

"Well, look what you've done to this place!" Charles exclaimed as he opened the fridge and started putting things away. Elliot started to help him. "No, lad, you go down to the Rolls. There are six more bags to bring up."

After they had stocked the kitchen, Charles smiled at Elliot and said, "Well, are you ready for your first driving lesson?"

"Yes, Sir," Elliot said quickly, "What do we do?"

"Well, since it's Sunday, and the roads are filled with cars, we'll have to go someplace where there is a lot of room and no cars.

"Where would that be?"

"How would you like to see Laurelwood High School," Charles asked with a smile.

"I'd like to," Elliot responded enthusiastically.

"We'll do more than that! I will personally introduce you to the parking lot."

Once there, Charles found that he was very nervous. He had never dreamt he would ever let anyone else drive the Rolls, let alone some teenager. But here he was, on the surface of the large empty parking lot, getting out of the driver's seat, walking around the back of the car, changing places with Elliot. Elliot walked around the back too. They passed each other at the trunk. Charles could see that Elliot was nervous as well. Both got in, feeling unaccustomed to their new positions.

With a sigh, Charles said, "I have been in this car for almost thirty years, and this is the first time I ever sat in this seat."

"Maybe we shouldn't do this," Elliot said, looking at all the dials and stuff on the dash before him.

"No," Charles said quietly, "I didn't say it for that reason. I was just stating what I felt was a very unusual situation."

"I agree," Elliot, answered, "I feel unusual too."

There was a moment of silence before Charles felt he had to push on with the task at hand.

"I think that the first thing we both must do, is to forget that this car is worth well over a hundred thousand dollars."

Shocked, Elliot could only turn and look at him. He suddenly felt that he shouldn't even touch anything.

Then Charles smiled and said dryly, "Then again, why should we worry when neither one of us own it?"

Elliot tried to laugh, but just couldn't bring himself to do it. Charles felt the same.

Charles explained all the parts and dials before the lad, what they were for and what happened when they were not used properly. Since the shift was automatic, Elliot was soon moving up and down the parking lot, becoming more and more familiar with each run.

Charles relaxed somewhat as he observed that Elliot learned quickly and that he respected the car as much as he did. After an hour of practicing, Charles had Elliot stop the car. Then Charles opened the door, got out, and moved into the back seat.

"Now, Elliot, I want you to drive me around the parking lot," Charles said, acting somewhat like the owner might.

Elliot, not to be outdone, said, "In which direction, Sir?"

"I think clockwise would be best."

"Certainly, Sir."

"Then after a while, depending upon the way I feel, we might go counter-clockwise."

"As you wish, Sir," Elliot replied, as they moved slowly forward.

Soon Elliot had his learner's permit, and they took to the streets. Charles taught him the rules of the road, and they practiced the different types of parking. Elliot learned quickly and soon became comfortable driving in traffic.

One morning, when Elliot had finished his jogging and was waiting for Charles to begin his lesson, he saw a Jeep coming down the driveway. It went past the house and headed for the garage. Elliot saw that Charles was driving. Charles pulled up in his beautiful suit and his silk tie, with his hair blown all over his head. He looked so out of place that Elliot couldn't help but laugh.

"What is it?" Charles asked.

"Nothing," Elliot answered, losing control again.

Charles waited until the young man stopped laughing. "Get in," he commanded.

"Where did you get this?" Elliot asked as he got into the passenger's seat.

"I rented it," Charles replied. "What I want you to do is watch my hands and my feet. This type of driving is not so easy, but it can be lots of fun." Then, as he put the Jeep into low gear and drove down the driveway, he added, "He who laughs last, laughs best."

Wondering what he was going to do, Elliot did as he was told and watched every move that Charles made. The chauffeur drove to the local mall, where he parked in an empty section of the huge parking lot and got out.

"Drive it around the parking lot," he directed Elliot.

"Aren't you going with me?" Elliot asked as he got into the driver's seat.

"No, I'll watch. But I will give you a hint." He pointed to the stick shift and said, "Do you see those numbers on the handle of the shift?"

"Yes, Sir."

"That's the order and direction of each shift."

Elliot looked down and saw that it matched what he had seen Charles do. It didn't look that hard. He moved the gearshift down and to the left. It made a terrible sound.

"Ah, don't forget to use your feet. The left foot is for the clutch."

Elliot had forgotten about that part. He put in the clutch and shifted down. No noise, smooth this time. He pressed on the gas. The motor went faster, but he didn't move.

"Your other foot!" Charles called over the roar of the motor. Elliot let go of the clutch, and the auto leapt forward. Elliot was almost thrown out of the front seat. Then the Jeep stalled. Elliot sat there, stunned. Now it was Charles's turn to laugh.

Elliot was getting used to the Jeep and liked the idea of the open cockpit. Charles had purchased a baseball hat and sat next to Elliot as they drove from neighborhood to neighborhood with Elliot becoming more and more confident.

The day before Elliot was to go down to take his written test, an unusual event took place as he was practicing driving. He came up to a stop sign and made his stop. To the right, on the far corner was the small church he had looked at during his first jog some weeks ago. Though it was now a weekday, the front doors to the little building were open. Elliot made a turn and drove slowly by the front of it. He tried to see inside.

"What is it?" Charles asked.

"It's a little church," Elliot said, still trying to look inside of it.

"I can see that," Charles retorted. "My question was directed at you."

"The first day I jogged, I saw this church. It was closed up then," Elliot answered as he picked up speed and went around the block. Once again he brought the jeep to a halt in front of the church.

"Somebody has fixed the gate," Elliot said.

"That's nice," Charles said, as he looked at Elliot. He watched the boy get out of the driver's seat and go around the back of the jeep.

"What are you doing?" Charles asked.

"I'll just be a minute," Elliot answered. He opened the little gate and walked up to the front porch. He walked inside. It didn't seem dark now, as it had the first time. The windows had been washed and the place smelled of cleaner and wax. Not noticing Elliot's entrance, a woman was industriously rubbing the base of the pulpit.

"Hello," Elliot said.

The woman looked up quickly, shielding her eyes because whoever had called out was standing in the brightness coming from the open doors.

"Hello?" she questioned.

"I'm sorry, I didn't mean to startle you."

"It's all right," she answered, sweeping hair back from her face.

"Is the church going to open?"

"Yes," she said, still only seeing the outline of the person standing there.

"Good," Elliot said. "I thought it was supposed to be open. Do you know when?"

"Well, we're not sure, but we hope in two or three weeks," Geri Lindquist replied. "Do you live around here?"

"No, ma'am," the voice replied. "Thank you. I hope I didn't frighten you."

"No, that's all right," she said. Then she watched as the figure disappeared out the door and down the steps.

He sounded young, Geri thought, but she knew that she would never recognize him if he ever showed up again. She went back to her cleaning, wondering what had gotten all over the base of the old pulpit.

The next day, the day that Elliot was supposed to take his tests for the driver's license, Charles knocked on his apartment door. Elliot had finished his run and was getting ready to swim.

"Hi, Charles," Elliot said as he was getting his towel.

"Would you mind missing your swimming today?" the chauffeur asked.

"No, that would be all right. What's happened?"

"Well, it's a little strange, but Mrs. Elsie wants to go with us when you take your driving tests."

Elliot thought this was strange, but he didn't think he should ask about it.

"Well, O.K., but it's not for three hours. My time at the DMV is at eleven-thirty."

"She would like to leave as soon as you're ready. Would that be all right with you?"

"Well, sure. I'll change then."

Elliot and Charles pulled up in front of the house in the Rolls. Elsie was standing on the front porch, waiting. Elliot got out of the front seat, opened the back door for Aunt Elsie, and helped her in. Elliot ran around to the other door and sat beside her. Charles drove off the estate.

"Are you ready for your written test?" Aunt Elsie asked.

"Yes, ma'am, I studied what they gave me," Elliot answered.

"Good," Elsie said as she touched Elliot's hand to get his attention and winking at him. Then she said, a little louder than usual, "It's all right if you miss one of the questions, Elliot. You don't have to get them all correct. Even Charles misses them some times."

From the front seat came, "That was eighteen years ago, Mrs. Elsie, and it was only one question. If you remember, they had changed a law and neglected to put it in the brochure. In retrospect, you could say that my mistake was really caused by bureaucratic negligence."

Elsie giggled and whispered to Elliot as she took hold of his hand, "I will never let him forget that one. Each time I mention it, his excuse gets more and more complicated."

"We're going to be really early, Aunt Elsie." Elliot said.

"We'll have to be very careful not to be late," she replied enigmatically.

Three weeks previously, when Charles had taken Elliot to get his learner's permit, Elliot hadn't paid any attention to direction. So now, as they were going to take his test, he had no idea where the DMV office was. The car stopped in front of the local Jeep dealership.

"We're here, Ma'am," Charles said.

Elliot looked across the street from the car lot, thinking that the DMV would be there. He could only see a McDonald's and a used car lot.

"Thank you, Charles," Elsie said, as she pressed the button for the tinted window next to her. As the window slid down, she pointed and asked Elliot, "Which one do you like?"

Elliot looked out and saw that they had pulled right alongside the showroom. Inside, standing between two brand new Jeeps, was a man in a suit who seemed to be smiling towards the Rolls. On one side of him was a black Jeep Cherokee, while on the other was a white four-wheeler convertible with roll bar and slightly oversized tires on chrome wheels.

"Which Jeep do I like?" Elliot asked, not understanding what was going on.

"Yes," Elsie replied, "which one?"

"Oh, the white one. It's a beauty," Elliot responded, still not understanding what Elsie's intentions were.

"Good for you," she said. Then she stuck her hand out of the car and pointed at the white one. The man standing between the two vehicles misunderstood and pointed to the black one. Elsie pointed the other way and then the man acknowledged her, also pointing to the white one. She rolled up the window.

"We'll wait here for you," she said.

"What do you mean?" Elliot asked.

Elsie reached into her purse and brought out an envelope. "You give this to the man who waved at us, and he'll give you your car."

Elliot looked at Elsie, then at the envelope in his hand, then toward the front seat at Charles. Charles had turned and was smiling back at Elliot.

"It's always best to do what she says," Charles said quietly.

"Aunt Elsie, this is a wonderful present. Thank you."

"I'm glad you like it," she said with a smile.

"She likes to watch people's faces when she gives them things," Charles said. "So did her husband. You should have seen her face when he gave her this car."

Elliot smiled, even though there were tears in his eyes.

"She cried too," Charles added.

"Thank you, Aunt Elsie. Thank you for everything, for the car, for being my friend, for everything."

"You're welcome," the old lady replied. They hugged each other, and Elliot got out of the car. He went into the showroom and handed the salesman the envelope.

The salesman opened it and took a check out of it. He saw the address on it, and said, "Wow, what a great way to buy a car."

"How did you know to be there like you were?" Elliot asked.

"Yesterday I got a call from a lady," the salesman said. "She said to me, `Do you have any pretty Jeeps?' I laughed and said, `Sure, lady, come on down and see.'"

"Then she said to me, `would you please put two of your prettiest in the showroom, and I'll come down tomorrow at nine."

"Now, I think this is a put-on, so I said, `How will I know you, honey?'"

"Then she said to me, `I'll be in a dark Rolls Royce, and I'll pull right up in front of the showroom.'" The salesman shrugged his shoulders, smiled at Elliot, and said, "Who would have thought it. Come on. I'll have the papers drawn up in no time."

Forty minutes later, Elliot walked out to the Rolls with the signed papers in his hand. Opening the back door, he said to Aunt Elsie, "It's all done."

"Good," she said, as she lifted her hand to him.

"Are you getting out?" Elliot asked.

"Certainly. You're not supposed to drive alone until you get your license, are you?" Aunt Elsie said, as she got slowly from the car.

"No, ma'am. Are you going to ride in the Jeep with me?"

By this time, Charles had gotten out from behind the wheel and had made his way to Elliot and Elsie.

"May I remind you, Mrs. Elsie, that you don't have a license," Charles said. "Elliot is supposed to drive with someone who knows how to drive."

"I will act like I have a license. I'm too old for anyone to question me."

"Aunt Elsie, the top isn't up on the Jeep," Elliot said.

Elsie smiled and opened her purse. She took out a clear plastic hat with flowers on it. She unfolded it and placed it on her head. "I thought of that," she said.

She did look comical. Elliot and Charles both smiled as she stood there smiling back at the two of them.

So, Aunt Elsie sat next to Elliot as the Jeep followed the Rolls to the DMV. One hour later, Elliot, temporary license in hand, drove back to the house by himself. Elliot noticed, as he followed the Rolls home, that Aunt Elsie had forgotten to take the plastic hat off as she sat in the back of the Rolls.

* * *

Harriet wondered why her daughter had come to her bedroom. As Harriet showered after her workout, her daughter made small talk, something about a skirt that didn't fit correctly and that she would have to take back, just small talk. Harriet decided to remain quiet until her daughter got down to the real reason why she was there. She never came to Harriet's room like this unless there was something she wanted.

"You don't seem to be very talkative," Tina finally said.

Harriet turned from her makeup table and looked at her daughter. She looked at the beautiful creature sitting on her bed and wondered why they had grown so unaccustomed to each other's company. She knew that her daughter wasn't here to just "talk". Those days of close companionship had stopped when Tina started wearing bras.

"What is it, Honey? What do you want?"

"I just thought it would be good if we talked sometimes," Tina said, as she moved to her mother's mirror.

"Uh-huh," her mother said as she deftly drew her eyebrow.

Tina had always appreciated the way her mother wore makeup. She remembered when her mother had taught her, and how she had made Tina pay close attention to every nuance. Tina glanced in the mirror, over her mother's head, at her own face. She wondered what she would look like when she was fifty. She saw that her mother had stopped filling in her brows and was watching her watch herself.

What the hell, Tina thought. "I've decided not to go back to college."

Tina saw that certain frown that would begin between her mother's eyes. Then her mother turned and looked directly at her. "You're supposed to go back Monday, aren't you?"

"Yes, but I'm not going."

"Your grades were passing last year; what's the matter?"

"I don't know what I'm doing there! I have no interest and everything bores me."

"You get bored wherever you are. Don't you know that?"

"That's not true!" Tina answered quickly, knowing that her mother was right. She knew it was true.

"What about Alex? Have you told him?"

"Yes, I told him."

"What did he say?"

"It really doesn't matter what he says. He doesn't run my life."

"Is he boring you too?"

The conversation was not going the way Tina wanted it to. She moved over to the bed and looked at a magazine her mother had been reading. It was on health and diet. What a bore!

"What do you plan on doing instead?" her mother asked.

"I'm not sure," Tina replied. She knew this wasn't the kind of answer her mother wanted to hear.

"All your friends will be back in school. If you think you're bored now, wait until there's no one else around."

"Maybe that's what I need," Tina said. She wondered what made her say that? Her mother looked over at her with a strange smile. "What you need, you should have had when you were eight!" Harriet said, then added, "I don't know if I want you around here all winter, doing nothing."

"Why not? Do you want to be alone?" Tina asked quietly.

Her mother stopped and looked at her questioningly. "What is that supposed to mean?"

"I just wondered why I would be in the way."

"I didn't say you would be in the way. I said I didn't know if I wanted you here, moping around, always telling me how bored you are."

"And you're not bored?" Tina said. She wondered if she wasn't onto something.

"No, I'm not. I keep busy," Harriet answered. She was beginning to understand why she and her daughter didn't talk to each other anymore. Tina was a pain.

"Maybe I wouldn't be bored if I started working out...with the two of you," Tina said, looking up at the ceiling.

Harriet glanced at her daughter. What did she mean by that, she wondered? "Well, it might help," her mother, said, "At least you would sleep better at nights."

"You wouldn't mind?" Tina asked.

"Mind? Two years ago, I asked you to work out with me. Do you remember what you said?"

"No."

"You told me it was too boring."

"I have a feeling it's not boring now."

"We start at nine o'clock," her mother said.

"I'll set my alarm," Tina said sweetly.

"I want you to tell your father what you've decided about school," her mother said as she got up from the makeup table and went into her dressing room.

"Daddy?" Tina said, surprised. "He doesn't care what I do, and you know it."

She came back out of the dressing room. "After two o'clock, today, I want you to go down to that library and tell him. And I don't want any arguments," Harriet ordered.

"All right," Tina said impatiently, "but it won't make any difference."

"Just do it," Harriet said, irritated at her daughter's laziness. She disappeared into her dressing room. As far as she was concerned, the discussion was over.

Tina got up and left the room. She had decided to start working out. Elliot got up too early in the mornings for her to be down at the pool to see him. This would be much easier, even though she might have to expend some energy. Besides, she wanted to see him up close.

She went to her room and called Alex. They were to have a date tonight, and she wanted to know where she was being taken.

"Hello?" Mrs. Alexander answered.

"Hello, Mrs. Alexander," Tina said, "Is Alex there?"

"Sure, Hon," Alex's mother said. Tina heard her call to her son, telling him that she was on the phone.

"Hi," Alex said. Tina waited until she heard the "click" of the other phone.

"Hi. Where are we going tonight?" she asked.

"How about a movie?" Alex said.

"That's not very creative," she said, wanting to do something a little different.

"What did you have in mind?"

She always got irritated when he asked her where she wanted to go. She liked the guy to make that decision. "That's up to you. You know I like to be surprised."

"O.K., I'll think of something else," he said.

"When you do call me up and tell me how I should dress."

"Then it won't be a surprise," Alex said, amused.

"You don't have to tell me specifically, just generally, so I'll know a little bit," Tina said. God, she thought, sometimes she even sounded dopey to herself.

"I know what you can do," Alex said, almost laughing. "Why don't you pack a suitcase, then you'll be ready for anything."

"Alex, that's not funny!" she retorted angrily. She was almost irritated enough to cancel the date, but then what would she do?

"Alright, alright, I'll call you," Alex said soothingly, knowing that she couldn't take kidding. He heard the click in his ear, then the dial tone. She was angry, he thought. He knew that she would make him pay for that remark.

He stood up and stretched his huge body. It was difficult, he thought, to be in love with a spoiled brat. Sometimes he felt like putting her over his knee and spanking that pretty behind of hers, but he knew that would most probably put an end to their relationship.

Maybe it's better that she's not coming back to the college, he thought as he went back to his weight lifting. I can find someone else. He almost laughed out loud at this thought. Who was he kidding? He'd had other girls at the school fall all over him, and he didn't care about any of them. He loved the little brat, and he ached every time he was away from her. Now he would have to travel home on weekends just because **she** was bored. And the coaches said they didn't like the players traveling weekends during football season. Now what excuse was he going to give to them?

* * *

As her mother had ordered, it was just after two in the afternoon when Tina knocked gently on the library door. She waited only a few moments before she opened the door.

"Daddy?" Tina said. He sat in front of his computer.

"Hi, Honey," he answered. "Come in, come in."

Tina entered and shut the door behind her.

The library, in years past, had been a place of mystery and had captivated her. When she was very little, and her father had been working in an office, she would quietly come in and sit in one of the long leather couches that were positioned back-to-back in the center of the room. Since she had been told not to touch the books, she would sit looking around her at the hundreds upon hundreds of books and wondering what was in them? Once, when someone had left the stairs down to the walkway that traversed three walls of the room, she had climbed up them. But just as she had gotten up on the walkway and was looking at the spines of the books, she got caught, brought down and spanked. She was told that such a place was not safe for little girls.

But even the scolding had not prevented her from daydreaming about the library. She would still visit the large room, cautiously walking along the lower selves and looking at the ornately bound spine of each book, trying to read the titles, wondering what they were about.

What the spanking couldn't do, the passing of time did. Tina's interest faded, and she soon stopped coming into the large, beautiful room. After that, even her dreams stopped venturing into the place.

So now, as she walked across its hardwood floor, the youthful memories of the room had long since faded. She passed the two long leather couches and walked to the huge bay windows overlooking the front lawn. Her father had set up his computer near the windows. She stooped and kissed his cheek. She noticed that though the computer was running, the screen was blank.

"How are you, dear?" her father asked. As usual, Tina felt that he was really thinking about something else and not really interested in her answer.

"I'm fine, Daddy," Tina replied, looking down at his face. He didn't look well, she thought. But then as far as she could remember, he had always looked this way.

"Mom asked me to come in and see you."

"About what?" he asked, turning to face her.

"I've decided not to go back to school this semester."

"Oh? Why not?" he asked politely.

"I feel like I'm wasting my time. I really don't know what I'm doing there," she said as convincingly as she could.

"Maybe you just need some time off," Graham said, looking directly at her.

"That's what I told Mom," the surprised girl answered.

She had never understood her father's thinking. His answer sounded to her as if it was making it **his** idea that she was not going back.

"Well, good. What would you like to do instead?"

"I'm not sure yet," she answered, wondering what kind of a response that would bring.

"Well, as soon as you find out, you should let your mother know. So she won't worry."

My God, Tina thought. He's not even in this world. She bent down and kissed his cheek again.

"I will, Daddy, as soon as I find out."

"That's a good girl," Graham said as he patted her shoulder.

As she turned to leave, she looked over at the wet bar, which had an open bottle of vodka on top of it. She wondered where her father had hidden his glass. It must be in his desk, she thought. It had to be close to him, because there had only been a few moments between the time she knocked and opened the door.

"Bye, Daddy," she said, as she opened the door to leave.

"Bye, Honey," he replied, without turning. Though he was looking down at the computer, she noticed that his hands were lying limply in his lap.

* * *

Elliot drove the Jeep into the area in front of the garages. Arnold watched from his upstairs bedroom as his cousin got out of the new vehicle and stood admiring it. Arnold made sure that he could not be seen as he watched. Next, he saw Charles pull up in the Rolls, get out, and join Elliot in looking over the new Jeep. Elliot opened the hood. The two of them moved around the front of vehicle and looked down at the motor.

Why the hell does everybody do that when they buy a new_car? Arnold thought, looking down at them. Why do they just stand there, like they know what they're looking at? And then what do they do? They just close the hood!

Arnold watched as they did that very thing. Now that's stupid, he thought as he walked away from his window and put his headset over his ears. Turning up the volume of his stereo, he flopped down on his bed, promising himself that he would never talk to that jerk cousin of his again!

* * *

Monday morning, Arnold's intercom started buzzing, and he heard his mother's voice telling him to get up. He opened one eye and stared at the speaker on the wall. He hadn't heard that thing all summer! Oh, God, he thought, school!

Even though his mother had stopped talking, the intercom was still activated and continued buzzing. He knew she waited to hear his voice.

"All right, ma! I'm up!" Arnold called as he rolled over.

The buzzing continued for a moment, then his mother's voice said, "No, you're not. Elliot said he would give you a ride to school, but you had to be on time." The buzzing persisted. Arnold eyed the thing on the wall but said nothing.

"Well?" the voice of his mother said, "do you want a ride, or would you like to take the school bus with all the freshmen?"

"I want my own car, damn it!" Arnold retorted to the speaker.

"Your car is in the junk yard, and you have no license until June. Now get up," the voice said, and the speaker went dead.

Arnold got up. He hated that school bus. Every kid who was too young to drive had to take that thing to school. He looked at his face in the mirror. He needed a shave. He looked down at his electric razor.

The hell with it, he thought, I'll go the way I feel. He pulled on a pair of pants, found a shirt hanging in his closet, and put on a pair of loafers, neglecting socks. He went into his bathroom and examined his tongue in the mirror. As usual, it was coated with a grayish scum. As he stood there looking at it, he remembered when some dork had once told him that if your tongue looked like that, then your liver did too. What a bummer of a thing to tell someone! Arnold brushed his tongue until it looked somewhat pink.

When he got down to the kitchen, Marny had breakfast ready for him. She didn't say good morning to him because she knew how he hated to be talked to in the mornings, mostly when he had to get up early. He sat down, as she placed brown, steaming pancakes in front of him, his favorite. He prepared them, making sure that each bite would have plenty of butter and syrup on it.

"Did Elliot already eat?" Arnold asked Marny.

"Hours ago," she said. "He's waiting for you by the garages."

"What time is it?" he asked.

"Seven-fifteen," she replied with a smile.

"Seven-fifteen!" he hollered. "School doesn't start until eight!"

"Take the bus," she answered indifferently.

He wolfed the last two bites and headed for the back door.

"You want a lunch?" Marny dutifully asked.

"I'm not carrying a brown bag anywhere!" he hollered as he left the room. "Why do you always ask me that?" he hollered as he ran by the back window, not waiting for an answer.

"Because you always get hungry, and you never have any money, you dodo bird," Marny calmly answered as she took his syrup-covered plate from the table.

Elliot saw Arnold coming across the lawn. He was beginning to wonder if he hadn't made a mistake in offering to give Arnold a ride. Would he have to wait for him every day? Elliot started up the motor as Arnold jumped in beside him.

"To school, James!" Arnold said with feigned arrogance.

Elliot drove out the driveway, noticing Tina standing at her window. Arnold saw her too.

"God, I've never seen her up this early," Arnold said.

"Your mom told me that she was going to start working out with her," Elliot said.

"Tina's going to work out? Impossible! She doesn't even like to walk to her car," Arnold said as he noticed a large envelope between the two seats.

"What's this?" he asked curiously, picking it up.

"It's my transcript from St. Maurice."

Arnold, smiling, looked at Elliot. "You mean to tell me that they trust you to carry your grades to another school? They must be nuts!"

"Why? They didn't know where to send them, and they knew I'd need them," Elliot answered.

Arnold noticed that the manila envelope wasn't even sealed. He pretended to look inside then looked over at Elliot.

"Did you make any changes?" Arnold asked.

Elliot laughed, and said, "What for? What good would it do?"

"It could keep your ass out of trouble, that's what it could do. I'd like to have my transcript for about an hour!"

He looked at the envelope again, this time really opening it enough to look at the contents.

"Are you going to tear it?" Elliot asked.

"Not if you'd let me look at it," Arnold said slyly.

Smiling, Elliot said, "Go ahead, but be gentle."

Arnold pulled the copy from the envelope. There were three sheets attached to each other. He looked at the first sheet, then the second, and then the third.

"What the hell is this?" Arnold asked abruptly.

"What do you mean?" Elliot answered.

Arnold, pointing at the sheets, said, "Are these really your grades since you were five years old?"

"Yes," Elliot said, turning down the street in front of the school and driving to the end of the block for the entrance to the parking lot.

Arnold was silent as he placed the sheets back in the envelope and put it back where he had found it.

"What the hell are you anyway?" he finally said to Elliot.

His manner was strange, almost hostile. "Oh, yeah," Arnold scoffed as he turned to leave. "Who's next, my sister?"

Elliot could only watch as his cousin walked toward the campus. What had happened, Elliot wondered. Arnold looked at my grades, Elliot thought, and then became angry. What did the grades have to do with friendship? Elliot wondered if it would have made any difference if he had had C's and D's. Would that have made them friends? And what did Arnold mean about his sister? Elliot sighed, not knowing what to do about the situation. He picked up his records and walked toward the offices.

The Admissions office was packed with students. Elliot saw a cardboard sign overhead, which read, "TRANSFERS". That line only had two students in it, both young girls, who were possibly sophomores. The girl directly in front of Elliot, as she waited her turn, brushed her hair. Elliot gave her plenty of room as he watched the brush go through her thick, red hair. It was silky and shiny, very pretty head of hair.

The girl turned, nonchalantly looking around her as any sophomore girl might do. Her eyes met Elliot's clear, thoughtful gaze.

He smiled and said, "Very pretty."

"What?" the girl responded, blushing brightly.

"Your hair. It's very pretty," Elliot said.

"Thanks," the girl said, as she quickly turned forward, blushing even more. With that, she put her hairbrush back in her purse.

Maybe I shouldn't have said that, Elliot thought. I think I'm going to have to be more careful about the things I say. Maybe I'm not supposed to speak to young girls.

The redheaded girl got a slip of paper from the lady behind the counter and was directed to another window. She didn't look at Elliot as she left.

The woman behind the counter wore granny glasses. She looked at Elliot over the top of them.

"Hello," Elliot said as he handed her his envelope.

"Hi," she said, opening it. She looked at the three sheets for a moment. "This is your transcript?"

"Yes, ma'am," he answered.

She looked at it again. "You went to the same school since you were five?"

"Yes, ma'am."

"If you're carrying your own transcript, it's supposed to be sealed. Didn't you know that?"

"No, ma'am."

Then Elliot said, "I'm afraid my school didn't know it either." He was concerned about starting off wrong.

She searched his face for a moment, before glancing back to the pages before her. "And these are your grades?"

"Yes, ma'am."

Elliot could tell as they looked at each other that she was having a difficult time believing this. She momentarily glanced behind her, then turned and went into a private room. Before she closed the door behind her, Elliot briefly glimpsed a man sitting behind a desk. A few moments passed before the door opened. The woman again looked over her glasses at Elliot and motioned to him with her index finger. Elliot moved around the long counter and entered the room. The lady left, closing the door behind her.

The man behind the desk sat looking at Elliot's transcript. He was heavyset, with a lot of hair on the back of his hands. He looked strong but out of shape.

"St. Maurice's Military Academy," he said, still not looking at Elliot. Elliot waited. The man finally looked up at him.

"Were you taught by Sisters or Priests?"

"Sisters, Sir."

The man looked back down to the transcript. "And these are your grades?"

"Yes, Sir."

"You know that all we have to do is call the school, and they'll send another copy."

"Yes, Sir. Mother Superior said that if one copy wasn't enough they would be happy to send more."

The man stared at Elliot. Elliot looked back. Then the man said, "Does St. Maurice's have a wrestling team?"

"No, Sir."

"What about boxing?'

"No, Sir."

"Well, Elliot, my name is Mr. Sala. I teach Algebra and Trig." He paused, before saying, "You lift weights?"

"Yes, Sir."

"Nothing else?"

"Else?"

"What about steroids?"

Elliot thought a moment and replied, "I'm sorry, Sir, I don't know that word."

Mr. Sala looked at him closely for a moment. He believed him. "All right, Elliot," Sala said, "Mrs. Henley will set up an appointment for you to meet your counselor. Open the door for me will you?"

Elliot turned and opened it.

"Helen," Mr. Sala called so the woman could hear him.

The lady with the little glasses left the counter and came to the door of the office.

"Fix him up," Sala said, handing Elliot's transcript to her.

"Yes, Mr. Sala," she said as she went back to the counter. Elliot nodded at the teacher and returned to the counter.

Mrs. Meecham, Elliot's counselor, met with him the next hour. She looked at Elliot's grades and laughed. She had been counseling students for years, and she had never seen anything like this transcript.

"Well, well," she said, so impressed; she was unsure what direction she should take with this new student. "My, my!" she exclaimed as she looked back down at the flawless transcript. Through the years, she had always felt very protective toward any student, who had excelled, knowing, without doubt, that she had been given this job to protect "these few" against the ordinary.

She looked up at him, smiled and said jokingly, "What college did you have in mind?"

Elliot paused, thought about the question, then said, "I've never thought about it."

"You mean you're not going to college?" She was astonished.

"I'm not sure."

"There must be something that you'd like to study?"

Elliot thought about this for a moment. "It all depends on what I'm supposed to do."

"Supposed to do?"

"Yes. With my life."

"Isn't that what we're discussing?"

"Not really," he said with a smile. "We're talking about what I should study."

She wondered what this boy was talking about. She had other brilliant students who acted strangely, so she thought it best that she overlook these unconventional remarks.

"What would you like to study here?"

He thought about this too. "Whatever you have, will be all right."

She laughed, wondering if this could be his sense of humor. But by the look on his face, she saw that he might be serious. "Didn't St. Maurice's offer electives... optional classes?"

"No, ma'am," Elliot answered, "they told us what to study, and we did it."

"Well, here we give you choices. Since you have taken care of most of your electives...even trig and calculus, I see, and ...'hermeneutics'... What is that?"

"It's a branch of theology that studies the interpretation of Scripture," Elliot answered enthusiastically. "What classes do you have on the Bible?"

"This **public** school system doesn't have religious classes of any kind," Mrs. Meecham said coolly. Elliot saw her stiffen slightly.

"Oh?" Elliot said, "That's too bad. Well, I like all subjects. What would you suggest?"

She looked once again at his transcript, using the time once again to gain her composure. It had not been too long ago that she and the principal had a great deal of trouble with a few "spiritual" students, who wanted special permission to have Bible classes on campus.

"Well," she said, "you might like to learn something about computers and business. What about a class in statistics?"

"That sounds good," Elliot replied. "I would like to learn about computers. My uncle has one, and it might be a good way to get to know him."

What a strange thing to say, the counselor thought.

"As soon as you find out what you're going to do with your life, it might be advantageous to think about what college you might like to enter," she said with feigned solicitousness. "With your grades, you would be accepted anywhere."

Elliot thanked her and took the list of classes that she made up for him. He smiled and left her office. She sat there, wondering what there was about the boy that she didn't like. She came to the conclusion that it was his attitude. Even though he showed respect, she had still felt uncomfortable around him.

By the time Elliot left her office it was nearing the lunch hour. As he left the building, the bell sounded. He walked out to the parking lot to get his lunch. He had put the paper bag underneath the front seat. As he sat down in the Jeep and opened the bag, he heard a voice behind him.

"What do you think you're doing?"

He turned and saw a large black man wearing a guard's uniform, looking at him.

"I was going to eat my lunch," Elliot said.

The black man took a few steps towards the Jeep. "Is this your Jeep?"

"Yes, Sir."

"I've never seen it before. You're new, huh?"

"Yes. This is my first day."

"Have you enrolled?"

Elliot brought out the paper from his shirt pocket and handed it to the guard.

"Is this all they gave you?"

"Yes, Sir."

The black man shook his head and handed Elliot back his schedule. "They were supposed to give you another paper telling you the rules of the school. You aren't suppose to be in the parking lot during the lunch hour."

"Oh," Elliot said, immediately closing up his lunch and getting out of the jeep.

"You're supposed to eat on campus, not here."

"Yes, Sir," Elliot said as he walked towards the school.

Elliot went over to the office and got a sheet of the rules. He read them and found them simple to follow, even though they didn't give the reasons for what they asked.

Elliot decided that during lunch, until his fifth period class at one o'clock, he would go see the swimming pool and the track area, maybe finding a place to eat over there. As he walked through the school he came to an area filled with students. They were eating, sitting on benches, around tables, and on the lawn.

That was when he saw Rachel Davis.

She was sitting on the grass with three other girls. He saw her push her long brown hair over a shoulder as she talked to one of her friends. Even at this distance, she's prettier than I remember, Elliot thought. She was wearing a white blouse and a dark skirt and had her legs tucked under her.

Elliot couldn't help looking at her as he walked along the sidewalk. Then he saw her laugh. He found himself smiling, actually feeling happy that she was happy. Strange, he thought. He hadn't taken his eyes off of Rachel. Elliot wasn't aware that Trish Hillman, Rachel's best friend and one of the four sitting on the lawn, was watching him, this new boy, watching Rachel.

"Rachel," Trish said softly, "Rachel, someone is watching you."

Rachel stopped her conversation and turned to Trish, "What did you say?" she asked.

"I said, Someone is watching you."

Now all three of the girls were suddenly interested and turned in unison to look in the same direction as Trish.

"Oh, this is great, girls," Trish whispered self-consciously. "Why don't we all just stand up and point at him!"

Elliot noticed that three of the girls suddenly turned their heads and all four were now looking in his direction. He knew that one of them had caught him staring. He wondered what he should do? Was it all right to go over and talk to them, to explain why he had been staring?

"Oh, my gosh," Trish whispered, "Here he comes."

Elliot walked across the grass and stood before them.

"I'm sorry, I guess I was staring," Elliot said as he looked directly at Rachel. "It was just that I met your brother, Lance."

She had either brown or green eyes; Elliot wasn't sure from this distance. But he did know that at this moment, they were looking at him with concern, probably wondering what he was doing here. Rachel was so pretty; she made you forget what you were going to say.

"He helped me pick out some clothes over at the mall," Elliot continued, trying to find a way not to make her feel embarrassed. He was beginning to feel that he had made a mistake in going directly up to the girls.

"How did you know I was his sister?" Rachel finally asked. She had a nice voice, soft like, Elliot noticed.

"I saw you talking to him during his break at the mall, and I asked him who you were. It was a few weeks ago."

He could tell that she didn't know what to say. He was becoming aware he had put her in a very awkward position. He was certainly learning what **not** to do around girls.

"My name is Elliot Reed," he said, as he smiled and backed off a step or two. "I'm afraid I'm a little new at this. I think maybe I've embarrassed you, and I'm sorry." He looked at her friends, nodded, and said, "Sorry, girls."

Then he turned and walked back to the path and continued in the direction he had been going. Well! Elliot thought. That certainly was dumb! His stomach had turned into one large knot! He took a deep breath and let it out, but it didn't help. He shook his head in disbelief. He couldn't believe how badly he had messed this up! "Oh, Lord," he muttered to himself, "let me not be put to shame!"

All four of the girls watched as he walked away from them.

"Wow," Trish said quietly. "He's certainly hard to look at."

Dottie, the girl who Rachel had been laughing with, said, "Will you look at him!"

The other girl, Evelyn, said, "I'm trying not to!" as her gaze followed him.

"How come your brother never said anything about him?" Trish said, turning to Rachel. Rachel didn't answer.

All three of the girls looked at her, then back at Elliot on the path. There was a moment of silence as the girls continued to watch Elliot.

"What do you think he meant when he said, `I'm new at this'," Dottie asked? All the girls looked to Rachel for the answer. Rachel looked back at them and said, "I was so surprised, I can hardly remember a word he said!"

As the girls laughed, they took one more look at Elliot, who was now nearing the corner of the gym.

"I wonder if he's a Christian?" Trish asked.

"No way," Dottie answered, pretending sadness. "Guys who look that good never have time to go to church."

Evelyn and Trish laughed along with Dottie, but Rachel didn't. She seemed to have a slight tenseness in her stomach. Unnoticed by her friends, she took a deep breath then sighed, trying to relax the tense area. It didn't seem to help. What was his name, Rachel thought - Elliot...Elliot Reed.

* * *

Standing in the east hallway, near the library door, Harriet looked at her wristwatch. It was one minute before two in the afternoon. Last night, after dinner, she had told Graham she would be down to see him at two but had not told him the reason why. She knocked on the door before entering. The huge room was empty.

She used to love this room. When she was a child, her brother Bertrand used to read to her here. Over in the corner, by the large bay windows her father had a large, comfortable leather easy chair. Bertrand would sit in it, and she would snuggle beside him while he read marvelous stories to her. Involuntarily, her eyes went up the shelves of books to one section of the far wall. The children's books were still there, their spines showing their titles, all of them, still there. But, Bertrand was gone!

She could hear the shower running behind the half-closed door to the bathroom. Over one of the long leather couches that sat in the middle of the huge room was a blanket. It was thrown over one end. Even the pillow was there. Graham slept here most of the time now. How long had it been since he'd come up to her in the middle of the night? She couldn't remember, nor did she care. She had learned to shut out those kinds of thoughts. She no longer thought about sex or about other things that were difficult. She had trained herself to think about things that brought her pleasure and held her interest and things that she could control. The shower turned off, and a moment later Graham stuck his head around the bathroom door.

"Ah, on time I see," he said as he disappeared behind the door. "One second."

Inside the bathroom, he quickly held a vial of Visine over his eyes, trying to put a drop in each upturned eye. His hand shook badly, but he finally managed. Slipping on a bathrobe, he hurriedly brushed his hair, turned off the light, and went into the library. He wondered what could bring her into this room?

"I'll try to be brief," his wife said.

"It's all right, Harriet. Please, sit down."

She sat in the center of the room, on the other end of the leather couches, but at the very edge of it. She hated sitting on them because she always felt so small, because they were so large.

Would you like some coffee?" He had a coffee maker perked on his wet bar.

"No, thank you. I'm trying to stop."

"Good for you," he said with a slight smile, as he sat beside her.

She could feel that her husband was already waiting for her to tell him the reason for her being here, even though he said he didn't mind. He no longer had small talk with her. That stopped years ago. Besides, she no longer expected it. What was more, she loathed this room and wanted to get out of it as soon as possible.

"I want to have a party for all the Reed executives and their wives," Harriet said without emotion.

"I see," Graham said, wondering what this had to do with him.

"And all of the subsidiaries."

"All of them?"

"Yes, from Europe too."

"My, my, that would be quite a party."

"Yes, that's exactly the kind of party I want. I want Reed Industries to take over an entire floor of a hotel, pick them up in limousines and treat them the way my father used to treat his executive officers.

"Highly commendable, my dear. Something that Bertrand would never have done."

"You're right, but that's not the reason I'm doing it."

"Doing it? You mean you've already begun?"

"The invitations have already been sent," she said, showing a thin smile at what she had just said. "I don't know if you can really call them invitations. I made it perfectly clear that I did not expect refusals."

"It must be an important party."

"I think so," she answered evenly.

"Is that why you're here, to tell me the reason you're having it?" Graham asked as he got up, deciding to have coffee after all. He was getting his usual morning headache, and he knew it would get worse without the caffeine.

"You're sure you don't want any?" he asked again as he walked to the wet bar.

"No, thank you," she said, watching him walk away from her. He always seemed to know just the wrong moment to walk away from things. Well, she thought, she would wait him out on this one. It was too important.

She waited in silence, looking out the bay window. Finally, he came back and sat down. He looks terrible, she thought. His eyes are puffy, and his skin looks pasty.

"So, what is this party about?" he asked, with that strange, amused smile that he put on so regularly.

"Since the day we buried Bertrand, something has been bothering me. I can't get it out if my mind," she answered.

"What is it?"

"There's no one from the family in Reed Industries. No one watches out for our interests."

"Harriet, Reed Industries made nine hundred million dollars last year. Its management is strong. It will continue to run just fine without Bertrand."

"I'm not talking about running it, Graham. I'm talking about watching after it! Who do we know that we can trust?"

"As long as the family holds the majority of stock, you don't have to worry."

"Yes, I do! I know I own the stock, with Aunt Elsie and my nitwit children, but I'm still worried! I want that company to grow and survive! No damn takeovers! No Japanese! No one!"

There was a silence. Harriet controlled herself and looked to her husband. "I...I don't know anything about business," she said, "or I would do it. I wouldn't even know what I needed to **watch**." She paused, knowing that it was time to say it, to tell him her plan. She looked directly at her husband. "I want you to do it."

"Me?" Graham retorted incredulously. "I'm fifty-eight years old, and I've been gone for five years!"

"How many times have you told me that you wanted to go back, to show them what you could do?"

"There have been too many changes. I couldn't keep up," Graham said quickly. He felt his back and chest pop out in sweat.

"Nonsense!" Harriet said sincerely. "My father told me that you were brilliant! You were just as smart as Bertrand and even more creative!"

"He said that?" Graham said, not believing her.

"Yes! And so did Joe Tidwell. They both wanted you to run the company with my brother."

Graham looked away from his wife. He didn't know what to say. His stomach had a sickening feeling in it, and he suddenly wished that she would go away. He didn't want her here, and he certainly didn't want to listen to her lies.

"You don't believe me, do you?" she said, feeling that even with these belated compliments, she was losing the battle. "Why do you think you and Bertrand never got along? He knew your potential. He didn't want the competition."

"It's too late," Graham said, suddenly feeling exhausted.

"No it isn't! The invitations have been sent, and I want the announcement to be made! I want you to go on the board and take an active roll in the direction of the company."

"I have work here I'm doing," he said lamely.

"Your writing? The novel you've been writing for five years? May I see it?" Graham was silent, not looking up from his empty coffee cup. "Graham, in five years, I've never asked anything of you. I've let you stay in this room. Maybe that was wrong, but it's what you wanted. But now...I need you."

"Harriet, this is ridiculous. You never cared about the business before. You only wanted the money. Now, even if it were sold, you would have well over a hundred and fifty million. Probably more."

"Two years, Graham. Just for two years," she said.

His head was splitting now, and he knew that if he got up to get another cup of coffee, his hands would shake so much he'd probably spill the cup. God, he felt terrible.

"I can't do it," he said. He was surprised how emotionless he sounded. Inside he was screaming at her.

"Oh, yes, you can. I need your brains. It's time you started earning your keep."

"I'm telling you, I can't do it," he said, feeling himself breaking up inside.

"You have three weeks. The party will be the weekend of the twenty-fourth. I expect you to be the gracious host, and, for the next two years, to do those things that you should have done twenty years ago." She controlled herself the best she could and got up from the couch.

Graham watched as she moved to the doors. He could see that she was near tears. He wondered if it was from anger or disgust. He decided not to answer her ultimatum. He knew she was waiting for his response. She had never looked so beautiful in years, but he found himself hating her.

As Harriet waited at the doors, she could see by the expression on his face that she was not going to get an answer to her demands.

"If you let me down on this," she said slowly, holding back her tears, "our marriage is through, and you'll be out of this house for good."

She opened one of the doors, stepped into the hallway, and slowly closed the door behind her. Once in the hall, she leaned against the door. She felt sick to her stomach. She hadn't had any trouble reading the look on her husband's face; he hated her. As she slowly walked down the hall, she continued to hold back her tears, now doubting her decision for the party.

* * *

Elliot didn't know that the school did not furnish gym clothes. His last class of his first day was sixth period P.E. He was unsure of what he should do. The instructor was already outside on the football field, waiting for the students to come out from their locker room. Elliot decided to go and at least watch and listen. When he got there, forty boys had gathered around the instructor.

"By law each student has to take physical education," the instructor was saying. "If you don't show up for this period, you will not graduate. Once here, you have to suit up daily, and pretend that you like physical exertion! You can pretend in three ways: softball, volleyball or soccer. Those of you who want soccer, stand over here." He pointed under a nearby goal post. "Those of you who want to play volleyball," he said as he pointed, "over to the court. And if you like softball, the diamond is across the field."

Elliot noticed that most of the guys looked bored and really didn't want to be there at all. Elliot was getting the feeling that his counselor hadn't really considered his needs as far as P.E. was concerned.

"Excuse me, Sir," Elliot said to the instructor.

He was looking down at his clipboard. All the boys seemed to be wandering about, trying to make up their minds as to which sport to play.

"Yeah?" the coach said, looking up at Elliot.

"I wonder if there might be swimming or track available now?"

The instructor measured the size of the boy in front of him and said, "What are you doing out here?"

"This is what my counselor gave me."

"Have you got your schedule?"

Elliot took it out of his pocket and handed it to him.

The instructor looked at it and smiled.

"Ah, Mrs. Meecham. No wonder. She hates jocks. You must have good grades," the instructor said.

"Yes," Elliot answered.

"Then she would take for granted that you didn't want to have anything to do with sports."

"I really like sports," Elliot said.

"Good. You said swimming?" the instructor asked.

"Yes, Sir."

"Go on over to the pool and see Mr. Sala."

"The Algebra teacher?"

"Yeah, he runs the swimming team. He might be over there with some of his team. I don't know his schedule, but they always seem to be there."

"Thank you," Elliot said.

"Yeah, sure," the instructor said. "And if you want to transfer over, let Mrs. Meecham know so she can make the changes."

"Yes, Sir," Elliot answered as he turned and walked towards the gym.

The outdoor pool, located on the other side of the gym, was regulation Olympic size. Elliot had seen it during the lunch hour after he had made his blunder with Rachel Davis. But now there were some swimmers in it. Mr. Sala was walking alongside the pool, talking to someone who was doing the backstroke. Elliot walked through the gate and stood at the far end of the pool. Mr. Sala saw him as a guy swimming the backstroke made his turn. Sala motioned to him, and Elliot walked over to him.

"Hi, Elliot. What do you need?" Sala said as he kept watching the student in the pool. Elliot looked down too. He saw that the swimmer was getting tired, not able to reach behind him like he should.

"The P.E. instructor said I might come over and see you. Mrs. Meecham put me into last period P.E."

Sala smiled and said, "She did, did she? That's what happens when you've got grades like yours. We've got a weight training program; it's sixth period."

Elliot walked along beside him. "I thought maybe I could swim."

"Did they have a pool at St.Maurice?" Sala asked.

"Yes, Sir," Elliot said, as he watched the swimmer in the water. His kick was wrong, and he was way too tense.

"You got some trunks?" Sala asked.

"No, Sir."

"Go into the gym and ask Andy for a pair. He's the guy behind the cage."

Elliot was given a towel with his trunks. He changed in the gym and went out to the pool. As Elliot was touching the water with his foot, Sala glanced up and saw him. This Elliot Reed had an extraordinary physique. Sala watched as he smoothly dove into the shallow end, staying underwater for about forty or fifty feet. If he can swim as good as he looks, we've got a winner, Sala thought.

Elliot broke to the surface and went into a smooth freestyle. Mr. Sala noticed that he moved through the water with such smooth, even power that it seemed as though he was using very little energy. His head turn was just enough to breathe, no wasted motion.

Sala smiled. He'd never seen a youngster with such power. The boy seemed to draw through the water without effort. The question was how long could the boy keep this up?

Sala went over to the side of the pool where Elliot was swimming and began walking alongside of him. Elliot's kick seemed almost slow to the coach. Yes, it was only a four kick. What could he do if he went to six or eight kicks per stroke?

Sala watched as the lad finished three hundred meters. Then, as he glided out of his turn, the instructor saw him pick up his kick count! Now the water fairly churned behind this powerful swimmer. The other swimmers, who had now stopped and were watching Elliot, laughed in surprise. It was as if he had gone into another gear! He sped down his lane, made a quick, smooth roll turn, and completed the next fifty meters just as quickly as the first. After another roll turn, he came out of it slowing to his regular four kick, finishing in the shallow end.

Sala watched as Elliot stood up. He saw that the boy was breathing hard, but he certainly wasn't exhausted, far from it.

"How much do you swim a day?" Sala asked.

"I try to do two thousand meters a day," Elliot answered.

Sala looked a long moment at the transfer, not really believing in his newfound blessing. "I think we can use you." Sala said, trying to hide his delight.

* * *

Graham Swindale normally took his first drink about seven in the evening, after he had finished having supper with his family. He had never felt that it was right that he should let his family see him when he was not sober. Besides, he had long ago told himself that he always had to eat properly, or he would get sick. But for the past year or so he didn't seem to care much about food. Even when he went to the evening meal and as good as Marny cooked, he still had a difficult time getting his food down.

But this night, he knew that he wasn't going to supper. After his wife had left, having told him what she had already done, he knew he couldn't face looking at her at the other end of the table. He hadn't moved from the sofa for hours. He wasn't sure of the time, but it was already dark before he got up to mix his first drink.

During those hours on the couch, he had tried to think of what he might say to her that could possibly change her mind about this damn party. What she was asking of him was impossible. Graham knew it, feeling it inside of himself. He could no longer be a businessman.

Years before, he had anticipated going into the office. When had he stopped wanting to go? It was certainly long before Bertrand had gotten rid of him. He never told Harriet, but he had been relieved when he was fired. Maybe that's what he should tell her? Graham knew that she hated her brother for something he didn't even care about, losing his job. How many times had Bertrand told him to stop drinking and to make some decisions concerning the growth of their company? Graham never even tried to stop. Oh, he had thought about it a couple of times, but that's as far as it went.

Graham was almost sure he knew when he stopped trying, but he couldn't hang on to it in his mind. It was when Harriet's dad and Joe Tidwell were still running the company. It was sometime when our kids were still little, during the times when he used to chase his wife around their bedroom, and they would laugh and laugh and laugh. Yes, Graham thought, it was during those times, when everything seemed all right that he had stopped trying. He was almost positive it was sometime when things were really good. Yes, he was almost sure, but then again, maybe not. Maybe he had always been like he was now and had only fooled himself into thinking he was a winner. Maybe his whole life had been worthless.

By nine o'clock that night, when the noises of the large house had subsided and there was no chance of anyone disturbing him, Graham reached that enjoyable state of drunkenness he looked forward to each night. Nothing was real anymore. He no longer had to think; his mind seemed to sink into a peaceful darkness. At times like this, he would sit by his computer or stagger amongst the books, occasionally even climbing the stairs up to the catwalk to sit alone in the dark. Yes, this was the time he liked the best. How many times had he reached this state? Many times! How many? Oodles, he said to himself and then laughed out loud.

Who had used the word oodles? Where had he heard that word before? It must have been when he was little. Only little people say "oodles." Yes, this was the time he really liked.

Then, a drunken thought struck him. One he had never had before. I never wanted to be an executive! Never.

"That's a lie," he said out loud to the books. "There was a time... there was a time," he said slowly, "when I wanted to do things."

But his addled mind answered, You never did. You're full of it.

"I am not!" he said aloud. "There was a time when I proved myself, when I did what was expected of me!"

Bullshit! His mind answered. You're lying to yourself!

Tonight he didn't like where he was. He didn't want to be thinking about himself or about what he had wanted to be or hadn't wanted to be! He poured himself another drink and drank half of it.

Only three weeks, his mind said.

"Go to hell," Graham said to the darkness of the library.

He didn't want to think about three weeks from now! He couldn't do it! He didn't care if it was three years from now. He could not do it!

"I can't do it!" he said out loud. He staggered to the light switches and switched them on. He blinked in the brightness.

A new thought struck him, one he had never had before. He stared at his desk and then staggered over to it. He turned on his desk lamp and then laughed, because it made no difference since the main lights were on.

Leaning stiff-armed on the desk, he dipped one shoulder and opened the bottom drawer. He stared in it, then took out his revolver and drunkenly examined it. He finished the drink he had, looked at the bar, placing the revolver on the desk. He went to the bar and poured another. While he was mixing it, he turned and stared at the gun again.

"I'm not afraid to look at you," he said to the black, inanimate object on his desk. "I'm not!"

* * *

Elliot's third dream that night was numinous in content.

**He was looking at his uncle, who was dressed in a corduroy jacket, the expensive kind with the leather buttons and leather pocket flaps. His trousers were wrinkled, but clean. He had on house-slippers. Mr. Swindale stood very still before Elliot and had his eyes closed.**

**"Hello, Uncle," Elliot said.**

**Graham did not answer, nor did he open his eyes. Then suddenly, a strange, grotesque hand slid from behind Graham and gripped his uncle's arm. Next a head appeared, a small head, about the size of a child's. But it was not human. At least Elliot could not think of anybody being so grotesque. It stared at Elliot with red, bloodshot eyes. Its mouth was wrinkled and small, having tightly drawn lips that looked like they were made out of leather. The thing's nose, if you could call it that, was pressed against its face more like two holes in the leathery skull. It's fiery little eyes finally blinked at Elliot.**

**"Who are you? I don't know you!" the creature snarled.**

**"I'm Elliot Reed. Who are you?"**

**He showed a little more of himself as his head moved forward with a jerk. "I don't have to tell you a thing!"**

**He had no neck and his head seemingly stuck to a skinny, emaciated frame.**

**"Why are you hanging on to my uncle" Elliot asked, feeling very uncomfortable.**

**"Stupid child!" it answered.**

**Elliot could feel himself becoming angry and afraid at the same time. This thing hated him. "You aren't supposed to be there, are you?" Elliot said quickly.**

**"Oh yes I am!" the thing yelled at him. "He asked me to be here! He wants me here!**

**"I'll ask him about that!"**

**The creature just laughed.**

**"Uncle!" Elliot said. His uncle's eyes stayed closed. "Uncle! Uncle," Elliot cried out, "Wake up!"**

**"Stupid child!" His watery eyes creased into slits as he said, "When this one dies, I might come and stay with you!"**

**"Is that what you do, kill people?**

**The thing just grinned at him. Elliot knew that this was too much for him. He didn't know what to do. "I'm going to ask Jesus about you!" he announced.**

**The creature stared at Elliot for a long moment, then slowly moved back behind the man that he seemed to be attached to. Suddenly his head shot back out, and it screamed out at Elliot, "Stupid child, stupid, stupid, child!" Then with his eyes burning with hatred, he disappeared behind Graham.**

**Cautiously, Elliot moved to his uncle's side and looked. The thing wasn't there. Where could it have gone, Elliot wondered? Could it have gone inside of his uncle?**

**As Elliot moved in front of Graham, his uncle's eyes opened. He looked at Elliot, smiled lopsidedly, and took a step toward Elliot. He stumbled slightly, and Elliot had no trouble telling that he was drunk.**

**Slowly Graham reached into his corduroy smoking jacket and brought out a pistol. Again he smiled at Elliot. He pointed the gun at Elliot, then laughed, drunkenly shaking his head. Next he moved the gun until it was pointed upwards, at eye level, between the two of them. He pulled the trigger. Blood bubbled and seeped over the edge of the upturned barrel.**

Elliot woke with a start, yelling, "No, Uncle! No!"

Without hesitation he leaped from bed, ran out of his darkened apartment and down the stairs. He raced through the backyard to the back door of the kitchen. It was locked. He tried the door to the washroom. It too was locked. He knew that all the doors of the house would be locked and there was no time left. He picked up a rock from the garden and rammed it through one of the small glass partitions in the kitchen door. He reached his hand in, twisted the handle and the door swung open. Jumping clear of the broken glass, he ran through the kitchen, down the long hallway to the far end of the house. He rushed to the double doors of the library, flung them open, and rushed inside.

The bloated drunken face of Graham was bent over his upturned gun, with the barrel of it stuck in his mouth. Elliot's uncle was drunkenly trying to get his thumb into the safety area of the trigger. Elliot ran forward, grabbed his uncle's hair, which flung Graham's head backwards and, at the same time, slapped at the revolver. It fell harmlessly to the floor.

"Wha...? Wha...?" were the only syllables that came out of Graham's mouth as his bloodshot eyes tried to focus on Elliot. Then he sobbed twice, with drool running from his mouth, down his face and onto the rug.

Elliot picked him up and carried him to one of the large sofas. Placing him on it, he took a blanket that was thrown over the top of it and put it over his uncle. Graham sobbed again.

Elliot heard a siren in the distance, then a noise down the hallway. Quickly, he went to the gun and took the shells from it, then placed the revolver in the top drawer of the desk. Momentarily unsure as to what to do with the shells, since he only had on his under shorts, he decided on the bookshelves. Going to the nearest one, he took a thick volume from its place and quickly thrust the shells in the rear of the shelf, then replaced the book.

As he turned from the shelf, Harriet and Tina entered the doors of the library. At the same time, the glare of headlights flashed through the windows as the police car sped up the driveway.

Elliot stood motionless in front of the bookshelves. Harriet stared at him, then looked over at her husband.

"What is it?" Harriet yelled. "What's happened?"

Elliot knew that he was not going to tell about the attempted suicide. He didn't know why he wasn't supposed to tell, but he knew he had to protect his uncle's stupid, drunken action.

"I asked a question, young man! What's going on in here?" Harriet demanded of her almost-naked nephew. The front door chimes rang.

"Elliot, it's three o'clock in the morning! Would you please tell me what you're doing in here?" Harriet demanded again. Tina had gone to the couch and was bent over her father.

"Is he all right?" Harriet asked her daughter.

"It looks like he's all right," she answered as she moved away from her father. He smelled terrible.

The chimes rang again.

"Tina, go let them in," her mother directed.

"Really?" Tina answered. "What for?"

"Because I'm not getting any answers from my nephew!"

There was an awkward pause as both the women waited on the young man.

Then Tina said, "Elliot, don't be stupid. What happened?"

The chimes sounded again.

"I'm sorry, but I can't tell you why I'm here," Elliot said. The feeling was stronger than ever within him that he should not tell.

"Tina, go get the door!" her mother snapped at her.

Tina left the room. Harriet waited. Elliot had not moved from his position near the bookshelves. Moments passed, then car doors slamming, a motor starting, and a car driving down the driveway broke the silence. A moment later, Tina came back into the room.

"What did you do?" Harriet asked her daughter.

"I told the police that my father got drunk and broke a window. I told them everything was O.K."

Arnold sleepily walked into the room in his pajamas. "Hey, what's happening?"

"Shut up, Arnold," Harriet and Tina said at the same time.

"You should have done what you were told!" Harriet snapped at Tina.

"And what would you tell the police? That your nephew likes running around in his underwear, breaking windows?" Tina retorted just as sharply.

"Who broke a window?" Arnold asked.

"Shut up, Arnold!" the women said again.

"Hey, I'm just asking," he answered. "What's he doing here?" he continued, pointing at Elliot.

Harriet walked up to her son and stabbed a finger at him. "I want you to go back to bed, right now!"

Arnold was about to say something.

"No! Not another word," his mother said quickly. "Leave, right now!"

Arnold looked over at Elliot and then shuffled from the room as Harriet went over to Elliot.

"I don't understand why you won't clear everything up for us? All this does is make us not trust you. It makes us afraid of you! Don't you know that?"

"Yes, ma'am. And I'm really sorry. But you don't have to be afraid," Elliot replied. He felt sorry he had put his aunt in this position, but he knew that he was not going to tell.

Harriet stood before him, staring, and getting more resentful by the moment. As she turned and marched angrily from the room, she cried out, "Damn it! Damn it to hell!"

Tina watched as she left, then went up and stood before Elliot. She smiled and tapped her index finger on his chest, and said, "You, my cousin, are turning out to be a very strange and interesting fellow."

She tilted her head slightly to one side. "Are you aware of something?"

"What do you mean?" Elliot asked.

"That you could have been on your way to jail right now?

"Yes, I am."

"Then you must also know, my odd, handsome cousin, that you now owe me a favor, because I kept you out."

Elliot, embarrassed, didn't know what to say.

"And I'm not in the least bit afraid of you," she said as she gently ran her palm over his powerful chest. "But I am curious," she persisted, "just how kinky are you?" Smiling, she turned and walked from the room. Elliot watched her leave, then went over and looked down at his uncle. Graham had either passed out or fallen asleep. Elliot turned out the lights as he left.

Elliot went back to his apartment and tried to sleep. It was fitful at best, and at five-thirty, when the morning was approaching grayness, he gave up trying. Getting up, he put on his running shorts and shoes. He felt a little tired, but once he started his morning run, he felt better.

He ran past the little park with the horse trail, then turned and took a new direction, running hard, not wanting to think about anything.

As he began relaxing, extending his gait, he thought about Rachel Davis but decided that those thoughts weren't that terrific either. He kept seeing her concerned eyes and remembered how she had looked when she sat on the grass. Mrs. Swindale probably wasn't the only one who thought he was a freak.

"Oh, Lord," he said out loud, "what am I supposed to do about everything? Who do I talk to about this?" He increased his speed for a few more blocks, then slowed and stopped.

"I saw a demon," Elliot said, standing there, sweating in the middle of the street. "I know what to do!" he said, as he turned and started back to the house.

After Elliot had showered and changed clothes, he went out on the porch and knocked on Charles's door.

Charles opened it. He was already dressed.

"Is Aunt Elsie going to church this morning?"

"She never misses a day," Charles said, straightening his tie.

"What time will you get back?"

"Ten minutes after eight," Charles said. "We haven't been off more than a minute in the last year."

"Could I go with you?"

"She would love it," Charles said.

The Mass seemed to take longer than the ones at school, Elliot thought. This priest was either slower than Father Tinian or Elliot was impatiently anticipating his meeting with the Monsignor after the Mass was over. Elliot calmed himself by praying about what he was about to do.

Upon meeting the Monsignor, Elliot was initially surprised. This man was a great deal older and was not the priest who said Mass. When Aunt Elsie introduced them, she mentioned that Elliot had been to St. Maurice. Then she left, going out to join Charles in the car.

"I've heard very good things about St. Maurice Military Academy," the Monsignor said to Elliot as they walked down the corridor. "Did you graduate from there?" the heavy-set man asked.

"No, Monsignor, I'm a senior this year, but I'm going to Laurelwood."

"Ah, I see. Well, at least you've had an excellent beginning."

"Yes, sir, I feel the same way," Elliot replied.

The Monsignor led him to an ambry, a recessed part of the wall, which contained two small benches. They sat down.

"What would you like to talk about?" the Monsignor asked.

"Demons."

"What?"

"I'd like to talk about demons and ask you what we're supposed to do about them."

Good Lord, the priest thought, all the men who make movies should be shot! He smiled at the lad and said, "I don't think you have to worry about them. I would suggest that we let the men who created them live with them."

Elliot wondered what the man was talking about. "I don't understand, Sir."

"Exactly, and neither do they," the Monsignor answered. "That's my point. All it does is cause confusion in our young people. Pretty soon, you teenagers start thinking they're real. My advice to you is to stop seeing them!"

He stood up and folded his hands over his protruding stomach.

"Seeing what, Sir?"

"Movies, young man, movies!"

Elliot watched the old Monsignor walk down the hallway. Elliot smiled, wondering what he had missed.

"Well, did he help?" Aunt Elsie asked Elliot as he got into the car and sat next to her.

"I'm afraid he really didn't understand what I was getting at," Elliot answered with a smile.

"Well, that's too bad. Maybe one of the younger priests might be able to help."

"Yes, maybe," Elliot answered, doubting if he would follow-up through Aunt Elsie's church.

"Is it something personal?" Elsie inquired, wanting to help.

"Not really. I wanted to talk about demons."

"Demons? What kind of demons?" Elsie asked, shocked to hear what this boy was thinking about.

"The ones who are in the Bible. The kind that belong in hell."

What a thing for a boy to think about, she thought. "You shouldn't think about such things," Elsie said kindly to her great-nephew. "A boy your age should be thinking about nice things; his future, his schooling, things like that."

Elliot smiled as he took his great aunt's hand and after a moment, thought out loud, saying, "My people are destroyed from lack of knowledge."

Aunt Elsie searched his face for a moment and then asked, "Who said that?"

"Hosea," Elliot answered.

"Well, you tell him to think about good things too," she admonished as she patted the boy's hand.

Charles dropped Mrs. Elsie at the house before driving the Rolls back to the garage area. Arnold was there, already seated in the Jeep, waiting for Elliot. Elliot got in and started the motor. Arnold was silent as Elliot looked at him and finally said, "I thought you were mad at me."

"I am, but I still need a ride to school."

Elliot put the car in gear and drove away from the house. Arnold looked at him twice during the short trip to the school parking lot but didn't say anything until they were parked. Instead of getting out, Arnold just sat there.

"Well?" Elliot questioned, in no mood to take Arnold's guff.

"I wanted to know what you were doing in the library at three in the morning, in your underwear?"

Elliot sighed and said, "I wouldn't tell your mother, and I won't tell you."

Arnold continued looking at him. "Was it something bad?"

Elliot thought about his question, and then asked, "Do you mean, did I do something bad?"

"Yeah."

"No."

"Was it something weird?" Arnold asked.

Elliot considered this and replied, "Yes, you could say that. Don't ask me anything else."

Arnold eyed Elliot before getting out of the car and walking away.

Elliot didn't see Rachel that day. In fact, he didn't even go to the lunch area to look for her. He ate his lunch down by the pool and walked the track area. There wasn't anybody out there. He prayed, still wondering what to do about his uncle. Why hadn't he been able to tell his aunt about Uncle Graham? What should he do?

While making a turn on the twelfth lap of his swimming workout with the rest of the team, Elliot suddenly thought about the little white church. It wasn't a vision, no picture came into his mind, just a thought. But, in the state he was in, Elliot decided to act on something as ordinary as a fleeting thought. As he swam he asked himself what had made him think of the little church. What was he thinking about just before he thought of that church? He couldn't remember.

As he stopped swimming in the shallow end of the pool, he stood, lost in thought. Now, he considered, what was it he thought when the church came to mind? It was really nothing in particular, just a fleeting thought about the little white building. It had just come into his mind.

"Is there something wrong?" Mr. Sala asked from the side of the pool.

Elliot walked over to him and said, "I'm feeling fine, but I've got a problem. Would you mind if I left early? I could make up my laps tomorrow."

"What's the matter? You need help with something?"

Elliot smiled and said, "Yes, Sir, but I'm not sure where to get it."

"What kind of a problem?" Sala asked.

"Spiritual," Elliot answered.

Mr. Sala didn't try to hide his surprise. "Spiritual?"

"Yes, Sir."

"Where you going? To a church?"

"Yes, I thought I would."

"Sounds like a good idea to me," Sala replied.

As Elliot got out of the pool and walked toward the locker room, Sala wondered what a seventeen-year-old could know about spiritual things and what kind of a problem could he have?

Elliot drove to the corner where he could see the little church. He pulled over and stopped. There was a man mowing the front lawn. Elliot watched him fighting the tall grass, then drove up in front of the little gate. Now, not only had the hinge been fixed, but also the fence had been painted. The man didn't notice the Jeep or the boy who stood by the fence. He was too intent on the unruly grass.

"Excuse me," Elliot said. The man didn't hear him. Elliot waited until the man pulled the mower back, ready to once again attack, then called quickly, "Hello."

The startled man looked up and said, "What?" He was in his late forties, had up a good sweat and was very red in the face.

"Could you tell me where the pastor might be?"

"You'll find him mowing the grass of his church."

Elliot laughed, and so did the pastor.

"I didn't know pastors did that."

"Keeps us humble," the man replied as he took a handkerchief from his back pocket. Elliot could see his hand shaking as he began wiping his face.

"Are you O.K.?" Elliot asked.

The pastor, feeling his concern, answered, "Yes, I'm fine, but maybe a little rest wouldn't hurt." He walked to the porch of the church and sat down. He motioned for Elliot to join him, which he did.

"Do you live in the area?" the pastor asked.

"No, sir, a few miles away. I was driving by."

"I see," he said as he smiled at the young man. "What can I do for you?"

"I'd like to ask you about demons."

The pastor was surprised. He tried to hide it but there was a change in his attitude as he shifted to look directly at Elliot. He was on the alert now.

"Demons? What makes you ask about them?"

"Then you believe they're still around?"

The pastor searched the young man's face. He looked like such a nice lad, but that didn't mean a thing. That's just the kind they would send, the pastor thought.

"Did someone send you here?"

"I'm not sure."

"I think you are," the pastor said abruptly. "Was it someone from the Board of Elders? You can tell them, since I'm no longer with their church, that I'm not any of their concern! And I'd appreciate being left alone! How did they find me?"

"I don't know anything about a Board of Elders," Elliot answered. "I just need some help."

The pastor was immediately aware of his mistake.

"Oh, my. I am sorry, son," he said, as he shook his head. "I'm afraid I'm becoming paranoid," he sighed and smiled at Elliot. "What's your name?"

"Elliot Reed."

"I'm Art Lindquist."

The two shook hands, then the pastor asked, "What would you like to know?"

"Do you believe that demons are here, today?

"Yes, they won't be disposed of until Jesus returns."

"Have you ever seen one?" Elliot asked.

"No, but I know of two pastors who have the gift of discernment, and one woman who saw five of them seated in the rafters of her church."

"You mean some of them run around loose?" Elliot asked quickly.

"Yes. Why? What did you see?"

"I saw one that seemed to be attached to a person."

"Possession."

"Yes, I think so. I saw it in a dream."

"In a dream? What do you mean?"

"My uncle was standing in front of me, and this thing came around from the back of him and starting talking to me."

"What did it say?"

"He wanted to know who I was," Elliot replied. "When I asked who he was, he said he didn't have to tell me a thing."

"Was that all?"

"No. I asked him why it was hanging onto my uncle, and he yelled and called me a stupid child." Elliot paused, then looked at the pastor. "Then the thing told me that my uncle asked him to be there. And then it said, `When your uncle dies, maybe I'll come and stay with you.'"

The pastor could see how shaken the boy was. "Don't forget, these creatures are liars," he reassured Elliot. "They'll say anything."

"I asked the thing if what he did was kill people? He just grinned at me," Elliot continued. "I felt very frightened of the thing, so I said to it, `I'm going to ask Jesus about you.'"

"Good for you!" the pastor said quickly. "That's the only way to handle them."

Elliot nodded and continued, "He seemed frightened and went back inside my uncle."

"Well, well," the pastor said, thinking the story was over.

"That's not all," Elliot added.

The pastor waited.

"After the thing disappeared, in my dream, my uncle opened his eyes. He was drunk."

"Is he an alcoholic?"

"I think so."

"Go on," the pastor prompted. He could see that the boy was beginning to have a difficult time of it.

"After my uncle opened his eyes, he pulled out a gun from the pocket of his jacket. He held it between us, pointed it upwards, and pulled the trigger. Blood oozed out of the barrel of the gun. I woke up then, and I knew."

"Knew what?"

"That my uncle was going to kill himself," Elliot answered. "I live over the garage at my uncle's home, so I ran to the house, broke a window, and went into the library."

"The library?"

"Yes, he seems to live in that room. When I got there, he was holding the gun and the barrel was stuck in his mouth. He...he was trying to get his thumb over the trigger..." Elliot said, near tears. He stopped, controlled himself and continued.

"I grabbed his hair and pulled his head backwards. The... the gun didn't go off. It fell to the floor."

"Sweet Jesus," the pastor said softly. "Thank you, Jesus."

There was a moment of silence as the two of them thought about what had just been said. Then the pastor asked, "When did this happen?"

"Three o'clock this morning."

Another pause.

"I take it you're here to ask what you should do next?"

"Yes, Sir."

"Well, first of all, let me tell you, you've been blessed."

"Blessed?"

"Yes. God trusted you to help someone."

"Yes, Sir. Now what should I do?"

"In the Bible, there's only one way. Demons have to be `called out'."

"You mean like Jesus did?" Elliot asked.

"That's right," Lindquist answered. "Except now, we use His name to draw them out. In the Book of Acts, Paul called a demon out of the slave girl. He said, `In the name of Jesus, come out!'"

Elliot smiled and said excitedly, "I remember. Then the crowd got so mad at Paul and Silas that they beat them and locked them in jail."

"That's right," Art said, smiling. He was getting charged up, as he always did when he talked about the Lord. "The Lord has certainly shown you what has to be done."

"Yes, Sir. To call it out."

"That's right and in his Name."

Elliot thought about this for a moment. "I wonder what my uncle will think about all this?"

"That's a good question," the pastor mused. "Is your uncle spiritual at all? Would he believe it if you told him what happened?"

"I don't think so. He goes to Mass every Sunday, but I don't think it means much to him. My great-aunt says he goes because his wife makes him."

The pastor shrugged, "Then he won't know what you're doing. He doesn't need to know what's happening. You don't have to have his permission to get rid of it."

"I don't?"

"No, this is spiritual warfare. Different rules."

"Where should I do this `calling out'?"

"Wherever you can."

"Not in church?"

"This kind of work can be done anywhere."

"Can I do it alone?"

The pastor smiled at Elliot. "I think that's what the Lord has in mind. If He thought you needed any more help than Himself, he wouldn't have given you the job through a dream."

Elliot thought about this for a moment. "Yes, I think you're right."

"Remember though..." the pastor said as he laid his hand on Elliot's shoulder...

"Yes?" Elliot responded.

"...Be careful, because your uncle will think you're talking to him. He doesn't know that he's possessed."

"What might happen?" Elliot asked thoughtfully.

"I don't know for sure, but from what I've heard, it can get pretty wild."

The two sat in silence for some time. Then Elliot said, "I have to do this, no matter what happens. He could try to kill himself again."

Art Lindquist looked at him, and said, "Yes, yes, he could. In fact, since he's possessed, you can bet on it." Then he thought for a moment and said, "But don't forget, it has to all be done through faith. You must believe that you have been called to do this."

"Yes, Sir, I know."

"You're going to make a difference to your uncle."

Elliot thought about this for a moment and then said softly, "That means that you have a hand in it too."

Lindquist smiled, and said, "In a way, yes."

"No, it's more than that. God knew I needed help, and he sent me where I was supposed to go."

Elliot and the pastor smiled at each other. With that, Elliot got up and looked at the lawnmower. Walking down the steps, he took hold of the little mower and started ripping through the tall grass. He found pleasure in using his power against things he could see, something he could manhandle with his strength.

The pastor, watching how easily the strong lad went through the weeds, said loudly, "Elliot!"

Elliot stopped. "Sir?"

"Where do you fellowship?"

"Fellowship?" Elliot asked, not understanding the word's meaning.

"Where do you go to church?"

"I don't!"

"You do now! Nine a.m. this Sunday."

Elliot looked at the man for a long moment, smiled, then went back to work before the tears came. He had a church!

Art Lindquist watched the lad push the mower through the heavy grass and smiled at the strength the young man possessed. Then the pastor slowly got to his feet and went inside the small church.

Each time he entered it, even after...let's see, he thought, how long had it been? Yes, this was the fourth_week...and even now he couldn't get over how small and poorly constructed the place was. He remembered when his wife and he had first found it. It looked about the size of one of the classrooms of their previous church. They had glanced at each other, sadly smiling, knowing that this would be a difficult beginning, wondering in their hearts if they had the strength to do it.

Art sat in the back pew and looked up at the cross. Tears came into his eyes. He blinked them away. He listened as the mower outside continued to whir through the grass. He knew that the Lord had just given him a little miracle...a sign. Yesterday, the boy he had hired to cut the grass called to say he was sick. Art knew he couldn't wait any longer so he decided to do it himself. And if it weren't for that, he wouldn't have been here today.

"Thank You, Lord," he said softly.

He got to his knees and said, "I pray for your young helper out there. I ask an anointing be on him as he faces his uncle, to do Your work. May the Holy Spirit give him the power and the words during the fight. I think You've already given him the heart of a fighter. Thank you for bringing the lad into your church, Lord."

Art looked once more at the cross. "Forgive me, Father, for forgetting that You are in charge of **all** things. Forgive me for being critical of this tiny little place. It's Your church, not mine. I thank you for letting me serve You, no matter where it is."

* * *

Lance Davis would be leaving for college in the morning. Rachel looked across the dining table at her brother. If she were going to ask him, she would have to do it now.

Her father, Rachel noticed, was feeding a scrap of food from the table to Archie, their overly fat Collie. Her mother, at the other end of the table, was smiling as she watched her husband do something he had asked his family not to do.

"That dog is going to die early if you don't stop feeding him from the table," Dolores said, good-naturedly.

Marc looked up from the dog to see that both his wife and daughter were watching him. "He keeps staring at me until I feed him something," Marc answered, knowing he had been caught.

"During the summer, we should keep him outside. He's getting too fat and lazy," Dolores Davis said, knowing full well that it would never happen.

Rachel looked at her brother again as he concentrated on his meal. "Lance?" she said.

"Ummm?" he said, not looking up from his plate.

"Did a boy ask you about me, when you were working at the mall?"

"What?" Lance said.

"About three weeks ago, maybe. He bought some clothes from you," Rachel said, proceeding to tell what little she knew.

Her mother and father were listening, interested in the new conversation.

Her brother finally remembered. "Oh, yeah, that's right. He bought about five hundred dollars worth."

"What did you tell him?" Rachel asked.

"He asked me your name, and where you went to school."

"And you told him?" her father asked, sounding a little irritated.

"It's all right, Daddy. Nothing bad happened," Rachel said quickly.

"Then what's the problem?" her father questioned.

"No problem," Rachel answered, a little embarrassed. "He just came up to us during lunch and introduced himself, that's all."

"I can't remember his name," her brother said, shaking his head.

"Elliot Reed," Rachel said.

"That's right, Elliot Reed," Lance said with a laugh. "I remember, he was a little square...sort of strange."

"What do you mean?" his sister asked.

"Oh, I said a couple of things to him, and his answers were kind of strange, like he didn't know what I was talking about."

"I don't see anything strange about that," his Dad said. "That happens between the two of us all the time."

Dolores laughed and agreed.

"Yeah, Dad, but this guy isn't old like you," Lance teased.

Now both Rachel and her mother laughed, looking at Marc at the end of the table.

He laughed too. "Maybe you'll learn correct English in college," his father retorted.

Dolores Davis focused on her daughter. There must be a reason why Rachel asked about this boy. Usually her daughter didn't care for the boys she met and never asked about them.

"Was he alone when he bought the clothes?" Mrs. Davis asked her son.

"No, he was with an older guy, gray-haired, really well-dressed."

"His father?" she continued questioning.

"No, I don't think so," Lance replied, thinking about it. "In fact, I think he even called the kid, Mr. Reed."

"Really?" Rachel said.

Lance thought some more. "You know something else weird? This Elliot Reed, he didn't know anything about clothes. It was like he'd never bought anything in his life. Really weird."

"Just like he was new at it?" Rachel asked.

"Yeah," Lance replied, "just like he was new at it."

Dolores Davis watched her daughter as Rachel looked down at her plate.

* * *

The Swindales supper that evening did not start on time and Marny was going crazy in the kitchen. First, Mrs. Swindale told her that Mr. Swindale most probably would not be at the table. Then ten minutes later, Mr. Swindale called from the library and said he would be at the table. Then Arnold came down and wanted to eat in the kitchen, but Marny told him he couldn't. Then he got mad, said some things he shouldn't have and walked out, yelling that he wasn't going to eat at all. But then after about fifteen minutes with his mother in the living room, he came into the kitchen, apologized to Marny and told her he would be there for supper. Then he went back into the living room with his mother. Mrs. Elsie, who had been in the dining room alone, came into the kitchen, wondering where everybody was. Tina, who never came into the kitchen, came in and actually sat down. Marny looked at her. "What is it, honey?"

"Where's mother?"

"I think she's in the living room with your brother."

"What are they doing in there?" Tina asked.

"I think she's telling him that if he doesn't grow up she's gonna kill him."

"Good. I'll help," Tina said with relish. "Where's Elliot?" she said offhandedly.

"He's the only one that hasn't been around. It's not like that child to be late," Marny said. "Is his white car over there?"

"I don't know," the girl said as she got out of her chair. "I'll go look." She went out the back door.

As busy as Marny was, that stopped her. That girl never did anything for anybody, and here she was actually walking somewhere! Marny thought something was strange.

Aunt Elsie stuck her head in from the dining room again, smiling and looking over the salads that were prepared on the table. Marny decided to at least feed her, since she was the only one in the family who wasn't crazy.

"All right, Mrs. Elsie, I'm bringing a salad to you. Who knows, you might be eating alone."

"All right, dear," Elsie answered, as she disappeared once more into the dining room.

Tina walked slowly along the path to the garages. She knew that Elliot's car wasn't there. She had been looking for him. As she walked passed the hedge, she saw his Jeep come into the driveway. She walked to the garage area as he pulled up.

"Hi," she said as he turned off the motor.

"Hi," he answered.

"You're late," she said.

He jumped out of the car and ran up the stairs. "Are they waiting for me?"

"Yes," she lied as she watched him run into his apartment. She paused, then went up to the stairs, passed Charles's place, and entered Elliot's apartment. She didn't knock but walked right in. She could hear the shower running. Looking into his bedroom, she could see that the door to the bathroom was closed. She smiled and looked around. He was a very neat boy... everything was in it's place. Good training, she thought. His bed was made, and the blanket on top was so tight it looked as though it might have "spring" in it. She took her finger and touched the center of the blanket. It did; it bounced right back into place!

"Now that is a `military' bed!" she said, laughing as she went back through the tiny living room and stood looking around the kitchen. She heard the shower turn off. Going back into the living room, she sat in a chair. She made sure she could see directly into his bedroom. She watched as he came out.

He had a towel around his waist. When he reached into his dresser, he brought out a pair of shorts, dropped the towel and started to put them on. Then he saw her. Naked, he moved quickly into the bathroom, not taking time to pick the towel up from the floor.

"Sorry," she said nonchalantly. "They wanted me to make sure that you came to supper as soon as possible," she lied again. "I guess I should have said something."

When he came from the bathroom in his shorts, he shut the door to his bedroom. She waited, amused and even slightly excited that she was most probably the first woman to ever see him naked. He was beautiful, she thought, every bit of him.

When he came from his bedroom, he was fully dressed. He stood and looked at her. She smiled at him.

"If some man spied on you...saw you naked, how would you feel about it?" he said straightforwardly.

"It would depend on who it was," she said, still amused.

"No, it wouldn't. It would surprise and offend you, no matter who it was."

Suddenly, she felt strangely uncomfortable under his angry gaze. She had faced many men before who had been angry with her and had always enjoyed it, knowing that it was only a game. But now... She got up.

"I didn't know you were so touchy," she said, straightening her skirt. "Besides," she lied, "it was just an accident."

He held the door open for her as they left the apartment, but she could still feel his silent anger. She felt embarrassed. Somehow she felt as though she were a little girl and had just received a scolding. She felt like being angry, but at the same time she wanted to cry and ask his forgiveness! She didn't like these feelings. Damn it, she didn't like them at all!

When Elliot slid the dining room door open for Tina, all the family was already there, seated, eating their salads. Aunt Elsie looked up when they came in, smiled as she greeted them, "Hello, children. Just in time."

Harriet didn't look up, but continued to eat. She picked up a piece of bread and put butter on it. Something she never did. She wished Elliot hadn't come at all.

Graham, playing with his food, didn't really pay any attention to them as they came into the room. He was preoccupied with how badly he was shaking; it had never been this noticeable before.

Arnold, who was waiting for his untouched salad to be taken away, looked at Elliot as he sat across from him. Then he looked sideways, as his sister sat at her place besides him. Why, Arnold wondered, are those two together?

Elliot closed his eyes and silently asked the Lord to bless his food and thanked him for all that had happened that day. He also asked God to forgive his anger toward his cousin. Finally, he asked for protection for himself when he met with his uncle. Elliot had made up his mind, while mowing the church lawn, to meet with his Uncle Graham tonight.

"Did everybody have a nice day?" Aunt Elsie asked brightly. Elliot was the only one who looked up and smiled. "Father Lucas wasn't at the church this morning," she continued. "He has the flu. Monsignor had to do the Mass." As she looked around the table, she could see that nobody was interested. She stopped talking and looked down at her empty salad plate.

Harriet rang the little bell, and Marny entered the silent dining room.

"Maybe you could take away for those who have finished their salads," Harriet said.

"Yes, Ma'am," Marny said, glancing around at the silent family. As she picked up Mrs. Swindales and Aunt Elsie's salad plates, she looked at the faces of each person. My, everybody seems gloomy, even young Elliot, she thought. As she took the dishes and started toward the kitchen, Arnold handed her his still-full plate. Marny sighed, added it to her stack and went into the kitchen.

Elliot looked over at Mr. Swindale. His salad plate was still full, but the man seemed to be ready to lift a fork-full up to his lips. Elliot noticed that Graham's hand shook so badly that he seemed to change his mind and lowered his fork to the plate.

"Uncle Graham," Elliot said.

Even though it sounded loud in the silence, Graham didn't seem to hear it. Elliot reached over and touched Graham's left hand. His uncle jumped slightly and looked up at him. He smiled and responded, "Yes?"

Elliot smiled at him and said, "Would it be all right if we talked together after supper?"

"After supper," Graham said, seeming to echo Elliot's inflection.

"Yes, Sir," Elliot quietly said. "It's important that I talk to you."

Graham didn't answer. Everybody at the table was waiting for an answer, but none came. Elliot didn't take his eyes off his uncle.

"Sir?" Elliot said, when he was sure he wasn't going to be answered. "I need to talk to you."

He touched his uncle's hand again. Graham gave a short little laugh and looked at his nephew.

Arnold was getting nervous. What was Elliot trying to do to his father? He looked around the room, wondering what the rest of his family was doing. Everyone was staring at Elliot.

Marny came in with a large plate of vegetables and set them in the middle of the table. As soon as she entered, she knew that she had come into the middle of something dark, something ominous that could be felt in her spirit.

"Excuse me," Marny said, apologetically. Immediately, she left the room, praying to herself even before the door had swung closed behind her. Oh, Lord, she thought, what's going on in there? She went to the kitchen table and sat, folding her hands in front of her. She would pray now, not going back into that room until she heard the bell!

Inside the dining room, Elliot held his uncle's hand. The young man didn't care that the rest of the family was watching his every move. He only knew that he was already in a strange battle, one that he didn't really understand.

As he held his uncle's hand, the word "dumb" came into Elliot's mind. True, Elliot thought, at this moment, my uncle is acting dumb, but why would that word come to me?

"Uncle, listen to me, now," Elliot said, as he squeezed Graham's hand.

His uncle looked at him. "Yes, what is it?"

"What the hell do you think you're doing?" Arnold interrupted, starting to get to his feet. He could see that his father wasn't acting as he usually did.

"Sit down," Elliot said menacingly. "It's important that you don't interfere. If you try, I'll make it so you can't."

Arnold hesitated. Elliot waited, still holding his uncle's hand but staring hard at Arnold. Arnold was afraid. He sat.

Elliot looked back at his uncle, who sat looking at him and wondering what was going on.

"What is it, Elliot? What can I do for you?" his uncle asked.

"I need to talk to you alone, please."

"Do you have a problem?" his uncle asked nonchalantly.

"Yes," Elliot answered quickly. "It's important that I talk to you alone. Could we do that now?"

"Well, I don't see why not. Have you had enough to eat?"

"Yes, Sir."

"Very well. Why don't we go into the library," Graham said, starting to get up. Elliot got quickly to his feet and helped his uncle to stand.

"Thank you, young man. Sometimes my legs go to sleep when I sit too long."

He walked unsteadily towards the doors as Elliot followed. When Elliot got to the sliding doors, he turned and went back to Harriet at the table. He leaned down and came near to her ear.

"Aunt Harriet, please, try not to be frightened or worried," he whispered softly.

He paused, looking at her face, but she seemed as though she were in a trance, not even breathing. Elliot straightened, went out the doors and slid them closed behind him. He put his arm around his uncle's shoulder, grasping to hold him steady as they walked down the long hallway to the east wing.

A word came into Elliot's mind, "Suicide." Then others followed, just words, standing alone in his mind: - "Suicide, Worthless, Hopeless and Drunkard! Why were these words coming to me? Elliot wondered. He knew they were certainly things that his uncle must be feeling, but why was he receiving these words?

Just before reaching the library doors, Graham shrugged Elliot's arm from him, took two or three steps on his own and opened the door to the library.

"Come in," he said, politely, "and we'll talk."

As Elliot stepped inside the room, his uncle followed and closed the door. Elliot watched as Graham passed him and went unsteadily to the bar.

"Would you like a soft drink?" his uncle asked.

"No, sir," Elliot said, following him. "I wonder, Sir, would it be all right if we talked before you had a drink?"

His uncle stopped putting ice in a glass and looked at the youngster. "What?"

Elliot stood across from him, on the other side of the bar. "Do you remember what happened last night?"

"What do you mean?" his uncle asked, reaching for the vodka bottle.

Elliot could see that the only thing that mattered to Graham Swindale was to have a drink as he was pouring vodka over ice.

Elliot was prepared to do what he had to in order to get his uncle's attention.

When he had finished pouring, Elliot reached over the bar, took the glass and poured its contents down the drain. His uncle watched him, open-mouthed. Elliot met his astonished stare.

"Young man, what the hell do you think you're doing?"

"I'm going to talk to you before you start drinking."

"Are you forgetting whose house this is?"

"No, Sir," Elliot said as he walked halfway around the bar and stood before his uncle. "I want you to do something for me, please."

"I'll put you right out of my house! That's what I'll do for you!" Graham said as he headed for the library door.

"Get your revolver for me, uncle! Get me your gun!" Elliot directed, stopping Graham short.

"What? What are you talking about?"

"I want to talk about last night. Get me your gun."

Graham hesitated, looking at his desk. He pointed and said to Elliot, "It's in there, the bottom drawer."

"You get it for me," Elliot ordered as he moved toward his uncle, who stood swaying ever so slightly in the middle of the room.

"What does this have to do with exactly?" Graham asked, wishing this boy would get out before he had to throw him out.

"I want **you** to get me the gun," Elliot said again.

Graham's clouded mind decided to change its tactics. If he stood still, if he didn't move, then the boy would have to leave. But Elliot walked up to him and looked directly at him, and Graham felt himself becoming so nervous that he could not look directly at the boy. So once again, Graham decided to change his strategy.

The best way to get rid of this young pest is to get him the gun. As Graham moved unsteadily toward his desk, he did not realize that he was nearing a mental breakdown. As he was nearing the desk he forgot why he was going there. He stopped, hesitated, looked at Elliot, looked at the desk, and then remembered. The gun, he thought, get the gun. When you get the gun, you can have a drink.

Elliot, instead of following his uncle to the desk, walked quickly to the library door. There was a key in the lock. He turned it and put the key into his pocket. He tried the handle. It was locked. Elliot walked back to the desk. Graham stood, looking down at the bottom drawer.

"Open it," Elliot insisted.

Graham opened the drawer. The gun was not there. Graham turned and looked at Elliot. "It's not here. Why don't you leave?"

"Try the top drawer," Elliot said.

"I don't keep it there," Graham said.

"But that's where it is."

Graham could feel himself getting angry with this rude adolescent. He yanked open the drawer and saw his gun. He pulled it out and said, "So? So what?"

"Tell me where the shells are," Elliot continued.

Graham glanced down at cylinder and saw that it was empty.

"So, you've taken the shells out of my gun. May I ask why?"

Elliot looked closely at his uncle, searching his face. He didn't believe that Graham didn't remember.

"At three o'clock this morning I came into this room," Elliot began. "You were sitting in that desk chair, trying to put your thumb over the trigger. The gun was pointed up toward your face and your mouth was over the barrel. You were slobbering over the gun."

"This is ridiculous!" Graham replied, heading once more for the bar. He had to have a drink. "I did no such thing!"

"You were too drunk to find the trigger," Elliot continued, following him toward the bar. "That's the only thing that saved you."

"You're an insolent little puke!" Graham snapped, his eyes glaring.

It didn't even sound like Graham Swindale.

"And you're right from the pits of hell," Elliot answered quickly, beginning the attack.

"What!" Graham screamed.

"Remember me? Look closely! I saw you, and I'm here to call you out!"

"Who do you think you are!" Graham hissed. "You've never seen me!"

"Oh, yes I have! And in the name of Jesus, I tell you to come out!"

"What!"

Graham's anger suddenly turned to fear. He looked around anxiously, slammed against the bar, and then ran towards the doors. "Shut up, you puke-head little twit!" he screamed at Elliot as he grabbed at the door handle.

"It's locked!" Elliot yelled. "You can't take him anywhere! You have to leave by yourself!"

Graham turned and said, fiercely, "He wants me here! He does! He does! He asked me here! You have no right!"

"No," Elliot said, as he came close to Graham's face. "My uncle doesn't want to be a drunkard anymore! In the name of Jesus, I call you out!"

Grinning suddenly, his uncle shouted out at Elliot, "I don't drink, stupid child! Oh, you are a stupid one!" With a laugh he pushed Elliot away, showing surprising strength.

Elliot felt his skin crawl as he looked into the inflamed eyes of his uncle. He now knew that the spirit he'd talked to in the dream wasn't the spirit of alcohol!

Dear God, Elliot thought, my uncle has more than one demon in him! In the hallway, those words that came into my mind! What were the names? They must be the names of the spirits within him!

"Who are you then?" the amazed Elliot demanded, moving to confront his uncle again. "There's more than one of you in there!"

Then Elliot stated out loud for the spirits to hear, "Thank you, Lord, for your warning."

"Get out of my way!" his uncle shrieked as he tried to move away from him. Elliot blocked his path. "I'll take you apart!" Graham cried, even though at this moment he stood petrified against the library door.

"What's your name?" Elliot asked, suddenly placing his palm on the chest of Graham. Graham slapped his hand away!

"Don't touch me!" Graham screamed, sliding along the door, away from Elliot's touch.

But it was already done. Elliot had found out what he wanted to know. "It's Suicide!" Elliot stated harshly, "I'm talking to a demon whose name is `Suicide'! It was **you** in my dream!" Elliot spit out, getting right into his uncle's face. "And now **you're** coming out of my uncle in the name of Jesus! You can't stay in the presence of that Name, you sniveling coward!"

"You...you stupid child!" Graham screamed at him. "I don't know you!"

"You know Jesus, though! And your ugly little friends know Him too! You all have to go! You're the boss, aren't you?"

"Shut up! Shut up!" Graham snarled. "I'll kill you!" With that, Graham gave a terrible, pit-smelling belch.

"Drunkard!... Hopelessness!... Worthlessness!... and Dumb!" Elliot screamed out. "Oh, dumb spirit, you're all bootlicking friends of Suicide! I call you all out in the name of Jesus! But it's you, Suicide! You're the unearthly leader in there! You've missed your turn! You're too late! I call you out now, in the name of Jesus of Nazareth... come out... now! Go to your dark place alone! My uncle's not going with you! Almighty God wants you out!"

Suddenly Graham pushed Elliot with such force that Elliot was thrown backwards across the room, sliding along the polished floor.

Then, screaming, Graham, rushed halfway across the room towards the bay windows.

"Stupid child! Stupid..." Graham screamed as he suddenly lifted his arms out in front of him, as if trying to fly. Then he fell flat on the floor, as if shot. He lay there motionless.

Elliot jumped quickly to his feet and shook his fist in the direction of the bay windows. He was filled with an anger he had never felt before. He screamed out, "And in the name of Jesus, I tell you to leave this house and never come back! Go to some dark, hideous place where you all belong, you scumbags!"

Elliot's body was shaking as he went and knelt by his uncle. Turning him over, he saw blood covering Graham's face. It was running from his nose and from a cut over one eye. His cheek was scraped raw.

Elliot got a wet towel from the bar and then sat down on the floor next to the bleeding man. He lifted his uncle's head and placed it on his lap and began wiping the blood from his face. Graham came to and opened his eyes.

"What happened?" Graham asked weakly.

"Demons," Elliot answered as he continued to work on his bleeding nose.

"Demons? Here?" Graham asked fearfully.

"Yes," Elliot replied.

Graham knew beyond a doubt that his nephew was right. He began to cry. Elliot held his uncle and said softly, "They're gone now."

"They were in me, weren't they?"

"Yes."

"I wanted to kill you," Graham confessed. "I had to get away from you."

"They're nasty things. They almost had you last night."

"I know," Graham confessed through his tears. "I lied to you. I remembered taking the gun from the drawer. And...and I remembered someone pulling my hair...and then seeing your face."

Elliot lifted the towel, checking to see if the Graham's bleeding had subsided. "I saw one of the demons inside you...in a dream," Elliot said, placing the towel back over his eye.

Frightened again, Graham said, "You did?"

"Yes."

"Oh, my God, you mean they have form?"

"Yes. They're spirits, but they have form. He was an ugly thing."

"Oh, dear God," Graham said, once more in tears.

Elliot held him and let him cry. Then, when the tears subsided, Elliot said, "He's the one who saved you."

"What?"

"God. He's the one who saved you."

"He did?"

"Yes, He's the one who knows what's inside us."

Graham thought about this, saying, "He gave you the dream."

"Yes," Elliot said simply, "It's always Him."

"Why did He do that for me?" Graham asked.

"Well, He loves you, and I think someone has been praying for you."

"Praying? Who?"

"Aunt Elsie. I think it's her."

Graham looked up at the boy, then tears filled his eyes again; he couldn't talk. He could only grab the boy's arm.

Elliot watched him for a moment, "I want to ask you something."

"What?"

"If you would have died last night, if you would have killed yourself, where do you think you would have gone?"

Graham stared at the boy, astonished at the thoughts that were going through his mind. Then, horrified, he replied, "I would have been with the demons."

"Yes," Elliot said, "And they live in hell."

"I never believed in hell before," Graham said.

"Do you now?"

"Oh, yes," he answered quickly.

"I have to warn you. They can come back," Elliot said firmly, knowing the exact words to say next to his uncle.

"What!" the startled Graham exclaimed.

Elliot quoted, "When an evil spirit comes out of a man, it goes through dry places seeking rest and does not find it. Then it says, `I will return to the house I left.' When it arrives, it finds the house swept clean and put in order. Then it goes and takes seven other spirits more wicked than itself, and they go in and live there."

"How do you know this?"

"They're not my words. Jesus said them."

Graham pondered what he had just heard. "Then what do I do?" he asked, near panic. He lifted himself off Elliot's lap and struggled to kneel in front of his nephew. Blood still ran down his face.

"I've got to know, Elliot! I can't stand to have them back. What do I do?"

"Jesus said, `He who is not with me, is against me, and he who does not gather with me, scatters'." Elliot could see that Graham was perplexed, not yet understanding.

Elliot smiled and continued, "It's simple, Uncle." He pointed a finger at Graham's chest and said, "Jesus has to be in there. His Spirit will fill up your house."

"How do I get Him to do that?"

There was a knock at the library door, then an apprehensive voice inquired, "Graham? Graham, are you alright?" It was Harriet, trying to open the door.

Graham didn't move from his kneeling position. "Not now, Harriet, not now!" he yelled out. He continued to stare at Elliot, and asked again, "Please, what do I do?"

"Jesus tells us that we're all sinners. And that's why He came down to earth, to help us. Ask him for help."

Graham thought about this, then with a rueful smile said, "Oh, I am that! I never thought of it that way, but that's certainly what I am... a sinner!"

He stared at Elliot for a moment, and then closed his eyes. After a few moments he opened them again. "What am I supposed to say to Him? What did you say when you did it?"

"I was four years old," Elliot answered.

Graham blinked in surprise at him. "Four?"

"Yes," Elliot replied. "Why don't you just tell Him what you feel and how much you need His help?"

"Will he really hear me?"

"God hears everything."

Graham looked at the boy. He believed him.

Graham closed his eyes, and began, "Jesus." It was as though he was testing the name.

"Jesus, I want to thank you for giving my nephew that dream. If you hadn't, I'd be dead, and in..." He sobbed deeply, unable to say the appropriate word. "Oh, Jesus, I need your help. I'm afraid of the way I've been. And I know I can't run my life by myself, and I can't have those demons back. I can't live like this anymore!" Lowering head to the floor, he sobbed again.

He raised himself back up to his knees and pointed to his heart. "I need You in here with me. I know I don't deserve You, but I've got to have Your help." He paused and thought for a moment. "And I'm sorry I went to church all these years and never really believed in You. Help me to live a different kind of life. And help me with my family. I'm really sorry, Jesus."

Graham couldn't say anymore. He just bent forward to the floor and began to cry. But God had already heard him, had already done what Graham had asked.

Graham finally sighed, got slowly off the floor and made his way to the couch. "I'm so tired, Elliot," he said, exhausted. He was asleep as he fell onto the sofa. Elliot covered his uncle with a blanket, lifted his head and slid his pillow under it.

Walking to the library door, Elliot took the key from his pocket and unlocked it. When he opened the door, he saw his aunt sitting on the hall settee.

"He's asleep," Elliot said.

"I heard him scream and... and cry," Harriet said. "What did you do to him?"

Elliot sighed, leaving the door to the library open. "He's alright, and I think he'll probably sleep until morning. I'm sorry, but your husband will have to answer whatever questions you have."

Harriet watched the boy as he walked down the hall and went into the dining room. She got up and anxiously looked into the library, unsure if she should enter. She couldn't see her husband, who was asleep on the couch facing the windows. She decided not to enter. Reaching in, she shut off the lights and then gently closed the doors. She walked down the hall to the stairs. Though it was only nine o'clock, she felt exhausted.

Elliot was starved. When he walked into the kitchen, Marny was at the sink, looking over at him and motioned towards the kitchen table.

"Sit there, Elliot," she said, drying her hands.

Elliot went and sat. She pressed a button on the micro, then reached into the refrigerator and brought out a large salad wrapped in plastic. She unwrapped it and set it in front of him. The silverware had already been placed.

"How did you know I'd be here?" Elliot asked.

She sat down across from him and smiled. She watched as he prayed for the food, then dug in. She stayed quiet for a while just watching the boy eat. They smiled at each other, and she just had to know.

"Something good happened tonight, didn't it?"

Elliot, who had a mouthful of salad, smiled and nodded affirmatively.

"Could we count it as a miracle?" the black woman inquired.

Once again, Elliot smiled and nodded.

"I knew it!" she said, getting up from the chair. "I knew it!" She clapped and did a little dance on her way to the microwave oven.

"Thank You, Lord, thank You!" she sang with her dancing, "Oh, I knew You were here tonight!"

* * *

Usually the girls had to rush from house to house, picking each other up, forgetting books or makeup or lunches, and then frantically drive into the parking lot and breathlessly run to their first classes just ahead of the bell. But this morning, things were different. They were fifteen minutes early. Trish was driving, and Rachel sat beside her. Evelyn was home with a cold, and Dottie had a dentist appointment at ten. As Trish signaled and pulled into the parking lot, she noticed a white jeep in front of them.

"Look who I see!" Trish said.

"Who?" Rachel said, looking at Trish. Trish motioned her head, and Rachel looked directly in front of them. Rachel recognized Elliot immediately.

"Oh, my Lord, look who's with him!" Trish exclaimed.

"Who is it?" Rachel asked, not able to tell from the back.

"It's Arnold Swindale!"

"Really?" Rachel said, her heart sinking at the thought of the two of them being friends.

"What are **they** doing together?" Trish asked, as she followed the boys and parked right next the Jeep. Rachel's stomach began to churn as she saw that she was going to have to say something to Elliot. He got out right beside her. If she opened the door, she would bump him!

Elliot glanced over and broke out in a smile. As Rachel started to open the door she felt Elliot take hold of it and open it for her. Smiling at him, she got out.

"Hello," he said.

"Hello," Rachel answered. She turned to acknowledge Arnold Swindale, but he was already walking away from the car toward the school. Rachel reached into the back seat to get her books and a roll of drawings for her art class; it was going to be an unwieldy armful.

"Need some help?" Elliot asked.

Suddenly, she was glad for the bulky load. Thank you, Lord, she thought. "Maybe you could carry some drawings for me?"

"Why don't I carry your books, and you carry the drawings?" he answered as took the books from her arms.

She felt giddy just standing so close to him. She reached into the back seat and picked up the drawings.

"Don't forget your lunch," he said, just in time.

She reached back again and picked it up. Rachel glanced over at Trish who was standing on the other side of the car, smiling like an idiot!

"This is my friend, Trish Lotter," Rachel said to Elliot.

"Hi, I'm Elliot Reed."

"I remember your name," Trish replied. "Feeling any better?" she teased.

Elliot got the insinuation and laughed. "Yes," he answered, "I think I'm back to normal." Rachel's friend didn't miss much, he thought.

"I'll see you at lunch," Trish said. "I've gotta go build a fire." With that she waved to both of them, turned and hurried through the cars.

"What does she have to do?" Elliot asked.

"She has ceramics first period. She's supposed to help the teacher with the kiln, but she's never there on time. Today, he'll faint." The two started walking towards the buildings.

"Are you an artist, too?" Elliot asked.

"No," she answered. "Trish is the artist. I enjoy it, but she is really blessed."

There was an awkward moment, with each of them wondering what should be said next. Then Elliot asked, as he walked behind her through the narrow passages between parked cars, "What's your first class?"

"Algebra," she answered.

"With Mister Sala?"

"Yes. Do you have him too?" she asked, wondering what he was studying and what his classes were.

"For swimming."

"Are you on the swim team?" she said, turning and looking at him.

"Yes," he answered, smiling as he saw her surprised look.

She was walking backwards now, looking at him. "My brother was on the team, backstroke and hundred meters free style."

Elliot could tell she wanted to hear which event he would swim.

"I think Mister Sala wants me to do the distances...fifteen hundred meters, maybe."

"Wow," she said. "Can you swim that far? Two laps and I'm pooped." She laughed and turned back around.

He smiled. Her eyes were a deep green, and he really liked talking to her. She was funny besides.

"Where did you go to school last year?" she asked as they walked side by side off the parking lot and onto campus.

"St. Maurice's' Military Academy."

She looked at him. "A Catholic military school?"

"Yes," he answered, looking at her puzzled face. "Is that bad?"

"No, it's just that...I've never met anyone who's gone to such a place." As soon as she had said it, she knew it didn't sound right. He must be Catholic, she thought.

"Maybe I'd better tell you about such a place," Elliot said, teasing. "While I was there, they never told me I couldn't tell someone like you about the place."

Rachel stopped on the sidewalk that leads to her classroom. She smiled and said, "I didn't mean it the way it came out, but I would like to hear about it."

"Is lunch too far away or should I come back for you after this class?"

Rachel laughed and reached for her books. "I think lunch would be soon enough."

Elliot continued to walk with her and looked inside her room. "Where's your desk?" he asked.

"Second from the front," she said as he put her books in her arms.

"You like to sit in front?"

"Yes," she said, wondering why he asked.

"Me too," he answered with a smile. "You see, already we have something in common." He nodded goodbye as he left. Rachel walked down the aisle to her seat. She was shaking, and her heart was pounding.

Elliot turned the wrong way once he had left Rachel. He had to do an about-face to get to his business class. He laughed at himself and felt great!

* * *

Graham woke with the sun hitting his face. He opened his eyes and looked at his watch. It was nine o'clock in the morning! He had slept twelve hours. His face felt tender, so he touched it. It hurt. He smiled and slowly lifted himself into a sitting position. No headache. Not even the slightest bit. He sat for a moment, looking around, just feeling what was going on. He felt...like...he might be someone else.

He considered the thought. Yes, it's true; I don't feel like myself at all. He had no headache; he didn't feel sick, and he didn't have that terrible "blah" feeling he always had. Now he felt...like he had never felt before. That was it! All right! He felt, new... sort of or something like it. He wondered what he should do? He certainly knew he didn't want to sit on the sofa any longer, but beyond that, he wasn't sure.

He stood up and looked around again. He couldn't get over it. He actually didn't know what to do! Before now, it never entered his mind that he didn't know what to do. He just never did anything. Before - that was what he thought he wanted to do, nothing. Now, he knew for certain, he no longer wanted to do nothing... but he didn't know what to do. He found this amusing. He walked to the bay windows and looked out at the morning, then stretched. He laughed out loud. When he did, he felt his face stretch.

"Ouch!" he said, as the pain went through his face. He felt it in his cheek, in his nose and even in his eye. He didn't care though. He just felt fantastic!

Walking to the wet bar, he looked down at it, then slowly closed its doors. He opened them again, and then closed them. He knew he was being silly, but he didn't care. He opened them and closed them again. He laughed, felt the pain again, and then went into the bathroom. He looked at his face in the mirror. He had a cut over a blackened eye and a swollen nose. He couldn't help but laugh. He touched his nose, felt the pain, and laughed some more. "Oh, what a face!" he said out loud. "You should mess with the floor more often!" He laughed at his own joke.

He stepped back from the mirror and looked himself over. His corduroy jacket, that he wore all the time, was shabby, and he knew it should have been discarded long ago. He took it off and dropped it on the bathroom floor. Once again he inspected himself. He decided he didn't like his pants or his shirt. They too were shabby. He took them off and dropped them on top of his jacket. Turning, he took his robe from the hook on the back of the door and put it on. Once more he surveyed himself in the mirror.

"Boo!" he said. Going to the sink, he gently splashed water on his face and hair, and quickly ran a brush through his wet hair. Picking up his clothes from the floor, he turned off the light and went through the library. As he reached the doors of the large room where he had spent most of his life for the last five years, he turned and looked at it. Shaking his head in disbelief, he opened the door, stepped into the hall and shut the door behind him.

He went through the empty dining room to the kitchen door. He peeked inside. Marny was there, but she didn't see him. Graham felt good, like he was about ten years old. Everything seemed so different to him.

"Hello," he said.

Marny jumped about a foot. "Oh, Mr. Swindale! I was some where's else!"

"I'm sorry, Marny." He came into the kitchen.

She looked at him. He never got up before noon. He had his clothes on one arm, and he was smiling at her.

"Can I take those for you?" she asked.

"No, but I'd like you to tell me where the trash is."

"Right inside that door," she answered, pointing.

She watched as he opened it and stuffed all of those clothes into the trash bin. He looked down at them, smiled, and then looked back at Marny. She watched him closely as he shut the door, walked over and sat at the breakfast nook. He smiled at her.

"Would you like to eat now?" she asked. He never ate breakfast.

"Yes," he said, still smiling.

"What would you like?"

"What do you have?"

"Fruit, cereal, eggs, bacon, ham, French toast, waffles, pancakes, toast, and that's only breakfast."

Graham laughed. "They all sound good. What do you suggest?"

Marny had never heard him laugh before. "I'm partial to a fluffy waffle with strawberries, and a side of well-done bacon," was her answer.

"That sounds delicious," he responded. "What would you drink with that?"

"I like an herb tea, `cause me and caffeine don't get along."

"Sounds good too. I'll take it."

As she started to get everything together, she looked over at him. He was still smiling at her. She smiled back and went about her work. The only time he had ever stepped foot in her kitchen was whenever he had walked through, she mused.

"How long have you been here, Marny?"

She stopped and thought about it. "I'm starting my twelfth year," she said.

"Well, I'm glad you're here," he said. "I've always enjoyed your food."

"Thank you, Sir," she replied, astonished.

He paused for a moment. Concern was in his eyes as he looked at her. "I'm sorry I haven't told you long before this."

Marny was somewhat embarrassed. She could tell that he really meant what he was saying. "Well, thank you," she responded. "I'm glad to be here, Sir." Suddenly she realized that she meant it.

"Good," he said as he stood. "I thought maybe I'd go see Aunt Elsie for a moment. Where would she be now?"

"She's in her room, reading. Then she'll nap from eleven to twelve."

"Good. I'll be right back down." He smiled and walked out the hallway door. Marny couldn't help but smile too as she said out loud to herself, "He's just like a child, Lord, just like a child!"

Graham knocked on Elsie's door and opened it. She was sitting in a rocking chair next to the window. She didn't try to hide her surprise. "Graham!"

"Hello, Elsie," he said smiling. Going over, he kissed her on the forehead.

"Graham... Graham... sit down, sit down."

Moving the chair from the desk, he sat next to her. She leaned forward and gently touched his swollen face.

"I had a wondrous fall last night," he said with a child-like smile.

"You did? Wondrous?" she asked, curious.

"Yes. I wanted to come up and thank you for praying for me."

"How did you know I did that?" she said in surprise.

"Elliot told me."

Her mind considered what he had just said. No, she thought, she was positive about this. "I never told Elliot that. I've never told anyone. That was my secret."

"Well, somehow Elliot knew your secret," Graham replied.

"That young man knows a lot of things doesn't he?" the old lady said with a smile.

"Yes, thank God," Graham answered. He reached forward and took her hand. "I want to thank you for your prayers, for not giving up on me."

Elsie smiled and mused while she looked at his swollen face. "Something wonderful has happened to you. You don't even seem to be the same person."

"I know," he answered quietly.

"Have you seen Harriet yet?"

"No."

"I think you should. She might want to meet her new husband."

"Yes, I want to see her too. Right now, I think Marny might be waiting breakfast for me."

"Good. Maybe a steak for your eye, too."

Graham laughed. "No, Aunt Elsie, this eye is like a badge. I'd like to keep it for a while." He kissed her on her cheek, and left the room.

Graham ate all of the breakfast and drank every bit of the tea. He watched three hummingbirds at a feeder in the back yard, fighting for position.

Marny came from the washroom, the whirl of the machines could be heard as she shut the door behind her.

"Where is Mrs. Swindale during this hour?" Graham asked.

"Between nine and eleven, she's usually in that weight room of hers."

"How long has she been doing that?" Graham asked, not even remembering when the snooker room had been redone.

"Nearly three years now," Marny said as she took his plate.

This man has been in a real fog, she thought.

"That was delicious," Graham said. "Thank you."

"You're welcome, Sir."

Graham got up and walked across the kitchen. He turned and looked back at the brightly lit room, with its nice view of the lawn and pool area from its many windows. "You've got a real nice place to work in, Marny."

Turning to look back at him from the sink, she answered, "Yes, Sir, it is nice." She watched as he left the room. "My, my," as she went back to her dishes.

Graham walked slowly down the hallway to the last room of the west wing. He stood before the door of the weight room and listened. Music was playing. He barely remembered that three years ago Harriet had asked him to come and see what she had created. He hadn't wanted to see it then, having no more interest in exercise than he had had in snooker.

Now, standing here, he tried to remember what it had looked like, but without success. He started to knock, then thought better of it. Pulling the door open slightly, he looked in. Harriet was seated on a machine at the far end of the room. She was pulling a metal bar down behind her neck, then letting the weights carried by the bar over her head. He could see that she was sweating and breathing rhythmically along with her work.

When he stepped into room, she saw his reflection in the mirror. Stopping immediately, she turned to him.

"Hello," he said.

"Graham," she said, completely caught off guard. Getting up quickly, she went over to him. She looked up at his face.

He smiled down at her. "You work hard in here."

"Are you all right?" she asked, looking at his cut and bruises.

"Yes, I'm fine. Thanks. Do you mind if I come in and watch?"

"No...not at all."

As he came into the room, he looked around for a moment, glancing at all the shiny equipment. He felt very nervous. "This is a beautiful room. And that outside area...are there fish in that pond?"

"Yes, Koi," she answered.

"Maybe I could go out there until you finish," he said, really asking if that would be all right.

"Yes," she answered, "it's a nice place to sit."

He hesitated, smiled at her, then went to the glass wall and slid open one of the doors. As he closed the door behind him, he smiled once more at her, and then went over to the pond. He pulled one of the chairs near the water and sat looking down.

Harriet went back to the machine she was working on and sat down, but she knew she wouldn't be able to finish her sets. She was really unnerved that he had come here. And what had happened to his face? She knew that Elliot had something to do with it, and it was because of her that the boy was in their house. As she watched her husband watch the fish, he looked up at her. He smiled at her. He looks different somehow, Harriet thought, lost, sort of, as if he's here because he didn't want to be alone.

The idea surprised her, knowing how farfetched it was to believe that Graham could ever be lonely. But that was what she found herself feeling. Maybe it's the way it should be. Maybe it's his turn to feel what it's like, she thought. She glanced once more as he watched the fish. She knew she didn't want anybody to suffer needlessly. Again, she was puzzled by her thoughts. Up until now, she had wanted to get even with this man. But as she looked out though the window at him hunched over in the chair, unshaven, and with a bruised face, she felt drawn to him.

How can this be, she thought angrily. How can he just show up like this, and I'm willing to forget what it's been like for the past five years? It's not fair! But there he was, and she found herself wanting to go over to him, to be with him! More than anything else, this was what she wanted. This just can't be!

She got up, took a clean towel from the shelf and went out through the glass door. Graham looked up and watched as she walked beside the waterfall, took a long, round can from behind it, and came to stand beside his chair.

"Give me your hand," she said, with a shy smile. He reached out, and she turned his palm up. She sprinkled fish food over his palm.

"Just put the back of your hand over the water." He did as she directed. She pulled up the sleeve of his robe.

"Now let your hand down into the water." As he did so, the fish swam right onto his hand and started eating the food that was floating above his fingers. They were actually cupped in his hand, and some were even nibbling at his fingers!

Graham laughed like a child and exclaimed, "That's wonderful! Did you teach them to do that?"

"I guess so. It just sort of happened," she replied.

She hadn't heard him laugh in a long time. And he seemed so interested, so alive. She handed him the towel so he could dry his hand.

"Don't you want to finish your workout?"

"No, I don't think so," she responded, looking away from his gaze.

"You certainly fixed a nice place here," he said, sensing that she was feeling a little uncomfortable.

"Yes, it is nice, isn't it?"

Strange, Graham thought, how nervous he suddenly felt around this woman. But this was a new kind of nervousness, one mixed with a curious excitement, as though there were things about this woman he wanted to know, things that he might be seeing for the first time. He thought about reaching out and touching her, but instead he said, "You look like you did when we first met."

Harriet flushed and then answered without looking at him. "I weigh about the same now. I think there's only three or four pounds difference."

She could feel his eyes on her. She glanced up from the fish and saw he was smiling at her. Even though he had a black eye, a swollen nose, and needed a shave, she liked what she saw in his face. She knew that she was being admired.

Oh, God, she thought, I'm such a pushover for even the littlest compliment...even a kind look! But as soon as she thought it, she was sorry. No, she said to herself. I can see that something is different about him. I'm **not** going to **feel** badly because he's saying something nice to me!

He lowered his head and looking down at his own hands. Harriet had a momentary impulse to reach out and touch him, but she waited, wondering and hoping.

"I threw my clothes away this morning," he said.

"What?"

"The clothes I wore all the time...my corduroy jacket, my pants, and that shirt I used to like," he said with a rather doleful smile. "I put them all in the trash."

Harriet was unsure if she should respond to him, so said nothing.

Graham glanced rather shyly at her before he continued. "I don't want to live like I've been living." He thought about what he had just said, but decided it was best to reword it. "No, that's not the truth at all. I have to say it the way it has really been. I don't want to die the way I've been dying."

He moved forward in his seat and spoke softly to his wife, "I want to tell you how sorry I am." He frowned slightly and added, "I know that being sorry isn't enough. Nothing can take away the terrible years I've given you. But I still have to tell you how I feel." He smiled kindly at her as he saw her searching for something to say.

"Please, you don't have to say anything," he explained, looking at her still-beautiful face. "These things that I want to say to you don't need answers." He hesitated and shook his head, not fully understanding what it was he was thinking and feeling.

"When I was standing outside the door, I didn't think you would want to see me or talk to me. I was sure you would tell me to get out. That it was too late. I wouldn't have blamed you at all." He paused and openly searched her face. "But you didn't. That shows how little I know about you." He sat for a moment, staring at her, then continued. "Oh, God, I've been a self-indulgent foolish man!" Tears came to his eyes as he sat there blinking through them.

"Oh, Graham," his wife said compassionately. "Graham, what's happened to you?" She felt his vulnerability, and it distressed her. He was suddenly telling her that the terrible unhappiness, the shameful lack of love that had been between the two of them was all his fault! And up until this very hour, through all the difficult years of their marriage, she had believed that was so. It was **his** fault, his drinking and self-imposed isolation had caused it.

Now, unexpectedly, she found herself wanting to take the blame with him, but she checked herself. No, she wouldn't do it.

Graham looked down at his hands, and then slowly brought his hand to his eyes and wiped the tears away. "I don't think this is a good time for me to tell you what happened, because I don't understand it myself." He looked at her then, and added, "I **want** to tell you, but it must be the right time."

"It's all right, Graham. I'm just glad you're here." The words slipped out, but she found she really meant them.

He searched her face for a moment. "You mean that, don't you?"

"Yes," she answered. "That is what I've always wanted."

He paused, not knowing exactly how to say what he knew he must say, "There's one more point...that goes along with throwing away my old clothes..."

"What is it?"

"I can't live in the library anymore."

She knew immediately that he was asking permission to come back to their bedroom. He'd never asked before. In the past, when he'd been in the library for weeks or months and then had come back for one night or even one hour, he had never asked, only taken.

"It's still your bedroom too," she responded, even though at that moment she wasn't sure what that might mean between them.

He watched her face as she said it, then nodded and said, "This must be terribly difficult for you. Maybe it would be easier for you if you could think of me as a stranger."

"How would I do that?" Harriet asked, startled at such a suggestion.

"I'm not sure. But I know that I feel like one."

She thought about this and surprisingly found herself taking a very direct approach. "Since you've been with me today, you could very well be a stranger. It's certainly true that I have no idea what you might say next. I guess I might be able to do that." She noticed that even the look in his eyes had changed. There was a chance that he was even more of a stranger than she knew.

"Good," he said as he stood. "I want to go look through my clothes, a shower maybe...an errand or two. Then I thought, if you'd like, we might go out for dinner tonight."

Now this, she thought, certainly sounds like a stranger! My husband never liked to go out.

"Yes, I'd like that very much."

"And what kind of food do you like?" he asked politely.

Now he knows I love seafood, and he hates it, she thought. She had paused too long.

"Don't forget now, we're strangers." he added.

"I like seafood. It's my favorite," she responded.

"What a wonderful coincidence! It's mine too!" he said.

She laughed. If she didn't know him so well, she would have believed him. He laughed with her and then said, "Would seven be alright?"

"Just fine," she answered. "How shall I dress?"

"Bring out the jewels," he said, but then thought better of it and covered himself. "Ah, forgive me. There is a chance you don't have any. In that case, wear the best you have." Smiling, he bowed slightly and left through the sliding door.

She watched him as he went out of the workout room into the hallway. Smiling, she curled her feet under her on the chair and thought, I'm dressing for dinner, and I'm actually nervous about it! After all...having dinner with a stranger!

* * *

During lunch period, while Arnold was on his way to the cafeteria for a sandwich, he saw Elliot sitting on the lawn with Rachel Davis and Trish Modder, "brown bagging" it. Elliot waved at him. He ignored him.

What does Elliot think he's going to do with Rachel? Arnold thought. She's the coldest fish at school. Even the jocks who tried to pick up on her all struck out. A cold, cold fish!

After Arnold purchased a sandwich, he went out the other door so he wouldn't have to see Elliot again. Besides, he was about to score on some crack.

After Arnold walked by, Rachel asked, "Is he your friend?"

"He's my cousin," Elliot replied.

"Oh," Trish said without thinking, "that explains it."

Elliot glanced at her, then asked, "Explains what?"

She blushed and looked quickly to Rachel for help.

"It's just that we noticed this morning, that if he was your friend, he didn't seem to want to spend much time with you," Rachel answered for Trish.

Elliot smiled and answered, "He's not my friend, but I'm working on him. He's a tough nut." He paused and then said, "Well, I'm here to answer any and all questions about St. Maurice.

"St. Maurice?" Trish asked.

"That's where he went to school last year...a Catholic military school," Rachel said, filling her in.

"Really? How long did you go there" Trish asked.

"Since I was five years old!"

The two girls looked at him, then at each other, then back at Elliot.

"You've spent all of your school life in one place?" Rachel asked.

"Yes."

"Did you like that?" Trish asked.

"Yes," Elliot said, with a smile. "I've got good memories about the place, and I had some good friends."

"There's a girl in my English class whose sister is becoming a nun," Rachel said. "What are they like?"

"Well, they're all different, just like anybody else. But they have one thing in common; they all really care about their work."

"Are you Catholic?" Rachel asked.

"No."

"You spent all that time in a Catholic school, and you aren't Catholic? How come?" Trish asked.

"My father didn't want me to be."

Both the girls had the same question on their mind. They glanced at each other, then Rachel asked, "Then what are you?"

Elliot thought about this before answering, "I'm not exactly sure." But then added quickly, "But I've got a church."

"Oh?" Rachel said, indicating her interest. Since her pastor had left, she had been thinking what it might be like to go elsewhere. "Which one do you go to?" she asked.

"It's a little white one, on the corner of Maple and Second Street."

Neither one of the girls could place it since it was on the other side of town.

"What's the name of it?" Trish asked.

Elliot didn't know because there hadn't been any sign. "I don't think it has a name yet. It's new."

"What denomination is it?" Rachel asked.

"I really don't know," Elliot answered. "I've haven't been there yet." He could see the look of surprise on Rachel's face.

"I just know it's my church because the pastor asked me to fellowship there. Fellowship, that is the right word, isn't it?"

"Yes, it's the word alright, but how do you know you can trust the pastor?" Trish asked.

"Because he knows the Word of God," Elliot said simply.

He could see that the girls had reservations about what he had just said. He smiled and remarked, "I always thought Thomas was a man."

Rachel caught on immediately, while Trish sat looking blankly at Rachel. Rachel laughed and said, "So, you think we're doubters, do you?"

"It certainly sounds that way," Elliot teased. "Of course, for doubters, there's only one way to find out."

"And how's that?" Rachel asked, already knowing the answer.

"You have to come and see," Elliot replied. "Both you Thomas's come with me Sunday and see."

Rachel and Trish looked at each other. Though both the girls went to the same church, their feelings about the changes that had taken place there during the past few months were quite different.

"I couldn't go," Trish said. "I'm in the choir."

"A little white church, huh?" Rachel mused with suspicious humor.

"That's right," Elliot added, "with a picket fence around it."

Rachel made up her mind. "Alright," she said, "I'll go."

"What?" Trish said, dumbfounded. "You haven't been to another church since you were born! What will your folks say?"

Rachel could never tell Trish that her parents were just as unhappy about the changes the church had taken as she was. Trish and her family were too close of friends, for too many years, to let her know that the Davis' no longer felt the way they used to.

"I think it will be alright," was Rachel's only answer.

After school, when girls went out to Trish's car, Elliot was sitting in his Jeep waiting for them.

"Hi," Rachel said.

"I was thinking, and I thought maybe, if you didn't mind, I'd take you home," Elliot said. "That way, I'll know where you live, and I can meet your parents and ask if it would be all right if you went."

"Really?" Rachel said, surprised. "You don't mind meeting parents?"

"I don't think so," Elliot answered. "Should I?"

"Oh," Rachel said, forgetting. "You've never met any before, have you?"

"No," Elliot answered, mystified. "Should I be nervous?"

"Parents don't like big bad boys who come to take their little girls away," Trish said, thoroughly enjoying the situation.

"Really?" Elliot responded, not knowing he was being teased. He looked at Rachel and said, "I just want to take you to my new church."

Both the girls laughed, and Rachel said, "My folks really aren't that way." She walked around and got into the Jeep. "Where's Arnold?" she asked.

"He never rides home with me after school. He goes places with his friends," Elliot said as he started the car. They waved at Trish and drove slowly from the parking lot.

As Trish watched them leave, she had a feeling that she was losing her best friend. Then, she thought, but if the shoe was on my foot, I would do the same thing.

Dolores saw the white Jeep pull up in front of the house with her daughter sitting in the passenger seat. Hurriedly, she took off her apron and went quickly to the back door. Marc, her husband, was in the garage working on an old car. He liked to find them, fix them up and sell them.

"Honey," Dolores said loudly, "we've got company."

"What?" he yelled. But when he came into the yard, his wife had already gone back into the house. He picked up a rag and wiped his hands. It had sounded to him like she said they had company. He had no idea who it could be in the middle of the day. I'd better go in and check, he thought. He wiped his feet before he entered the house.

From the kitchen, Marc Davis could see the young man who was talking to Dolores. Marc glanced at his daughter and immediately noticed the look on her face as she watched this boy. Marc had never seen her look at any young man like she was looking this one. A picture is worth a thousand words, he thought. As Marc came up to them, Rachel greeted her father with a smile.

"Oh, Daddy, this is Elliot Reed," she said.

Elliot turned and smiled at the man with the rag in his hand. It looked like he had been working on a car. He smelled of solvents, just like Charles did sometimes.

"Hello, Sir," Elliot said.

"Hi, Elliot," Marc said, shaking his hand. The boy looked strong enough to lift cars.

"I hope you don't mind me dropping by like this?"

"No, that's fine. Would you like to sit down?" Marc asked as he led them into the living room.

"Thank you, Sir."

Dolores sat next to her daughter, while Marc remained standing.

"Go ahead, Elliot, you sit, I'll stand," Marc said, pointing to his clothes. "This is no time for me to sit."

Elliot sat, then said, "I came by to meet both of you and to ask if it would be alright if Rachel went to church with me on Sunday?"

Marc decided that maybe he should sit. This boy sounded serious. "Just a minute," he said. He disappeared into the dining room and came back with a wooden hard-backed chair. He placed it near his wife and then sat.

"What church do you go to?" he asked.

Elliot smiled and then looked to Rachel. She understood.

"He doesn't know the name of it, because it is just getting started," she answered for him. "There isn't even a sign out in front. It's a little church over on the other side of town."

"At the corner of Maple and Second," Elliot added.

"Well, how do you know about it?" Marc asked Elliot.

"I talked with the pastor, and he helped me with a problem. Then, as I was leaving, he asked if I had church...a place to fellowship. I said no, so he told me to come there. But I knew I was supposed to go to that church even before that."

"How did you know?" Dolores asked.

"The first day I was here, I saw it. It was empty, but I knew it wasn't supposed to be."

"How did you know that?" Marc asked.

"I'm not sure. Just something told me. The next time I went by, a lady was cleaning inside. She said the church would be opening in a couple of weeks. Then a couple of days ago, like I said, I had a problem that I needed help with, and I went by. There was a man mowing the lawn, and he turned out to be the pastor."

"He didn't say what denomination he was?"

"No, Sir. Is that important?"

"Maybe, maybe not," Marc said. "What was his name? Maybe I could find out?"

"Art Lindquist," Elliot said.

"Oh, my God," Marc exclaimed.

Elliot was completely surprised at the looks on all their faces. They seemed to be in shock. Then Rachel's mother began crying. Mr. Davis put his arm around his wife and just stared at Elliot. Rachel was smiling widely, and there were tears in her eyes.

"What is it?" Elliot asked, looking at Rachel.

"Art Lindquist was our pastor until six months ago. He was fired. One Sunday, he was there, and then he just disappeared. Mother's been praying for him."

"Wow!" Elliot said softly, seeing Mrs. Davis still crying. "Maybe we should all go to the little church Sunday."

Dolores Davis looked up. Tears were still in her eyes, and she suddenly had to laugh. She wouldn't think of going anywhere else! Marc Davis saw the humor in it too and laughed with her. Rachel joined in, and then so did Elliot.

As they quieted, Rachel said, "Trish asked me what my parents would say when I told them I was going to another church."

Everyone in the room thought about this for a moment, then broke out in laughter again.

* * *

Harriet hadn't seen Graham all day. She dressed for dinner, went down to the library to look for him, but the room was empty. She went to the dining room. Aunt Elsie and Elliot were eating alone.

"Have you seen Graham?" she asked Elsie as she walked into the room.

"Oh, Harriet," Elsie exclaimed with a smile, "you look ravishing!

"You look beautiful, Aunt Harriet," Elliot added.

"Thank you," Harriet replied, pleased at the attention.

"I can't find Graham."

Marny opened the door from the kitchen. She stopped dead in her tracks, steam coming from the teacup in her hand. "Oh, Mrs. Swindale, you are an eyeful! My, that is one beautiful dress and what you do to it!"

Harriet couldn't help but be very pleased. "Thank you, one and all. Marny have you seen Mr. Swindale?"

"No, ma'am, not since breakfast."

Harriet looked at her wristwatch. "It's five to seven, and..."

The front door chimes rang.

"Would you like me to get that?" Elliot asked.

"No, you finish eating. I'll do it," Harriet said. "Besides, I'm too nervous to sit."

As she left the room, Elsie smiled mischievously and whispered, "What a nice surprise. Oh, isn't this a wonderful surprise!"

Elliot and Marny had no idea what she was talking about.

Harriet opened the front door. Graham stood smiling at her. He was wearing a white dinner jacket, dark pants, a beautiful light blue shirt and a dark silk tie. He had shaved and had his hair cut. Though he had a little bandage over his blackened eye and his nose was still swollen, he looked very handsome. His smile broadened as he stood looking at his wife.

"Oh, Harriet, you look unbelievable," he exclaimed, reaching out and taking her hand.

He led her from the threshold, closed the door behind her, then took a few steps backwards and looked at her again.

"You are the most elegantly beautiful woman I have ever seen."

Harriet found herself unsure of what to say. But she did feel exactly the way he had just described. She felt elegant and beautiful.

"Thank you, stranger," she said softly as he took her arm and led her down the wide porch steps.

It was a warm September evening, with the setting sun throwing long shadows over the driveway. The Rolls Royce, with the passenger door already opened, stood idling. He led her to it.

"My purse and wrap," she said.

"Ah, certainly. Where are they?"

"Just inside the door."

Graham ran up the stairs into the entry and then back. He handed her both items.

"No Charles tonight?" she asked as she took her things.

Graham went around to the driver's seat and replied as he got behind the wheel. "Charles might not understand...two strangers having dinner."

Harriet noticed a single rose lying on the dashboard. She glanced at Graham. He was smiling at her. Picking it up, she saw that there was a small note attached to the stem. She read it.

"Good evening," it read.

She smiled and looked at Graham. "Good evening to you, too."

Glancing down at her rose, she waited for him to start down the drive, but they didn't move. She knew that Graham was still looking at her. She glanced up at him. He had such a gentle, loving smile that she could only shyly smile back and then had to look away. I'm being loved, she thought, and she didn't know how to react. She felt anxious, almost nervous. Had she felt this way when she was younger? If she had, she couldn't remember it. Had she felt this way when she first met Graham? No. By then she was the one in charge, the first to decide things even when they concerned the things of the heart.

Just then Tina drove up the driveway in her Thunderbird. She saw the Rolls and started to pass by, then saw her mother and father sitting in the front seat. She stopped.

"Daddy?"

"Yes," Graham said politely.

"Mommy?" Tina said, still shocked.

"Yes," Harriet said with the same polite formality that Graham had used. With that, Graham put the car in gear and drove slowly down the driveway.

Tina closed her mouth as she turned her head and watched the stately automobile.

My God, what has happened, she thought. They don't even look like the same people. And his face, what happened to it? Even with the bandage and black eye, she was struck by how handsome he looked. Tina turned off her motor, leaving the car in front of the house. She knew she was late for supper, but maybe not too late. She hurried into the dining room.

"I just saw Daddy and Mommy driving away in your car, Aunt Elsie," Tina said as she sat down across from Elliot.

"Yes, I know," Elsie, replied as she ate her dessert.

"Charles wasn't driving."

"Yes, I know. Your father asked your mother out for dinner, but not Charles."

"Daddy looked wonderful," Tina said, watching Elliot. She noticed that he had fresh fruit. He never seemed to eat sweets.

Marny stuck her head into the dining room. "You're late, child."

"It couldn't be helped," Tina said abruptly. She didn't like being talked down to by Marny, even though she knew she was supposed to help herself if she was late.

Marny stared at her for a moment, before disappearing into the kitchen. Tina wasn't sure if was going to get served or not but decided to wait and see. She turned her attention to Elliot. He continued to eat, ignoring her.

During the past few nights before going to sleep, Tina had remembered Elliot, naked, as she had seen him in his apartment. She found she couldn't sleep when she thought about him, because it led her to start wondering what it would be like having him in bed with her? From those thoughts, her mind had begun planning how she could get him there. She hadn't been sleeping as easily as usual.

"How's school?" she asked casually. Elliot looked up in response.

"Just fine. I like it," he answered. Her eyes always startled him; they were so lightly colored. But there was something cold about them, too.

"What classes are you taking?" she asked, putting nothing behind her words.

"Mostly business and computers. They told me I'd already completed my required courses."

"Business, huh?" she answered. "It's a bore, isn't it?"

"Not so far," he replied, pausing. "At St. Maurice's, the Colonel had a book on the industrialization of the United States. I liked it."

"You're not going to be a businessman, are you?" she asked, knowing the history of her family and hating it.

"I'm not sure what I'm going to be," he answered. "What would you like to be?"

"I'm not sure either," she answered while she thought, but I do know that you, my handsome cousin, are going to be asking me different kinds of questions in the near future. The same kind of questions Alex asks after we make love. `Do you love me?'...`Was it as wonderful for you as it was for me?' Then, in her fantasy, she heard Elliot say, `I love you'...just the way Alex would always say it to her.

Marny came through the door with a salad and main course, which she set before Tina. Eying her once, Marny said, "What do you say, girl?"

"Thank you, Marny," Tina said with a condescending smile.

Tina's attitude did not go unnoticed by Marny. Someday girl, it's gonna all turn around on you, the cook thought as she picked up Elsie's dessert plate and went back into the kitchen.

* * *

Graham gently took Harriet's arm as they entered the restaurant. As the headwaiter led them to their table, Harriet saw another rose placed across her empty setting. It, too, had a small note attached to it. She sat and opened it. It read, "Thank you for having dinner with me."

"You're welcome," she said to Graham as the waiter placed a menu in her hand.

Harriet knew that Graham had never done anything like this before. When he had given flowers in the past, it had been a dozen hurriedly picked up on his way home after work. Those times she would react with a smile, a little peck maybe, and then place them in water on the dining room table. As far as she could remember, he had never mentioned seeing them.

Graham watched his wife as she smelled the beautiful rose. He enjoyed giving flowers this way. The look on her face as she read the card, and the smile she gave him were very gratifying to him.

Harriet looked over the menu and ordered her favorite fish while Graham ordered a chicken dish. She noticed that he ate very little, instead mostly talking and watching her. He drank only water during the meal, and they both said no to the wonderful dessert tray.

"They have a very special blend of coffee here," Graham said, knowing how much she loved it.

"Really?" she paused, and then frowned slightly. "I've been trying to stop."

"It's a chocolate-almond, from Europe," he said, knowing her tastes.

"Oh, my," she exclaimed, her eyes widening. Chocolate was her favorite, and almonds were not far behind. "Maybe just one cup."

Graham smiled at her, motioning to the waiter, who came quickly to the table.

"She would like your chocolate-almond coffee."

"Of course. And for you, sir?"

"Nothing, thank you."

The waiter moved quickly away.

I didn't remember seeing it on the menu, Harriet thought. How did he know such a thing? She decided that she would say nothing about it. As long as he knew, that's all that mattered. This new man was very mysterious indeed.

The waiter returned with a beautiful, ornate glass filled with a dark, steaming liquid. As she began reaching for the glass, the waiter placed another plate near her coffee. On it was a small, square, black velvet box. She glanced at the waiter, who smiled, nodded politely and moved away. She looked at Graham. He was smiling at her, watching her closely. She could smell the chocolate and almond.

"It really is Chocolate-almond."

"Yes."

"It wasn't on the menu," she said softly.

"They said if I brought the grounds, they would prepare it."

She laughed and said, "Oh, Graham."

She looked to the small black box, picking it up, but not opening it.

"What is it?" she asked, loving the anticipation.

"It's smaller than a bread box," he said softly.

She laughed and opened it. It was a golden broach, with three tear-shaped emeralds set in it. It was breathtakingly beautiful.

"Oh, Graham, it's magnificent," she exclaimed.

"Yes, it is. As soon as I saw it, it reminded me of you."

"Graham, it's...you're..."

She found she couldn't continue. Her throat constricted as her eyes filled up, and she was suddenly crying. She couldn't stop herself. Graham reached across the table and took her hand. She grabbed hold of his fingers, while she cried softly into her napkin.

Slowly she stopped, regained what she could of her composure and said quietly, "Graham, please, take me home."

Graham motioned to the waiter, then placed a credit card on the table. As Graham stood and went to hold the chair for his wife, he said quietly to the waiter, "I'll pick my card up tomorrow."

"Of course, Mr. Swindale. Thank you and good night."

As they left the restaurant, Graham considerately put his arm around her waist, and she leaned against him as they waited for their car. Once inside, alone in the darkness, she moved as close as she could to him and cried. As he put his arm around her, he gently kissed the top of her head. Then his eyes filled up with tears, making it impossible to drive. He pulled off the road, just outside the parking lot of the restaurant. There, they held each other and cried together.

* * *

Elliot woke, startled, not knowing what had wakened him. As he looked at his clock, he heard a knock on his door. It was three-thirty in the morning. He got up and went to the door. Opening it, he saw Arnold leaning against the rail. Even in the dark, Elliot could tell there was something wrong with him.

Elliot opened the screen door and went to his cousin. In the pale moonlight, Elliot could see that someone had given him a beating. There was dried blood around his nose and mouth, and he had a look of pain on his face, even though he was trying to hide it.

"Could I come in?"

Elliot put his arm around him, opened the screen door, and led him to the living room sofa. As Arnold bent, he moaned in pain.

"They pushed me down a flight of stairs," the slender boy said softly. "Then they hit on me, and one guy got me with his boot."

"We need to get help," Elliot said.

"I don't want my folks to know about this."

"You need to go to a hospital."

"I'll be alright. Just let me stay here tonight."

Without another word, Elliot stood up and went into his bedroom. Quickly, he put on his clothes. He went into the bathroom, splashed cold water on his face and hair, and went back to Arnold. His cousin hadn't moved, not even in an attempt to lie down.

Elliot leaned down, put his arm around him, and said, "O.K., let's go."

"Go where?"

"We're going to the hospital."

"I don't need that, just a place to rest."

"Since you've come for my help, I'll do what I think best. You don't have to do anything except what I tell you."

Arnold looked mournfully at him and said, "Why can't you just act like a friend?"

"That's exactly what I am doing," Elliot said, deciding to lift and carry him. "But you don't know it."

"What are you doing?" Arnold asked as Elliot lifted him up.

"I'm carrying you to the car."

"I can walk!"

"Shut up or I'll go get your dad."

Arnold stopped arguing but winced when Elliot pick him up.

He was skinny, almost nothing to carry at all. His shoulders, Elliot thought, feel a lot like Felix's did. "Heavenly Father," he prayed silently as they went down the stairs, "protect my cousin. If there is anything wrong inside, keep him safe until we can have it fixed. I lay my hands on him now, in the name of Jesus." Elliot thought of Sister Teresa, and the day in the classroom years before, when she had prayed for him.

Elliot carried him quickly down the stairs and placed him in the Jeep.

"Don't move," Elliot directed, turning back to the apartment.

"Where are you going?"

"I forgot something," Elliot answered as he ran across the drive area and back up the stairs. He knocked on Charles's door. He knocked again and then once more. A light came on, and Elliot could see the outline of Charles.

"Who is it?"

"Charles, it's Elliot."

Charles opened the door.

"Arnold's been beat up. I'm taking him to the hospital. How do I get there and how do I pay for it?"

"It's Memorial, off of Broadhurst Avenue. Is Arnold conscious?"

"Yes."

"He knows the way," Charles told him. He paused, thinking. "Just a moment." A few seconds later he returned with his wallet and handed Elliot a plastic card. "This is Mrs. Elsie's admission card for Memorial. They'll accept him immediately. Just tell them he's family."

"Thanks. I might have to call you later. Is that alright?"

"Certainly. Does the family know?"

"No, but I think Mr. Swindale should be told."

"I'll take care of it," Charles responded.

Elliot turned and bounded down the stairs and ran to the Jeep.

"You know where Memorial is, don't you?" he asked Charles.

"Yeah."

Elliot started the car and drove down the driveway. Once again, he took up his silent prayer, from time to time glancing at his cousin.

* * *

Graham answered the second buzz of the house phone.

"Yes?" he said, as he rubbed his numb arm that had been around his wife. He listened intently as Charles explained what had happened.

"Thank you, Charles," he said, as he hung up the phone and glanced at Harriet. She was awake looking at him.

"Arnold's been beaten up. Elliot's taken him to Memorial."

They both got up quickly. Harriet, nude, reached hurriedly for her undergarments. Graham, also without clothes, sat on the side of the bed, reached into the nightstand and got out a small telephone book. Looking in it, he dialed a number. He waited a moment.

"Harvey, Graham Swindale. Arnold's been hurt and taken to Memorial. We don't know the seriousness of it, but I would like you there." There was a moment's pause, and then Graham said, "Thank you" and hung up.

Harriet was almost finished dressing in her sweats. "He'll be there?" she asked.

"Yes. He'll leave immediately." They dressed and left the room without any more conversation.

* * *

Charles had been right about the admittance card. There were no questions asked as the admittance nurse took the card and ran it into their computer. Arnold was placed on a gurney and rolled into a screened area. A doctor and a nurse entered with him.

Five minutes passed, and then the young doctor came back into the waiting room.

"Do you know how long he's been like this?" the doctor asked Elliot.

"No, sir. Can't he tell you that?"

"He's unconscious," the doctor replied and then paused. "Are you part of the family?"

"Yes, sir, I'm his cousin."

"He has internal bleeding. We're prepping him now, and his doctor is on the way." He turned and left. Elliot continued his silent prayers.

Three minutes later, though Elliot didn't know it, Harvey Mercer, the Swindale family doctor hurried through the emergency doors and went directly to the operating room. Three minutes after that, Elliot saw his aunt and uncle coming towards him. He stood to greet them.

"What's happened, Elliot?" Graham asked.

"The doctor told me he had internal bleeding, and they were prepping him."

Graham turned quickly, went into the hallway and over to the admittance nurse. "Has Doctor Mercer come in yet?"

"Yes, Sir, but he's in the operating room," she answered quickly.

"Thank you," Graham said, appreciating that the hospital had someone on the desk who paid attention to what was going on. He turned and walked back to the waiting room. He sat next to Harriet and took her hand.

"Harvey's here. Now all we can do is wait."

It was an hour before Harvey Mercer finished. He was smiling as he came up to the three of them. "He's going to be fine," he said as he shook Graham's hand and kissed Harriet on the cheek. He had delivered Arnold seventeen years ago.

"There was internal bleeding. His blood pressure was quite low. It's fortunate you brought him in when you did."

Graham and Harriet looked at Elliot.

"You brought him?" the doctor asked, looking at Elliot.

"Yes, sir," Elliot answered.

"Good for you," he said seriously. "Another hour or so and it would have been too late.

"Oh, my God," Harriet exclaimed.

"Knowing my son," Graham said, "you probably had to drag him here."

"He was in too much pain to fight," Elliot replied.

"Do you know what happened?" the doctor asked Elliot.

"Arnold told me he was thrown some stairs, beaten and kicked."

The doctor shook his head and turned to Graham and Harriet. "He'll be here a few days. I'll keep a close watch."

"Good, Harvey. Thanks for taking charge," Graham said, patting his friend on the arm.

"Thank you, Harvey," Harriet said. "We really appreciate how you take care of our family."

Harvey Mercer smiled and answered, "It's a pleasure, Harriet."

Harriet returned the smile and at the same time, chided herself on not having Harvey Mercer and his wife on her mailing list for the party. She would send an invitation as soon as she got home. She watched as Harvey turned to Elliot. They shook hands and introduced themselves.

My God, she thought, I owe my son's life to this boy, and I've got him sleeping over the garage!

It was six o'clock in the morning when Elliot climbed the stairs to his apartment. He hadn't planned to wake Charles, but then he noticed that his door was open. Elliot saw Charles, dressed and reading in his front room. He knocked on the door.

"How is he?" Charles asked as he came to the door.

"He's doing just fine. He'll be home in a few days."

"Ah, that's good news. Mrs. Elsie has been waiting to hear."

"How did she know?" Elliot asked.

Charles smiled and answered, "The house phones are just one open line. One buzz is for Mr. Swindale, two buzzes for Mrs. Swindale and three for Mrs. Elsie. Mrs. Elsie says she can never remember, so she picks up on all of them."

Elliot and Charles smiled. Then Charles reminded him, "Would you like to make it later, about picking up your suits?"

Elliot had forgotten about his appointment at the tailor's. "No," Elliot answered, "eleven will be fine. See you then."

Elliot wouldn't miss going down and trying on his new clothes. He had to have them for the next day when he was taking Rachel to church. He smiled as he kicked off his shoes and flopped into bed. He was too tired to undress. He reached up, set his alarm clock and fell asleep.

* * *

Graham and Harriet stayed at the hospital until their son was moved to his room. They looked in on him before driving home.

It was a beautiful Saturday morning, clear and already warm. The streets were still nearly deserted. They were driving Graham's Continental, which meant that Harriet couldn't sit right next to her husband.

"I like the old cars better," she said.

"Old cars?"

"The ones without the bucket seats...just one wide seat."

Graham glanced over at her. She was smiling, looking very alluring. This is amazing, he thought, here it's been less than five hours, and I want this woman again!

"Yes, I agree," he said, then added, "Are you still tired?"

"How do you mean that?" Harriet responded, smiling slightly.

He laughed, "Am I that obvious?"

"Yes," she said softly, teasing, "Because I'm just as <u>tired</u> as you are." He paused, and then said in pretended seriousness, "Do you think eighty-five would be too fast in this neighborhood?" He did increase his speed, but only slightly. Harriet placed her hand lightly on his shoulder, wanting to touch him, to remind him how much she wanted to be with him.

* * *

At seven a.m. Sunday morning, Elliot was already trying on his light-colored suit. He wasn't supposed to pick Rachel up until eight-thirty. He couldn't remember which tie was supposed to go with the suit. He had three suits and eight ties, six shirts and two more pairs of shoes. He had told them he didn't need that much, but Aunt Elsie insisted. And Charles always carried out her orders.

Elliot decided on the dark blue tie to go along with this light suit. He remembered Charles saying something about contrasts and this tie certainly did that. He looked at his watch...seven-ten. What was he going to do for the next hour? He had already done his running, showered, eaten, and cleaned up his apartment. How early could a person arrive without the Davis' thinking that he was entirely crazy? He decided to go visit Arnold, see if he was awake. Elliot knew he had to fill his time doing something.

At seven-ten, Rachel was standing before her mirror in her slip trying to decide which dress to wear. She had three out hanging up in front of her closet, wondering which one he would like? One thing for sure, I don't have any idea what Elliot likes or doesn't like.

She wished she knew more about him. Though they talked at lunchtime and when he brought her home after school, she still wished she knew more about him. The trouble was, as soon as he left her, she always had something else she wanted ask about him. But when she saw him, she would forget to ask, because she was with him. And so it went.

Now it was Sunday, and they were going to see Reverend Lindquist's new church. Elliot said it was small. She wondered how many people would be there? How would any one from his old church know that he was there? What if they were the only ones there for him?

She heard the heavy-slippered steps of her father as he went into the bathroom. Had she remembered to pick up everything? Yes, she remembered. She also made sure she didn't use too much of the hot water for her shower.

She finally decided on the light blue dress. She slipped it over her head, hoping that Elliot would come a little early so they could drive slowly to the church.

* * *

The hospital halls were quiet. Elliot walked down the hallway of the fourth floor, glancing in each room as he made his way toward Arnold's room. He didn't see any visitors. Maybe he wasn't supposed to be here this early. He did see two nurses talking near a drinking fountain, but they didn't pay any attention to him. He kept walking.

He came to Arnold's room and looked in. The other bed, the one next to the window, was empty. Arnold had just put down a glass of water on the stand and was looking in Elliot's direction.

"Hey, man," he said softly.

Elliot smiled and pulled up a chair. "Hi, Arnold. How are you doing?"

"Lousy. They cut me open."

"I know. You were bleeding inside."

"Yeah?"

"Haven't you talked to the doctor?"

"Yeah, maybe, but I must have been a space cadet. I don't remember anything."

"Doctor Mercer told us you would have died in another hour." Elliot watched as that registered with Arnold.

"No bull?"

"He told us right after the operation. I was there with your mom and dad."

Arnold's face, usually filled with malice and resentment, was softly subdued, showing concern with what he was hearing. Then he asked, "What did my folks say?"

"Your mom cried and your dad was too surprised to say anything."

Suddenly Arnold reached out and took Elliot's arm, weakly holding on.

"When that guy kicked me, it hurt so bad...and I was even high... and I passed out. When I came to, there was nobody there. They left me at the bottom of the steps. I knew I had to get home. I don't know how I walked it."

Elliot watched his cousin's face. All of Arnold's expressions were genuine now, nothing forced or put-on.

"Can I do anything for you?" Elliot asked.

"Yeah, you can give me some of your muscles," Arnold replied, trying to not make it a joke.

Elliot smiled and answered, "I can show you how to put on some of your own."

Arnold stared at him, considering the offer. "Do you mean it?"

"Sure," Elliot said, "if you're willing to play by different rules."

"What rules?"

"No drugs."

Arnold didn't have to think about this. "I can do that."

"What about cigarettes?"

"What does that have to do with lifting weights?"

"You'll have to learn how to run too."

Arnold thought about it. "No cigarettes, huh?"

"Right. And no more junk foods...and good sleeping habits."

"Wait a minute, wait a minute! What the hell is this, basic training?" Arnold demanded.

"That's right. That's exactly what it will be for a while. But then, when you're stronger, when you start gaining weight, I'll teach you how to protect yourself. I'll make it so anybody who wants to mess with you will think twice about it." Then he smiled and added, "And they'll end up not doing it."

Arnold searched Elliot's face and believed him.

Something deep inside Arnold happened, right then! He knew what he wanted to do. He really wanted it so nobody would mess with him. And he knew that he could do it! He didn't know how he knew, but...he knew.

"When do we start?" he said weakly. He was getting tired.

"You think that you can do all those things?"

"For sure." he answered, suddenly feeling very sleepy. Maybe someday he would tell Elliot that it had been his own friends who had beaten and kicked him. Maybe he would tell his cousin that he had stolen some crack from them. Still, they shouldn't have kicked me like that! Maybe...someday... But right now, he only wanted to go to sleep. Arnold felt Elliot's hand patting him on the shoulder as he fell asleep.

Elliot stood motionless until his cousin's breathing became regular, then he quietly prayed out loud, "Thank you, Father, for sparing his life. And I thank you that my cousin and I are becoming friends. Keep us safe and give Arnold the new strength he wants... first in body...and then in his mind and spirit. In Jesus' name."

* * *

Elliot was only fifteen minutes early to the Davis' house. Rachel answered the door. She had on a blue dress and looked sensational. She had a small purse and a Bible in her hand.

"You are so beautiful," Elliot said enthusiastically, looking at her smiling face. He saw her redden. "Shouldn't I say that to you?" he asked quickly.

Rachel laughed and answered, "No, I like it...it's alright... It's just the way you say it."

"How should I say it?"

She blushed again. "No, you say it just fine...the way I... but...I... can't explain it right now," she said, looking behind her. "Mom and Dad aren't quite ready, but they said they could find it on their own. Should we go?"

"Sure," Elliot said, standing aside as she closed the door behind her. They walked out to the Jeep. Elliot had a difficult time not staring at her. Out in the bright sunlight, she looked even prettier. He helped her into her seat, then stopped short as he walked around the Jeep. The top, he thought. I should have put up the top! She's going to get blown all over.

He got into the driver's seat.

"I should put up the top."

"What if you drive slowly?" she asked.

So, he drove only ten miles an hour causing people to honk and stare at them as they went around them and some other things not worth mentioning. Elliot kept to the side streets as they talked and laughed together, inching their way to church.

When they approached the church, Rachel asked if Elliot would park around the side, out of sight. She wanted to be sure to surprise the pastor. So Elliot did.

"Before we go in," Elliot said, "I want you to explain what you meant back at the house."

"You mean about your compliment?"

"Yes."

"I just felt like we didn't know each other well enough for you to say something like that, the way you said it."

"Oh. You mean it was too personal?"

"Yes. It's not that I don't want to hear it from you...it's just that I need... Oh, I don't know how to explain it."

"You want to know me better, so that you can say the things you want to say after I give you a compliment," Elliot suggested.

"That's right," she replied, pleased and surprised at his understanding. But then, as she thought more about it, she laughed and said, "But even then, I still might blush!"

Elliot laughed with her as he helped her from the car. They walked around the block until they could see the front of the church. There was no one out in front, not a soul, but the two doors were open. Rachel stopped Elliot and looked at her watch.

"It's ten minutes to nine," she said, trying not to sound too concerned.

"There's plenty of time yet, maybe..."

"Excuse me," a man's voice said from behind them. They turned and saw a little old man and his wife looking up at them.

Elliot took Rachel's arm and moved off the sidewalk.

"Sorry," he said to them.

They didn't move ahead, but stood there looking at the young couple.

"Do you know if it's going to be open?" the old man asked, throwing up his thumb toward the church.

"Yes, Sir," Elliot answered. "Today's the opening Sunday."

"Well, it's about time! It's been closed for three years. We live up at six-ten Maple," he continued, flipping his thumb in the other direction. "And they won't give me a driver's license anymore. If this church isn't open, we don't go!"

"You haven't been to church in three years?" Elliot asked.

"That's right," the feisty old man replied. "But we read the Word every day. Don't worry, we know how to get fed on our own!"

"Do you happen to know the pastor's name?" the old woman asked softly.

"Pastor Lindquist, ma'am," Rachel answered with a smile, "Pastor Arthur Lindquist."

"Does he preach God's Word?" the old man asked.

"Yes, he does," Rachel answered. "And he lives it too."

Rachel's response caused the old man to laugh. "Oh, he does, does he? Good for him! The last fellow that pastored here sells insurance now."

"Allstate," his wife added.

"Couldn't make a living! Can't blame him for that!" the old man added. Then he took his wife gently by the arm and said, "Let's go see if we can get our old seats." They smiled and nodded in unison at the young couple as they made their way toward the open gate.

Elliot and Rachel looked at each other and smiled. "I wouldn't want to take his seat," Elliot whispered. Rachel laughed, nodding in agreement. They waited a moment before starting to follow them into the church, when Rachel noticed her father's car coming down Maple.

"Elliot, there's Dad's car. Maybe we should wait and all go in together?"

"Good idea," Elliot answered. They watched as the Chrysler pulled up across the street. Mrs. Davis got out first and saw the kids. She waved. They waved back and went to the edge of the street to wait for her parents to cross.

"We thought it would be nice if we all went in together," Rachel said.

"Good idea," her dad responded as he took his wife's arm. All four went through the little fence and up to the church.

There were eight people already inside, including Geri Lindquist, who was at the piano, playing softly. She saw the Davis' as soon as they came through the door. Astonishment came over her face, then she smiled broadly and began playing, "Amazing Grace," which was Dolores Davis' favorite hymn.

Dolores went immediately towards the piano while Marc selected a pew near the middle for all of them. By the time Dolores got to the front, Geri had stopped playing and stood. The two women hugged each other, with tears rolling down their cheeks.

"Oh, Geri, I was so worried for you and Art."

"I thought about you so much, Dolores, but I couldn't let you know where we were. We moved out of the church's house the very next day."

"I understand," Dolores replied, smiling at her. "I'm just so glad to find you.

"This is a miracle! How did you find us?" Geri asked.

"You're right; it's a miracle. I'll tell you all about it at lunch."

The two women smiled at each other, hugged again, then Dolores went back up the aisle to her family.

Art Lindquist was alone in his small office behind the sanctuary. For the past half hour he had been praying, at least most of that time he had been praying. His mind was not settled and his heart was not at rest, as he wanted it to be. But then again, why should he be at peace? Was this the time for it? He got up from his knees and picked up his Bible. He was in a new battle, and he had to continuously remember it. "I will not be discouraged, for the Lord my God will be with me wherever I go," he said out loud.

Checking in his Bible to make sure he had his notes, he went though the door into the sanctuary. He had no false expectations as to what he would find in the sanctuary. The important thing was, it was nine o'clock, and he was adverse to tardiness.

As he walked out and glanced at his wife; he knew something good had happened. She was crying. Looking at the congregation, he immediately saw the Davis family, Marc smiling broadly at him, Dolores, Rachel, and...Elliot Reed? Art smiled broadly at them, and then began the worship service by welcoming his small congregation.

"Good morning, everyone. My name is Art Lindquist, and this is a church of Jesus Christ. My wife, Geri, and I believe that He is the Savior of Mankind...the only One!"

Art heard an "Amen" from a little old man sitting with his wife in the second row.

Pastor Lindquist smiled at the couple. As Geri played, they all worshiped God together through song.

Elliot loved it. He'd never sung songs like this to God before. It was wonderful. He watched as the people stood, raised their hands, worshiping. He saw Rachel give herself over to worship, with tears flowing from her closed eyes. Everyone knew the songs they were singing. Elliot knew he would have to learn them as soon as he could. Maybe Rachel would teach them to him. He closed his eyes and raised hands, letting the music fill him up. Sometimes they would sing a song twice and then he would be able to sing some of the words.

After the worship, the pastor preached about Jesus and the importance the Savior should hold for the man of today. Pastor talked about His followers and disciples, and how important their walk was after Jesus had gone up to be with the Father. Pastor Lindquist paralleled this to Jesus' disciples of today, telling how their walk must be the same even though two thousand years had passed. Elliot drank in every word.

After the sermon, the pastor said there would be Communion next week, and starting in two weeks, there would be a Sunday evening service. He also mentioned that tithes could be placed in the basket near the door. For the first time, Elliot felt badly about not having money. He wanted to give something but didn't have anything to give. Elliot watched as the people put in money, and Mr. Davis dropped a check into the basket.

Pastor Art stood at the back door, greeting everybody as they left. He shook hands and talked. Elliot noticed when the pastor and Mr. Davis faced each other and hugged, that there was something special between the men. Elliot thought of Felix Skinner.

The pastor then greeted Rachel and Elliot together.

"Well, well, what a surprise," he said as he gave Rachel a hug. "Isn't it a wonderfully small world?"

"I've missed you," Rachel said to her pastor.

"Thank you," the pastor answered. "I've missed all of you more than you can know." He patted her cheek and then turned his attention to Elliot.

"Hello, young man. You took me at my word, and you brought three of my closest friends with you."

"I want to thank you for this morning. I've never been to anything like this before," Elliot replied.

"You're welcome," Art said, then added, "How is everything else?"

Elliot smiled and said, "There were five of them, and they all left."

"Five?" the surprised pastor repeated.

"Yes, Sir."

"I want to hear all about it. One of these Sundays, I would like to hear about it."

"Yes, Sir," Elliot answered, looking forward to it.

"Good. And how is he getting along now?" the pastor wanted to know before the lad left.

"He's fine, Sir. Someone else moved into his house," Elliot answered with a grin.

"Praise God," Art said excitedly. "I want to know all about this."

"Yes, Sir."

Elliot and Rachel moved down the steps to where her folks were waiting. Rachel wondered what the Pastor's and Elliot's conversation was all about, but she didn't think she should ask.

"Honey," Dolores said to her daughter, "we're going to stay and have lunch with the Lindquist's. Would you two like to go along?"

Rachel knew her mother would rather the adults be alone this time, to catch up on the past few months. "We'll go ahead," she answered.

"Goodbye, Elliot," Mr. Davis said, shaking his hand. "We'll see you soon." Rachel was pleased because she knew what her father's words meant; he liked Elliot.

They walked back to the Jeep. As Elliot helped her in, he paused before going around to the driver's side.

"What is it?" she asked.

"How would I go about finding a job?"

"When would you have time? You swim almost every afternoon, and then with your studies..."

She watched him as he thought about her reply. "What made you think of that?" she asked.

"Because I never have money. I have everything I need, but I never have any money in my pocket."

"Don't you get an allowance? When Lance was in high school, Dad gave him an allowance."

Elliot looked at her. "Didn't he have to do something for it?"

She nodded her head. "Yes, he had to do odd jobs around the house and get good grades. If he didn't, no allowance."

"I couldn't ask them. They even gave me this Jeep."

"How do you buy gas for it?" she asked.

"My great-aunt gave me a gas card." Reaching into the glove compartment he showed it to her.

"Wow, it's a gold Visa with your name on it," she said.

"What does that mean?"

"You can buy anything with this... even get cash."

"Really?"

"Is she rich?"

"I think so. Charles drives a Rolls Royce."

"Who's Charles?"

"Her chauffeur."

Rachel laughed and said jokingly, "Elliot, lying is a sin."

Elliot looked at her, and then smiled, knowing what he was going to do. He jumped into the driver's side and starting the car, he asked, "Is it O.K. to drive faster now?"

"Sure. Where are we going?"

Elliot didn't answer as he turned the Jeep down the street and headed for home.

When they entered the neighborhood, Rachel looked over at Elliot. As a child, she had ridden through these streets with her parents, who loved to look at the mansions and dream. When Elliot put on his turn signal and turned into one of the huge estates, she gasped, "Elliot, this is not funny."

But he kept driving, right up the driveway, past the beautiful home and up to the garages. There was a silver-haired man, dressed immaculately in white duck pants, white short sleeve shirt, and white deck shoes, washing a Rolls Royce.

Elliot stopped the Jeep beside the Rolls. "Hello, Charles."

"Hello, Elliot. How was church?"

"Just great, Sir." Then, straight-faced, he said, "This is Rachel Davis."

"How do you do, Miss Davis."

"Hello," she responded, still in shock. Neither remembered the other from the mall.

"Did you find this young lady at the church?"

"No, sir, I took her there."

"Ah, I see. Well, if you had, I was thinking about going with you next week myself."

Elliot broke out in laughter and looked at Rachel. Clearly, he knew she had received a compliment.

"Is Aunt Elsie busy?" Elliot asked.

"I doubt it. We're going to visit Arnold at four."

"Do you think she would mind a visit?"

"I think she would enjoy it immensely."

Elliot turned the car around and waved at Charles, who waved back as Elliot drove up to the front of the house. Helping Rachel out, he led her in through the front door.

"Oh, this is wonderful," Rachel said, looking at the marble entry way and the beautiful staircase.

"She's upstairs," Elliot said, as he led Rachel up the staircase.

"It looks like a movie set."

"It does?" Elliot asked.

"Don't you go to movies?"

"No, but I've seen them on television."

"You've never been to a movie?"

"No," he answered, smiling at her. "Do you want to take me to one?"

"I guess I'll have to. You don't have any money," she teased.

At the door of Aunt Elsie's bedroom, Elliot knocked and opened the door slightly.

"Aunt Elsie?"

"Elliot? Come in, come in," he heard her say. He opened the door and saw her sitting in the sunlight next to the window.

"Aunt Elsie, I want you to meet someone. This is Rachel Davis. Rachel, this is my great-aunt, Elsie Reed Tidwell."

Elsie smiled and looked closely at the girl as she held out her hand; the young lady took it. Elsie noted that she was beautiful and looking into her eyes, was reminded of Susan Rydell Reed. She saw kindness there and intelligence.

"It's nice meeting you, Mrs. Tidwell."

"Thank you, dear. But I never go by Mrs. Tidwell anymore, just Aunt Elsie."

Rachel smiled and nodded her head in agreement.

"Did you two meet at school?" she asked, looking at the girl.

"Yes," Rachel answered, "He introduced himself one day,"

"Do you like him?" Elsie asked, wanting to observe her under pressure.

The question startled Rachel. She knew she could only tell the truth. "Yes. Yes, I do."

"That was a good question, Aunt Elsie," Elliot said. He too could tease. "Whenever I want to know anything about her feelings, I'll bring her here."

"Now, now, nephew...there are many secrets that Rachel and I will never give away," Elsie remarked, smiling at the girl. "Liking you is only the beginning. She could drop you tomorrow."

Rachel laughed, liking this spirited old woman. "See there, Elliot. We women stick together,"

Elliot smiled, enjoying it here with these two. Walking over to his great-aunt, he pulled the gold credit card from his pocket.

"Rachel told me that this wasn't just a gas credit card."

"Did you think it was?" his aunt asked kindly.

"Yes."

"I keep forgetting you don't know anything about our world. "That card will buy anything you want up to ten thousand dollars."

"I've been keeping it in the glove compartment of the Jeep!" he said in amazement. "Why did you give this to me?"

"How are you supposed to have money?"

"I could work," he suggested.

"When?" his aunt asked. "Besides, that will come soon enough. Right now, you are supposed to prepare yourself for work."

"You've given me so much," Elliot said, squatting beside her chair.

"God has given this family a great deal. We must all begin to realize this fact. He expects us to use it wisely and to remember that it all belongs to Him. Your father didn't know that."

"I do," Elliot answered seriously.

"I know you do. That's why I could give you that card." She patted his hand as it rested on hers. "Why don't you go take her to lunch before you lose her."

Elliot and Rachel both laughed as Elliot stood up.

"It was a pleasure meeting you, Aunt Elsie," Rachel said. She found no difficulty in saying nice things to this old woman.

"I hope we see a great deal of you around this house," Elsie responded as Elliot bent down and kissed her cheek.

"Bye, Aunt Elsie. Say hello to Arnold from his cousin, when you see him."

"I will, young man, I will."

Elsie watched as they left the room. Here is one relationship that is going on my prayer list immediately, she thought. How fortunate Elliot is to find a girl like her.

* * *

Tina Swindale knew nothing about how close her brother had come to death. When she returned home Monday afternoon, she went directly to her room. As was her plan, she succeeded in not being seen by anyone. Her friend Donna had come home from college and had a party that lasted for four days for her twenty-first birthday. For Tina, it had been a time of little sleep, too much drink and boring men. Besides, it didn't make that much difference about the guys, since it was her time of the month.

When she entered her room, she threw her valise in the corner, stripped and stayed in the shower for fifteen minutes. She was shaking and felt very weak from lack of sleep and food. She set her alarm for suppertime and crawled into bed. She was so tired, she didn't even think about Elliot.

Graham got to pick up his son from the hospital a day early. Over the phone, Harvey Mercer had told him that the patient was doing fine and wanted to go home. Graham joked with Harvey, telling him that it was certainly an unusual occasion when his son stated that he wanted to be home.

A male nurse wheeled Arnold to the car and as Graham started to help his son into the car, Arnold waved him off.

"I can do it, Dad," he said. Getting slowly from the wheelchair, he cautiously moved into the seat of the Continental. Graham shut the door after him.

Graham decided to be quiet, to see if his son wanted to talk. There was silence for the first mile or so. Graham could feel his son looking at him as he drove. He glanced at the boy.

"What?"

"Did I almost die?"

"Yes."

"What was wrong with me?"

"You were bleeding inside."

Graham was silent, thinking about it.

"That night, I wanted to stay at Elliot's place. If he'd let me stay, I'd be dead?"

"Yes," Graham replied, realizing once again how much he would have missed his son. "When a son dies, I believe a part of the mother and father die too." Graham said quietly.

Arnold looked at his father and said, "No more cocaine, no more pot. I quit `em all."

Graham looked back at his boy. "Good for you. That's really great, son."

After watching the road for a moment, he looked back at his son. "I quit booze, too. No more for me."

Arnold saw his father smile at him. Arnold felt good inside. He was glad to be going home.

As Tina left her room, she heard laughter from the stairs. When she got there, she saw Elliot carrying Arnold up the stairs. Down below she saw her mother, father and Aunt Elsie, smiling and watching the boys.

"What's going on?" Tina asked.

"Tina? When did you get home?" her mother said looking up at her.

"A couple of hours ago," she answered. "What happened?"

Elliot smiled as he carried her brother past her and on down the hall towards his room. "He can't climb stairs for three more days," Elliot said.

"Why not?" she asked, paying more attention to how Elliot's arm muscles were bulging. She wanted to feel them.

"That's what the doctor told us," Elliot answered, kicking the partially opened door with his foot.

Tina looked downstairs, but her family had already gone from view. Hurriedly, she went down the stairs and into the dining room.

"What's going on with Arnold?" she asked.

She looked to her mother for an answer, but it was her father who replied. "Your brother got beat up and almost died Friday night."

"Oh, my God, what happened?"

"He had internal bleeding. Elliot took him to the hospital. Harvey Mercer said that in another hour it would have been too late."

As Marny came in with the salads, Harriet watched her daughter, wondering where she had been for four days. She was somewhat irritated that Tina had neglected to tell anybody else where she was either.

At that moment, Graham asked, "Where have you been for the past four days?"

It surprised Tina that her father would question her. "I was over at Donna's," she answered. "She was home from college for her birthday."

"Your mother and I would appreciate knowing where you are from now on," he stated.

Tina started to take a bite of her salad without realizing that her father was waiting for an answer.

"Is that understood," he persisted.

Looking up, Tina saw everybody at the table was staring at her. "Yes, Daddy," she said quickly.

He had startled her. Slightly irritated and a little hurt by her father's unfamiliar behavior, she wondered what had been going on in this house for the past week.

Harriet, as she began eating her salad, smiled ever so slightly at what her husband had just done. "Oh, my," she thought, "I certainly am living with a wonderful stranger!"

* * *

One of the boys Tina had met at Donna's party called her that week, asking her to go out. She said yes, even though she really couldn't remember exactly which one he was. Even so, it was better than sitting at home.

He took her to dinner, then dancing. She drank a little more than she should, because she found it easier to keep up a conversation. The boy was nice enough; even though he did ask her if she would like to go over to his place after they had danced a while. She, in turn, asked him if he thought she was a one-night stand, and he apologized.

He took her home, and she allowed him to kiss her goodnight. When he asked if she would like to go out again, she told him to call her, even though she knew then that she would never go out with him again. He wanted to walk her to the door, but she told him it wasn't necessary.

Arnold, awake in his bed, heard the car drive up. He looked at the clock. It was two-thirty. He had been sleeping so much that now he was wide-awake. He carefully crawled out of bed, finding an easy way so as not to stress the stitches in his belly. He looked out of his corner window. He didn't recognize the car. As he started to go over to the TV to turn on a late, late movie, he saw the passenger door open and his sister get out. She stood watching as the car drove out the driveway.

She remained standing still for so long, that it made Arnold curious. When she finally did move, it was not in the direction he had expected. Instead of coming to the house, she turned and looked behind her toward the garages. She stood like that for a long moment, then once again turned and started moving toward the house.

But, as Arnold continued watching her, she stopped again, looked down at her feet, then turned around and walked toward the garages.

"Where the hell are you going at this time of night?" Arnold said out loud to himself. He thought she might be drunk, even though she seemed to walk straight enough.

He continued to watch as she stopped at the stairs to the apartments, took off her shoes and placed them on the cement. She took one final look around her and started up the stairs.

"Well, well, will you look at you, bitch," he said softly, shaking his head in amazement. "I know you're not going up there to see Charles." Then, a large branch from the black walnut tree blocked Arnold's view.

Tina was so excited she could hardly breathe. She quietly moved past the window and door of Charles's darkened apartment, then stood at Elliot's screen door. She was concerned about the door making noise. She found herself wanting to giggle. She suppressed it. Ever so quietly, she inched the screen door open without even a squeak. She reached in and turned the knob of the door. It wasn't locked and even opened without the slightest rub.

Most cautiously, she moved in and gently shut the screen door. She didn't make a sound. Then, turning the knob quite slowly, she moved the door until it reached it's closed position.

There was enough light in the room so she could see the outline of the furniture. Something white was over the end of the couch.

She listened for Elliot's breathing. She couldn't hear him. She moved closer to the bedroom door and listened again. Yes, she could hear him now. She could see that the whiteness on the couch was his jacket. Quietly, she undid the buttons to her blouse, took it off and slipped out of her skirt.

My God, she thought, I feel like I'm going to faint. She grabbed hold of the sofa, finally feeling the giddiness ease. She had never felt like this, never! She loved it. She put her clothes over his jacket, then took a deep breath and let it out slowly.

She moved into his bedroom as quietly as she had come into his apartment. There were two windows in the corner that threw some moonlight into the room. She could see he didn't wear a top while sleeping. He was on his back and one of his muscular arms was wrapped around his head. She wanted to touch the hair under his arms as she stood looking down at him. He was beautiful, and he had been driving her mad.

Was this the way it was supposed to be, she thought? Was this the way you should feel toward someone you were about to make love to? She had never felt this way before. She knelt down by his bed and put her palm gently on his chest.

"Elliot," she whispered.

Startled, Elliot awoke. "What?"

"It's alright," she said soothingly. "Don't be frightened."

"What is it? What's the matter?" he asked.

"Nothing. There's nothing wrong. I have to talk to you, to be alone with you."

"What?" he said.

"It's the middle of the night. No one knows I'm here."

"I don't understand. Is there something wrong?"

She smiled and took his hand. "Elliot, there is nothing wrong. I came here tonight because I had to...I want to be with you."

"Be with me?"

"Yes. I want to sleep with you tonight."

"We can't do that. Tina, you're my cousin."

She had drawn his hand until it is almost touching her lips. "Elliot, you don't have to worry about anything. I take the pill, and no one will ever know." She gently kissed his fingers, and then dropped his hand to the top of her breasts.

He drew his hand away and sat up in bed. "Tina, I can't do this. You can't be here."

She looked at him for a moment, slowly standing. "Look at me, Elliot." Elliot saw that she was standing in her underwear.

"Tina, stop it! Your father took me into his house. He trusts me. He's my uncle."

She sat down at the side of the bed. "He won't know anything about it." She reached out to touch him.

Elliot grabbed her wrist, holding her still. "What about God?" he said to her.

"God?"

"He knows exactly what's going on now. I won't break His laws."

"What are you talking about?"

Elliot took her other wrist and gently moved her back until she had to stand up. He was kneeling on his bed now, looking into his cousin's eyes.

"You have to leave now. What you want me to do is a sin against God. I won't do it. I won't ever do it."

Though he's seemed to be barely holding her wrists, she could not move. She wanted to break free; she wanted to strike out at him, but she could do nothing.

"Let me go."

"Will you leave?"

"Let me go, you bastard!" She was near tears now and her lust had suddenly turned into embarrassment and anger.

Elliot let go of her. As soon as he did she struck out at him, trying to dig her long fingernails into his eyes. Once again, he quickly took hold of her wrists, this time standing with her. She felt like a child in his grasp. With a strength that could have easily frightened her, he drew her into the living room. He saw her clothes on the sofa.

"I want you to dress and leave. When I come out, I want you gone." He let go of her wrists and stepped back into his bedroom, shutting the door.

She felt thoroughly humiliated. She stood at the closed door, wanting to kill him but knowing she couldn't. She knew that there was nothing she could do to him...not at this moment. Slowly, she picked up her skirt and put it on. She looked at the closed door and vowed that she would get even with this "holier-than-thou" bastard! Oh God, how she hated people like him!

"You bastard," she said softly to the door, "I'll get even, you self-righteous bastard!"

She reached for her blouse and put it on. As she went to the front door, she stopped, turned back, and picked up his jacket that was draped over the couch. She took it and went silently out the door. She moved quietly past Charles's apartment and down the stairs. She carried her shoes back to the house. Her rage didn't diminish until she had stood in her shower for a long time...planning.

Elliot didn't hear her leave. He looked through the small apartment before going back to bed. As he stared up at the ceiling, he was frightened. It hadn't been easy. He had wanted to see her, to touch her, to take her clothes off of her. He saw how beautiful she was, and he had been tempted. When Tina touched him, he had wanted to touch her in return. He knew that if it had been Rachel, he could have never resisted. Now, he couldn't sleep.

* * *

Graham had to smile at Harriet as they walked down the hall from their room. When they went downstairs to breakfast, he had playfully patted her behind. She hadn't even realized it because she was paying much too close attention to a list she had in her hand, a "to-do" list for the party.

"It's only four days away," she had said to him, while he was shaving.

When they were in the lower hall, just before going into the dining room, he said, "Let me see that list."

She stopped, looked at him and handed over the list. He looked at it for a moment and said, "If two of us worked on this, it should only take half as long."

"Really?" she asked, "Would you mind helping?"

"I would consider it...for a price," he said in mock seriousness.

"So, it's finally come down to that. Crassness! You'll only work for pay," Harriet said in return, loving his games.

"It's the only way," Graham said as he put his arm around his wife and brought the list between the two of them.

"Now, let's look at this list. If I check the limousine service, make sure of the hotel rooms, and get in touch with the catering service... what would that be worth to you?" All the time he talked, he drew her closer to him, with the list becoming of less and less importance. As he finished, he kissed her. She kissed him back.

"Well, let me see," she said, acting confused. "Since you put it that way...I think it would be worth...anything you want."

"There, you see! Crassness can be fun!" He kissed her lightly, and they went into the dining room laughing.

Elsie was already there, having her coffee and waiting for the rest of the family. "What's so funny?" she asked.

"My husband and I are in a labor dispute," Harriet said as she sat down.

"Is it settled?" Elsie asked, looking at Graham.

Graham only smiled and lifted his eyebrows.

"I'm taking it under consideration," Harriet said as she smiled toward her husband. He smiled back.

Marny came in with two juices and the morning paper. She handed the paper to Mr. Swindale, placing the glasses before them.

"Good morning, Marny," Graham said. "How are you this morning?"

"Just fine, Sir."

Then Harriet asked her, "Have you seen Elliot this morning?"

"Yes, ma'am, he took Arnold's breakfast up to him, then he went to school."

"Did he eat?" she asked.

"He told me he already ate over at his place." Marny answered. "I'm beginning to think he doesn't like my cookin anymore."

"I haven't seen him for three days," Harriet said. "Is he alright?"

"He seems to be," Marny answered, even though she felt there was something bothering the boy.

"The next time you see him, will you tell him I would like to speak to him?" Harriet asked, folding up her list.

"Yes, ma'am," she said as she went back into the kitchen.

"I wonder why he leaves for school so early?" Harriet pondered out loud.

"He has a girlfriend," Elsie offered.

"Really? How do you know?"

"He brought her over to the house last Sunday."

"Where were we?" Graham asked.

"You'd already left to visit Arnold. Elliot brought her to my room."

"What did you think of her?" Harriet asked.

"I liked her. She's sensible and a real beauty."

"I thought I was the only one that had a woman like that?" Graham said.

Later that morning, seated in the library, Graham easily took care of the things on Harriet's list. He made all the necessary calls, double-checking to make sure that everything was ready and would run smoothly. He didn't want his wife concerned about any of it.

During the last two weeks, he had taken care of a great deal more than she knew. His computer, though it had remained unused in the past years, now gave him direct access to all Reed Industry information. The inner company memos, board meeting notes, R&D workups within Reed subsidiaries, plus their capital expenditures, projected profits, pertinent developments for acquisitions both in the near future and long term were all there for Graham's perusal.

With this newly acquired access, he familiarized himself with the direction the company had taken since he had been gone. The only thing missing was the inner thoughts of the late Bertrand Reed. But as Graham studied all the information, fitting the pieces together, he began to see that even Bertrand's brain was there, his thoughts, future plans, his failures (there weren't many), and his special loves were all set out before Graham.

Something wonderful happened to Graham as he saw Reed Industries before him. He became excited about going back to it. He saw ways where he could make a positive difference. A few areas needing improvement jumped out at him, glaring errors of judgment, misunderstandings between departments and even some mistreatment of subsidiaries. Bertrand, Graham could now see, had been weak in communications, in understanding and coping with personalities. And these unsolved dilemmas were costing the company tens of thousands, maybe even millions!

But just as important, Graham recognized that Bertrand's attitudes had certainly caused men in management to hold back their intuitive thoughts and their creative ideas. Who could afford to give of themselves when it was usually flung back at them or ignored entirely?

Each day that Graham delved deeper into the workings of the company, he thanked God for the new excitement coming over him. His enthusiasm seemed higher now than when he was young. He knew, without hesitation, that he could make a difference to this company. He thanked his Lord for many things during the two weeks that he worked on the computer. Excitedly, he uncovered more bits than he had ever guessed.

He decided to memorize the names of all the men, no matter what their position, who would be at the party. He memorized their strong points and their weak ones. He memorized their wife's name, their children's and even their dog's if that information was available. He brought in a fax machine and had Reed Industries send him a picture of each president, vice president and board member that would be at the party. He was going to be prepared. His wife was one smart lady for thinking of such a party. He thanked God for her too.

Later that same afternoon, when Elliot got back from school, Marny told him that Mrs. Swindale wanted to see him. He found his aunt in the upper hall; her arms full of new towels that she decided belonged down in the workout room.

"Hello, Aunt Harriet."

"Ah, Elliot. I wanted to talk to you."

"Would you like some help?"

"Yes, thank you," she said, transferring the bundle to his waiting arms. "I want them down in the workout room," she said as she watched him tuck the lot of them under one arm.

"Aunt Elsie told us you have a friend," Harriet said.

"Yes, ma'am. Her name is Rachel Davis. We came by the house after church."

"I'm sorry we missed the two of you. Maybe you could bring her to the party."

"What party?" he asked.

"Oh, my, I've forgotten to tell you. Next weekend, your uncle and I have invited all the executives connected with Reed Industries to join us. They'll be coming from all over the United States and Europe."

"Wow! How many are coming?"

"With their wives, there will be a little over a hundred and fifty."

"You're sure I won't be in the way?"

"Nonsense," she said as she opened the door to the weight room for him. "You're family. Graham and I want you there."

Elliot followed her over to the shelves and placed the towels on them. "Thank you. I'd like to come. What would be the best time to bring Rachel?"

"Friday night, for sure. There will be an orchestra and dancing. Do you like to dance?'

"I've never tried it."

Harriet smiled, not surprised at his answer. "I think Rachel has her work cut out for her."

"I'm afraid you're right," he said. "I just hope she wants the job."

Harriet went to the small refrigerator and opened it. "What would you like?" she asked as she reached in for a small bottle of spring water.

"The same would be fine," he said. She handed him one, then slid open the glass doors and went out to the lawn chairs. Elliot followed her. She reached up, took the fish food from the rocks and sprinkled food for the Koi. After she sat, Elliot sat across from her. They both watched all the fish as they ate.

"I have to tell you something," Harriet said, twisting the lid from her bottle. Elliot watched and did the same to his.

"I owe you an explanation and an apology. First, I put you over the garage in that empty servant's quarter, because I was angry at your father." She paused and took a sip from the bottle. "Did you know that your father and I hadn't talked to each other for over five years before he died?" she continued.

"No, ma'am."

"Well, I'm ashamed to say, we hadn't. And I took you out of the military school because Bertrand had wanted you there, not because of money. I was angry with my brother, and it had nothing to do with you. I'm sorry for that."

"It's all right, Aunt Harriet. I'm glad to be here."

She paused and looked at his young, handsome face. Surprised at herself, she reached out and took his hand.

"We believe if you hadn't been here we would have lost our son." She paused, then continued, "When I went up to his room yesterday, he really talked to me for the first time in...I don't know, years...it seems like. He told me that he was going to start workouts with you as soon as the doctor says it's alright."

"Yes, we talked about it in the hospital."

"He also told me he's been using cocaine and other drugs for the last three years."

"He almost died, and it frightened him."

"I know, but now he wants to be like you, Elliot."

She knew that she was embarrassing the boy, that he didn't expect anything like this, but she had to tell him for her good. How could she be so happy now and have things like this bothering her mind? Everything had to be cleared up. She pressed the hand that was in hers.

"There's something else, just as important," she continued. "I thought you did something harmful to my husband that night in the library. I don't know what happened, and I'm really not asking you to tell me, I just want to thank you and tell you how wrong I've been." She smiled at Elliot and patted his hands. "Your uncle is now...well, he's wonderful, and I don't know how to explain it. He's like...like a wonderful stranger."

Elliot smiled at her, seeing how much she loved her husband. He thought of Rachel.

"I just wanted you to know how wrong I've been and how I feel about you now."

Elliot smiled and placed his other hand over hers. "I'm glad we're friends. That's the way it's supposed to be!"

Once again, this strange young man surprised her. She laughed and stood up. He stood too, and they smiled at each other. Then they stepped forward and hugged each other.

That's what friends do, they hug, Elliot thought. How many years had he been thinking or saying those same words?

* * *

Near dawn, the morning before the party, Elliot had the following dream:

**He was seated in a high chair, in a kitchen. At least that was the perspective he saw things from. When he looked directly in front of him and downwards, he saw an assortment of food on the high chair tray: a partially**

**eaten piece of toast, a quarter of a peeled apple with a bite out of it, a half a slice of bacon sloppy wet at one end, and a baby bottle half filled with milk. Looking up, he saw a woman seated at the kitchen table in front of him, reading a newspaper out loud. Elliot watched her as she read the newspaper.** He woke up.

"Ida," he said out loud. Yes, he thought, it was Ida. He closed his eyes, visualizing her face again. Now, Elliot thought, I'll never forget her face again.

He smiled as he drifted off to sleep again. He immediately dreamed the same dream again, seeing the same scene in its entirety. But after it ended he continued to sleep until five thirty, his usual wake up time.

* * *

It was nine o'clock when Arnold woke Friday morning. The sun was coming through the window, blinding him. He smiled. He felt good. He tested the inside of his mouth by smacking his tongue against its roof. Though it wasn't great, it didn't taste like it usually did. He wanted to take a big stretch, but he knew better.

He got slowly up from bed, stood, lifted his pajama top and looked at the bandages on his stomach. He peeked a little. Everything looked O.K. in there. He just saw a thin red line running part way across his stomach below his belly button.

No matter. He felt good. His head felt clear, no headache, no pain behind his eyes, and his body felt good too. He went into the bathroom.

His dad had come up and visited him last night. He had told Arnold about the party they were having for all the bigwigs. He made it clear that he didn't expect Arnold to be there, that it was O.K. if he missed it. Arnold could tell by the way he said it, that it really was all right to miss it, but his dad wished he could be there. Arnold had thought about it after he had left. Surprised at his own thoughts, he found himself considering it. Maybe he wouldn't go to the dinner at the hotel because he didn't want to go downtown, but what about going downstairs for the party afterwards? That's what he considered last night before he fell asleep.

Now, he looked into his bathroom mirror. "Oh, brother," he said, "look at you! You think you're going to a party lookin' like this?" His stringy hair hung around his shoulders and his beard, patchy as it was, was at least three weeks old. And the six earrings in his ear... He knew he looked like hell. Staring at himself, he reached up, moved his hair out of the way and took his earrings out. He opened the medicine cabinet, took out his safety razor and searched around until he found a new blade. He lathered up and shaved, making sure he got all of it...pausing though, at his mustache. What the hell, he thought, if you're going to do it, do it!

Off it came. He couldn't shower yet, but he did take a sponge bath, before he dressed. He formulated a plan, but he knew he would need help.

He was too late for breakfast with the family, so he went into the kitchen. He could hear Marny in the laundry room. At the refrigerator, he got out the milk, saw some strawberries, and searched around the cupboards for cereal.

Marny came into the kitchen, saw him, then saw the milk and strawberries on the breakfast nook table. My Lord, she thought, the boy's gonna make his own breakfast! Then Arnold saw her watching him.

"Hi, Marny. Where do you keep the cereal?"

"Up above you. How are you feeling?" she questioned, watching him carry a box of oat bran over to the table. He had never eaten anything like that before. And look at that clean shaven face, with no earrings!

"I'm feeling pretty good. How about you?"

"Me?" she answered. "I'm O.K., but I didn't have my stomach cut open either."

"It's feeling good," he said with a laugh. "Hey, this cereal is pretty good. It's supposed to be good for you, right?" he asked her.

"Elliot says it is," Marny answered, wondering what was going through this child's mind. He watched as she worked over the chopping block.

"Do you think Charles is home?" Arnold asked abruptly.

"He's over there somewhere," she answered.

Arnold finished his cereal, slowly got up, carried his bowl to the sink, and put the milk back in the refrigerator.

"Bye, Marny," he said as he went out the back door.

"Bye, child," she said as she went to the window and watched him walk slowly toward the garages.

Arnold found Charles under the hood of his mother's Continental. Arnold looked under it with him, saying, "Hi, Charles." Charles looked up and saw him.

"Ah, Arnold. How are you mending?"

"Pretty good. Every day I seem to be moving around better."

"Good, glad to hear it," Charles said as he closed the hood of the car.

"Could I ask you a question?" Arnold asked, knowing that Charles didn't like him very much.

"Certainly."

"Do you remember when you first came here, when I was little?"

"Yes, you were eleven."

"Yeah, that's right. Well, do you remember giving me a haircut?"

"I do indeed," Charles said. "You told your father you wouldn't go to the barber shop anymore, because you thought the man was going to cut off your ear."

"Yeah, that's right," Arnold answered with a laugh. "That's what the barber told me he was gonna do if I didn't sit still. I believed him. But then you told my dad that you would give me a haircut."

"I gave you four or five, if I remember correctly."

"Would you mind doing one more?"

Charles looked at the boy for a moment, then smiled and said, "I don't see why not. You wait here."

Going upstairs, he got his shears, scissors, comb and a sheet. When he came down, he went into the garage and brought out a high chair used at the workbench. He put it in the sun; close enough to the garage so the extension cord would reach.

He motioned to Arnold, who sat, and placed the sheet around his shoulders.

"How short do you want it?" Charles asked.

"Not as short as yours," Arnold countered. They both laughed as Charles began on the long, stringy mass of hair.

As he was cutting, Arnold asked, "Would you mind doing something else for me?"

"What would that be?"

"Could you rent me a tux and all the rest of the stuff?"

Charles had noticed that the earrings were gone. "Do you need it for tonight?" he asked.

"Yeah. I guess the dinner will last until about eight and then they'll come back here. Is Aunt Elsie going to the dinner?"

"She wouldn't miss it," Charles answered. "As soon as we finish this haircut, I'll go see what can be done for you. What color would you like?"

"Whatever you think," the boy said.

Charles nodded, then paid attention to his task.

* * *

Tina called Alex at his fraternity house early in the week. She told him that her family was having a very important party, and she wanted him to take her to it. Alex told her yes, even though he knew he had a practice that Friday afternoon. He would have to make up some excuse to the coaches because the ride home took four hours. He would even have to miss a math class to get to Tina on time. He promised to pick her up at six for dinner before the party.

The coaches weren't even mad when they heard the reason. In fact they told him to have a good time! Alex decided the best excuse would be the truth. "Reed Industries was giving a major party for all of its bigwigs," and he was invited. The head coach ate it up. After all, Bertrand Reed had been an alumni and had always given a bundle in support of the college, including athletics. Alex got to go with their blessings.

As soon as he got home, he shaved and jumped into the shower. Tina didn't like it when he was late and always showed it by pouting for an hour or so. After the shower, he got on the scales, 267 pounds. He had lost two pounds. He had to be careful. He wanted to hit

290 by his junior year. He had to work out more and eat better. He made a mental note to eat plenty of pasta tonight; carbohydrates were what he needed.

He put on his tux, looked at himself in the mirror and drove to the carwash before going to pick up Tina.

When he rang the Swindale bell it was two minutes before six. Tina answered the door. She always took Alex's breath away but tonight she looked utterly fantastic. Her black cocktail dress fit the way Alex liked. He enjoyed watching other men drool.

Standing on the porch, Alex could only smile and nod his head. God, he thought, I'm glad to be her boyfriend! More than anything else, even more than going to the pros, I want to marry this girl.

Without a word, Tina came to him and stood on tiptoes, kissing him gently on the mouth. She had never greeted him like this before.

"You look wonderful," she said without smiling. Alex noticed that there was something sad about her, something different.

"Thanks," he answered, really appreciating how she seemed to be caring about him. Then he added, "Are you alright?"

"Oh, I'm fine," she replied, sounding rather melancholy.

"You sure look beautiful," he said, wishing he could express his feelings a little better to her. He knew that he always said the same thing.

"Thank you'" she said nicely. "Would you like to take my car tonight?"

Alex liked her new turbo Thunderbird, and it would be a lot more comfortable than the bucket seats in his old Porsche. "Sure, honey, it would be more comfortable," he said to her.

He drove his car back to the garage and parked it out of the way. She drove hers out of the garage and moved over, so he could drive. He climbed in, and she stayed as close as she could to him. He looked down at her as she put her arm around his huge triceps and put her cheek next to him.

There's got to be something wrong, he thought, she never does things like this.

"Tina, what's wrong with you?"

She paused for effect and then said, "Nothing. I'm just glad you're home." She looked at him with a pensive smile and added softly, "We'd better go or we'll miss our reservation."

She sat close to him during the ride to the restaurant, saying very little but always touching him. Alex wished they didn't have to go eat, he just wanted to drive around all night with her just where she was, just like this.

Tina's favorite food was Italian, but tonight Alex noticed that she ate very little. He ordered extra pasta and even ate most of hers. During the meal, he also noticed that she looked at him often. When their eyes met she would smile then glance away.

During dessert, she started to cry. It was not the kind of crying that caused people to turn, but instead, just a soft, mournful, private kind of weeping. It deeply touched Alex.

"Tina, Honey, what's wrong?" Alex asked as he reached for her hand.

She took it, then said through her tears, "Oh, Alex, I just can't get it out of my mind."

"What?" he asked, hurt because she was hurting.

She shook her head, then answered softly, "I...I can't talk about it here...not with people around."

"O.K., Honey," he said, getting the waiter's attention. "Check," he said as the waiter came toward them.

While waiting for the attendant to get the car, Alex put his arm around Tina, and she stayed very still, leaning against him. When the car arrived, Alex went around and helped her into the seat, waving the attendant off. He handed the boy a tip, then carefully shut the door after making sure she was seated. As they drove through the parking lot toward the street, Tina said, "Alex I think you should pull over."

He did so immediately, stopping in an area where there were no cars.

"What is it, Honey?"

"I want you...to go into the trunk. There's something you have to see."

Alex looked at her for a moment, then shut off the motor, took the key, and opened the trunk. As the lid came up, the only thing he could see, besides the spare tire, was a white jacket. He picked it up, looked at it for a moment, and then took it to Tina.

"This?" he asked as he got in.

"Yes."

Alex unfolded it, looked at it again and noticed that the front pocket was ripped. "What does it mean?"

"I tore that, fighting him off," she said, moving away from him.

"What?"

"He started taking off his clothes...he..." But she couldn't go on, she was crying.

"Tina, are you saying you were raped?"

"No, he only tried...twice."

"Twice? Who the hell are you talking about?

"One night, a few weeks ago, he broke a window in the kitchen and came up the stairs. I heard him breathing outside my room. But the police came, and we all heard the sirens... but he must have run down stairs... probably confused. My mother and I found him with Daddy in the library. He...he was just in his underwear."

"Who the hell is this?"

"I...I thought maybe I was wrong, maybe I imagined him being up there. I didn't want to get him in any trouble."

"Who? Who is it?"

She put her fingers gently over his lips, quieting him. She went on with her story.

"A few nights ago, I went to a late movie. When I came home and parked in the garage, he was waiting for me. He asked me to go up to his place, to go to bed with him. When I said I wouldn't, he...he took me by my wrists and backed me up against a wall and rubbed himself against me...saying that he had to have me. Then he began touching me."

She couldn't hold back the tears now. Alex put his arms around her, comforting her.

Alex knew who it was... "up to his place" she had said. Over the garages, that's where her cousin lived.

"It's your cousin, isn't it?"

She cried all the more, hiding her face in his huge chest.

"I'll take care of this," Alex said ominously, stroking her hair. "When I get through with him, he won't be able to touch anyone, anywhere with anything!"

* * *

The dinner at the hotel was a success. Reed Industries met in the special dining room at six. There was an exceptionally good string quartet that played while they had cocktails. Harriet accompanied her husband as he made his way to the different couples, introducing himself, saying hello, making every person feel comfortable.

"How did you know all these people?" she asked him as they were sitting down to eat. He only smiled, gave her a kiss on the cheek, and whispered how happy he was to be here with her.

The food was excellent. Harriet's idea of serving two entree's on the same plate, a beef tornado and a lightly seasoned filet of fish in a lemon sauce with capers, worked very well. She had devised a way of separating the sauces of each by spears of asparagus settled on a line of swirled potatoes. The other vegetable was served separately. The head chef had done a masterful job of creating a very nice look.

Harriet heard some of the comments from her guests, unaware that she had been the creator, telling how unusual and yet delicious they were together. When Graham heard the same comments, he smiled at his wife, knowing full well how much time and thought she had spent on this dinner.

Even, Bill Bryant and his wife, who Graham had wanted at their table, commented on how delicious everything was. Earlier in the week, Harriet started to say something to Graham about having **that** lawyer seated at the same table with them, but decided against it. Things were too good now, she had thought at the time; so let Graham decide who he wanted to have around him. She really didn't care anyway and found that she wasn't really angry with Bill Bryant anymore. In fact, she wasn't angry any more with anyone.

As the dessert was being served, Graham stood, took a spoon and tapped on a glass. Harriet was as curious as the rest of the guests.

"Ladies and Gentlemen," he said, waiting for the murmuring to die down. "My wife and I will be leaving a little earlier than the rest of you. We want to make sure that our home is in order before you arrive."

There was some laughter from a few people. Graham smiled, then continued. "We want you to take your time over this wonderful dinner. After you've finished, there will be transportation for all in the front of the hotel. Please notice that there are six of you at a table, and that is exactly how many each limo will handle comfortably." He paused and looked around him. "I can't tell you how much my wife and I have looked forward to this time together. We want to welcome all of you into our home, to do some dancing and some talking, so we can begin to know each other. I believe that the future holds some wonderful things for this organization of ours, and that the best way to begin to prepare for it is by becoming friends."

Graham moved behind Harriet's chair as the people started clapping. She stood, smiled, and then taking her husband's hand they walked together from the dining room.

The ride home was quiet. They both commented on how well the dinner had gone. But beyond that, there was just a peaceful silence. Harriet looked at her husband as the lights from the dashboard gave his still-handsome face a strange, rather serious look. She never knew before this very moment that she could love a man so much. Her heart was full. How long had it been, she wondered. A month? What had happened to him that night in the library? How could any man make such an abrupt change? And why didn't he still have a craving for those things that had kept him in such bondage for so many years?

Tonight, she had watched him closely during the whole affair. While other people were drinking, it didn't bother him at all. Why wasn't he affected by what had gone on in his life before? There, in the darkness, Harriet found herself wanting to know how he managed all this.

Since Graham had requested that the band members and the caterers park on the street to make room for the limos, as they approached their home, the city streets near their entrance were filled with cars. As Graham turned into the estate, he saw that all the lights were on in their house.

But then something else gripped his attention. Someone was hurrying down the driveway toward him, desperately waving his arms up and down as though signaling for help. Graham turned on his high beams.

"Oh, my God! It's Arnold!" Graham said.

"What?" Harriet said, looking out the windshield. It was Arnold in a tux, waving his arms excitedly at them. Graham sped up and reached him.

"It's Alex!...by the garage! He's got Elliot," he said breathlessly. "He's trying to kill him! Hurry!"

Graham pressed the accelerator to the floor. As his high beams hit the turn past the house, he saw Alex and Elliot in front of the garages. Alex had him and was doing his best to smash in his face. Tina was there, standing to one side, and another girl, who was trying to get Alex off of Elliot. Graham slammed on his brakes, leaving the high lights on the fighters, and jumped from the car. Harriet followed.

"Alex! Alexander!" he shouted at him. Alex stopped and looked into the bright lights, seeing the silhouette of Mr. Swindale. His face was enraged.

Graham walked up and stood before the two boys. He could see that Elliot was still conscious, but there was blood all over him.

"Alex, this is Graham Swindale. If you hit him again, I'm going to make sure that you spend the next few years of your life in prison. Do you understand?" There was still a crazed look over Alex's face as Graham moved closer.

"Let go of him now," Graham commanded, with all the calmness he could summon. "Right now, Alex."

Graham saw the huge arm relax that had held Elliot prisoner against the garage door. Elliot's knees gave way slightly. Graham went forward to help the boy.

"Now step away," Graham said, in the same tone of voice.

Alex did so, his face losing that frenzied look.

Graham heard someone sobbing in the background. It was the young girl. Harriet went to her and put her arms around her. Graham glanced at his daughter and saw her looking coldly at what was going on.

"Alex, Tina, everybody into the house."

Alex looked to Tina, who hadn't moved. This giant was waiting for her to move.

"I said, get into the house, and do it now," Graham ordered sharply, now close to losing his temper. He looked directly at his daughter. She lowered her gaze and moved toward the house. Alex followed.

"Can you walk?" Graham asked Elliot.

"Yes, Sir," Elliot answered. "He was just too big and strong."

"He's like a bull," Graham said.

"He just jumped him, Dad," Arnold said coming up behind them. "Alex called him a son-of-a-bitch and hit him."

"Can you walk into the house?" Graham asked.

"Yes, Sir," Elliot said, looking over at Rachel and Harriet. "Rachel, are you alright?" Elliot asked.

Rachel had calmed now and came up to Elliot. "I'm fine, Elliot... it's you."

"No, I'm alright. He just got me in the nose and one on the side of my face. He's so strong, it's like getting hit with a hammer."

They all walked slowly to the front door, while music drifted from behind the house.

When Graham came into the entryway, he saw Tina and Alex standing next to each other. Alex's shirt and cummerbund were splattered with blood. Scurrying about behind them, carrying hors d'oeuvres and drinks to different rooms, were the caterers.

"Into the library," Graham directed.

Without a word, everyone started down the hall.

Arnold came into the entryway just as his family was going into the library. He had moved his father's car and locked it. He walked down the hall to join them. When Arnold entered his father looked at him and said, "Are you alright?"

"I'm O.K."

"I think we should lock the door. We don't want the caterers coming in during this."

Arnold turned the key, then went and sat down on the sofa. His mother was sitting nearby and smiled at him.

"There are towels in the second drawer of the wet bar," Graham told Elliot. Rachel went with him to help. Tina stood by the bay windows, looking out to the lawn. Alex, looking down at himself, went over, moistened a towel, and worked on cleaning his shirt.

"We have about twenty or twenty-five minutes to get this sorted out, then we'll have a hundred and fifty people here," Graham said as he walked over and stood in front of Alex.

"Were you the one who started the fight?" Graham asked.

"Yes, Sir," Alex answered.

"I'd like to know the reason for it."

Alex paused, looked over at Tina, and said, "Ask him," motioning toward Elliot with the towel in his hand.

As Graham looked at Elliot, Alex moved away and joined Tina by the window.

"I don't know why," Elliot replied, standing still as Rachel wiped the blood from his face. "When we drove up, he got out of Tina's car, came over to me and started swinging."

"You know the reason for it!" Alex insisted.

"Why don't you tell us, Alex?" Graham said, walking over to the windows. Turning, he looked directly at his daughter, whose beautiful face was expressionless. She acted as though she didn't belong here, like this dispute was beneath her, and she shouldn't be expected to participate. But Graham knew that whatever had happened out at the garages, she had something to do with it. Alex was her puppy dog, her St.Bernard. He would bite only when his mistress spoke.

"Alex, you have always been welcome in this house, and you've always acted responsibly. I want to know what happened down there, and then I want this settled. It **has** to be done right now."

"It happened twice!" the huge lad said, looking over at Elliot. "Why'd you let him stay at your house after he broke the window? Didn't you know he'd try it again? Don't you know he's a freak?"

"The window?" Graham said, looking over at his wife. "What window?"

Harriet didn't want to say it, but she was afraid things might go back to the way they had been. Oh, God, she thought, why did this have to come up? Please, don't let things go back the way they were.

"Harriet, can you help me with this?" Graham asked.

"About a month ago, the house alarm went off at the police station," Harriet answered. "In the middle of the night someone had broken into the house. We found Elliot in the library with you. He had broken a kitchen window to get in."

"How was he dressed, Mother?" Tina probed. Her voice sounded cold and impersonal, as she was acting.

"He...he was in his underwear...just his shorts."

"And what reason did he give for being there?" Tina continued questioning her mother.

"We asked him, but he wouldn't tell us," Harriet responded, watching her husband's face.

"Ask him where he was before that!" Alex blurted out.

Graham looked at Alex, then turned and walked over to Elliot. "This was the night of the dream, wasn't it?"

"Yes, Sir."

Rachel couldn't understand what she was hearing. What had Elliot done? Did Alex have a valid reason for doing what he did? If so, what was it? And Elliot was found in the middle of the night in his underwear? She felt a sudden emptiness. What did Alex know that Elliot seemed not to want to talk about? Rachel was frightened.

Graham turned back to Alex. "Before Elliot came into this room that night, he was sleeping."

"No he wasn't," Alex answered harshly. "He was upstairs in this house!"

"Upstairs? What do you mean?" Harriet asked.

Alex looked to Tina, but she was still looking straight ahead, unwilling to participate. "Ask him where his jacket is! What happened the other night in the garage, you creep?"

"What are you trying to say, Alex?" Graham said sharply. "Just say it!"

"He's been after her! He tried to rape Tina!"

There was stunned silence in the room. A moment passed, then abruptly, Arnold laughed. Everyone turned and looked at him.

Slowly the boy got from the couch. He went over and stood in front of Alex and Tina.

"What night did this attempted rape happen?" he asked the two of them. Alex looked at Tina.

"Wednesday night," Tina said without looking at her brother.

"About two-thirty in the morning?" Arnold asked his sister, smiling at her.

She paused, measuring her brother. She knew something was wrong. He never smiled like this unless he had something on her, something she didn't know. "No, it was much earlier," she replied, turning away and trying to ignore him.

"No," Arnold said, "if anything, it was really a little bit later, closer to three in the morning."

Arnold's gaze went from his sister to the huge man standing next to her. Arnold felt sorry for him. He knew that the big oaf just loved the bitch.

"You've been had, Alex." Arnold looked back at his sister and found that he felt sorry for her too. She's a spoiled, **silly** broad, he thought. That's all she is.

"I saw you get out of someone's car that night and walk over to the garages," Arnold said without emotion. "I thought maybe you were going to get your car, to go somewhere. But instead, you did something really weird. You took off your shoes, left them on the cement, and walked up the stairs to the apartments."

"That's a lie!" Tina snapped, spinning to face him.

Arnold looked at her for a moment, slowly shaking his head as he continued. "No, it isn't." Glancing at Alex, he said, "It's the truth, Alex."

"She told me she went to the movies, and when she got back he was waiting for her inside the garage," Alex said while watching Tina's face. "And that he began touching her...she even cried when she told me!"

Arnold moved away from them and went to the wet bar. He stood next to Elliot and Rachel. Graham went to his daughter and stood in front of her for a moment. Her chin was trembling and her face was filled with unveiled resentment. Graham knew by looking that she was the liar, not Elliot.

"I want you two to sit down," Graham said softly. "Please, we don't have much time. In fact, I'd like everyone to sit."

Alex looked down at Tina, then moved to the couch by himself and sat. Graham took his daughter by the arm and sat her next to her mother. Arnold sat on the edge of the couch. Elliot led Rachel to the computer chair, while he sat on the desk next to her.

"My daughter has just been caught in a succession of lies. Undoubtedly, there was no rape attempt. Most probably, there was an attempted seduction of her cousin that failed, and my daughter's lust turned into revenge. Who else would avenge her, but the man who loves her." He looked at Tina for a moment, then moved over and placed his hand on Arnold's shoulder.

"But she's not alone. My son was a cocaine addict and a thief. A week ago, he almost paid the ultimate price for it." Graham paused and quietly continued. "It's strange, but I can't bring myself to judge my children. I can't even find it in my heart to be angry at them." Graham moved away from his son and stood before the group again.

"I'm certainly sorry what happened to Elliot, the abuse he had to take because of my daughter. But I know he can take it." Graham looked at Rachel, then back to Elliot, smiling at both of them.

"Instead of judgment and anger, I believe it's time for me to bring out all the filthy laundry of the Swindale family."

He paused, and looked at his wife, "Would that be all right with you, Harriet?"

"Whatever you want, Graham," she answered.

"Yes, I think this is the appropriate time," Graham said quietly. "A month ago, that night when Elliot broke into the house, he had just had a dream, an amazing dream. Because of it, he ran to the house, broke the window and came **directly** into this room."

Graham paused, trying to visualize what the next scene must have looked like, then moved to where Rachel was seated at the desk. "He found me seated here, drunk, leaning over my upturned revolver with its barrel in my mouth. I was trying to put my thumb on the trigger."

Harriet heard herself moan.

"He yanked my head up and slapped the gun to the floor."

Graham paused, "Of course I don't remember much of it. I have to take Elliot's word for it."

Graham reached into the drawer and brought out the revolver. "But I do know one thing, I still can't find the bullets to this gun. Where are they, Elliot?"

Elliot walked to the bookshelf, slid out the wide, heavy volume, and retrieved the shells.

"Where was Elliot when you came into the room, Harriet?"

"Right where he is now," she said, wanting to cry with gratefulness for still having her husband.

"Yes, of course, where else?" Graham asked, nodding.

"The next night, during dinner, Elliot asked if he could talk to me. My family certainly remembers that...the way I acted at the table. The two of us came in here."

Graham thought for a moment, remembering exactly the way it was. "I went to the bar to fix myself a drink. It was time, you see. Every night, for years, I'd gotten drunk right here in this room. This night, I poured myself a drink and watched as Elliot came over, took the drink out of my hand and poured it down the drain! I couldn't believe it! A seventeen-year-old boy doing that...to me!"

Graham looked over at the bar then walked behind it, taking his place where he had been that night.

"But you see, I didn't know anything about his dream. And I couldn't remember much of what had happened the night before." He stopped. He could feel a rush of feeling coming up from his guts. Tears suddenly blurred his vision. He looked down at the bar, trying to control himself.

"Tell us about the dream, darling," Harriet said gently, so much wanting to help him.

"Ah, yes, the dream. Elliot?" Graham asked.

Elliot nodded his consent.

"In the dream, Elliot saw me standing, drunk, in my corduroy coat. He saw a `being' come partially out of me, and he talked to it."

"A being?" Arnold said, his eyes widening.

"Yes," Graham said, "a small, ugly creature with grotesque features and fiery eyes."

"That's ridiculous!" Tina said sharply.

"No, they're real," Rachel interjected. "Demons are in the Bible."

"Yes, exactly," Graham said quickly, acknowledging that Rachel was right. "And they inhabit people sometimes. Elliot told me they were demons. And this being who was inside of me had a name."

"A name? Really? What kind of a name?" Alex asked, wide-eyed. The huge lad believed what Mr. Swindale was saying.

Graham looked to Elliot.

"They seem to be named after the work they have come to do," Elliot answered.

"Yes," Graham continued, "Names like, Drunkenness, Hopelessness..." Graham couldn't finish the list as a sob come from him.

"...Worthlessness, Dumb...and Suicide," Elliot said, finishing the list for him.

"Yes," Graham said, "five of them were inside me."

"Five of them?" Alex asked. "How did they all fit?"

"They're spirit beings," Elliot said. "Space is not the same for them."

"What happened? What did you do?" Harriet asked her husband.

Graham picked up a wet towel and wiped his eyes, surprised at how much emotion was still behind these things that had happened to him. It was almost like he was going through them again.

"First Elliot told me what I had tried to do the night before... commit suicide, and I found myself actually hating him. I wanted to kill him." Graham looked at the door, then walked toward it. "But then as he questioned me about the gun, I tried to run out of the room. But he'd locked the door."

"I thought you said you wanted to kill him?" Tina said, disbelief hanging on every word.

"I did, but at the same time I was so frightened I felt like I had to get away. Strange feelings were fighting inside of me."

"What did you say to the demons?" Harriet asked, looking at Elliot. Elliot didn't answer her, but only smiled and looked to his uncle, knowing it was his story.

Graham slowly placed himself against the door as he had done that night. "He...he looked right into my eyes, and then called them out of me," Graham said with a degree of wonder in his voice.

"You mean they listened to you?" Arnold asked Elliot.

"Yes, if you know they're real, and you deal directly with them, they listen," Elliot answered quietly.

"What did he say to them?" Harriet asked her husband.

"He was right here in my face," Graham said, motioning with his hand. "He was this close. I remember how loud he got, how he called them by their names. And he called them out in the name of Jesus. And as soon as he said the name, Jesus, I knew I had to get out of the room! I couldn't stand being there. Then, he mentioned the name `Suicide', and I felt, if I didn't leave I would die. I began running for the bay windows."

As he was telling the story, Graham moved away from the door and toward the bay windows. "I remember my arms going out, like this...and I felt as though I could leave the ground... And then, everything went black." Graham looked over at Elliot.

"The demons left him, and he hit the floor. It knocked him unconscious."

"When I came to, Elliot told me what had happened. I'd never felt such fear. I knew everything he told me was true. And then...he told me they could come back."

"And just how did he know that?" Tina asked.

"Jesus says so in the Bible," Rachel answered, finding it difficult not to become irritated at this beautiful troublemaker.

"She's right, that's exactly what Elliot said to me," Graham acknowledged. "He told me how Jesus knows about demon's habits, and I believed him."

"What can you do so they won't come back?" Harriet asked, never wanting her husband to be like he had been.

Graham smiled and said, "I've already done it. Jesus said we're all like houses. If we get it cleaned up inside and then the demon comes back and finds the house empty, he'll go get his friends, move back in, and it will be worse than before."

"So what did you do to fill up your house?" Arnold asked, wondering if he might have demons in him as well.

"Elliot told me I could ask Jesus to come inside my house. So I did it."

"Is He in there?" Alex asked in awe.

"Yes."

"I thought Jesus was supposed to be in heaven?" Tina said, almost sneering at what she was hearing.

"He is," Elliot replied, "but the Holy Spirit, the Comforter, is in Uncle Graham. The Father sent Him."

Tina was not about to accept an answer from Elliot, and she immediately refuted what he said. "Ridiculous," she muttered.

"Dad, how do you know He's in there?" Arnold asked his father curiously, ignoring his sister.

Graham paused for a moment, surprised at how wonderful he felt talking about Jesus and what had happened to him. "I know he's there, because...I don't want to drink anymore. I don't even think about it."

"I can vouch for that," Harriet said. "He can be around people drinking, and it doesn't phase him. He could care less."

"Another thing..." Graham continued, smiling at his wife as she talked about him. "I feel like...like I never knew what love was before. I love my wife so much now, I can't leave her alone."

Harriet blushed, and said quietly, "I can vouch for that, too."

Everyone laughed except Tina.

"Now, let me tell you why I told all of you this..." Graham continued. "It's to let you know that I've been given a new life. I came within an instant of dying and being with those terrible creatures forever. So now, I've started over."

He looked at his family and their friends, "I get a chance to start over with all of you." He had tears in his eyes again. "And now I can tell all of you that I love you...every one of you, and I want us to become a real family...something we've never been."

There was a long silence as everyone sat with his or her own thoughts. Then Graham said, "What about you, Alex? How are you feeling?"

"Me, Sir?"

"Yes. Are you alright with everyone in this room?"

"No, Sir," Alex answered, understanding what Mr. Swindale was getting at. He looked over at Elliot, then got up and went over to him.

"I really did a bad thing to you," Alex said. Then, pausing, he thought for a moment. "Even though I never really got you good. I've never seen anybody move quicker than you. I couldn't get a clear shot until I got you up against the garage. How come you never tried to hit back?"

Elliot smiled, "You're too big."

Alex watched the younger boy's face, not really knowing what to believe, then said, "I'm really sorry for what I did."

"It's alright," Elliot answered. "It's all over now."

Alex could tell by looking at Elliot's face that he had been forgiven. The two young men smiled at each other, then Alex gently pounded Elliot on the shoulder and shook his hand.

Then the big lad looked out the bay window and saw a string of headlights coming up the drive.

"Cars are coming, Mr. Swindale."

"Well, here they are. Why don't we all go out in the entryway and greet our guests?" Graham said.

As everybody started leaving the library, Graham motioned to Harriet to come over to him.

"Wait a moment," he whispered to her. Then he moved over to Arnold and gently took him by the arm. The three of them waited until the others had walked from the room. Then Graham smiled at his son.

"I want to tell you how nice it is to have you here. I can't really tell you what it means to us."

Moving forward, he hugged his son. Arnold hugged him back. When they separated, Graham moved to one side, and Harriet stood before her son. Arnold came up to her, and they hugged.

"You look marvelous!" she whispered to her son, "Just marvelous."

The three of them walked out to meet their guests.

As the people came in, all dressed in their finery, Rachel stayed very close to Elliot. There were so many things she wanted to say to him. She too, like Alex, wondered why he hadn't fought back.

There were times during the fight when Alex left himself open to attack, and Rachel had seen it, but Elliot never took advantage of it. He didn't try to run either. He stayed, protecting himself as best he could, but ended up taking a beating. She had never seen anything like it. As she thought about it, she took his hand.

Elliot greeted a couple from Scotland. He paused, looked at Rachel and smiled while he continued to talk to them. She really didn't care to listen, she just wanted to stay near Elliot. Oh, there were so many things she wanted to say to him!

Then, she heard a familiar voice in her ear, "Hello."

There stood Aunt Elsie, smiling up at Rachel. Rachel took her hand, then felt a slight pull. She leaned forward, as Aunt Elsie whispered in her ear, "What happened to Elliot's face?"

"He had a fight with Alex," she whispered back to the old lady.

"Why would he do that?" Elsie asked.

"It had to do with Tina," Rachel said, hoping that would be enough of an answer.

"Ah, that girl," Elsie said, shaking her head and smiling wistfully. She gave Rachel a kiss. Rachel watched her make her way over to the stairs. She saw Arnold take hold of his aunt's arm and slowly escort her upstairs. That was nice of Arnold, Rachel thought.

She heard the music outside. She knew Elliot didn't know how to dance, and she wanted to teach him. She wanted him to hold her, so that she might tell him all the things that were going on in her mind. She wanted to hold him. But people kept streaming in from the limos, smiling, looking at the grand house, talking to Elliot and the rest of the family. Rachel smiled at them, but she was really lost in her own thoughts and feelings about the person standing next to her.

Then suddenly, without Rachel even realizing it, the two of them were alone. No more people, no more small talk, just the two of them standing in the large entryway with Elliot looking down at her.

"Hello," he said.

Now she could say all the things she had been thinking! Now she could tell him how proud she was of him. How she hadn't understood, but now did. Do it now, she told herself.

"Hello," she answered.

"Should we go out and watch them dance?"

"Yes," she answered, knowing now that she was a coward.

A portable dance floor with soft lights around it had been placed on the lawn beyond the swimming pool. The band was playing.

Elliot watched, as Rachel stood beside him, still tongue-tied.

"It doesn't look too difficult," Elliot said. The band was playing a slow number, and the men were holding the women close.

"It isn't," Rachel said, irritated at her own timidity.

"Let's give it a try," Elliot said.

They went to the edge of the floor, and Rachel turned to face him. She placed her hand on his shoulder and felt his arm go partially around her waist. Their other hands folded into one another. Elliot had yet to move. She looked up at him and saw him looking down at her. Slowly, she moved closer to him, until their bodies were touching. His arm encircled her waist entirely now. She found herself breathless, undone. She was beyond helping herself; she had to look to him now.

"We should move, shouldn't we?" he said, becoming weak in his knees. This was more than he had ever thought it could be.

"Oh, yes, please," Rachel responded, feeling his chest against hers.

"What should I do?"

"Whatever you want. I'll follow, no matter where you go."

When she said it, she knew that her words meant much more than dancing. But she didn't care, because she knew that she wanted only him. For her, from tonight on, everything in her life was now different. Now, she knew who she wanted.

Elliot touched his lips to her forehead, then moved his left foot. She moved with him. He moved his right, and she followed. He felt her body move in oneness with his and knew instantly that there were depths to him that he had never felt before. It was all he could do not to stop dancing, not to take her in both of his arms and crush her to himself.

The music stopped, and they separated. Both were terribly shaken, not even knowing where to walk. They made their way to one of the small tables near the dance floor and sat down.

"Would you like something to drink?" Elliot asked, his breathing still erratic.

"Yes, please," Rachel answered, still unable to think clearly.

Elliot got up and walked towards the house.

* * *

Alex believed that he had lost Tina. More than that, he knew he had never had her. He wondered to himself if it wasn't better this way. He was finally aware that she could do anything she wanted with him. There was no doubt that he was a wimp and really stupid about her. Though he felt embarrassed, he decided he wouldn't leave the party but would talk to the people, greet them, make them feel at home, just like Mr. Swindale had asked him to do. Since Mr. Swindale really did care about him, it was the least he could do.

Alex soon found men who were interested in football and wanted to hear about his college and the team. Everybody was really impressed with his size. Besides, he always enjoyed the attention. He started having a good time.

Tina watched Alex as he moved through the crowd of people. They all looked at him, in awe of the monster, as he smiled and talked to them, shaking hands and being polite to the women. Tina felt sick. She had been caught, and she hated the feeling. And besides, now, nobody would talk to her.

She thought Alex would leave the party after the way she treated him, but there he was, just as though nothing had happened. The bastard! How could he do it? And he never looked at her. What was worse, she could tell that he wasn't even playing a game with her; he really didn't care where she was!

What was she supposed to do now? She couldn't stay at home, not after this, and she didn't know what she could do on her own. She wished she were back in school. At least there, she could find something to do. Would her father let her return? Would he still be willing to pay her way? She doubted it. What was she to do? She wandered through the party, smiling and saying hello, wishing she were anywhere but here. Halfheartedly, she looked for her father.

* * *

At the refreshment table, Harriet was talking to a woman, when she saw Elliot, excused herself and went up to him.

"Are you enjoying yourself?"

"Yes, ma'am."

"I saw you dancing. How did you like it?"

"It's...really something," he said, trying to put the appropriate words to it and knowing he fell short.

"Yes, it is. I'm going to have to find Graham and try some of it." She smiled at Elliot. "Rachel is a beautiful girl."

"Yes, she is," Elliot answered, once again knowing that he has not really describing Rachel the way he wanted to. "In fact, she's absolutely astounding," Elliot said, knowing that even these words weren't good enough.

Harriet looked at her nephew. He had all the signs. Good for him, she thought. They are certainly beautiful together.

"There's something about her I can't describe," Elliot said, trying to explain his feelings for her.

"Yes, I know," Harriet answered.

"You do?" Elliot said, wondering how she knew.

"Of course, young man, I'm in love too."

Elliot searched her smiling face. "That's what it is, isn't it?"

"Oh, yes," Harriet answered. She reached up and gave him a kiss on the check and added, "And if you're really fortunate, it will get worse."

At that moment, Bill Bryant and his wife, Evelyn, came up to the drink table.

"Hello, Harriet," Bill said, wanting to thank her for placing them at the head table.

"Hello, Bill...Evelyn," Harriet said as she took Evelyn's hand. "I'd like you to meet Elliot Reed."

Elliot knew he had heard the name, but where?

"Hello, Elliot," Mr. Bryant said. "I'm the lawyer who wrote the letters to your school."

"Oh, yes, Sir. I knew I had heard your name before. It's nice meeting you. Hello, Mrs. Bryant."

"Hello, Elliot," Evelyn said. Her husband had told her all about the surprise Bertrand's will had given the Swindale family. He's certainly just as handsome as his father was, she thought.

"Could I ask you a question?" Elliot said to Bill.

"Shoot."

"Do you still have my early records, when I was a baby?"

"Yes, we have all of them."

"Do you have the name of the lady who watched after me? Her first name was Ida."

"I'm sure her name and all the pertinent information would be in there."

"Could I come down to your office and look at them?"

"Anytime."

"Tomorrow?"

"Saturday?" Bill asked, suddenly seeing something of the boy's father standing in front of him. When Bertrand wanted something, he wanted it now.

"What time would you be there?"

"Would nine be too early?" Elliot asked.

"Ooh," said Bryant feigning pain, "you are a task-master. What about nine-thirty, since this is a party night. I'll meet you out in front of our building at nine-thirty."

"I'll be there. Thank you, Sir." Elliot shook his hand, nodded at Evelyn and Harriet, then picked up two soft drinks and headed back to Rachel.

"He's got a grip like a vice," Bryant said to Harriet.

"He's quite a young man," Harriet said, watching Elliot walk back toward his table.

Bill Bryant could tell by the softness in her voice that something had happened to change Harriet's opinion of this lad. He wondered if the bruises on the boy's face had anything to do with it?

* * *

Graham felt a tap on his back as he stood talking to the president of Europa Fibers from Scotland. They had been in the living room for a good half hour.

It was Tina.

"I'm sorry to bother you, Daddy," she said.

"No, sweetheart, it's all right. Mr. Donnelly, this is my daughter, Tina," Graham said.

"It's a pleasure," the Scotsman said. "I've taken enough of your father's time. You take over, Lass. I'll search out me wife." He smiled and moved out of the room.

Father and daughter looked at each other. Then Graham reached out and gently touched her cheek. "Why don't we go dance together?" he said, taking her by the arm.

Graham was grateful it was a slow number. He hadn't danced in years, and he knew what a good dancer his daughter was.

"You don't seem to be mad at me at all," Tina said.

"I'm not," he said, meaning it. This new thing with Jesus in him was just as amazing to him. "You did wrong. You were found out, and it's over. You're still my daughter, and I still love you."

"What should I do now?"

"I suggest that you go back to school. Right away."

"That's what I want to do."

"Good. You'll have to work hard to make up for the few weeks you've missed, but you can do it."

They danced together for a few moments, then Graham said, "You don't believe what I said in the library, do you?"

She decided to tell him the truth. "No, I don't."

"I think maybe Arnold and Alex did."

"Alex hasn't even looked at me. He's found out about me."

"Prove him wrong."

"How?'

"Change. He's loved you since you were six."

"I know. How do I change, Daddy?"

"Well, you might start believing your father," Graham said with a smile.

"You're mad at me?"

"No, not really. It's between you and God."

"I don't believe in Him either."

He looked at her and smiled. "I know you don't. But if <u>you</u> were right, I'd still be an old drunk." He gave his daughter a whirl, then kissed her forehead. Then he felt another tap on his back and turned to see his beautiful wife smiling up at him.

"My turn," she said, smiling and kissing Tina on the cheek as she cut in. Graham took his wife into his arms.

"We haven't done this in years," he said.

She was silent, then pulled away slightly and looked up at him. "You've never loved me like you do now, have you?"

Graham thought about it for a moment. "No, never like I do now."

"Then I really don't have to pretend. I really am with a strange, new man."

Graham laughed and said, "That's true."

She moved closer to him, and they danced in silence for a few moments. Then she said, "This month has been like a honeymoon, Graham...something more than we've ever had."

"Yes," he said, "It's been unbelievable."

"When we go upstairs tonight," she said, looking up at him, "I want you to tell me what you said to Jesus. Is that alright?"

"Sure," he said, taken by surprise. "Why do you want to know that?"

She was quiet for a moment, then moved closer to him, holding him, and whispered, "Because I want to know how to be new too."

* * *

Elliot and Rachel sipped their soft drink and watched Mr. and Mrs. Swindale dance. Then Elliot said, "Rachel, I can't hold things in anymore, about the way you look or the way I feel about you."

"I know. It's alright now," she said, looking at him.

"It is?"

"Yes. You can say anything you want now."

Elliot wondered what had happened to change her mind? He touched her hand. She took his. "Holding you in my arms, being next to you, was more than I imagined."

"I know," Rachel answered, looking directly at him. "I felt the same way."

"You did?"

"When you left to get our drinks, I wanted to be with you. I wanted to go over, take your hand, and stand next to you. I want everyone to know that I'm yours...just yours."

"I feel the same way about you," Elliot responded, looking into her eyes. "This is love, isn't it?

"It is for me. I've never wanted to belong to someone before."

"That's what I want to. I want to belong to you."

Elliot moved his chair around next to hers. They held hands and watched the people dance.

* * *

After Arnold took Elsie to her room, he walked around the party, ate a little food, did a little talking, and got tired quickly. That fight between Alex and Elliot had shaken him up. He decided to go up early, to get plenty of rest. No more screwin' around at nights, he told himself. He was going to do exactly what he had to, to get strong. He was tired of being skinny and damn tired of the wrong kind of friends.

He saw his dad out on the dance floor with his mom. He waved, then motioned that he was going upstairs. His dad smiled and nodded that he understood. They look good together, Arnold thought as he started to leave the dance area. As he turned to go, he saw Elliot pick up his chair and move it around next to Rachel's chair. Then Rachel took his hand, and put her head on his shoulder as they watched the dancers. Man, Arnold thought, how wrong was I about Rachel. She loves that dude, no doubt about it. He turned and went through the house, picking up a couple of little fancy sandwiches and a soft drink on the way out. That's what I want, he said to himself, I'm tired of being alone. I'd like a girl, and a nice one, too, someone like Rachel.

* * *

Elliot and Rachel were quiet during the ride home in the Jeep. He had put the top up, and they listened to the radio.

"I have to go downtown to see Mister Bryant at his office. Would you go with me?" he asked, as they neared her home.

"Sure," Rachel said, smiling, thinking how simple this was. She didn't have to make a decision. All she had to do was say yes.

"Why are you smiling?" Elliot asked.

"It seems so simple now. What I want the most is to be with you."

Elliot thought about this, then said, "Is this alright with you, Rachel?"

"It's a new way for me to feel, but it's wonderful."

"I want to do things you want to do too," Elliot said as he pulled up in front of the house and turned off the motor.

"It's simple," Rachel said with a smile. "Tomorrow you have something you want to do, and you want me with you, so we both get to do what we want."

Elliot looked at her for a long moment in the darkness of the car, and then laughed. He opened up the door and went around to help her out.

"What? What was funny?" she asked.

"I think love is funny. The Colonel once told me that one of the most important things for a man to do was to include the woman he loved in whatever he was going to do."

"The Colonel was right. What's funny about that?"

"How come I'm worried about whether you're going to like what we're going to do?"

Rachel thought about this as they walked up to her house.

"Maybe it's because you don't know me yet."

Elliot looked at Rachel's face as they stood on the porch, the light from the living room throwing shadows across their faces. "That could be. Or maybe it's because I love you so much I'll always be concerned about whether you're pleased with what we do together."

"I like that reason better," she answered softly.

They moved nearer to each other. He touched her face with his fingers. She smiled and placed her hands on his sides. He felt himself jump slightly inside. His hands went over her shoulders, and he drew her to him. Her arms went around him, and they kissed.

Dancing is good, but nothing like this, Elliot thought as he kissed her partially opened mouth. He kissed her for a long time, finding that he didn't want to stop. But he did stop.

Rachel opened her eyes and smiled at Elliot. "I'm pleased."

Elliot touched her face again, and then put his palm on her cheek. "When I hold and kiss you, I forget everything."

"I know. I can only think of you too," she answered.

He searched her face, and then said, "It's up to me, isn't it?"

"Yes."

"He kissed her softly, once more, then opened the front door for her. "Eight-thirty? Is that alright?" he asked.

"I'll be ready," she responded as she went into the house. She was glad he understood, because she would have kissed him all night. She went into the living room.

"You're in early," her mother said, greeting her from the couch where she was doing some sewing. Her father sat watching basketball from his leather chair. The sound was low on the TV.

"Elliot and I have something to do in the morning."

"Did you have a good time?"

"Yes. I found out what I'm going to do for the rest of my life."

Dolores stopped her sewing and looked closely at her daughter. The television screen went dark as her father turned toward his daughter and said, "What did you say, Honey?"

"He's the one," Rachel stated.

"You know for sure?" her father asked.

"Without a doubt," Rachel said as she kissed him good night. She went over to kiss her mother.

"I was hoping it would be him," her mother said, holding her daughter's face in her hands. "He's special."

"I know," Rachel said, "He's wonderful." She gave her mother a long hug. "God's blessed me, Mama. He's just blessed me." She smiled at both of them and went up to her room.

Marc watched her walk out, then looking over at his wife.

"What about college?"

"Her priorities have changed. Elliot comes first now." She glanced up from her work and saw that her husband was still looking at her, most probably thinking about what she had just said. She smiled and added, "Just like someone else you know."

Marc knew exactly what she meant. He had always felt that he had been first in her life. He got up and went over to sit next to her.

"I wonder what we're supposed to do now?" he said.

Dolores smiled and said, "Prepare ourselves to receive a son-in-law, I think."

* * *

Elliot and Rachel parked in front of the attorney's building. It was nine-fifteen. Ten minutes later, Mr. Bryant walked from the building and came out to the Jeep. He had a large envelope in his hand.

"Hello, Mr. Bryant. This is Rachel Davis."

"It's a pleasure, Rachel," Bill said as he handed the envelope to Elliot, "I made a copy of everything we have for you. You've got it all."

"Thank you, Sir."

"My pleasure. I'm on my way to hit the little white ball around. Do you play golf, Elliot?"

"I learned a little bit when I was at St. Maurice. It's a lot of fun."

"And it's good for business. We'll have to play sometime," Bryant said as he waved and went back into the building.

Elliot opened the flap of the large envelope and took everything out of it. He handed part of the papers to Rachel.

"I want to find the name of the woman who took care of me when I was little. It should be in the back..." After reading for a moment, he said, "Here...here it is," he said excitedly. "Her name is Ida Wilcock...and she lives at 4233 Evans Way."

"I know where Evans Way is," Rachel said.

"You mean it's here, in this city?" Elliot said, incredulous.

"Sure, over by the old County Hospital."

Elliot was trying to think back. "I don't understand. I wouldn't forget an airplane ride. I was sure she lived somewhere around St. Maurice, but that's five hundred miles away."

"Do you remember the car that picked you up?

"Yes, it was a long, black car, probably a limo."

"How long was the ride?"

"I thought it was a short time, just a few minutes."

Rachel is smiling now. You were five years old, weren't you? The drive could have been six or seven hours."

"You must be right. I don't know how anybody could forget their first airplane ride."

"I won't ever forget mine," Rachel said.

"When was yours?"

"I haven't had it yet," she said with a laugh. Elliot laughed with her and then started the car. As he was pulling out into the street, he said, "Ida Wilcock was the one who told me about Jesus."

"I want to meet her."

"Let's do it right now," as he moved through the early morning traffic.

They found 4233 Even Way and silently looked at the old house.

"Do you remember it?" Rachel asked.

Elliot shook his head, "I'm not sure."

"Maybe it's a different color now," she said. The shades were drawn, and the lawn looked long and unkempt. Rachel was afraid it was no longer occupied.

They went up to the porch, and Elliot knocked on the front door. He knocked again. There was no answer. Elliot stepped back and looked at the front of the old house. "I think I remember it," he said, troubled that he wasn't sure. They went down the front porch and looked at the house again.

"It doesn't look lived in," Elliot finally concluded.

"No, it doesn't," agreed Rachel, taking Elliot's hand. "Why don't we go next door and ask?"

"O.K. Maybe they'll know." Elliot led the way to the house on the right, because there was an old car in the driveway. Not seeing a doorbell, he knocked. They waited and then saw the curtain move slightly. A muffled voice from behind the door said, "What is it?"

"I wanted to ask about Ida Wilcock, the lady that lives next door."

"She's not there."

"I know. Do you know where she is?"

There was a long pause. Elliot looked at Rachel.

"Please," Rachel said, "She raised him when he was a little boy."

They saw the curtain part again, and a wisp of gray, stringy hair showed in the darkness.

"She's at the hospital," the old voice said.

"Does she work there?" Elliot asked.

Another pause, then from behind the unpainted door came, "No, young man; she's dying there."

Elliot stared at the dirty glass of the window. Rachel put her arm though Elliot's, pressing him to her. She turned them, and they went down the stairs.

"I know where the hospital is," she said as they got into the Jeep.

Arriving at the hospital, they went up to the fourth floor. "What room did the nurse say?" Elliot asked.

"Four-sixteen," Rachel said, looking at each door as they went down the hall. She didn't like hospitals. In fact, her grandma had died in this one. "There...there it is," Rachel said.

They looked into the darkened room. There was a window at the far end but the shade was partially covering it. They went in. Both beds had patients in them.

Elliot led the way as they looked in the first bed. It was a heavy-set woman, and she was asleep. Elliot looked at her face. No, Elliot thought, this isn't her.

He went and stood at the foot of the next bed. The woman was on her side, facing the partially curtained window. Elliot moved forward, in front of the window. He saw that her eyes were closed, but her mouth was moving. He recognized her immediately. He turned and nodded his head to Rachel, who was directly behind him.

Quietly, he pulled up a chair for Rachel, and then bent down over Ida Wilcock. He watched her tired, thin face. She certainly didn't look like the woman in his dream, not now, but it was she.

Elliot could see that she was praying. He waited, looking at her face. All the love he had for the woman when he was a child came back to him. Memories began flooding through him, the kitchen table, the bookstore, the walks in the early mornings, and the kisses she gave.

Her gaunt hand was near the edge of the bed, thin and weak looking. Elliot took it.

Ida wasn't startled. Most probably it's a nurse, she thought, though they didn't seem to come into her room as much as before. She opened her eyes slightly, not wanting to stop talking to Jesus. In the haze of the morning light, it looked like it might be a young man looking at her. She blinked, trying to focus better. Yes, it was a boy, and he was crying, tears running down his face. He came closer, kissed her on the cheek and put his arms around her.

"Good friends always hug," she heard him say.

"Elliot," she cried out weakly. "Oh, Elliot, I dreamt about you. You were a little baby in your high chair..."

"...and you were reading the paper at the kitchen table," Elliot continued. "I had the same dream."

"Could I have another hug?" Ida asked as she grasped the front of his shirt ever so weakly.

Behind him, Rachel had stood and was gently leaning against his back. She cried softly, once again feeling the same pain that she had felt when her grandmother had died.

"Ida, I have a new friend," Elliot said, "and she wants to meet you." Rachel leaned over the old lady, and then kissed her cheek. "My name is Rachel, Ida". Ida slowly raised her hand and touched her face. "Now it's your turn," Ida said softly.

Three days later, Ida Wilcock died.

* * *

In April, Bill Bryant handed an oversize letter to Elliot that the law firm had received from Saint Maurice's. It was a wedding invitation for the marriage of Colonel Whitcome and Amelia Skinner, to be held in the school's chapel. It was to be in the last part of June, after Elliot's school was out. Elliot replied that he would be happy to come, and that he would be bringing a friend.

Rachel took her first plane ride and held Elliot's hand as they knocked on the large doors of the school. The door opened. Elliot recognized the Sister but didn't remember her name. She smiled recognizing him too, then lead them through the spacious waiting room, and then to the door leading to the outside parade grounds. They walked the cement walkway leading to the chapel.

Elliot was surprised at how few people there were for the wedding. Since school was out, very few of the students were in the school, which Elliot knew would be the case. And it seemed like less than half the Sisters were there. Then Elliot saw Sister Teresa as she smiled and waved at Elliot. He stopped at her aisle, and they touched hands. Sister Teresa smiled and acknowledged the lovely girl on his arm him.

Felix Skinner was in the second row, standing, smiling and motioning for Elliot to come forward and sit with him. Wow, Felix thought, look at the girl with him! He continued to stand until they came and sat down next to him. He and Elliot grabbed each other and hugged, and as they did Elliot said, "This is Rachel." Felix was two feet from her, and now she was even more beautiful. She held out her hand, and he shook it. Wow!

Father Tinian came out the side door by the altar, opened the small gate and came and stood on the same level as the pews. He saw Elliot and acknowledged him with a smile. As he did, the Colonel and Mrs. Skinner came from a door at the rear of the chapel and walked down the aisle. Elliot noticed the Colonel had lost more weight and that Mrs. Skinner looked lovely. They were both so very happy. Beside Elliot, Skinner sat with tears of gladness in his eyes, twitching slightly so that he would not cry out loud. Rachel sat on the other side of Elliot. He took her hand.

It was a simple service, and Father Tinian was really enjoying himself. Elliot wondered if he'd ever done this before. He must have, he did such a good job. After the words had all been spoken, the Colonel kissed his new wife. Elliot found himself with tears in his eyes, remembering what the Colonel had been like just a year ago. God was so good. Both the people standing up there smiling at each other deserved one another. Elliot glanced back at Sister Teresa. Tears were coming down her cheeks. She saw Elliot's looking at her, and she smiled through her tears. Then the couple turned and walked down the aisle. He'd never seen the Colonel with such a smile.

The reception was in the main waiting room. The Colonel came up and took Elliot's hand, as did Amelia with the other. "You know," said the Colonel, "if you hadn't left school when you did, this wouldn't have happened."

"It's all because you came to visit us to say goodbye to Felix," the new Mrs. Whitcomb said.

"I think it was because the two of you dried dishes together." Elliot answered with a straight face. They both laughed, and Amelia gave him a kiss on the cheek, and said softly, "That's for being Felix's friend."

During the reception Elliot kept looking at Rachel, concerned, that since she knew no one, that she might be uncomfortable. But she always smiled at him and seemed at ease. Nearing the end of their time there, she pressed his hand, and whispered in his ear, "Before we leave, could I see part of the school?"

"Sure. What parts?"

"Where you lived when you were five years old."

"Really?" he answered. She smiled but said nothing.

After asking Father Tinian, they went out the door to the parade grounds, climbing the two flights of stairs.

"They said they put us on the top floor because we were so noisy, and none of the older kids wanted to hear us."

They entered the dorm. As usual all the beds were made, even though the cadets were gone for the summer.

"Which one was yours?" she asked, as she looked at all the rows.

Elliot walked to the back, near the Sister's rooms and stopped by the second bed from the door. "This is it. Why did you want to see it?"

"I want to know everything I can about you." She sat on the bed. "Sit down with me and tell me something about you that I don't know." He joined her and paused for a long moment. Rachel looked at him, waiting for a response.

"Aunt Elsie and Aunt Harriet want me to go on to college."

"Do you want to?"

"Yes, I think I do. There's so much to know."

"What would you study?

There was another long pause as Elliot searched her face. "You. I want to study you for the rest of my life." She didn't know what to say. "I don't want to go anywhere without you. I told my aunts that."

"What did they say?"

They agreed. "Every young man needs a friend." Aunt Elsie said, "Next to God, a wife is the best friend you can have."

"My mother got married right after she got out of high school. She says she's never been sorry."

"Then you'll marry me?"

"Elliot Reed, the sooner the better."

They kissed on that little bed and looked forward to the future.

THE END

LaVergne, TN USA
28 September 2009
159271LV00006B/2/P